By the same author

POETRY

Whatever Love Declares
After the Armies Have Passed
In Memory of the Future

FICTION

An Egyptian Bondage and Other Stories
Bearing Gifts
Death Comes for the Behaviorist
Transmigrations

TRANSLATIONS

Geza Csáth: *The Magician's Garden*
(from the Hungarian)

Forugh Farrokhzad: *Bride of Acacias*
(from the Persian)

Miklós Radnóti: *Under Gemini*
(from the Hungarian)

Nicolai Kantchev: *Medusa*
(from the Bulgarian)

Sándor Rákos: *Catullan Games*
(from the Hungarian)

Anthology: *The Face of Creation*
(from the Hungarian)

ESSAYS

Lee Mullican's Guardians

AS EDITOR

American Poems: A Contemporary Collection

Siren Songs & Classical Illusions

Jascha Kessler

McPherson & Company

SIREN SONGS AND CLASSICAL ILLUSIONS
 For information, address the publisher: McPherson & Company, Post Office Box 1126, Kingston, New York 12401. Publication of this book has been assisted by grants from the literature programs of the New York State Council on the Arts and the National Endowment for the Arts, a federal agency. Designed by Bruce R. McPherson.

Library of Congress Cataloging-in-Publication Data

Kessler, Jascha Frederick, 1929–
Siren songs and classical illusions / Jascha Kessler.
p. cm.
ISBN 0-929701-22-4 (alk. paper) : $12.00
I. Title.
PS3561.E67S57 1992
813′.54—dc20 92-6642

ACKNOWLEDGMENTS

Parts of this book have been published, sometimes with different titles and usually with varying details of text, in the following places: *Kayak*, *Ascent*, *The New Lugano Review*, *Gallimaufry*, *The Kenyon Review*, *Confrontation*, *Agni Review*, *The Spirit That Moves Us*, *Prism: International*, *The Smith*, *The Michigan Quarterly Review*, *The Missouri Review*, *Chelsea*, *The Grammercy Review*, *Arete*, *Bottomfish*, *Crosscurrents*, *Jacaranda Review*, *Jeopardy*, *Midstream*, *New Letters*, *Nimrod*, *The Malahat Review*, *Pulpsmith*, *The Village Advocate*, and *Writ 19*. Some pieces appeared in the anthologies *Contemporary American Satire*, *Epiphanies*, and *Sinn und Sinn-Bild: Festschrift zum 60. Geburtstag von Joseph P. Strelka* (Switzerland), and in chapbooks published by Jazz Press, Illuminati, and Treacle Press. Two stories were awarded prizes in PEN Syndicated Fiction competitions. All but one of the stories in the collection *Classical Illusions* (McPherson: 1985) are included.

Lyrics quoted in the story "Sybil" are from the song "Dominator Soul," recorded by Killing Joke for Malicious Damage, a division of Rough Trade Records, Ltd., London.

Printed on pH neutral paper.

First Edition.
Manufactured in the United States of America.
1 3 5 7 9 10 8 6 4 2 1992 1993 1994 1995

CONTENTS

What song the Sirens sang, or what name
Achilles assumed when he hid himself among women,
though puzzling questions, are not beyond all conjecture.
—*Sir Thomas Browne*

Siren Songs & Classical Illusions

Orfeos

ON THE MORNING of December 31st, the phone rang. My old friend the photographer, back from Macedonia. He was exhausted: he'd had five fashion models to himself for a month! Would I accompany him to Connie's for New Year's Eve? He was ashamed to go alone. Well, he was afraid of Constance, that black beauty from Philadelphia. They'd broken up and she was grieving.

I'd seen his folio of their Mexican adventure. It was all Connie: marketplaces and streets, cathedrals and cafés, Mayan ruins and the great lake of Chapala. Sweet Connie, naked and sweat-beaded in their dingy hotel rooms across seven thousand miles of Mexican byways. He'd left her behind in that sway-bottomed brass bed somewhere, blanched gray by fever in that roach-ridden dump. His assignment in Macedonia had come up. Her wide brown eyes stared from the last glossy portrait, patient with the knowledge that their love was finished. And he had been able to gaze safely back at those eyes only through the lens of a camera. Those shoulders, those long breasts, that belly with a thimbleful of silvery perspiration.

Beautiful people, Connie's friends, dancing all night in her whitewashed coldwater tenement flat in Hell's Kitchen near the docks. Ebony, yellow, mocha women: models, dancers, artists. Beefy black men and wiry black men suavely dressed: con men, PR men, cops, singers, ex-athletes, crooks. No one speaking: all childless, separated, like us. Drinking. Dancing. All night long never uttering a word, never meeting one another's eyes, and never touching: the men on one side of the empty room facing the women on the other. We danced the Chicago, the St. Louis, the Kansas City, the New Orleans, the San Diego, the Honolulu. Dancing. Drinking. Despairing. Towards midnight she came in, kissed Connie, smiling wanly at her, and took her place in the rank of dancing women. She did not speak to me. I heard her silence in the blasting music.

About 4:00 a.m. we walked out. We went down into the subway and took the Broadway Express. It was jammed with bleary revelers like ourselves. We sat side by side. At 125th Street, I got up, and she followed me. We took the White Plains Express, which ran screeching and rattling into the fogged dawn of a frozen January. When we got out at the last stop, no one was left on the train. The old planks of the station platform boomed hollow under our feet. She trailed after me, trusting yet uncertain. I was taking her to see P.S. 99, the school I'd attended more than half a lifetime ago. There had been empty lots around it then, swampy land washed by the Sound. Children used to fish there with string and bent pins and balls of white bread.

She walked behind me, and I listened to her heels clicking along as we paced slowly eastward down the long slope to the Sound. Concealed in the plumes of frost rising from the naked earth alongside the icy sidewalk there were coiled bronze vipers, tongues flickering like tiny red and black pennants, their hiss faint and menacing. I pointed them out to her, hoping she would keep close behind me in the middle of the narrow way we were following.

As we neared the end of that empty street, the iron band along the horizon over the black waters of the Sound turned lighter, suffused by a gray rosy hue. The sun was coming up on a new year.

Then we halted where the sidewalk broke off at the edge of the marsh. Reeds stuck out of the ground, frayed calamus, hollowed and bent, clacking frozen in the stony breeze that stirred, rolling in from the east ahead of the wintry dawn. Thin ice like cellophane wrinkled over the dank shallow-cratered land. The place would never again be the warm pool of my summery childhood years. That had drained away and been replaced by this cold, tar-blackened morass.

So many fish once swam here, I said. Just see how it is all dried up! "Time passes," she said quietly from behind me, and took her hand from my shoulder.

A Prophecy

THIS AFTERNOON, a colleague said he suddenly had something else coming up, winked, and handed me his ticket to a sold-out session of the international society to which he belongs. Thus, at 9:00 p.m. I find myself at the Empire Pavilion at the Decennial World Congress of Philosophers, Intellectuals, Theologians & Scientists. Though I'm not a registered participant of PITS, the usher takes the ticket anyway and leads me to a seat down among the first rows. I am apparently a little late, for there is already someone at the lectern. Naturally, it's somewhat embarrassing to be conducted down the aisle when the house is filled with attentive listeners. But it doesn't seem to bother people as I shuffle across their laps to my seat right in the middle of the row. They are engrossed by the speaker, a tall tweedy Englishman of about sixty, poised with his left thumb casually hooked in his waistcoat pocket, his right hand taking off and elegantly replacing thick horn-rimmed glasses. His delivery is cool, as only Oxbridge can offer: an authority that convinces not necessarily with argument but by its mere ease.

His report is somewhat lengthy, yet so well-constructed that it's possible to follow even without having heard his introduction. Subject? Humanity. At last he comes to his peroration, which ends somberly capped by a hushed assertion meant to impress: "And so, one must inevitably conclude that, finally, we are all to go to the lakes. It is there, soon, in those cold black waters, that we shall find our next, perhaps our final, residence. Provided, of course, suitable preparatory measures are taken to enable us to assume the new form of life required by the lakes . . . ."

I find myself laughing out loud. He stops in mid-drawl to peer down at me with surprised eyebrows, his expression itself politely enough asking, "How can this long-considered conclusion, supported by overwhelming signs, as well as by the evidence of things seen, be *laughed* at?"

I respond by standing to address the audience. Ladies and Gentlemen, I say, Surely you do realize that we have already *been* there?

They stare at me, astonished, transfixed.

So I continue, Have you already forgotten that we came from the lakes? Surely not! Forgotten how we lived beside those deep, cold, maternal waters? Don't you remember? That was our way of life. In the beginning! Once upon a time! And to think that we've come only this far since then! It's enough to make one weep! To think that our next steps should lead to the source we hoped to have abandoned forever. How absurd! How banal! And how bad! Bad, because retrograde! And worse, because antemillenial! And worst of all, because anti-millenial! Think again, Ladies and Gentlemen! I shout. Look into the light, for that is where we must be headed! Look into the light!

I plump myself back in my seat, arms folded across my chest, face lifted in challenge towards the panel of distinguished conferees arrayed on the dais behind tonight's speaker.

People shift uncomfortably in their seats, glancing at one another and again at me, unsure what to make of my laughter, unsure how to take my refutation of the ponderous arguments adduced and my objection to the prophecy pronounced by that insidiously pessimistic speaker. The Englishman gazes at me perplexed, then checks his papers, as if searching for a clue to his error. He colors, ever so slightly flustered. There is a rising hum through the Empire Pavilion as, confused, confounded, they begin discussing this bomb that I have thrown into their grave deliberations. For it is true, isn't it, that we have left the past behind forever?

Afrodite

BECAUSE IT WAS HIGH SUMMER in the Mohawk Valley, and the tumult of July's thunderbolt-riddled days had passed, I meditated in peace in my study on the second floor of the Greek Revival house we lived in, built long ago in the early 19th century, and rebuilt again in the 1950's into two apartments. The downstairs place was inhabited meagerly by Gertrude and David and their boys, all off camping in some gulch at the bottom of the Grand Canyon, he tapping at two-billion-year-old strata for specimens of proof for his geology classes, she wrinkling deeper into what she'd become, angular, hollow-chested, confused, the boys wallowing in the Red Colorado River clay, hardening into spasmodic sticks. It was peaceful now without their tromping and bellowing below. The paperweight on my desk was a big fossil scallop shell he'd brought back three years ago as a souvenir of the times when Arizona had lain beneath the foaming waves of archaic seas.

Now the ghosts of the two old spinsters, last of their line, to whom this house had belonged once, could ascend from the earthen-floored cellar and stump through their apartment, as they never cared to do when the Crawleys were home during the academic year, perhaps preferring to wander about fretting, or to squat beside the washers and dryers on the south side where gelid sunlight lit the muddy panes cut in the foundation wall, offering them a little cold comfort. We preferred it like that too: our little boy had seen the sisters in his room one evening and screamed from his crib, pointing over my shoulder as I soothed him, telling them to go away, go away. . . . More than once I'd been aroused from sleep as they paced down the long hallway of our apartment, making faint shoe-creaking sounds, not on the floorboards, and raising the hairs of my body like the spicules of a sea urchin. My wife never woke, though. Her name is the same as the younger of the sisters. When they passed through the rooms they'd occupied for nearly ninety years, even the squirrels in the vast attic above us ceased their midnight gambols and stopped trickling their acorns down inside the thick walls. In summer, though, they took some light and air in the Crawleys' place, and never disturbed us at all. It was a compromise: I had asked them, out loud, to stay out of the children's rooms, since it was no good for little ones to be scared by old ladies who aren't there. Keep to the Crawleys', I implored the empty air, you can share the space with their bodies, they won't even notice you, and stop troubling our wits! That was a reasonable request, I thought, since we paid rent to the College, not to them. And that was that.

All morning I'd been meditating in my study under the front gable, shaded by the canopy of great, ancient elms surrounding the house. It was quiet across the road: the fraternity houses were shut down for the summer. So was the home of Ulysses S. Grant's daughter, she having died last winter at eighty-eight. Robins hopping on the lawns, heads cocked for grubs, the jays fighting around as usual, the wren tending her tiny nest, flitting in and out of the eave like a blur in one's vision, cardinals, orioles, and doves visiting through the morning hours. My wife was out back under the apple tree in the garden with the children. Occasionally a pickup rattling by on the cobbled road, and a cow lowing far down in the valley. The cicadas of August tuning up for the afternoon's tedious static.

Meditating, if it can be termed that, sitting two hours looking out at lawns, the road, the old white houses behind their hedges on the other side. I'd come to realize that somehow, somewhere, I had lost my self. I had no idea where to look now. Yet it waited for me. Nearby, perhaps. Or far off. But not here. We'd parted one day without even a farewell, like former friends at a crossing, and gone our separate ways. And here I am, thirty. The road I'd taken had come abruptly to an end. No track led on from it now. Must I go back all that way to the fork? Then what? I might go on, always hoping to catch up, and knowing time lost is lost forever, like myself. So I sit here at this roadside in the Mohawk Valley. And wait, wondering how to proceed. It has been three years now. No one, it seems, can tell you. You are alone. Absolutely. My meditation this morning says simply, It's useless for an object to seek the subject which it is. Only the subject could seek, and the subject cannot find itself by seeking. Because what's sought is necessarily elsewhere than that which seeks it. The sought-for is in a different moment of time, and in a different region of space, from those moments of time and space occupied by that which is seeking. If you could have it, you wouldn't be seeking it. Seeking it, yourself, is vain. It can be presented to you, though. How? and by whom? It depends.

I got up feeling the book-lined walls of my little study closing on me as if to blot me out, in the way I had just obliterated a gnat by closing my fist. Queenie, our golden retriever, got up with me. I went down the stairs and stepped out on the verandah. It was nearly noon. Beyond the shade of the elms, the sun floated swelling up to its height. I crossed the lawn and walked up College Road to the Grant house, slipped through the garden and went out back into a copse that shielded it from the winter gales, walked down the path that dipped through among those trees, and climbed again to the pastures running beside an old apple orchard that spread out along the crown of the long hill heading away from the College. This hill was a ridge stretching ten miles north and south, paralleled by similar rolling hills to the east and the west. I was walking southward through the old pastures. Here and there the mounded green grass was mined by groundhogs and rabbits and cropped by horses some faculty kept. In the springtime, cows from the adjacent dairy farms were let out here to forage after the long months of silage. There were always crops of common field mushrooms battening on the manure, and giant puffballs white as bleached skulls. Last week's rain had brought them out, and I could see many "Yoricks," as we called them, lying here and there where they'd popped from the ground. I regretted having left the basket on the porch.

No shade out here, and no breeze now. To my right, the apple trees, full of small green fruit. On my left, a pair of horses standing side by side at the barbed wire, head to rump, switching the flies from one another's face. About a half-mile ahead, the trees I was making for: a tall, second-growth forest in which you could escape the sun to rest beneath the shadowing alders and beeches, breathing in the tang of rotted log and leaf-mold and ferns, where trillium sprouted in lavender and white choruses. In this wood, there were no directions: the sun scatters into a diffuse greeny light filtering through the thick layer of branches, and only the faintly traced track winds through to come out nowhere. . . down a narrow ravine where a brook flows clotted with green slime. Wild grape covers that deep ditch and its slopes, and not much else but sumac and poison oak. Swarms of midges and mosquitos hang over it. In this wood it is always silent, except for the rasping of a crow floating between the tall,thin treeboles. Sometimes a pair of phoebes calls sweetly in the depths, echoing. But not disturbing the heavy stillness. In there, misery is assuaged for an hour. And, emerging afterward by the same path you have taken in, you are even glad to be back in the empty light once more on the meadows and pastureland, and heading somewhere again, home perhaps, with a few huckleberries and blackberries garnered along the way and staining your hands blue. A palliative, if no remedy.

As I looked along the track and the wall of that wood ahead, I felt the midday light glancing about at violent angles, and not just pouring down over the fields. I blinked at the strange, invisible shafts flickering around me. The ground seemed suddenly to be thrumming, a sound louder than the usual buzz and hum of the bees hovering over the clover and the daisies, milkweed and Queen Anne's Lace. A low susurration, and behind it a muffled low roaring that seemed to rise out of the grass on which I walked. The ground of the faint track seemed springy, elastic, a thick carpet spread upon a lake. As though there were no flinty granite beneath but a dark, and a warm, sea, and I was treading on matted weed. Dizzied, I kept on going. There is solid world here, I said to myself, plain, simple, poor, meagerly alive, but solid.

The yelping of the bitch stopped me. She was poised up ahead, alert, her tail stiff and high. She scented something. Then she began coursing back and forth, her nose to the track. I saw what her nose was thrilled by: just before the gate into the forest, right in the middle of the way, a great, ten-point buck faced us, his antlers lifted high. The bitch hadn't seen him. She kept her nose to the ground she was eagerly traversing. The buck watched her coming. He also gazed at me where I stood, his ears flicking. No one had ever brought down such grand game in these parts, where there's not enough forage or cover for the likes of that stranger. I watched Queenie as she began running towards him; he stood his ground watching me. Then she lifted her muzzle and saw him too. With a crazy, strangled bark, she rushed him. Casually, the stag turned, his head twisted back to keep me in his view, and snapped his white rump, bounding away into the dark wood, the retriever in wild pursuit. I called out to her; it was useless. I could hear her baying fade into the echoing forest, fainting away as the buck led her off in chase. That fool might never find her way back. Nothing to be done now.

I kept on anyway. As I neared the spot, I saw that the dried grasses were crushed near the track. The stag had bedded down here. I stopped to pick up a clump of coarse red hairs snagged on a twist of briar beside his couch. The sunlight flooded down terribly then, as if a boiling cauldron had been tipped out overhead from the zenith. The roaring low rolling hum out of the earth grew until it sounded like surf thundering in. What was this? I swayed. I felt myself being forced down, the ground coming up for me. I yielded: I dropped to my knees for the first time in my life. Something was sweeping at me. The air split apart before its progress. What I felt was the pressure of its coming. I couldn't look up from the earth. I stared at the stag's lair, the tangled grasses and the tiny purple clover and daisies enmeshed among the broken stalks. The space about me was thickening with light and heat. It drummed. Far off, I heard the last belling of that maddened bitch, down and over the little valley to the west it seemed, miles off now.

And I knew what it was.

Afrodite! I shouted that name. At the same instant I was flung on my face. I did not dare to look up. Calmly I lay there, thinking, This is extraordinary: you have not sought this: neither have you deserved this: yet it has come: there is no remorse, no panic: she is here: there is only joy: brilliant joy: it will not stay: be thankful. Laughing and mumbling tears, full of a gratitude I had not known was in me to offer, I gave thanks. I called out to this bombarding passage of light and immense heat—this noise and power erupting from the earth and pouring like a wind over me, and passing steadily by like a great vessel—Afrodite! Io, Afrodite!

When I returned some hours later, my wife sat on the verandah, rocking the child in her lap. A glass of sherry was in her hand, the bottle at her feet. She smiled at me, reaching up to tug a straw from my hair.

Queenie came home the next day, matted with mud, her tawny coat a mass of burrs, her pads swollen and bleeding, her chest caved in, broken-winded. She drank her fill and stretched out to sleep for a whole day and night.

The Foundation

THE FEBRUARY RAINS ARE ENDING here in Southern California. The sky is a flat light turquoise hue this morning. On the plum and apricot trees in my garden the buds are swollen, their tiny white nipples tipped with a rusty pink. Hummingbirds dart about the orange trees, which are covered with white blossoms clustered among dark green leaves, all washed and polished, free of the dust and grit blown in from the deserts to the north and east during the January heat waves. All the lawns are sparkling with last night's late shower, and the male robins, on their passage north from Mexico, are tugging at the worms that have surfaced or pouncing on the grubs newly hatched, five or six plump brutes together, not at all battling for nesting territory, since their speckle-breasted consorts are still a week behind them in the migration. Spring has arrived.

With springtime too come letters of rejection. The mingled scents of orange blossom and nightblooming jasmine, though rich and syrupy on the cool washed air flowing in from the Pacific, are not enough to lift one's spirit. This year I am not sanguine, for I think my project cannot have interested the foundations, much as it concerns me. Deafened words. My thesis has asserted itself irresistibly over my lifetime. How? Because I have noticed a change. Not in myself, but in those addressed. I have not changed my text: the masterwork is the same. The creation remains vivid—suggestively, eternally new. And yet, scanning the faces before me, watching ballpoint pens suspended above blank notebooks, drawing tangled webs in the vague air, I have begun to perceive the sentence I utter appear to dissipate before reaching their minds. Although they seem to listen hard. The Words Are Deaf. I put my thesis: it is language: the world is passing through a cloud of unknowing: the living word is scrambled in its passage between lip and ear: yet the earth endures: here are the robins, the orange blossoms: here morning sun and cool vapors rising from wet roofs.

In the mail there is a letter for me. The large envelope is an impressive heavy parchment. I open it and remove a single white sheet of the same quality. It has been twice folded. When I have spread it crackling before me on my desk it is elephant folio size, covered with dark words written in clear bold Uncial hand.

It says, simply: "Welcome! We, Lords of Perigord, and Curators of the Abbey of Thélème, take pleasure in greeting you on your entrance into our community. We are delighted that you have accepted our invitation. We trust your stay will be long, your study original. You will find treasures waiting here for you. May we call your attention to the Caves. Most especially to the caves beneath the Caves. Which caves have Caves hidden within. The rest is up to you. And so forth!"

I turn the letter over. Nothing more is written. I turn the envelope over. Nothing else is written, as if my name and address were enough for the message to reach me. A grant, an odd sort of grant. No funding, no termination. Only a fool would accept.

Sphinx

ONE EVENING IN JULY I was walking the dog. It had been a scorching day, and very smoggy. First Stage Alert all afternoon. Now, at eleven, it was tolerable, though still hot: the air was smoke-singed and tasted bitter because there had been no rain for seven months—yet another drought year in Southern California. Sirens whooped a few blocks away on the boulevards north and south, fire engines hooted, and the hot night's din roared everywhere. It was, however, relatively quiet down the dark side streets.

From one of the little frame cottages built in the early decades of this century, a faint voice called. I stopped. A cat perhaps? But it had called to me, I thought. In the faint street light filtering through the cedars the house appeared to be a forest green faded with age, the color of stagnant algae staining a swampy pool, streaked with the black tars that drip from our skies. The grass of the lawn was dead in patches and rank with dried mustard weed. The cottage was surrounded by huge clumps of spikey agave cactus. It was a woman's, or child's, voice, calling to me for help. The dog crouched, whining. I went in.

The place was cobwebby, layered with stale dust, filled with a fetid, desiccated air, as though not a window had been opened in many years. It had the sour taste of newspapers that have crumbled over a lifetime into microscopic flakes that float about, clogging, gagging the throat. A house, I thought, like Miss Haversham's, though I wasn't aware of having had any great expectations. I walked through the empty, cluttered parlor and stopped. From the back there came the piteous voice again: an old woman's quaver. She was crying to me for help. I went down the fusty hall to her bedroom where I found the poor thing lying all helpless on the floor. I lifted her in my arms. She weighed no more than a child. Her skin was scaly and dry as a serpent's. Her hair was tangled, sour and clotted, and she had dry sores on her cheeks. Her dark eyes were luminous in their shadowed hollows, lit by feverish points, and her lips were stretched and chapped over her dry protruding dentures. A sack of bones she seemed when I had laid her out on her huge rats' nest of a bed, and she moaned a little in pain and hunger, her arthritic hands barely able to hold the glass of water I fetched to her mouth. Two diamonds were set in her huge old earlobes, sparkling in the dim glow from a little crimson lamp on her night table. On her knobbly fingers she wore a ruby ring, a great star sapphire, and a lustrous pearl the size of a cherry. I opened the shutters, though she feared the draft, and I let in what weak, hot air there was outside. She was grateful then. Her voice was cracked and hoarse, and yet piped like a child's too. Hardly a voice at all, but a miaowing and a rasping. "Are you married, young man?" I have gray hair, I said, and a wife. "Children too?" She gave me those, I said, and the dog. "Then you are a happy man," she said, coughing again as she sipped the water. Yes, I answered. "Well then, remember what I say. What you predict comes true." Of course, I said. She closed her eyes, slitted them rather, and leaned back against the headboard, her long jaw thrust forward, the waxy teeth protruding even further so that she whistled and clacked. "Don't be too sure!" she said.

I told her I'd call the social services people when I got back home. And I did that.

A few weeks afterward, I saw a realtor's sign on the lawn. In two months, nothing remained: the bulldozer came and razed her house into a mound of splinters in an hour; the trucks came and carted it all away by noon. Three months later there was an apartment building with twenty units and a swimming pool and sauna on the site, fresh new bluegrass on the lawn out front, and the realtor's pennants advertising vacancies. Within two weeks those were gone, and the garage below filled with Jaguars, Stingrays, Cobras, and the like. The drought broke: we had November rains washing our city clean again.

A lawyer's letter came in December. She'd left me everything. When the estate was finally settled, there would be a quarter of a million. A small fortune for us. A week later, another letter came: her distant relatives were suing: they had been displaced by me: I was an interloper. They claimed that I had dared to trespass; that I had found the old creature dying and forced her to write me into her Will. That I was a criminal, a fraud. That I was the usurper. And that I would never have dared to enter her bedroom if I'd been a happy man.

Of course I explained to the Probate Court that I was only an innocent. That I had done a mere kindness one late evening, called out of my way. That her own family had left her there on the floor of that midden to rot. That I never expected thanks for doing what is right, let alone the property and a fortune.

The verdict came in the spring: Not Proven.

Rhadamanthys

Of all times for my car not to start. Late for the last lecture. He'd promised a summary discussion touching on all that he had to teach us, including such problems as had heretofore resisted our reasonable formulation: the source of judgment, the distribution of responsibilities between the logician of the left hemisphere and the esthete of the right hemisphere, and the unplumbed well of energy from which flows love and death in a single yet ambiguous stream labile in nature as time. Et cetera.

I had to roll the car down out of the driveway, after calling the garage for the towtruck. They came along and laid on the jumpcables in ten minutes, after which I drove there to have a hot charge put on the battery. That took half an hour more. Even so, I arrived only fifty minutes late . . . to find the others shuffling out. At the lectern stood Professor Freud, stacking examination booklets. I murmured an apology for my tardiness. I had not been late before, in fact. He raised his eyebrows at me quizzically as I panted, winded from the three flights I had taken loping. My car wouldn't start, I said. He grunted, sceptical. As far as I was concerned, it was a likely story. I knew better than to insist on the truth. Instead, as was I believe my right, I simply asked him what was going on here.

In that low voice of his, that voice nearly a whisper, and which had caused us to lean forward tensely week after week just to catch his precise utterance, he observed simply that I was too late: "I have just given you your final examination."

But this was to be your last lecture, I protested. The exam's next week! "I am sorry for you," he shrugged. Sorry! How could you have done this! Whom does it serve! Time is needed in order to think! You promised to review all this matter in the end! "Yes, I have usually done so. Nevertheless, I decided to give the test today, and finish things up for good." He indicated with a wave of his hand the questions written in small Italic script on the blackboard with dark blue and bright yellow chalk. For a moment I studied them, uncomprehending. They seemed to be nonobjective statements about our everyday life; they had nothing to do with the themes he'd discoursed upon all these many weeks. And who could have answered them in this one brief period we had? Fifty minutes for essaying Process & Probability; Work, Waste, & Compensation; Appropriating Silence? And other topics too! I said, But surely, Professor, I can make it up? I'm perfectly willing to take another exam whenever you wish to give it. "No, no," he whispered smiling, "now that you have seen my questions, it is impossible. I will never let you make it up. Too bad. However, I am sorry for you."

I stared at him as he grinned up at me through his crisply curled salt and pepper beard. He didn't flinch; but he did play for time, fumbling in his jacket pocket for a box of matches, averting his glance as he relit the soggy stump of his short black Swiss cigar. I said nothing, because I knew there was now nothing to be said.

Still, I stood my ground: he'd have to pass around me to leave the room. Sucking at his cigar, he waited. He knew how to wait. I had to speak at last. So, I said, I've missed my chance. "Yes, well. You came too late, you know." I beg your pardon? I said ironically. He did not reply. Keeping his eyes on me, knowing that I knew that what he taught was now mine in any case, and that he had committed the unforgivable, he gathered up the papers, that firm little man, tucked them beneath his arm, and came towards me.

Naturally, I stepped aside. Nodding curtly once, he went out. It was all over. Resisting the rage that gathered in me, a force that seemed to rise from my toes, I drew a deep breath and held it for a few seconds. Then I turned and walked out into the vacant corridor. The Professor was striding towards the exit with that pace he'd learned on his Alpine walking holidays. As he passed through the door he tossed the bundle of examination booklets into a trashbin. Then he was gone, a puff of thick Brasil tobacco smoke hanging in the air behind him. It floated a little while, and thinned away into nothing.

Ikaros

DOWN SECOND AVENUE driving stop and go through racketing thunder and rancid blue fumes in the rush hour, eight lanes of trucks, buses, and cars inching towards Manhattan Bridge on the last Friday of June as the sinking sun spreads, flattening, a pale red like an erythrocyte dying. On the corner north of Delancey there's Tuli, Tuli Knoepflmacher. Tall, thin, sloped shoulders. A muzhik's reddish-brown beard to his belt, matted and tangled. Worn Indian moccasins on his long feet, fraying holes in the knees of his baggy jeans, and a black-green tartan flannel shirt draped over his small behind. It must be Tuli. I sit jammed behind a garbage truck halfway up the block. I honk him. He's carrying a fat bundle of leaflets under his left elbow, and passing them out to commuters stalled like me on the Avenue. If I know my Tuli, it's more of the same: anarcho-pacifist literature full of tortuous analysis, denunciation, exhortation, excoriation. Terrorism of the sleepwalker, though gentle in its way, because not yet plugged into organized power. I honk him again. His head turns slowly: it is Tuli—those great brown liquid eyes full of dreaming wonder. He stares, and doesn't see me.

Seven years since graduation. In fact, we didn't take that last step officially: we strolled away from Brooklyn College through an April shower. Our credits had accumulated till we were far beyond degree requirements. Somebody had run a check on us at last. So we were expelled, with Highest Honors. "What's wrong with intellectual curiosity?" Tuli asked the President. The answer we got was, "Nothing. But you're occupying minority space." "I am a minority of one, sir," Tuli came back sweetly. "Beat it now—before the Comptroller flays my ass!" And it was curiosity that had kept us hanging around, a couple of Phi Beta Kappa bums—as well as yet another undeclared war that was consuming young men's bodies like bulbs in a Times Square marquee. I took shelter working at my doctorate in biophysical chemistry. And I got something nice done with a five-year grant from the National Science Foundation: heart-cell metabolism, functions of lipids, lipoproteins, lipoids, lipolysis. Leading me to my next project: lipoma processes: the fatty tumor, benign and other. My future lies in California: Sunday morning I fly out, and goodbye to all this. But what's Tuli's thing? From the look of him, he's gone right on with his poetry of poverty, his preaching, his principle.

Principle. What we had. Our true plenty. Perhaps. Tuli ignores my horn. He gets hooted all day. He continues shambling among the cars, coming up the line, thrusting his leaflet into open windows, smiling, saying his word of peace—that soft smile says it's peace. When he reaches my rusty, shuddering, blatting contraption, I lean over, throwing the door open. I know he'll recognize me, and I know he'll show neither surprise nor pleasure. Everything is as it is. Even time signifies nothing for Tuli. "Hello," he says in that same low baritone, and flops in. What a smell! Sour as mildew, a Bowery bum's smell. When did you give up on washing? "I wash myself. These are my clothes this year."

Simple as always. Before we're over the Manhattan Bridge and out to my mother's in Flatbush, I know where he's at. While I'm in the library and lab for seven years, he's adhering to principle: honesty, resistance to social warfare, resistance to social crime, resistance to criminal work, resistance to the darkening of intellect and the occultation of the soul as systematically organized in America, specifically emanating from Manhattan, the rock of evil. Twice-married; twice-deserted and annulled. What woman could sue him, and for what? To put him in jail, because he demonstrates we're all prisoners to begin with? When he alone, pacifico-anarchist, struggles towards freedom? And so he does, taken care of now by one friendly female or another: harmless, humorous, helpless. Fed by whoever finds him in the street or climbs the ancient flights to the seventh floor somewhere below Houston Street, to the clubroom of his Society for Anarcho-Pacifism, where there's the reliable Gestetner duplicator still, cartons of blank paper, a coffeemaker, some rickety folding chairs with their missing wooden slats in the seats, the barred windows opaque with fifty years' grime, a platform made of old crates, and the oak lectern from some long-lost school auditorium, the NRA fridge with the coil on top and still working, and mouse droppings everywhere in the corners of this abandoned factory loft. He dosses beneath a thin khaki Army blanket on a decrepit piece of carpeting laid on a workbench, when it's free of leaflets and stapler waiting to collate the Manifesto. Nothing's changed since I first saw it as an anarcho-pacifist of sixteen. Posters, handbills, proclamations: all the light of the future originates there. He is now its source and messenger, the old leaders being gone, swept away into Social Security and after. The ink-smudged sheets with their red and black letterings do not shout slogans—they argue, reasonably and patiently and impossibly, for the Kingdom of Heaven on Earth . . . now . . . if we listen to the dialectic, and if we hear. Really, it's quite simple, simpler than even Moses could have supposed. Of course it is. But easy it isn't. Whoever said easy? Even falling asleep, even death isn't easy. And yet, why not? As Tuli has said always, "Only drop your mental chains, only reach up, reach out, and soar, up, up, and away . . . ." Gravity, Tuli, gravity, I have replied. So far Tuli's up there still, sustained by friends, ex-wives, fond girls, as though he's winging really on his own into the light. Say one thing for him: unlike the other dreamers, Tuli respects science. And math talent? He proved a fundamental theorem in ergodics at eighteen. Perhaps it scared him. Science is mine too, he said, to enjoy or not, as I choose. He chose his own truth. Which he offers yet. Do I see that? he asks. And I say, I do, I do see, as we sit stalled on Manhattan Bridge, gazing out over the old Navy Yard and the Lower Bay towards the Statue of Liberty out there down towards the southwest. I see us together, Tuli, in midflight over the doubts weltering below, hateful monsters with terrible slashing teeth and ravenous gullets hiding scaly-sheathed in the unillumined depths. From which terror, may we be safe. And we shall be safe, I add—if we're prudent. "Prudent? What's prudence got to do with principle?" Laws, Tuli, there are laws. Many laws yet unknown. Ignorance is dangerous. Willful ignorance is sin. "So you've held. You know me, though." I know you, but Tuli, do you know yourself? "I do, I do," he mutters, looking down into the spreading scarlet stain on the turbulent, gray waters. "And I know that what I must have is more than what I know. It's up there," and he points skyward, "where the light comes from."

So we have resumed the conversation at the beginning, after seven years. No great distance covered, it seems. This has nothing to do with radical thought, or plastic bombs in toilet stalls, a burst of submachine fire in the waiting room, hostages lying against the walls, ankles tied with lamp cord. It's that we're right where we have always been—at the beginning, starting out once again, like waking in the morning. If what happens is waking, when the alarm clock jars. Thirty seasons pass; we grow beards; we work at something; varied bodies come within our reach, and go again. Yet we have not launched ourselves. Our wings are folded. We stand looking out over the surrounding sea that must be somehow passed, if we're to begin to think. Construct a raft? when the shore's patrolled day and night, the waters roughened by wind and current in perpetual conflict? Meanwhile I've found my solution. Tuli though has his principle. And his principle and my prudence will never fly together. Pity.

At my mother's we take a light supper of cheese, salad and sardines and smoked fish, buttermilk, olives, and black bread. Tuli soaks in the shower while she washes his rags and dries them. Before our eyes then, the bum's transformed. Young Tuli once more stands here: curly-bearded, red-cheeked, big brown glowing eyes, a shine to his curly locks too, and that clear skin, that light olive complexion that is like a fine suede. Handsome: layers of anarchopacifist dirt had obscured him. He waits in my striped robe, that comes down to his ankles, while she patches the jeans. He smiles at us, and we smile back. My mother has always had a tender protectiveness for the poor homeless child, as she calls him. Even for these brief hours she's happy to have him back, so that she may work her domestic magic upon him. "Tuli, Tuli," she keens with joy, "don't throw yourself away, my sweet boy, don't go chasing after a vision. You're still nice. Be good to yourself, Tuli. And listen to me: be a man, after all." He answers her plea simply, "I hear you, Momma." But she knows him better than he knows himself. As we go into the night to hunt up some dames I know down in Brighton Beach, she calls after us, "You hear me, Tuli? So why don't you listen!"

The chicks are okay: we see a good show; take a walk on the boardwalk; spend a long hour after midnight in their pad. Like old times. As we're strolling towards the street where I'd parked, we find ourselves going a dark stretch—streetlights all out, smashed by rocks—and so we review the constellations visible at this late hour over the Atlantic. It's something we used to do, parsing the Zodiac on summer night rambles. Suddenly, we both take an awful fall together—into a hole in the sidewalk two feet deep and three across. Fortunately, nothing's broken, we find on checking ourselves over. We sit stunned for a while at the rim of this pit, rubbing our legs and cursing the Borough of Brooklyn, the city and the society that permits such a clear and present danger to its citizens, in which no one cares enough to remedy even such an obvious evil. It is an execration we used to utter in antiphony, in the old times. And nothing has changed: it's only worse.

We look at one another. We sigh, and get up and work in silence to fill this awful mantrap. Handfuls of dirt scrabbled from the vacant lot here; sticks, stones, tin cans, and bottles, whatever broken bricks or chunks of concrete we can pick up from the demolition of the burned-out tenement across the alley. We fill it. Then we stomp on it until it's tamped level with the jagged edge of the ruined sidewalk. A sweaty, frantic hour in silence. We're fouled by the effort. Naturally, there's no water anywhere around here.

On the way to Manhattan, Tuli asks me to stop the car on the Brooklyn Bridge, just as we're passing midpoint. He needs air, he says. Wants to walk the rest of the way home himself, across the bridge, and up Manhattan to his loft on lower Broadway. I will not argue with him. I can't keep him. We always acknowledge the primacy of desire. Principle, he calls it. I call it anarchy. Anyway, I'm tired, and want my bed. The final report's due in tomorrow. Sunday morning I'm flying to the Coast, and my new lab.

I let him out. At the Manhattan end, I swing around, heading back again. As I pass him and see him striding west on the boards that run down the center of the bridge, I give him the horn again. He seems to wave, a slim shadow in the starlight.

The week has passed swiftly. It's my first time in San Francisco. There are bridges here too, newer spans, immense ones. A letter comes. Tuli's jumped from the Brooklyn Bridge, and landed in

Kings County Hospital. Back broken in three places. In deep coma. Maybe he'll live. Maybe not. My mother's matter-of-fact. Probably, she adds, he'll live: if he can be picked up alive out of the East River at four in the morning, then he can be set back on his two feet to start in all over again.

I write back to say that I've been well-received here. They've waited for my coming. My place in the lab's set out for me, and I can begin to work. I have even landed a nice sublet in a new tower: it looks down on the Golden Gate, on the Bay, and out over the Pacific. I've landed safely, and everything is better than I imagined.

Proteus

SIX DAYS IN La Paz. The high, pure blue cloudless sky of Baja California, the white and tawny sands at the end of a thousand miles of desert peninsula. Some of the world's greatest fishing, they say: giant tuna, swordfish, immense sailfish leaping like missiles out of the sapphire sea. Six days of expensive trolling the depths: sonar, depth-finders, radio-sounding, radar . . . and not even a strike!

Enough science! This was my seventh and last day. I'd given up all hope. So I put out into the Pacific in a simple fishing boat this time, one mast, and two other fishermen I'd met in the bar, Italians or Greeks with lots of money and no luck, like me. We'd rented the leaky vessel and were making a mess of our adventure. They weren't sailors either. Late in the afternoon, burned out by sun and bloated with beer, we lay wallowing, oars shipped and dingy canvas limp, far from any glimpse of land. But we had lines out and had been drifting for hours on the slow greasy Pacific swell, unmanaged and unmanageable. Rod and reel abandoned, we lolled tired; drunk; bemused; silent.

I felt a tug on the line tied to my wrist that was by then tangled around my ankle. Then there was a furious jerk. Fish on! I yelled and began pulling in hand over hand. The other two lay sprawled on their thwarts, laughing. I dragged up loop after loop: how had I ever let a hundred feet get away into this empty deep? Then just as the leader came up, the line went slack. He'd got off after all.

But no. When I yanked at the last three yards , there was that thrilling flash below the surface. I hauled away—and brought up a silvery blue fish . . . about seven inches long!

We looked at it. It was recognizably a sailfish: the beak or bill was just forming out of clear gelatinous cartilage, and its future sail was still but a rainbow-hued, spikey, tender membrane.

I said, Let's get this hook out and free him. Let him grow up and roam the world. Who knows if we won't meet again some day? I held him out on my palms to display him to the others, and his big blue luminous eye looked up at me, intelligent.

Psyche

ASLEEP FOR YEARS in broad daylight. In the dark of Michigan. Though seldom fast or long asleep at night. Restless; thrashing. But waking up now, I think. After seven years' hard labor in the Boutique de Bellezza. Sales girl to manager. My penance. And no one to help me—no guide, no friends, animal or vegetable. Just the hard floor beneath the suave carpeting to support my weary legs. It seemed as if these legs had been wandering the wide world these seven years, though they hardly even took me through the whole store. But beauty was good to me at last. I had thought it never would be good for me.

Nights he's been here with me. My husband. And nights are good because he's been here. Thank god for the nights he's given me. My loverboy. Who came to me from out of nowhere. Same old song. Respite from my rich little world.

And it all begins privately, exclusively, at Entrance 1, a special door for affluents from Grosse Point and Birmingham who wear gloves and veiled hats even in summertime, and a tall black doorman who also wears gloves to help them out of their limousines. And no one ever complains about our way of handling rejects —it's even easier to return things than buy them: we take back about 15% of what's sold, and no questions asked. It's the cheapest advertising we know of. We were about the first to put a price tag on everything, and stop the haggling that's gone on for thousands of years; and we were the first to put in basement levels with lowered prices for everyman and everywoman. If something goes wrong at home, we'll page a customer anywhere: our switchboard's second only to the Pentagon's, we like to claim. And it's for serving, not destroying. We have more of everything, and we sure have everything. Our workers and salespeople can take breaks in a 50-bed Silence Room. After 5 years with us, no one can be fired unless the President approves. Full pay for sick employees, because that's when they need it most. Elevators, 51 of them paneled in warm, polished woods and operated by girls in gray who wear white gloves. Four banks of escalators that go up 12 floors and end, where else? in Toys. After a month of New Orleans and Mardi Gras, spring turns us into a gigantic flower show; summer, and we're a tropical paradise, an island in the South Seas: little atomizers fill the air with fragrance; fall brings us the new cars, parked right among the clothing shops—always some lovely theme done up in an extravaganza that sparkles out of the gold-gleaming brass drinking-fountains. The largest toy store, as big as a city block, the largest pharmacy, the largest book store in Detroit. Four restaurants on 13, and one of them our elegant Georgian Room where the exotic wood tables are oiled every morning, sugar comes in sterling bowls, and food is served on specially made English china set out on hand-stitched Irish linens. Fifty-one giant window displays face the broad sidewalks, and the animated Christmas pageants on Woodward Avenue gather joyful crowds of young and old for weeks during the darkest hours of December, climaxed by the parade every year: floats, clowns, acrobats, bands, and, bringing up the rear, Santa himself, the real, the one and only Santa Claus, all the others who stand and ring their bells for the Salvation Army shabby facsimiles, his humble helpers. Rich or poor, people are served by us from birth and then right through life: there's truly no need we cannot fill, for ours is the mother of all stores. And, just as though I were to be dismissed, driven out in disgrace, this is the world that will vanish should my trust in my own good fortune be shaken. It would be a lot to lose. And yet I can see the end coming, like bankruptcy. There are new suburbs and new roads, and all the roads lead away from the center.

It's a strange world, yet mine is stranger still, almost impossible to contemplate objectively once you leave Men's Furnishings or Designer Clothes and step into its heady circle, as though into the heart of the labyrinth. My languorous girls lounge about, beautifully groomed and dressed from the tips of their bright shoes to the perfect ends of their glowing coiffeurs. They glide unhurried amongst the glittering refractions of crystal and chrome lit by hidden tinted globes. They are made up to demonstrate the latest techniques and trends, drastic models of the season's hued patterns, hot or cool, motley or pale, garish, refined, glossy or even rough mattes, extravagant layers of stuff that seem nearly as thick as velvet masks. They calmly display and apply the wares proffered by the various houses from the sample kits at the different counters: palettes of powders, alchemically mixed oils and cremes, and their long, honed, lacquered talons click against the vials of perfumed waters or essences. Beauty's shrine at the entrance to the department store temple, where they do their woman's office for women, serving seductively, yet chastely, too, as I take care to ensure. Oh, but it's an ancient, an immemorial sell.

Passing through my circle on the way to shirts and ties, socks, underwear, and sweaters, men only glance our way; but instantly their eyes grow smokey, their eyes glaze as they step into the invisible steam of fragrance that billows up from the counters. Sometimes they stare at us for a long moment, though they see nothing, stunned by the power of the cosmeticians' compounds. Sometimes there is reflexive stiffening, even fear shows in their widened pupils, perhaps because our faces, bathed in the unctuous radiance so cunningly designed for the boutique, must seem to them merely what they are: masks of a beauty that is obviously not even skin-deep: masks of faces that have been plucked, polished, painted with expressions fixed as though for some unknown ceremony that is about to commence—though at this altar it obviously it never does. I have watched the passing men and watched that little flinch of fear. Terror rather. For the girls speak softly, the girls almost chant, invitingly, as they murmur and coo to our clients, or brush and dab onto their faces secret formulas prepared for each alone. When they laugh, it's sweet, complicit laughter, never brazen, never coarse. And that terror is linked to puzzlement, it seems to me: for some of us are slim girls, some are sleek women, and some handsome, ageless crones.

My Boutique de Bellezza is for women only. If not for Woman. What do we sell? Never ourselves. We sell the form and image of Beauty itself. And generous counsel concerning its application, not its use. Never never. What would any one of us know of the uses of Beauty? Not more, and probably less than most other women know. Not once and never in seven years was my hand kissed or even brushed by a man's breathless parted lips; not once did a man's misting, troubled eyes gaze up into mine. What would he have seen but the blank questioning gaze in them? Friendly and impartial, if accommodating, too—but only as far as the cashier's. Oh, occasionally some fellow in banker's pin-stripes will pause a moment to sniff a sample of scent sprayed on the thin white wrist or the creamy blue-veined back of my hand boldly held to his thrilling nostrils. He inhales, he pretends to savor, to judge; and he buys, staring tranced into the depths of the remote night, far from that proffered tender, gold-braceleted hand. I can see him hesitating later, confused in his sensual trance, far away from us all, who by that late hour will long ago have creme-rinsed it off, packed up, and left by the service door, hurrying to catch our buses home through the sleeting night and the dismal blackened shabbiness of downtown Detroit.

Merchandizing glamor is not glamorous work. Mostly it's tedious; sometimes irritating. Hesitancy, caution, perplexity, unformulated doubts surging up from the bottomless well of self-doubt tug our clients this way and that. At last, looking speculatively, deeply into the mirror, they find themselves face to face with anger, and then despair. For, of course, women know better: they have been hopefully trying on this and that beauty year after year, knowing all the time it's actually sinister nonsense. Because what you see is never, never what you get. Still, it gives them the courage to step out mornings or venture into the night. Oh, to have the peaches-and-cream glory of an eighteen-year-old Irish dairymaid—without having to endure the sidelong mean oglings of tired, drunk, or daft barnyard Irish boys of forty. And who can show you how to have such complexion—well, an expensive facsimile—who but we, Hudson's salaried vestals, our nylons rustling as we float about in our gold-glimmering and crystal grotto, we, who serve the the most luscious goddess of them all. And you, our bored, curious, and constant if restless votaries, you listen to our singing, and you do as we advise without ever truly seeing us—and you pay, ladies, you go on paying your whole life long.

My job at the Boutique de Bellezza is nice work, though not too clean. Luck, steadiness, endurance—after seven years I'm manager. My goal's attained. I've bought a fine house of my own and furnished it all too. I have learned to labor and to wait. Rewards are still possible. But I was still alone.

Yet suddenly I am married. The Little Princess and the Stranger. It came to pass, what can I say? As though I were ordering the scene to be carved in high relief on my own marble tombstone, I still see myself standing transfixed in my boutique at the moment he appeared. That thick light is timeless, an emanation of orange shading into amber and persimmon hues. It is five minutes to five. How long has he been standing patient and silent behind me? And I hadn't even sensed him there. I only felt my hands hurting, my empty hands, as though I had been twisting and knotting my fingers together for hours. To the day I die I will hear myself saying, my voice pitched sharp, compressed by an anxious fatigue and sounding mean in my own ears: Listen, girls, we'll just have to clear this mess up Monday morning, so let's have all your outstanding tickets. A blizzard's on the way. I don't want you out there tonight on buses that'll be caught in drifts. Get going, leave the paperwork to me. I'll call a cab for myself.

Twelve relieved salesgirls scamper for their lockers. My assistant, Halina, who's been here five years and is like a sister to me, pauses. Go on, I don't need you, I say. Go, go! I'll straighten everything out. If I'm snowed in there'll be plenty of time to think about it. Did you ever see such a mixup? There must be ten thousand dollars missing here today. I can't imagine how you could all be so careless—or have these registers gone haywire? Halina doesn't move; her full, carmine-brushed lips are rounded to an O, and she is staring past me, the nipples erected under her pink silk blouse, her breasts rising and falling as though she'd just climbed a flight of stairs. Are you all right, Halina? I ask, turning to see who's there.

Someone's there indeed: a tall, a towering man. As I remember this, it seems to me I cannot make out his features. They are blurred, as if my eyes were filling with tears, or as if I trembled just as the camera of my memory focused and shot. I do see his elegant form, the fine gray plaid suit, a pink carnation in the lapel, a silvery thick silk tie, the dazzling white of silk shirting, and the strong tanned hands with their two massive rings that seem to have been cast in a basketweave of bright liquid gold, a big ruby mounted in one, a big diamond in the other. I still hear his voice, firm, deep, direct, calmly asking me—as though it were an ordinary Saturday afternoon on a mild spring day—for a bath oil, a present for his mother, something with a lasting scent. And though the store's closing and the snow's storming out there and it's just plain too late to think, I serve him. I only remember wondering vividly why Halina, that chatterbox, had not warned me, why she seemed strangely muted. I hand her a large flaçon to giftwrap—Bain de Venus. I think I managed to write up the sales slip and take a crisp $100 note from him. And yet it's altogether unclear. He must surely have said something more, and I must have replied . . . because he waited for me, and I let him chariot me home in his white Thunderbird, almost invisible amidst those flurries of frozen feathers whirling out of the black caverns of the night. And I let him come in from the December blast that was howling over Detroit, its icy diamonds heaping into mounds that had already shut off the sidestreets and were beginning to block the boulevards.

From that night on I have known nothing but his voice. A voice that speaks low to me, words that never make sense—and why should they? And those hands that caress me, that quiet me, ah, what hands, and those arms that carry me off to peace each night. My fingers and my lips have traced and touched that satiny skin of his everywhere each night for a year now, a year that seems endless. And yet his face at that first meeting remains altogether hazy in my memory, though how well I feel the contours of those features. I wonder why, when I can still suffer in my bowels the dizziness of those first moments as I turned towards him. Yet I cannot see his eyes at all, or his face—what blinds my recollection?—as though I had been about to faint with alarm at the day's botched accounting, which isn't like me. And what makes me think it was love that came then, from out of nowhere, as the song says? Love at first sight—that's to laugh. More like the sun exploding. And since then, that silent flare of sun brightening in my mind's eye by day, unbearably dazzling my mind at night. I am not dreaming. And yet.

Halina has been at me for the last few months. Who is he?

Where'd he come from? What's his name? What's he like? What does he do? At first she said nothing: but her eyebrows spoke for her, raised a little when I showed her an engagement diamond before Christmas as if to say, "In one week!" and raised a little higher when I shrugged off the idea of a honeymoon, and returned after New Year's with a wedding band. She kept still for six months, working very hard to please me, and helped by taking over routine chores in the boutique I'd always kept in my own hands, as if she meant to give me more time to float on the stream of my new pleasure, and spare me from spending my strength at work, although she couldn't imagine that I was full of new energy, of the happiness that generates more happiness out of nothing. Love cannot be "used up" like some jar of royal jelly that holds just so many ounces of essence. But these last three months she's been piqued by my silence, until she couldn't contain herself and simply came out with it over lunch one day: Was my marriage some kind of secret I was keeping—not just from her, but from myself too? What was it all about? She didn't get it.

She hurled question after question at me, compelled by a courage that took all her strength, because she knew she was in the wrong to ask me about my new husband, let alone what she was asking. After all, she's not my sister—it wasn't her affair. Yet I understood what she was unaware of in her fit: she wore the same face as on that late December afternoon, as though even then she must have thought it might be the only time she'd ever see him, and her breasts rose hard again in her blouse. And peering from beneath her concern was a mean, slit-eyed hankering to lay eyes on him again, coupled with a bit of feverish hot and dry lust I could sniff coming from her lap. She was anxious; perhaps I'd never grant her that wish. And I never will, though I wouldn't say it in so many words. I couldn't even if I wanted to. It isn't up to me. In the first place—he'd be angry. Although he's never been anything but gentle and kind, even in his throes, I somehow sense in him an enormous hidden power, a reservoir of molten wrath I never want to see poured out over me. And then? The truth is I'm scared to let anyone know about him. It's not selfishness or jealousy, I know that. It is not simply my privacy, what's intimate, personal—rather it's something to do with my sense that whatever I do know of him, what I've learned during those black winter nights when we have ravished one another, is never to be told in words, or compared with anything else. It is purely itself. Its acts of passion are absolute. And that puzzles me, because how can a thing be so palpable, so plain to me that it's part of my flesh, and yet at the same time be ultimately unknowable . . . although I was not part of him at all, and never would be.

And that is what my little Halina somehow must have guessed, or read in my smiling silence. Oh, she is a cunning little bitch! She believes her curiosity's normal, inoffensive. "Love is blind." She actually said that over coffee last week. And then I had to listen to what's going on with her friend . . . . Halina's got a classmate who's twenty-seven, a beautiful and very smart lady, she says. And a few months ago this Melissa broke her engagement to a lovely guy she was living with, because she *fell in love* with a sixty-two-year-old man who started up a conversation with her while they were both jogging around the lake. "Now she's *totally mad about* that jogger, and she thinks, get this, 'He's gorgeous, sexy, masculine, brilliant, very rich, and decent—because he's been married to the same woman for forty years'! This man swears to high heaven that he 'loves' Melissa. But no way will he take her anywhere in public; and he'd never consider divorcing his wife—because he's such a *devoted family man.* So what does he do? After they jog every morning, he 'sees' her for about forty-five minutes, at her place, of course. And hands Melissa five hundred bucks a week, in cash, naturally! Because he can't take her anywhere or buy her presents. Maybe his check would tell her too much? And Melissa simply refuses to date anybody else because she's so wrapped up in that guy." Halina just can't get it through to her that she's out of her mind wasting her time like that, five hundred smackers a week or not. Besides, a whore can do better than that. It's not "love" when a woman won't listen to sense or logic—it's a mental disorder!

I shrugged at her story. So? So she goes for another cup of coffee. Take her mother now. Fine example, her mother. She got married for the second time a few years ago to a man of fifty-nine, " . . . old enough to be her father," Halina intoned without realizing how silly she sounded, and takes off on a second honeymoon around the world. And ever since, they've gone on acting like a pair of teenagers. I said it sounded ideal to me. Halina shook her head dismally. I could see she was nerving herself for the next thrust. "My mother told him everything about herself, about the family, about the cashbox. But—does she know doodoo about him? 'He treats me like a queen,' she says, 'he gives me everything I want,' she says. But his past is none of her business, he tells her. My everlovin' eye! I asked him myself one day, and he told me off too. *It's none of your goddam business!* I haven't talked to him since, and I never will. After all, he's your husband, I told her. Suppose the police are after him? Suppose he has big debts? What about bastard kids that could pop out of the woodwork any time and say, 'Hi, Mom!' And maybe there's another wife stashed away? Or even two? But she's afraid to ask him again. What are you so scared of—you're his wife! And what's her reason? She's afraid he might fly away! Bird in hand, you know. And my mother just smiles at me like she's been born again. Jesus!"

I don't know what to say to that. Except that I am happily married. Maybe I've told her too much already. Halina thinks I'm in the dark, fast asleep, rocked in the cradle of my ignorant womb; she thinks she can wake me, hold up a lamp, show me a mirror in which the love she sees in my face will be reflected. She doesn't even know what she thinks, or what she wants; she only knows she itches to find out something that can bring her no satisfaction, and even destroy whatever happiness has been given me. What good would that be to either of us?

The warmth that smolders in me is like the soundless flames of an invisible fire eating through a seam of coal that will explode if ventilated and bring down my world in ruins. My world is not merely these female quarters in the Boutique de Bellezza: my world is the whole palace of this great store, where everything's much better than just good. There is no need that this place cannot fill: more than 100,000 transactions a day, conducted on 15 floors and two basement levels; a fleet of 300 dark green trucks delivering 10 million packages and over 900,000 pieces of furniture a year to homes around Detroit. And our trucks are not just merchandise vans: our drivers are helpers the people of Detroit admire: they stop for disabled cars, they push cars stalled in snow, they fix tires;

they start furnaces for elderly folks on cold days. Our drivers are our messengers, and they stay on their routes for life, as familiar to households as the bread man, the egg man, the milkman. As for creature comforts for our clients, there's a room where mothers can nurse their infants and change their diapers; there's a fully staffed hospital where we treat up to 200 customers a day for everything from scrapes and cuts to heart attacks. If a lady tears her stockings, we provide a free pair on the spot. We have available clerks who speak fourteen languages, just to cope with our immigrant populations. Seven hundred five fitting rooms; 13,000 meals a day served in our restaurants and cafes; storage for as many as 83,000 garments in our fur vaults.

Halina's making too much noise with her spoon, stirring cold coffee. "Happily married . . . ," she says. "Don't you consider you have a legal right to know something about your husband?"

Of course I do.

"Well then, where does he work?"

Somewhere in Detroit.

"How do you know?"

That's what he tells me.

"What does he do, how much does he make, what does he owe, is there anything saved?"

I don't know.

"Any insurance? Who's the beneficiary?"

I don't know.

Halina frowns, thinking hard, pretending to hide her hot curiosity. But it has to come out. "I can guess what your life's like with him." I wish you wouldn't, I say, you're bound to say silly things.

"No, no, it's for your own good," she hisses at me. "I bet he never has any friends over, right? I bet he never mentions any names. Nobody ever calls him at home. But he must have friends and associates, because he goes somewhere every day, doesn't he? Have you ever asked him any questions, for god's sake? Tell me that!"

At first I did, but invariably he just said, 'Don't worry about it, darling.'

"Don't worry?" Halina's laughing at me. "The hell I wouldn't worry if I were you!"

Thank god, Halina, I've got a good job. I make all the payments on the house myself. I pay for improvements. But he pays utilities.

"The heat and light are his, hunh!" Halina jeers.

And the phone too, I add. But I buy my clothes. He buys his.

"There's more," Halina says. She reaches across the table and takes my hands in her smooth, strong fingers, and holds them fast. "Tell, baby, tell!" She fixes her wide green eyes on me, and I stare into them.

He never gets any mail.

"I knew it! Call the police."

Oh, Halina, don't you think I went through all that. He's never been arrested for anything, he's never been in jail, and he's never paid any fines. He's clean in every way.

"Why haven't I seen him again?"

He wouldn't want you to. If someone comes to visit me, he goes into our bedroom and stays there. I've begged and begged, but he won't come out. And when my guests go, he scolds me for opening the door without warning him. Sometimes I think he doesn't even like me answering the phone.

"Listen to me now." She grips my hands so hard my rings hurt me. "That man's either paranoid or hiding out. Why else would he be so secretive?"

I don't know. I like his name. Eric's a nice name. It's like him somehow.

"He didn't look like any Eric to me the time I first saw him here. Chances are you married a phony name. Something sure is strange. Why can't you look at it straight? I'd get a private investigator on him. I wouldn't get in bed another night with such a mysterious man."

My turn to laugh. Oh yes you would, Halina! If you even came by for a cocktail, I don't believe you wouldn't find a way to get near him, even for just a touch of his hands. Halina goes crimson—I've never seen anyone blush like that—behind her ears, up over her scalp, her throat mottled purple and pulsing. But still she comes on strong.

"What's his mother's name, the one he bought that damn jug of Weill Parfum for? What's she like?"

It was only bath oil, Halina . . . but I haven't met her, no. She lives in Europe somewhere. And her name's different from his—you know, remarried a couple of times.

"Oh what a load of bull! You're in real trouble."

Nothing I can't handle, I whisper.

"What? You don't even see where you're going! Anything might happen and who could help you then? You better find out who he is. There's just got to be more!"

Halina, I know what there is for me to know. It's enough. I can live with it.

"I wouldn't spread for him. I wouldn't let him sleep with me another hour without telling me everything. Keep the hell after him!"

But I know enough.

"Your cunt may know, but you don't."

That's not nice talk, Halina.

"Nice talk she wants? Listen to me, cunt—one more night of what you're getting from him, and you could be dead. I say it for your own good."

What do you want me to do?

"Take a good look at him."

I'm afraid . . . .

"What's to be scared of?" She speaks to the coffered gilt ceiling of the Georgian Room: "Afraid of her own shadow. You'd think I was telling her to clip his wings!"

Halina, what do you want from me?

"Promise me something: check him out. All I ask. Please?"

I promise.

We took the elevator down to the boutique. My ankles were watery. She shook me good. I'm awake now. I am going to shed light on my own life. And that will put an end to it. If the news is bad, if I am married to ugliness, all my pleasure in him will turn hateful. If it's beautiful news, I'll never forgive him for keeping the secret from me. Either way I lose. Him. Everything.

Cheiron

NOW LOOK, SIR, excuse me—you mean he takes the poison willingly?" Yes. "Because he thinks he's not coming back?" He knows it. "It's goodbye, just like that?" Yes. "All right, say he can do better than become a shitbeetle or lizard like us. But he could escape from prison, and teach us how. So we could make it to a bear, a baboon, a porpoise even?" That's all over now. He's going on, going out, going up.

Ames throws himself back in his chair, wincing as if he's been clubbed. The others are silent, drowsing as usual or fiddling with their pens or staring up at me, as puzzled as he is. Their eyes are clouded with ignorance. They are young. Ames rests his head against the cinderblock wall behind him. Its rough, ash-gray surface makes his straight, thick, dark blond hair look like a muddy patch. His eyes are brown, his face long, the skin a dulled pink with rusty, flaring cheekbones. He knots his brows in pain, his thick lips drawn tight.

Two days ago he was baffled by the Ladder of Love. For fifty minutes he grasped it, rung by rung, ascending carefully, a creature made to climb. And then, near the top, hearing that there was another step, and learning that it led to the highest kind, but seeing it looming far beyond his reach, inexplicably distant, he hung there, biting his lip so hard it bled. What troubled him? "Yes, I see it, sir. But—" Well, Ames? "—it has no reason from within itself." The others were confused, vexed by his protest. They shifted uneasily in their seats, as if they'd felt a wave of nausea passing through them. Ames looked down because he'd felt drops of blood on his hand. Holding it before him with horror, he'd reached for his handkerchief with the other and dabbed at his chin. I'd watched that blood trickling down and said nothing: he'd been listening hard to the silent argument that filled the air in this room, turning and unfolding. Finally he'd said, "So, he went to this old mysterious wisewoman to learn the reason?" Yes. "And what did she tell him?" She told him what he says she told him. "But it's a secret!" Yes. "And after that, there's even more?" Yes. "I don't believe it." Suit yourself. "But he did?" We know only what is reported here. "What is reported here . . . Sir?" What is it, Ames? "It comes from a witch!" Whom else? Ames had dropped his head. One hand held the bloodied handkerchief to his mouth, the other drummed its fingers on the opened, blank notepad before him.

This morning he doesn't drum with exasperation. He writhes in silence. One can only wait. We all wait with him. Ames will bring it forth, when he finds it. He stares out the window. February in the Mohawk Valley. The hills and the valleys have been buried ever since early November beneath layer upon layer of snowfall, each packing on a foot over the former crust. The brief thaw of late January had glazed the world with ice, coating the trees, their limbs, branches, twigs, with a sheath of crystal: the woods beyond the nearby golf course are a stiff, glistening network of diamond cables and wires by day, a glowing, scribbled frieze by starlight. The very earth seems to have stood still during the week's cold snap: bright and blinding during the short days when the thermometer crawls up to ten degrees, and blueblack during the long, still nights that crack and glitter at twenty below. The porches are menacing cavemouths, with long fringes of heavy, murky stalactites. When we walk in our thick boots over this blanketed, cold world, the ground crunches dryly. Everyone marvels, feeling good because it's not the usual moist and storming sleet and snow tumbling down from low swarms of brutal dark clouds, but hard, clear, opened outward to the vast space of the illimitable heavens. The sky is white with visible cold again this morning, the dazzling, refracted glare of the small, cold sun above. We wait, staring out at the scene. Then, three crows come across the panorama of the wide window. Flapping heavily, slowly, patiently, half-gliding, half-winging, they pass above the shapeless, smoothly contoured earth, seeming to float on a swift current upward toward the crest of the hill. Their cawing pierces the thermopane, a conversation of cynical, braying sarcasms. Easily they swoop up, circling suddenly, slipping over the other side for good.

Ames speaks abruptly, "But it's not fair!" Fair? "What about us?" Who, us? "All the rest left behind here. Grandfathers, husbands, and young people. Mothers, babies. Abandoned forever." So it seems, Ames. "Doomed here. Cockroaches, mice, frogs. Snakes and slimy funguses. Your dog, your cat—they were living souls once." Perhaps, I say. "But he has no right! He can't leave us here like this." Ames' face mottles up, his eyes filling with tears. Some of the others smile at me with happy derision; some turn to stare at him. You have a point, I say: it is unfair . . . but what can we do? "He just swallows that poison and goes away, when he knows we have no chance of making it to the top of his ladder, of getting out of all this down here. Well, I won't buy it—we have souls too." And you think each soul is entitled to salvation? "Hell, yes." I mean, Ames, you'd better wait for Jesus then. He'll come along in a few centuries to fish you out of the pool of oblivion. You can sing along with the Christ in heaven, and not freeze beneath the eternal ice of creation like a beetle waiting for spring. "I haven't got three hundred years to wait for Jesus." Too bad. "So, he just turns his face to the wall, forgets his friends, and passes on. It's cruel. I need his answer now." But you have it, Ames. "I do?" Yes: he's asked you for a favor, Ames. "What's that, sir?" Sacrifice your rooster to Asklepios for him. "Why should I?" In payment for having been healed. "Now I don't understand you either, sir." Folding my arms over my chest, I say: Death, Ames, is the cure.

Now they burst into laughter, all but Ames. Unsure laughter: for a moment their ignorance has cleared, and they rejoice in clarity. Will they remember in an hour, before their thought is turbid once more? But Ames is angered. "Not me!" he shouts, "Not if I have to come back like some mangy weasel in some godforsaken hole. And that's only if—if I'm lucky."

The bell rings. Ames slams his chair back into the cinderblock wall, scoops his books together. The noise of his raging is obscured by the crashing, sliding, grinding of the other chairs in the room, the stomping of heavy boots, and the fading laughter of the others. He leaves by the rear before I can shake him from his stubborn dismay with a kind, lying phrase.

Despite the steel frost, it's a busy weekend beginning for the College. Parties; the place overrun with girls from Wells, Vassar, Skidmore, even distant Holyoke. Cars slithering over the ice, smashing crudely into snowbanks; crowds of young people struggling up the Hill or whirling down again on toboggans from party to party, intoxicated and wild in the bonebreaking chill; the girls' laughter and shrill cries audible from far off through the limpid atmosphere. Hundreds of lively bodies: some even wearing shorts and sneakers, their hardy knees red with cold. We older ones generally stick to our own bars this weekend, after the Friday night cocktails. Too much develops in these mixers for anyone over thirty to take for very long: whole cellars awash with beer so that one must walk through on planks; armchairs with half-undressed, long-haired beauties floating by; deafening bands, mad dancing, and dozens of bodies heaving on the floors of the wide fraternity ballrooms in the dark small hours. And yet, after two nights and days of this intense festival, there they are Sunday morning walking in the light between the walls of snow, bright-faced and innocent, to Chapel, where our kind, good Colin—a Shakespearean actor before becoming a pastor—delivers them a savage lesson from Calvin's primer.

Late Sunday evening, I stand before the deep punch-bowl, lapping up steaming, spicy, mulled red wine provided by our Assistant Dean, a sociologist. Sidney wishes to become the Dean: he hopes that they will come to think it's time at last for a social scientist to take over from the tradition-bound classicist drunk. Being men of business, the Trustees should have sense, he thinks. But of course they are alumni of this place too, and loyal to the dimmed past. In the middle of my conversation with Chaplain Colin on the limits of unmediated pain, and the blessings of our needful anodynes, of which the greatest is oblivion, Sidney interrupts to ask me what I think of young Ames. I look down at this short, plump hypocrite and reply, An intense boy. "Well, he's gone," Sidney says. His work is okay, no reason for him to drop out in midyear. "He's gone, I said. They took him off an hour ago. Maybe he'll live." Sidney rolls his bulbous eyes upward, a sort of chipmunk he seems to me, puffing his cheeks out with easy words. I dip my cup into his bowl again and ask what has happened.

"We don't know. I thought you might," he leers, prompting me. I answer by raising my cup overhead, pouring a bit over the tablecloth, and drinking it down in one gulp. "The fellows say he got liquored up Friday night early at the start of the Chi Rho mixer. He was in and out of things. They had a big one over there, looking their prospective pledges over. The usual. One fine lassie from Wells says he took her on a talking jag, and she missed most of the dance. Then he went silent, she says, and disappeared."

Which tells us nothing, Sidney. What happened? "He disappeared. At four a.m. they found his clothes outside the gym. Twenty-five below by then." So? "So he was gone. They say he flashed in at the Alpha Delts', the Tau Omegas', and who knows where else. Drunk out of his mind, or whatever. And naked. In that frost. With a wreath of withered oak leaves for a scarf. With a hockey stick in one hand, and a dead, plucked chicken in the other, for Christ's sake! They couldn't catch him. He ran through the Houses like a demon, screaming and getting everybody up." What was he saying? "Nobody knows. Made-up words. I thought you might know."

I dip my cup again, and look down at Sidney. I know how to wait. Sidney coughs. "They found him in the woods out back on the other side of the hill over the golf course. Stiff and blue. Covered with crusted, icy blood. Must have thrashed through the woods. Maybe they'll pull him through. He won't come back here."

Did you call his people? "You don't think much of me as a Dean, do you." Your wine, Sidney, is balm to me, I say. "Of course I called them. Ames did too sometime during this weekend. Told them some nonsense about breaking out. They thought he had one of his allergic spasms, and advised him to lay off sweets for a while. They're Christian Scientists, you know." Are they really, I say. "He also told them he wouldn't let himself be caught by the Greeks. They suggested he avoid the frat-rushing and go Independent if he liked. Maybe that's why he tore through the Houses, you think?"

Sidney, I can't say. "Well, I thought you'd be the one to know." Why? "Because in the ambulance he came to for a minute, and seemed to think you were there. His mentor, sort of?"

I guess he won't make it here, is all I say. "Perhaps that's what bothered him? Every year some don't," Sidney opines, ladling me out another cup of the hot wine punch, "and it's hard to tell which ones will, and which ones won't. I believed Ames was one of the strong ones."

So he was, I say. "I never believed he would be exceptional, though." Lots more where he came from, I say, hordes of them out there.

Sidney lights another cigarette, looking up at me accusingly. "You are an inhuman bastard." His folks must be very rich, Sidney, for you to be so upset about it. "Very, very rich."

With that bitterly spoken phrase, Sidney dips up a cup of wine, not for me, but for the President's wife, who has been expecting him to come and serve her. I dip for myself, turning back to the chaplain, who observes, "God only knows why there has to be so much pain in this affair."

And He's not telling, I say.

To Kolonos

AFTER THE JUDGMENT, after the great bronze doors had boomed shut behind me, I was alone with my life. I stood there dazed at the injustice of it all, recalling the silky image of that cool beauty in her pale gold dress I once escorted into these halls—I'd just met her in Prospect Park. The spree followed after I found myself pacing very slowly behind her down that same grand flight of marble stairs I'd ascended years ago, remembering myself as a groom with her on my arm. Today, my new white Rolls Royce Corniche waited in the judges' blue zone; on its hood my young son, clad in greasy deerskin like the barbarian he is, squatted insolently, his legs tucked under him. I stopped at the bottom of the steps: a dime lay on the grimy sidewalk. She stalked ahead, alone as always towards the car, erect, her once long russet hair now steel-gray and brutally cropped in the latest styling, though still long enough to cover the fine mesh of creases on her neck and the cords that held her head so proud and high. Her hips rocked undulant, the noon sunlight flashing from her sheer, satiny skirt; her full body, in that deep scarlet jacket the color of clotted blood, swept forward, carried clickclick on those firm, strong legs that stepped clickclick into her own future. Our boy watched us both, jeering and nodding his head in that mannered way adolescents have, affecting sagacity to conceal their compulsive cynicism. I was glad to realize I should never again be in his jeans—nor her bed. She'd loved me, and left me. She'd used me, perhaps to further the dynasty of the race. Nonetheless used me. I stooped for the dime. My son winked in a shallow show of sympathy. His pity mocked me.

To the judge it made no difference that I could produce tapes, made in my own car! that demonstrated the fact of her amorous trysting with her lover. No difference that my lawyer held out to him that white raw silk skirt mottled with the faint yellowed albuminoid spatterings of his semen, which she'd wiped between her thighs like any slut after taking him propped against a pillar of her own porch—her husband snoring upstairs after a long day's trudge through the fouled flights of tenements in Spanish Harlem and Hell's Kitchen, and a longer evening toting up accounts at the office. No difference whatsoever that she'd squandered our inheritance on a discothéque that merely fronted for her crowd's traffic in cocaine and heroin. His Honor could see that I, as her lawyers insinuated, was a wiseass, an adventurist, a tactless fool, in general, a born patsy—although Justice Lyman Ulick O'Toole never once lifted his purple, warty, whiskey-veined nose from the dossier on the bench before him. He summarily decreed us separate, "to prevent further violence," and moreover forever divorced. Joan had gotten to him before I could.

I descended those stairs stripped, as poor as I'd been on that frozen afternoon when I picked her up where she wandered as if lost among a grove of naked oak trees by the stagnant pond in Prospect Park. I wasn't even a slumlord anymore. Now I knew why my wife's chorus of retainers and hangers-on called her Tiger. My son cupped his hands and held them out to me, obsecrating. I tossed him the ring of keys: to the house, office, the boxes in the vault at Manufacturers Trust, and the Rolls. Playing milady's page-boy, he opened the rear door of that magnificent chariot for her: she slipped in and seated herself glossily on its plump, leather cushions. Playing chauffeur, he started the engine and backed out: she was already chatting on the white telephone, no doubt hitting up her next connection. No wonder it was so hard for just anyone to get into her discothéque: she controlled the best stuff around.

Five minutes later the first drink was down my gullet. I started with boilermakers only a block from that courthouse and Foley Square. Sometime after midnight, I found myself below-ground at Times Square. It was the first time I'd been there since I was a tireless acned youth of seventeen wandering with the crowd. How had my white suit been ruined? Stained, and torn across the knees, vest buttons ripped off, the right sleeve slashed from shoulder to wrist. Nor could I recall the way I had come up to midtown, though I knew it had been a long day's journey on foot from bar to tavern to pub. And my daughter was with me now, trying to take me through a turnstile, holding me by my left elbow with as firm a grip as a sixteen-year-old could manage with her little hands. Had she been the one who guided me this way? I must, I thought, get her away from here. Or had she said it: I must get home to my old parents, uptown, wasn't it? To Larchmont. And safety. Before I was mugged and stripped by the gang of black kids who hovered near the change booth, or the Puerto Ricans waiting around the stairway to the trains below. Thousands of people were passing by, coming and going, yet no one seemed to see them. I could be thrown down and stomped to death, and never be noticed or rescued.

Through the turnstile I lurched and down the stairs, shoved yet held back stumbling. And where was I then, which platform the right one for me? Trains thundered in, stopped, discharged and swallowed people, and pulled screeching away into the alternate tunnels. In the quarter-century since I had stood in that place, it had changed: glaring fluorescent light, bright new signs, new vending machines, even new trains, spray-painted elaborately with the graffiti and logos of the wild demotic gangs who ravished our many-gated city by night, and looking like hallucinated steel worms. I couldn't find my bearings: masses of late-night folk swirled round me as though I wasn't there: they were grim and yet chattering like birds and monkeys as they got on and off through doors that shot open and banged shut. I leaned against a post, distressed, waiting for my daughter to find me once more, put me on my own right train. She had led me here. Left me here. But she was gone now, and I was too drunk to consider what way to turn to find her. The laughing Puerto Rican boys had followed me down, and stood a few yards off, deterred perhaps by the black cop who eyed me as he swung his nightstick in elaborate loops as some veteran officers do. Which way uptown? I asked him. "Take the shuttle, man, and transfer," he pointed behind me and strolled off whistling. Transfer? Where to? I wondered, and answered myself aloud, To hell!

Another train roared in and I let myself be swept aboard in a knot of teenagers coming all dressed up from their prom, the girls in long dresses of pastel pink, green, or blue, the sallow boys in ill-fitting dinner jackets, their bowties askew on their throats, their faces pasty after the beers and pizzas. Filled with their noise and drowsing old people, the train jerked away into the sweltering blackness of the tunnel. I clung to a pole in the center of the car. The signs had changed inside too: this train's destination was as unfamiliar to me now as its origin. The letters seemed to double and dance in my watery vision: I had lost my glasses somewhere along the way too. All I could make out was BROADWAY EXPRESS. But it used to go to Woodlawn, didn't it? to the cemetery at the end of the line? I'd been there as a child once, the family plot perhaps. And now my own child's gone. Where had I lost her? How much longer could I stand there, clutching that stanchion for dear life as the train hurtled and rocked, heading somewhere through the dusty earth.

Maybe I could find a seat forward in the next car? I made my way through the massed kids, who paid no attention to me even as I lurched through them, swinging forward from strap to hanging strap as local stations passed the train in a blur of speed. Did I see familiar faces glancing up at me now and again? Old women, the three surviving of my father's nine sisters? No: whatever would they be doing here at such an hour? Besides, during the past twenty-five years of my absence I had changed: heavy, grizzled, and now ragged and filthy as any homeless Bowery bum.

The next car was nearly empty: only that knot of murderous boys at the other end, who turned and stared at me as I hopped in and the door slammed behind me. No one would risk coming in here with them. I was tired, though. I didn't care anymore. I flopped to a seat and sank into stupor as the train roared and rattled on.

Sharp taps on my left shoulder. Here it comes, I thought, squinting down, unable to raise my head. But the feet before me were set in the heavy, black patent shoes of old women: thick ankles swollen over them, stocky calves bulging with varicose veins held tight by elastic sand-brown support-stockings. I lifted my face. It was my old aunt, Frieda. The other two were stepping fearfully yet boldly through the opened door, the hot, sooty draft behind them whooshing gumwrappers and newspaper sheets along the car's floor. Jennifer. And Eleanor. Once upon a time, they were all of love to me.

Freida smiled. "Is it you, precious boy? Why did you pass us by?" For god's sake, I wanted to say, tell me where to get off before it's too late. "Where do you want to go now, precious?" Home, I heard myself choke, a word that had never come to my lips before. "He wants to go home" asked Jennifer. "Now?" Eleanor chimed in. Where is it? I implored. They conferred, standing before me and blocking the sight of those ruthless boys. "We miss you," said Frieda. "Why don't you visit us?" I couldn't speak anymore: my head was breaking into pieces, my teeth seemed to shake in my jaws. I couldn't even focus on them. "Come with us," said Jennifer. "We've gone away from the Hillside Homes. We're all up in Larchmont now." So I heard, I said. "We'll take care of you," Eleanor crooned. "You were always our favorite." And Frieda sang, "Do you remember when—" No, I can't go home, not the way I am. I wept. "Never mind," they chorused. "You look finished, but never you mind."

I must have passed out. I was lifted by brusque tugs at both my wrists, hauled with my arms outstretched over two pairs of shoulders, shuffled from the stilled train into the dewy obscurity of the night's final hour. I was led along the vague platform of the last station and down a last flight of steps. A taxi, as the old constellations waned. An entrance, the elevator of a new building. Supported still by those three old women, whose heads scarcely reached to my heart. The dry skin of their arms was papery, their breath sour. Silent, they guided me gently, gently. A door opened, and there was a burst of morning sun into the rooms. I glimpsed the ancient furniture they had brought to this new highrise condominium way past the end of the old line. Far below, I could see treetops in a park.

Then, down a long corridor until at last they let me fall onto a bed. My daughter's voice was speaking low and musically beside me as the curtains were drawn. What was she saying? "I'm here, Daddy. I'm going to be with you for good."

No! I thought. No, you mustn't! I have nothing more to say to any of you now.

Aeaea

THE THREE VIRGINS, they called us at Vassar. I don't know, even now, if we were wise or foolish. But we've each seen something of life: one in New York, one in Chicago, and one in Beverly Hills. We meet up often enough, passing over this wide wilderness, to and from on the career trails, the marriage and separation trails, wandering from sacking and slaughter with our booty, from conquest and humiliations, wedding banquets and sanatoria, fat farms, dude ranches and communes, islands en route, and adventures.

The Three Virgins are now divorcees again. And I have been trying recuperation at a fortnight's seminar of sensitivity training in the mountains of California over the Pacific. My gyroscope's almost reset yet again: after the last breakup, which left me stripped and drifting, I feel like I've been refitted for another journey. But where to? What god have I offended, I ask myself, that such stormy mischance rules my way? It's a question that has no answer, I think, because I am not, after all, the only one in these straits. Each of us has suffered her trials.

When my plane landed in Chicago I called Cissie. And she told me Celia flew in today too. We could have another reunion: it's been a year. There was nothing we'd have to say: it had all been said over and over, for ten years now and more. Cissie as much as indicated that when I entered, telling me to get my fancy things on right away: we're off to a party. Celia was almost ready, and then in she walked from the bedroom, pale and shining. I showered and dressed and made up. Then our brandy toast, the same one as ever, "Bon Voyage!"

The buzzer rang, and Cissie said, "My date, our escort and driver. Be nice to him, girls, he's shy—and loaded." She called into the intercom that we were just descending to him. "Made ten million before he was forty. Corn futures and hog bellies. Retired. Went into training. Now he's a rabbi."

The party's in a penthouse on the Drive: forty storeys up, all glass wall. Behind us, Chicago stretches glittering to the west and out of sight over the horizon. Below, Lake Michigan steaming and heaving as the evening lengthens out. Towards midnight it turns utterly black, nearly invisible, because the July sky is hot and full of low stagnant thunderclouds. These affairs are all the same: white fur wall-to-wall, fifth-rate paintings signed by modern masters on all the walls, ditto lithos in frames that cost far more than the prints, heavy plastic constructions with shifting fluorescent colors inside, cubes or spheres or tall oblongs, and glass and chromed steel abstractions that get in the way. Fifty-seven varieties of hors d'oeuvres.

Cissie and her sweet plump little rabbi are old hands up here in speculators' heaven. They introduce Celia and me quickly to the possibles among the swillers and boasters. Most of them are not from Chicago, it seems, but had stopped off on their wanderings and found what they wanted. The great grain terminal and hogbutcher has enough to hold them fast, and make them rich in less time than it takes to raise a child to the age when it can be shipped off to college on its own. A loud party.

Celia settled on a black lawyer about six feet and a half high, and had gotten far along and down to cases with him by midnight. "He's part man, part The Machine," she hissed at me on a pass to the john. Sounds okay. He's handsome, walnut-colored, poised, and looks extra good among this demotic bunch of crass males, half-bearded, scraggly-haired, paunchy-jowly, pudgy-pinkies, all snorting at the trays—but all all-confident and dangerous. These didn't seem ready yet for the mineral baths and ego-revitalization sessions the same types huddle at on the Coast. I don't know if it's better for them or not: I'd just spent the last days, as I say, with those identical swingers and swingees, naked in the hot tubs, touching and stroking and eyeballing, plumping all the naked misery together in midlife, under the guidance of the oracular therapist. Though here they didn't do primal whining and elaborate charts of their life-patterns. They shouted about politics, power, campaigns, and fixes, and stood before me dressed to the teeth. But is there a difference, if you look into their eyes?

Our host is something else again, besides being a zillionaire, as Cissie prompts me. And with a wife and grown son. Oh, where? "Iron Mountain," says he, "know where that is?" Can't even guess. "North, 'way north of north, top of Michigan. Great country. Mosquitoes, Hemingway. Got a lodge up there. Fly up weekends, when I can get away." Right now you're tied up though? "Can't you see?" and he gestures at the crowd with wide arms. "They eat me out of my profits. But business never stops here, you see." I could see. He's forty-five, built like a rolling barrel; hairy black knuckles over smooth hands with nails manicured and polished, the little rings with big diamonds bright on both pinkies; shadowed cheeks and cleft black chin, oily skin and bulging, sweaty black eyes; square feet and shoulders thick enough to shove an ox over. And he never stops moving: smoking constantly, eating away at his own rich table all evening, gulping Maalox tablets and washing them down with 20-year-old single-malt scotch. Booming, raspy voice, hoarse from shouting orders into the world. And with it all, a grabber: there wasn't one woman in the place I didn't see him grope in the course of four hours, including me: a paw on the breast, a clutch at a crotch, two hands—between canapes and drinks—on the backside. Wild, inconsequential squeezes. Never a pat or a stroke, no; but bizarre snatches just like those of a nursing child. Only, those hands could hold a good piece of you, and they bruised. It was funny, somehow, and went on in time with his words, his eating, his jokes, his noisy good cheer and domination. It was not funny, either, because it wasn't sex. I have never seen anything like it, in all these years of wise and foolish virginity. Cissie apologized, "I should have warned you. They say he's like that at his own parties. Outside, he has a sense of reality, they say."

I would say that he's a lost man, I remarked. "Yes," Cissie agreed, "and his wife loves him faithfully."

At one a.m. the party broke up in exhaustion. Yet he isn't finished with us. Cissie and her date, Celia and big black lawyer, our host and I are dropping forty storeys in the elevator. Going sailing. His yacht's parked just out there where the green light's blinking at the end of the dock, and it's waiting for us now. *Escape II*. A big sailboat. Sleeps ten. At the gangway, the rabbi stops, holds up a forefinger, looks about at the heavens, the low dense clouds glowing pink and white from Chicago's grid, and intones,

"My children, no wind, and it's coming on to rain. Let us go home to bed on dry land. Today's another day." Cissie stands there frowning over the water in the middle of the plank, lifting her silver lamè skirt to her knees, and mutters only, "For crying out loud, Jonah." Our host drives us all aboard, and before we know it, he's got her untied, cast off and moving out. The black lawyer's wearing a fancy yachting cap full of gold braid like a commodore: he's got the galley opened up, drinks coming, and we are slowly shoving along into Lake Michigan. Host has turned into captain, with a sailor blouse tugged over his burly chest, a pair of anchors embroidered in gold thread on the collar, and tucked in crooked behind: his hairy feet are bare on the planking: he's raising canvas with mighty haulings: and then he's running up and down, placing us in our positions, yelling at us and bellowing out nautical phrases at Cissie, Celia, and me: "Lee, there! Hardalee! Mizzen mizzen! Belay that tackle, matey!" And somehow, we get far out into the darkness before we know what has happened.

The lawyer is now seated before the mainmast, his yachting cap down over his brows, a tall drink in his lap. Before slumping into sleep, he says, "Always wanted to sail away from that place. Shit."

And all the time this voyage has been getting underway, our captain has been a demon of action: shouting, swearing at us, sweating, grabbing at hunks of cheese and bread, pouring glasses of scotch, lurching up and down the length of his sailboat, squeezing our tits at every pass, commanding the sleek *Escape II* as though it's headed for war. But there's no getting out of this now. Where are we going? I ask finally, struggling with the wheel, first left, then right, trying to understand his ejaculations. "Ten points alee! Bring her about, blast you!" and so on.

"Yar, Yar! Keep it yar, girls, that's the only thing that matters now."

Well, it seems our destination is still Chicago, up the Lake Shore somewhere, "to the Northwestern," whatever that is, a new jetty at his new corporate offices maybe. Though there's nothing out there in any direction now: utter darkness. We're exhausted. Not him: he's eating, and burping, and groping at us alternately every time he passes alongside and shows us "how to make yar." And despite it all, the three of us are laughing: our long skirts flung aside, our shoes and stockings stripped off. The three of us in the hot air filling the world over the lake waters, pale white shadows in the gleam of the running lights, wearing only our bras and panties, our hair coming down wet and wild, Cissie wearing her glittering necklace and Celia with her diamond earrings and bracelets . . . and he in his sailor shirt and jockey shorts—some crew.

But we get nowhere at last. Three a.m. Dead, flat calm. The lawyer wakes up and says simply that in the absence of any favorable wind, the best thing for this expedition to nowhere would be swinging round and going back. Our captain's standing behind me, pressing hard up against me, his arms covering mine, his hands clasping my hands to the spokes of the wheel. "How the hell do we do that?" he says. "Well, switch on your diesels, man, and put her about southeast or something."

"The hell you say," he roars, holding me there. "That's not yar. I want everything yar, yar, dammit! and yar it'll be, or nothing!"

And so we wallow into the first weak gray of dawn, which reveals the east to us, and nothing more. A fine, thick mist of warm rain envelopes *Escape II.* Shivering, half-naked under a blanket, looking like poor strayed cows, Cissie and Celia huddle curled up in the arms of the black giant against the mast up front. And I stand pinned to the wheel, the compass floating dreamily in a slow circle before my eyes, while our captain paces stubbornly behind me, drinking, munching, lecturing the greasy swell of green-gray waters. Yar, I could tell him, is nothing. And nothing's yar. But I don't.

Calliope

AN INVITATION TO A GALA housewarming at the new home of the media celebrity. They've been constructing that house on La Mesa for a year and a day, it seems, but when the walls went up around the property nothing could be seen as you walked past but the red-gold copper sheathing on the roof—which cost over a half-million, it's said. The massive electronically-activated iron gates reveal a driveway of granite cobblestone. At night the tennis court's tall standards tint the surrounding trees a poisonous blackish-green; a glowing misty dome of bluish light usually hovers over the place. Strolling by, you flinch when the vicious clamor of three or four black mastiffs erupts, and they go tearing back and forth behind the wall, at each pass hurling themselves slavering at the gates.

This afternoon those brutes must be chained to their kennels. The long, winding, tree-shaded street's lined with Porsches, Maseratis, Jaguars, Mercedes, Rolls Royces, Lincolns, Cadillacs, and a half-dozen ivory or silver stretch-limos decorated with streamlined TV aerials and telephone antennas. A valet service of chattering young Chicanos in scarlet bolero jackets trimmed with gold braid like operetta hussars greets arriving guests and whips their cars off into the dark side streets, from which the perspired and panting boys emerge running in a relay. There is a curving flagstone walk up to the imposing white building with its windowless walls. Propane burners line the way, driving away the cloudlets of fog that have billowed in from the Pacific all evening. Bowing waiters and butlers from Ma Maison's catering service wait patiently in their black tuxedos just inside the open front door, which is a low entrance that you have to stoop to enter, as if it were a cave's mouth, a hogan's or kiva's door.

Inside, it's immediately ultra chic: indeed, the doorway gives upon a great, high-ceilinged hall. A tour de force, this futuristic blend of medieval/cum antique/cum archaic, reminiscent of palace and temple at once. The naked, rough-plastered, windowless walls are painted a warm gray—there's a tint of rose in that hue—and decorated with fine, large abstract paintings that give the impression of being windows into deep, blank landscapes, sometimes depthless, sometimes a maelstrom of passionate colors, as if you stood on the plains of Mars or the surface of Jupiter. Rich Oriental rugs cover the cold black slate that paves the floor. The furniture is massive, chairs, couches, cabinets, but all hand-carved from a sleekly polished rosewood. There is fine silver and exquisite crystal. The only source of light seems to be an airy luminosity that pours down its purplish, foggy light over us from an octagonal opening in the center of the high, coffered ceiling. Looking up, I watch the clear sky turning slowly sapphire-blue: it is still dusk and only Venus sparkles there, seeming to reflect the sun that has just sunk beyond the watery horizon to the west. At the other end of this salon there is a great tapestry that looks like a Miro painting, and beside it a tall, narrow, curtained doorway reminiscent of the entrance to a sanctum. The flooring at that end is teak parquet, and it looks like a small stage because there is nothing on it at all.

There are about forty guests, all in black tie and designer gowns; even the press people and party-crashers are formal. They stand about, sipping from champagne flutes, chatting in discreet tones, waiting for a cue for the party to begin. The hostess is late. Yet there is nothing for it but to be patient as the first hour passes into a second and the steely hemisphere of the full moon can be seen moving over that opening overhead like the belly of a vast, floating ship. As though I'd been her impresario, her producer, or even her lover once upon a time, I seem to know her, though to these people who've come to drink and bask in the glow of her hospitality she's a mysterious personage. Our hostess is always late. She can be as late as she likes. Anyone with any hope at all will stand and wait.

A smooth man approaches me as I stand at the bar, getting my glass filled for the seventh time. By his manner and voice, his few observations about the rugs, he would seem to be a Foreign Service hand. There are of course a dozen of his sort here, Consuls, First Secretaries, and the like: quiet, intelligent, dignified realists who know how to cover boredom and irritation, since their careers consist largely of ceremonials that consume their days. He wants to know what that hole is up there in the ceiling.

The skylight, I tell him. We look up at it a while.

"A skylight," he murmurs in a contemplative voice. "Obviously it's a skylight. But it has no glass. Don't you find that peculiar? What the hell kind of skylight is that?"

I glance over the heads of the crowd, thinking she may be already among us. Then I whisper to him, Actually, it's not. It's a smokehole.

"A what!" he says, astounded.

Well, yes—a smokehole.

"What I thought I heard you say. Let me get a refill while I take that in. Now, do go on. . . ."

It's to remind her of her origins.

"That woman?" He seems baffled by my words. "Barbaric?"

Well, yes. Her beauty, that astonishing strength some of us have felt, that aura of the exotic—those talents come from her childhood. No matter how she may appear today, she's not in the least civilized. In the end, that hidden truth cannot be concealed. So, this smokehole was built into her new mansion as a token. What it says is, She has dwelt in tents, in sod houses, in log halls where the fireplace burns in the heart of the room, not down at one end.

"Ah," he says, "so you mean to tell me you're someone who's had an opportunity to—"

—Privilege rather. Isn't that what you meant?

"Whatever. Tell me, when you . . . that is, when she—?"

There is the noise of hushing from people. The room goes utterly silent. Everyone has turned to face the curtain. She now stands before it, magnificent, taller by a good head and shoulders than anyone here. In our absorbed conversation, we had not seen the lifting of that veil before the sanctuary. We had missed her entrance upon the little stage. And now there she is: benign, glorious. Like a goddess, one hand on her hip, the other held out to everyone in greeting. From head to toe she wears a shimmering celestial confection by some Paris couterier that seems to hide nothing of her generous attributes, yet somehow covers them all.

Hermes

CASUAL AS ALWAYS, careful too, I sip my Lillet at the little white cast-iron table in the garden near the freely turning mill wheel. The mill turns, the water splashes, grinding only the hours away. The willow's very old; its cooling ombre reaches far out over the thick, viridian turf that plunges, dank, moss-lumped, over the bank of the brook purling out from under the ancient building whose dark granite blocks are blackening with lichen. Two silver swans float in the pool behind the weir, and a waddle of young geese gossip as they strip away at the waterweeds near the opposite bank. But for the telephone wires going out over there, you would hope you were in the slower times of the last century, when such afternoons might have been enjoyed for their own sake. An occasional fatty and spiced cloudlet wafts invisibly past from the kitchen: this house is now a country inn on the southern reach of the Cote d'Or. Three Star. Those who know pause here before tooling up to Beaune for the auctions after the grapes are put away. I come a week early, park the aging Aston-Martin conspicuously out of the way—all waxy silver and chromed wirewheels—and wait. I am neither alive nor dead. I just happen to be here. It's but one of the possible seasons of the year on my regular Continental Tour. I'm not expected here, as I might be in Cannes, say. Cannes isn't for me, not even the film fair. Once too often was once too much. Well, one adapts to circumstances. Anyway, I prefer these old heaps of stone along the roads. Why not work from them, if one must? So I break from the gate in Burgundy, Station One. I have various private names for the twenty fortnights of my working season. This one is named after the house: Le Moulin d'Argent. It has been lucky for me.

An ancient district. As you walk into town from the inn, you pass beneath a Roman arch, a great gray square pile over the road. Up a steepish street to the dusty Place de la Liberté, a gravelled square bordered by tall chestnut trees. This month it's filled again with that broken-down gypsy charivari. After my aperitif, I stroll round, always stopping to pot a few clay pipes on the turning wheel with the old toy rifle at a dear 5 fr. per load. By now I'm acquainted with the tricks of this crazy gun: I break a dozen pipes each time. Grandpa's patient with me, for a Frenchman. Of course, I let him keep the change from a 50-fr. note. Money still buys tolerance. Not everywhere; but in these less-visited spots, yes. And I hand over the stuffed animal to a little girl from the orphanage. A week, and I've given eight of the silly critters away. The Sister takes care to send a different child wandering out of the file towards me after I've done shooting. They watch solemnly, complicit: there is breathless silence until monsieur puts the rifle down, receives his prize, and turns at the applause, delighted to see the children halted on their promenade, as though they happened along just as he was shooting. One reaches such understandings in France. Everything has been known. I can even recall who I am myself, from the soft twitter of the stooped old Sister: "*Voilà le jeune monsieur!*" That "jeune monsieur's" the sweetest jewel I've ever been given. And I must be fifty by now. Though who's counting.

On my return, there is a fire-engine red Bentley sedan docked alongside my car. Export plates. Only Americans would have one done up in that color: for a gag. Vermilion leather too. I think my party must be waiting, though I've expected them for a week now. Stroll down the old wagon lane back to the garden for another vermouth. There they are, ensconced at my table in the deepening double shade of dusk, their faces blanked by huge sunglasses with mirror lenses. Their heads turn to follow me. What can they see? I hesitate, and they gesture: will I join them? They have surely appreciated the taste of my car, the sort of vintage machine their sort rally in at Palm Springs. Nice folks, the Greens, Hank and Marge: accommodating. Tuxedo Park, New York. Floating awash in their own gravy. Thrilled at finding this inn, nearly empty too, after having been lost a whole day coming from Lausanne over the wild hills and getting miserably stuck in a rainstorm somewhere back there in those forests, not a bed to be found, my God! Switzerland bordered by Appalachia . . . but is this house as good as the Red Guide indicates? Better, I say. Terrine is unmatchable for 50 kilometers. Crayfish hors d'oeuvres should not be missed. Take the whole menu gastronomique, I suggest, just as it's offered, day by day: at 75 fr., and with old Chambertins, they can complete each day in sheer delight, and so cheaply too. There are also a few things worth looking at in this place.

"We didn't plan to stay," says Marge.

"There's a schedule drawn for us," says Hank.

"Golly, though, it's quiet here. What's to see, anyhow?" says Marge, opening it for me.

The Last Judgment over the portal of the Cathedral, for one thing. That's worth an afternoon.

"For that nonsense?" she snorts.

It's fine stonecarving. You'll look at it, and you'll see. And that Eve swimming naked on her side like a mermaid, offering her fruit to the man she loves—who wouldn't taste of it?

"Well, all right. Maybe."

"It's not that strict, honey," says Hank, lighting up a five-dollar Monte Cristo, and ordering another double scotch-and-soda. He commences telling me that they're actually headed to some big affair next week, by invitation. Oh? Well, it seems his senior partner at Bache, Halsey and Stuart's an Honorary Chevalier de l'Ordre du Tastevin . . . something from his mother's side, Hank thinks, vineyards they picked up under Napoleon . . . and quite the gourmandizer Charley is! but the poor fellow's suddenly off to China next week—you go when they call you—some oilwell-drilling deal . . . Bee, Aitch and Ess means investment banking, in case I didn't know . . . Well, of course I do, I say: I've worked with your folks. "You have? What line?" I'm in the communications thing, I reply, groping. But Hank knows all about that: not that he's done any of the underwriting for the new satellites over the Pacific; but he knows—and what is my part? I satisfy him with: a piece of the pickup-relay mechanism, a couple of patents on some resonators: an idea I got from my training in music. That nonsense was enough for him, after I'd told him the Aston-Martin was my first purchase with the first royalties. Hank likes my wheels, Marge approves the cut of my Beverly Hills tweed jacket, the discreet suede walking shoes . . . So, they're carded to the Tastevin shindig? Then this little inn can start their training, is my suggestion. You don't want to seize up with indigestion: you'd better build to it. "That so?" says Hank, disbelieving. Sixty courses of Burgundian cuisine in three days—just about the richest on earth these days. "My goodness," Marge exclaims, "I'm going to have to run the dogs myself when I get back." Dogs?

And Marge gives me the salient item, as though I were starting to collect an obituary file on her, "I breed Afghans in Tuxedo." Well, I mightn't have guessed that. Golf maybe, from the rangy limbs, the tanned leathery face, the brown-gold graying hair cropped straight. But it's dogs. The rings on her hands are interesting: if she travels about in that car, wearing that dazzle of diamonds by daylight, then what's snoozing in the safe back home? Not that I've glanced at them since they'd flashed out as I came into the garden. I go on with my advice, telling them about the Tastevin ceremonies, the chefs' new line of cooking this year, the rare wines they will taste. In response, they ask me to dine, not supposing I would refuse them. Somehow, I'm a little off my feed this evening, I say. "You look spunky enough to me," says Hank, in the way a man tiring of appeasing his lady would. But my way is to send signals on several frequencies, part noise, part sheer redundancy. They pick me up, but they cannot tune in. Making for confusion at the subliminal. Fatigue; then more havoc. I can work faster when they're unaware they can't even discriminate what it is. "What's the matter?" Marge implores, impulsively leaning forward to lay her jewelled paw on my upper left arm, her eyes behind their bright mirrors swimming closer. She presses my triceps, letting her long, freckled breasts droop freely, exhaling a gust of her musk. Though the muscle satisfies her, still I must respond to her concern.

I do, reluctant. My mother's gravely ill, I say. It's upset me. And I'm annoyed too. "Ah," she sighs in that brazen cracked voice of the first-generation outdoorsy woman. A voice that pleases me, though: it's full of the fret of hard whelping, tennis, and lawn parties. Reality that cash buys. She was doing well enough in Bath, I continue, comfortable, considering her age. But she had a whim to see Greece once again—her people came from there, she always said . . . "I knew there was something about you!" . . . But I think she imagines it: most likely some Classics teacher she once had a crush on—there were such people once in the public schools, you know. "How cynical you are—and your own mother dying!" How did you know that? I say, surprised. "She's sensitive," Hank comes in, suggestively again, patting her knee. "She's a good eye: conformation tells her a lot." Wanhope's wan hope. He would help me to help myself.

I haven't heard from her for ten days. She swore she'd call me here after she got up into her Arcadian hills. "How fascinating," Marge croons, apropos of what? It's down in the Peloponnesus. You wouldn't like it there, it's nothing but dying villages. Never was much more, except for boasting and producing mercenaries. Superstitious from the very beginning, and between Byzantine and Turk, things only got worse. She goes to her mountain, Cyllene. Her father, she calls it, her strength! All nonsense. Pointless. I'm boring you.

"No, no. Go on," Hank says. I don't go on. Why make up more than I must. The past doesn't exist, and there's too much to remember, once you begin to discover it. Marge is titillated and wants more. She is a handy, practical dame, a type easily disoriented by a mystery withheld. She takes it to be sexual. Her nostrils flare. As though sex were still the mystery. Or my dying mother. Fantasy, fantasy. To get hold of herself as we're climbing to our rooms to prepare for dinner, she asks about the ring on my little finger, an emerald-cut yellow diamond of say 35 carats. "That's a real heirloom, isn't it." No, just my father's—he said he'd won it in a poker game on the Orient Express, from one of Goering's boys. "Luck, or skill?" jibes Hank. Both, and more—he had to take the finger with it. That's a deft touch: Marge blanches. When her color comes back, the horror will glow with lust. "I've got things worth a lot more," she says, "but nothing with any background to it." Famished she is, like all these new folks, for history. Which is easily supplied. Harder providing truth. For a reasonable facsimile of that, I go down right away, call Paris and have the telegram sent to me. It will do.

The garçon brings it discreetly two hours later with the check, which I take over protest. We have had a repast of duck and venison and Scottish salmon —I take care to touch almost nothing of the dishes we were sharing about for variety's sake. We have coffee, and light up two more of Hank's Habanas. I am listening to her stories about her shaggy dog. Champion Rondina Tiger Rosay, a silver-and-gold Afghan hound, who took his 69th Best of Breed in Richmond last week. She extracts some polaroid glossies from her Gucci rucksack. Quite a dog, my eyebrows say with amazement. "You must imagine it takes endless hours to get that perfectly splendrous coat." Yes, of course. "Well, no. You couldn't be more mistaken. Grooming him's much less work than that! I never touch Rosie with a brush during the week. He's bathed every five or six days. I use a hair-conditioner by Helena Rubinstein, and I experiment with women's shampoos. Every hair's brushed dry with a 1200-watt blower, and the whole process takes only two and a half hours. I rely on long pin brushes. The longest parts of Rosie's coat are ten inches, and will continue to grow just like human hair. The texture's a pure beautiful silk, so it doesn't mat. Exercise is terribly important for his coat, since it stimulates circulation."

She must be playing me the tape she uses from one dogshow reporter to the next. I lap it up. She believes she has me now. It doesn't faze Hank. "I roadwork Rosie religiously every day for three miles: he runs beside the estate wagon around the lake in Tuxedo Park, and the last half-mile's straight up the mountain. And proper diet's essential, including balanced vitamin supplements. I'm sort of a health freak," she laughs, "raw meat, cottage cheese, raw vegetables, fruit, and about one-third a daily portion of good quality, dry kibble. That keeps Rosie in the pink." I lope ahead to the conclusion: For all those Blue Ribbons? "You got it! I just turned in my 1973 wagon with 175 thousand miles on it. Why, the new one's clocked eight thousand, and that's only over the last two months! I got my first Best in Show with Rosie's mother, a beautiful bitch named Bluejay's Gold Passion. That was in 1973, when Hank was made First Vice-President of Bee, Aitch and Ess. Good year for us," she giggles. "I give Hank a Blue Ribbon, and he gives me a diamond choker to go with the bracelet." Fair enough, I murmur. "Oh, better than that," Hank says, ambiguously. "We both worked our butts off for ten years though, didn't we, darling," she says. "I guess we did," Hank says, and sighs. He will agree to anything. "Of course, it was Hank who revived the Tuxedo Park

Kennel Club. That old crowd let it go to hell years ago: too busy in Palm Beach. Someone has to keep tradition up. So why not us?" Why not indeed. Diamonds and dogs. Life goes on. "Hank's busy: busy busy busy. He's a judge of several breeds, and secretary of the Larchmont show too. Oh, not Afghans, if that's what you're thinking! That would be, uh, conflict of interest. After Watergate, it's—" She's at a loss. Hank helps out, "It's not done." "That's what I mean, it's just not done."

But I reassure them, I wasn't thinking that at all. Marge is skeptical. Narrow-eyed, she says, "Then what were you thinking? Come on, 'fess." I take the telegram from my breast pocket, hand it over. MAIA DEAD STOP FUNERAL STOP CAN YOU COME STOP WAITING FOR YOU STOP LOVE. A tiny gasp of contrition, and sympathy too. Marge reaches out to clasp my hand in hers. She's sorry, her eyes liquid. "You must go. We'll miss you, of course." Hank is very helpful, "Look, don't worry about the car. We'll putter around a few days. You just go along. We'll keep an eye on it." I'll garage it, I say, you have somewhere to get to. "Oh, no!" they protest. Better yet, since your Bentley's a bit big, why not use my car, and tool around the back roads: there's lots to see. That's it. They take my keys greedily. I've tied them down here.

I go up and get the shoulder bag that's already packed and waiting. Come down, tell them goodnight, and call a chauffeur in from town. Before dawn I'm in Dijon. Hop to Paris. Air France to New York; a first-class nap in First Class. My kit's in the vault at Irving Trust. Cab over to Tuxedo Park. Not quite midnight. Rondina Kennels in the directory. Afghan hounds are silent; the help's asleep. Sometimes dogs are allergic to strangers, so I quietly drop by to say hello. The fence is unlocked. Rosie's a friendly brute, and all his show-training has accustomed him to visitors. Still, he's restless, alert and smart. A few pats, a tussle, and then a generous squirt of Mace: he will sleep out the night. Their house is a big pile of fieldstone: brokerage Victorian, pre-Depression model. Alarm's an old one too. Three minutes and I'm inside. Library safe needs thirty seconds. Not enough in it. There must be more, I can sense it. Nothing in the master bedroom. The upstairs parlor, however, is now a trophy room. The new Mosler's tucked behind an oil portrait of Rosie's mother, Champion Gold

Passion. Blue Ribbons cover the whole wall, and there are shelves of silver cups and statues of Afghans on pedestals. Ninety seconds for this one. A nice lot of things, as Marge says, but nothing heirloom. About 250 thou, I guess.

By two-thirty I'm back in town, closing the bar at the Pierre with a glass of port. And then to bed. In the morning, business: the kit returns to the vault, the glass goes into my Fagin's box on 46th Street. Shlomo's a genuine phony. If you passed a huddle of Hasidim on Sixth Avenue, you wouldn't pick him as the ringer if your life depended on it. Even fasts on Yom Kippur. My estimate's good: quarter-million retail. Shlomo counts me out fifty grand. I might do better elsewhere. But I've known him all my life, it seems. If he ever thought of twisting me, he knows he wouldn't get my ring, an heirloom from Goering's buddy he covets. As long as I wear it, I'm safe from the like of him.

By nine, I'm taking a cognac over the Atlantic. Back on the road to Moulin d'Argent by afternoon. I hope Hank and Marge have enjoyed their two days of sightseeing. As the driver pulls into the court I remember to pin the little black silk ribbon to my lapel. The Aston-Martin's standing there covered with white dust. Good. As I step round to the garden, where they'll be seated under my willow, drinks in hand, I notice on my left sleeve a long and bright strand of silky hair, silver-and-gold-tipped, from champion Rondina Tiger Rosay's breast. Nice dog. Nice folks. They'll have a hell of a time at the Tastevin banqueting this weekend. Let them eat till they drop.

Kronos

THE FELLOW WORKING in the carrel ahead of me was departing. He screwed his fountain pen into its cap, slammed three tomes shut, scraped back his chair, stood with ponderous rustling, stretched, sighed, and clumped off through the narrow aisle between the stacks, letting a gargling, hemorrhoidal fart as he turned at the end towards the exit.

Two p.m. I remained to shuffle some data and collate my sources, my pen reluctantly scratching out a last few key phrases before my watering eyes. After such a winter, to miss this so-sweet day? By three p.m., I knew it was all over with me, even though my time here is brief and my research scarcely done. Still, I could think of nothing essential lacking for the four lectures commencing tomorrow at the War College. One always imagines there is so much more that needs to be known. And there is of course really no end to it, or this discipline of ours is meaningless.

It wasn't my first visit; but this time I looked forward with a sense of purpose: I have a question for the officers. Like everyone else, officers have been trained to give answers ever since they were children. Anyone can give you an answer: just come to the Library of Congress and seek: you'll find it all here waiting for you. But it's time they were made to feel the agony of propounding a question.

I gathered myself up. Passing the next carrel, I glanced in: Egyptology. Strewn over the scarred little desk, beautiful drawings laid out on parchment: vessels with covers in the likeness of jackal heads, cat or hawk heads. Death his subject, then? A title neatly lettered on the front of his spiral notebook: VICISSITUDES OF DEATH: NECROPOLI OF SERAPIS IN THE LOWER KINGDOM FROM THE FIRST DYNASTY TO AKHENATON AND AFTER.

I opened it. "Burial urns, vases, Canopic jars: they all tell us

. . ." his study began—and broke off. Not even the first sentence framed. Washington is irresistible in cherry-blossom time.

I went down and outside, where I stood dazzled, looking out at the scene before me, what I could see of it without sunglasses. Tourists were scrambling down from buses, parading in small groups up the Mall. The great government buildings lined the wide green swath, and traffic was heavy. The monument pointed its immense obelisk into the pale sky like a fanciful, frozen rocket some geometer of antiquity might have imagined. I wanted to go down and walk about among these visitors in this gay spring afternoon, to sniff the moist, flower-scented breeze, and forget the inexorable drift of things military. Where is there an end to it, after all. Besides, to believe in the importance of what one knows is dangerous. It fixes one's thought, and then any mere novelty can knock one over, like that. And what else does each day bring but pure surprise?

I'd been aware as I stood leaning against one of the stone lions guarding the entrance to the Library that someone was near me, on my left. Slow, stertorous breathing. Then the sound of two dragging steps, and a shadow thrown over me—immediately I felt the loss of that hopeful Easter April sunlight. I glanced sidelong down. Handsome, well-polished English shoes bespoke bootmaking that wears a long time. Thick wool trousers of a light brown, salt-and-pepper Donegal tweed with rather large, old-fashioned cuffs. I looked up carefully: a smoking jacket of maroon silk velour with black satin-matte lapels looking a faded gray, washed out in the slant, afternoon rays. A fine white shirt of Sea Island cotton in a thick basketweave, custom-tailored obviously, and a green woolen tie. The man was well over six feet. And he was old, old: a wrinkled throat with a great knobbed Adam's apple, heavy jowls, the skin blotched by pink patches and freckles spreading large as pennies. A handsome if vestigial dignity. Real age is still hard to come by. Yet this man was familiar: that erect posture, the deeply seamed yet gentle strong features, the pale, creamy blue eyes that stared straight ahead with that remote and thoughtful gaze of the truly ancient. White hair, straight and well-groomed. He must have been a hundred years old. The mouth was open in a fixed smile, perhaps because he breathed so heavily. And he swayed, the way a redwood patriarch swings like a slow pendulum if you lie on the forest floor on your back and look up at it lazily and long. Did he see anything I couldn't see, far off, beyond the monument? His right arm came up then and rested on my shoulder. I understood. He wanted my support down the wide steps to the street. Well, why not? I rose from my half-reclining position against the lion's pedestal and started down. At each step he rapped the lucite cane he carried in his left hand against the risers, as though counting the flight of stairs. It came to me who he was: our former chief of staff. General Marshall: Soldier and Statesman, as it reads on the postage stamp. Of course he would have been around a hundred.

His big-knuckled, rope-veined hand gripped my shoulder with a strength one would not have thought the old man had in him. I took the wide steps cautiously, the giant shambling after me in those fine shoes, the weight of his ramshackle frame thrusting against me as I leaned backward to keep myself from being thrown headlong. What was he doing there? Where had he come from? Senile, probably. He must have wandered out of the geronts suite at Walter Reed, and wound up lost in the Archives of the Library of Congress. That great man whose foresight had saved Europe from economic disaster and chaos and eventual subjugation—this is what he'd come to at the end? Magnificent, yes, but a ruin. He said nothing. I hesitated on the sidewalk; his hand on my shoulder impelled me into the road, and we crossed, stopping traffic. I assumed he wanted to walk on. Well then, I should lead him along this lengthening balmy afternoon. I'd come out for a stroll anyway. Later, I could hail a taxi, fold him into it, and send him back where he came from.

We entered the Mall. Marched forward. People stared at us. I—with my shabby stained trenchcoat and worn attaché case, a balding scholar, round-shouldered and listing to port under the weight of the old man's arm as he tramped, half-shoving me, half-following. And he—but nobody seemed to recognize him. Don't they remember how much they owe to his generous vision? I heard myself murmuring as we went, scarcely imagining he could hear me coherently. It's a shame, I was saying, that people forget so easily, so soon. That I was honored to encounter him. That I happened to be studying some aspects of the origins of strategic thinking, trying to bridge the discontinuity between the history of the world that ended in 1945 and our new situation, which had materialized from one day to the next and swollen in a single generation far beyond the logical parameters of conventional historical analysis. Of course, nothing novel in all this to him, I mumbled apologetically. But for us, who have had to conceive the new, contingent terms of our existence, let alone our survival, yet apparently have not really comprehended them even after so many years, it's a task we should continue to struggle with, didn't he agree? No response. Stared straight ahead and far off, lurching along on my left, lifting that transparent cane and rapping the concrete every so often, as if erratically punctuating my harangue, or testing for hollow places beneath the walk. His stride was long, with a sort of double-jointed hitch that threw me off balance because of the momentum of that lanky form, coordinated by a mechanical jerking, it seemed to me, and moving forward by sheer will alone, as if he'd collapse if we halted for a breather.

Near the monument were steps off to one side leading underground to the Men's. He staggered on ahead of me. I followed, anxious that he'd stumble, fall and snap one of those old, long limbs or pop a clavicle. But he dashed down awkwardly enough, tripping and catching himself, yet remaining on his pins. Inside, he went and stood at a urinal. I took the adjacent one. For many long minutes he gazed before him, seeming not to focus on the multicolored palimpsest of graffiti, an index of banal, sinister, and silly contemporary apothegmata. I finally went to wait at the exit, not knowing whether I ought to stay. At last he returned silently, that phlegmy bubbling in his throat, laid his right hand once again on my shoulder and followed me up, where we resumed our dogged march.

Not once had he acknowledged my words. Could he really hear, did he actually understand me? Was he merely bored—indifferent, indulgent? His grip, though, was urgent enough. I didn't know what to think. So on I went as before, half-leading, half-guided, talking as though lecturing our majors and colonels, doing away with ingrained, outmoded attitudes and responses, preparing the ground for the question, a question both necessary and strategic. A thread of white, frothy spittle oozed from one corner of his rigid, opened lips: it moved down his chin and lay looped over the black silk of his left lapel, soiling its red ribbon of the Legion of Honor. I did not dare to wipe his chin. It would have been an insult to the dignity of his hundred years. Or perhaps not. I didn't know what ought to be done with him.

We'd gone almost a mile and were approaching the end of the Mall, where there's a slope up to the street and a bridge. The path we had taken went on beneath it into darkness, towards an underground vault barred by a heavy iron gate. The sky above had purpled. The rush hour roared by out there like rolling thunder. I wanted to glimpse the yellow flash of taxicabs in it; but there weren't any. Instead, the bridge seemed to be lined with people regarding us in silence. Tourists? No cameras. Odd. As we approached, I realized what it was about them. They were short: their heads barely topped the stone railing. Big heads, too, and vivid faces, like a massing of mongoloids. A class of exceptional children out for an airing? But where was their teacher? No—now I made them out: Wolfman, Snow White, The Marx Brothers, Dracula, Porky Pig, Mickey and Minnie Mouse and Goofy, King Kong, Elmer Fudd and Bugs Bunny, Daffy Duck, and Frankenstein's Monster. They jabbered, they squealed, they pointed down at us, mockingly, menacingly. I stopped. The old man paused with me, panting, and squinted up at them from beneath his shaggy white eyebrows.

A stone fell at my feet. Then another. They were hurling rocks at us. One struck me sharply on the shin. Another whizzed right at my head, but I got up my attaché case in time to block it. They had our range now—we were going to get hit. A flat one skimmed dipping down and banged the old man on his upper thigh, smack in the groin. He was astonished, seeming to wake for the first time from his stuporous yet insistent forced marching. A croak issued from his chest, a voice long disused. "Aliens!" he bellowed, "They've come at last! We're being invaded!"

No, General, it's not what you think.

"Got to get to HQ!" he rumbled, "Got to sound Red Alert!"

Listen, my dear General, you don't understand: they're children.

He lifted his cane, babbling, shaking it like a sword of light at them up there, and staggered back as more stones hurtled down at us. One hit him a glancing blow in the face: a long cut opened from his right eye to his jaw, and swelled with a thin, jagged red line. He let go my shoulder and crashed off to the side, groaning, "National Emergency!"

We retreated until we were out of range of their missiles. They were yelling at us: wild, weird cries, screeching indistinguishable words, their chorus of jeering laughter sounding like nonsense, like formless curses.

Suddenly he tripped over the curb and lay spread on the wet grass, still muddy from the recently melted heavy snowfall that had brought April's cruelty to us. His arms and his legs were strewn at stiff angles; he seemed to be merely a broken skeleton inside that tweed. He looked up at me: his slate-blue eyes were clear—prophetic eyes that looked through me and beyond. "Tried to warn you. Don't say I didn't try! Knew they would come. They're here now! God only knows if we can win this one. Get me to HQ. Got to warn them all! Before it's too late!"

General, I whispered as I bent over to calm him, trying to catch his wrists as he flailed at me. Sir, Sir—listen to me, Sir. It's not the end of the world—it's only children! But he resisted my grasp, he was too strong, too heavy, too old to raise up again. I couldn't manage it: I slipped and fell on my butt to sit sprawled beside him.

He lay there on his back weeping, pleading with me, his slashed cheek dripping a crimson that matched the color of his silk jacket, his thickened tongue licking at his withered lips, his green tie twisted about his throat, his big chest heaving, his eyes glazing, fixed on me with the urgency of a seven last words. With a great effort he held his breath, quieted himself. I was aware that the late afternoon light had vanished, that suddenly we seemed to have been dropped into a darkness that would receive no light from above. He nodded his head as if to accept our situation, as if to acknowledge this terminal solitude. And then he said, with the chilling, contemptuous authority of an old, old man who gazes into the dark mirror of the world and sees the evidence of things unseen, "No, you just don't understand, do you!"

Teiresias

SATURDAY MORNING we decided to travel all the way downtown for a change. It was one of those memorable days when March has just blown itself out and April has not yet warmed and gathered its damp tinctures of sulfuric smuts. We were after nothing really but a view of the fast-flowing waters of the Bay, of the Statue of Liberty, and the great bridges arching east and west, and the shapeless forest of gray hulls and masts in Brooklyn, like the dead trees of a great swamp. No one is crowded then in the shadowed canyons of the financial district; on Saturday morning the over-reaching walls of stones and glass refract clouds and the sky in harsh cubistic angles. Only strollers, shoppers for oddments, traverse the narrow streets, thinking of hardware, exotic lumber, surplus paper, sundries, electronic gear, and salvage. The offices are silent, dark, rank upon rank above the old, winding abyssal streets. Alpha to Omega: the first Dutch cowpaths and village tracks, now paved over yet persistent beneath asphalt, enduring the unimaginable mortgaged future entailed in the skyscrapers. Only a very deep frozen granite plug into the magma beneath the mantle of Terra could sustain the weight piled up on Manhattan Island down there near the Battery. One feels lighter, smaller than an ant in that district. But on such a Saturday morning, noontime, springtime, one's soul caroms about those breezy canyons, free for an hour from the corridors of work in our pharaonic temples.

Up Nassau we wandered after circling the tip from Wall and out along the railing over the sparkling, tangy bay waters. We looked into old stores, with their high ceilings and carved oaken lintels. Now and then, to the east and the north, a glimpse of the high decks of the Brooklyn Bridge swaying quaint and stolid over the East River. We stopped somewhere at the end of Nassau Street before a dusty store window. Judging from the anchors crossed over the first storey, the building must have been a chandler's warehouse in the 1800's. Most of it seemed derelict now, boarded up. But the door was open. Let's go in, I said.

Such an array of ill-sorted junk: hardware, war-surplus equipment and clothing, canteens, webbed belts, boots, tents, mess kits and rubberized ponchos, rusted machetes and trenching tools, all laid out on rickety tables and stacked up on metal shelving, up to the high ceiling where weak bulbs dangled from naked cords. Anything can be found in a store like that. Sometimes the quality is fine: reams of 24-pound rag paper; big old ledgers with creamy stock, wide margins, deckled edges and leather binding. I saw a display case stacked with cigar boxes, and asked the proprietor—who had come out now and stood there in baggy striped pants and ravelled wool cardigan of faded scarlet, silver-white-haired, pink-faced, smooth-shaven, and smoking a fine meerschaum on whose bowl a mermaid swam forward like a Naiad on the bowsprit of a clipper—if by some chance he had any vintage Habanas tucked away there? You never know. "No, nothing like that," he said puffing away rather contemptuously, I thought, even sneeringly. Well, what was in those fine Monte Cristo boxes? He reached down and handed me one: instead of Churchill Corona Coronas, it held shiny clips of neat copper and brass fingers, oiled 7.65 ammo. I see, I said. "So you do," he replied, taking the box and placing it back carefully with the others stacked up in the case. Would you perhaps have a good shotgun for me? "If you like, I might have something for you, yes." He turned towards the partition that divided the store. My wife frowned at me, but followed after.

We went round to the rear of the store. This part was much cleaner than the front: the floor waxed, the cabinets highly polished oak and walnut, their glass clear. In the middle of the floor stood a pair of .50 caliber machine guns on tripods, World War I types. They looked ready for use, belts of rounds draped out and folded in their metal boxes like metallic tripes. There were bazookas on fine old mahogany tables; there were grenade launchers, recoilless rocket guns, 200mm mortars, automatic cannons, a Bofors anti-aircraft gun. In the cases, pistols of all sizes, and rifles in the cabinets, Brownings, Mausers, Mannlichers, M-1's, M-16's. My wife picked up a Kalashnikov assault rifle and hefted it. I turned the wavering muzzle away and said she ought to keep her finger off the trigger. "This is more like it," she said, cradling it under the crook of her arm like a guerrilla and sweeping in a circle. I said she should keep her fingers out of the trigger guard.

The proprietor stood up from behind the large case then. He'd been stooped over and fussing in a low drawer. He smiled wanly at me around the amber mouthpiece of his pipe as he held out a large gun. "This is what you might be wanting, I think. Something extraordinary." I took it from him. It was an old shotgun, a make I didn't recognize. It was quite beautiful, and I said so. The stock was burl walnut; the breech of heavy silver, engraved all over with a forest of flowers and curvetting stags and leaping hounds; the barrels were blued to perfection, satiny, oiled; the trigger guard gilded and velvety to the touch. Perfectly balanced: it went up against my shoulder as though made for me. It broke apart at a touch: the action was almost liquid. "Traps, hunting, whatever you like with a weapon like this," he said, puffing away. I turned it about, just to enjoy the feel of it, and noticed a silver plate sunk in the heel of the stock. It had letters engraved in elaborated Gothic script. When I made them out I was surprised: entwined with minute patterns of stylized small game and oak leaves, the name was mine. What a coincidence!

The proprietor, who was watching my wife toying with her deadly, Russian automatic weapon, raised his eyebrows shaggily, but said nothing. Neither did he move to warn her himself or take it from her, though it made me uneasy, her behaving that way behind my back. She hated guns, so I thought she was being sardonic. I wanted her to look at this shotgun of mine. It's quite a coincidence! I said again. "I don't know," the proprietor finally replied, still watching her, "but we could find out, couldn't we." I only wish we could, I said.

He hauled out a great old record book then, dropped it down on the countertop, and began thumbing through it. It was like the registers you still see sometimes in some decrepit spa in Europe somewhere, full of names and numbers written in every kind of hand, splotched here and there, and glowing in the faded inks of all the colors of the rainbow. How old was that book? I wondered. The proprietor was in no hurry. He seemed to relish the chance to browse through it while I waited: I could see the pleasure he took in it, as though running over the pedigrees of fine old guns of the last two centuries reminded him of the very weapons themselves. That must be a rare catalogue, I said. All yours? "So it is," he said. "So they were." The paper was heavy, deckled; the early signatures were almost faded out or illegible with weevil holes. The latter third of the volume was, however, still unused, and the paper fresh as though it had been bound yesterday. Seems up to date, doesn't it. "Yes," he mumbled, running his arthritic and tobacco-stained finger down a column, the nails of that gnarled hand broken and black with dottle—he had a way of tamping the hot wad in his meerschaum down as though he couldn't even feel the fire of the glowing ember he puffed at. "Here we are," he said in a voice that showed no happiness in having found the record of this gun. A neutral voice, bored in fact. "There are only two others like it. This one has had but three owners since it was made . . . oh, about 1928 or 1929,1 should imagine." Where does it come from? "It's a German make. Can't you see that?" He was sneering at me. I suppose so. Well, how did it get to America then? and how did it come to you, I said. I was almost shouting at him. Well?

He shrugged at me. He wasn't telling. He pointed at the names in the ledger again. I couldn't read them upside down, and all I could make out was that it had been sold three times. After the War, the space went blank. I'll buy it, of course. I had decided right there. "But can you afford an item like this after all?" he said, not to me but to my wife, as though she were the one to ask. I turned and held it out to her. Whatever it costs, I said, we're buying it. She tucked the light and dangerous Kalashnikov weapon under her arm again and stood there, legs apart, looking sceptically at me and my shotgun. I admitted the price seemed rather high. But, I said, the name on it was mine, too. And so. . . . "And so?" she said. That was my reason, I said. She demurred, "Strange, yes, but—" But nothing! The point is, who's that original owner! How did he come to have my name!

She wasn't listening. The proprietor had stepped round me. He was putting the leather strap of that Kalashnikov over her shoulder. He was showing her how to release the safety catch. She followed his bony fingers with her long, soft ones. My own voice sounded dim in my ears, so long ago, and far away.

Bacchæ

I STOOD IN A LONG LINE of derelicts, shes and hes and whatevers, downtown at the Grand Central Market. There was one butcher stall that gave out old meat. Illegal, probably, but the Health Department looked away. There were too many of us for the Salvation Army to feed, and the missions were bankrupt.

It was nearly at closing time, as usual, that we stumbled into place, and the great shed was emptying. Our raggedy file shuffled forward, wheezing, shaking, sour old sterno drinkers, piss-ass wino bums, degenerated kids. We were the last of the men, and I was nearly last in line. It was the end for us.

As I neared the counter, I noticed a large tray full of longish, pale, white, semi-transparent meat veined with clotted bloody threads in a colorless sac, more a tripesy tissue than flesh. About the size of smelts they were, glistening oilily. The big scar-faced butcher with the missing thumbs stood there up high with his bloody fists on his bloody-aproned hips.

What're these, I asked.

"Them? Oh, them's prostates."

Prostates? Where'd you get prostates?

"Well, don't mention I told you, but—the ladies likes them. They generally go in there clawing, about an hour after a man's dead. They're no good later. But, fresh like these, they're real nourishing. And cheap. Women's food."

I was nauseated at the idea of eating corpse meat, fresh or no, starving or no. Worst, a gland from behind a dead man's scrotum . . . !

Well, I said . . . and turned away.

The butcher grinned benignly down at me, understanding what I meant. Then he cocked his head to one side, pointing his fist that way too. I stopped and listened. From outside the market, from the darkness of Broadway, I heard what I thought were sirens in the distance. Police? No. Not sirens either. Ululation. Confused cries, faint in the distance, a desolate chorus of wailing, yet coming closer all the time.

Pan

I SELL AND SERVICE FLUTES: nickel-steel, silver, gold. A hundred symphony orchestras in the country, give or take a dozen. Any town with a central high school has its marching band. I'm always on the road now, supplying parts for junky ones and tackling the harder job of refitting good ones: my fingers are trusted by finicky players. A regular schedule's not easy to set up because symphonic seasons vary; but this past year I've managed to get back to Houston for a week at a time every so often. Lettie's there.

Actually, I'm from Boston, where I worked for the best flutemakers in America; but after my wife walked out and took my three little girls with her, I got restless and went off on my own. It wasn't hard to get up a list of good clients: my touch is appreciated.

My wife said she didn't know how she'd stood it so it long. For seventeen years the music of the flute never touched her. But one Sunday morning she woke up with a scream, and ran wild. She was like a wasp bumping against a windowpane, sweeping angrily back into the room while everyone ducks, and then flying at the glass and bumping it madly again and again. Not exactly bothered by my fluting, though there was a sort of underlying irritation. It seems I never once finished a piece I started—here some bars of the faun's afternoon, there some measures of gypsy tarantella, or a phrase of fugue, the rest left hanging. Never a climax; never a resolution; never any song sung to the end; never a march that got somewhere. She raved at me that it was all just murdered melody!

I'd never realized that. I just tootle on someone's defective instrument. Like any technician, I listen to pitch and tone, not music. Maybe it was those ascending scales that got her, the constant repetition of the same single note as I tested the flute, up and up, and over and over, one note at a time. Low tones thrilled her when we were first married; but it was the upper registers, those really high notes that finally got to her. I'd spoiled the sheen of moonlight on the snow. Everything shivered. It was those damn frequencies, the vibes I set going everywhere in the house. She said it drove her up the wall—she couldn't even bear the sight of dust motes skipping on the sunbeams that slanted through our bedroom on a winter morning. At least that's what she cried out. Eventually she hated anything to do with flutes—the sound of them, even the sight of them—by which I think she meant the sound and sight of me. My girls loved me, though. When they were little they called me Papa Piper and danced for me in their nighties like flowers at bedtime. And when they were about starting to turn into gangly, prancing virgins, they called me their Mister Pied Piper.

Best thing to do was open the window and let the wasp fly out before you got stung. She moved south, to Virginia somewhere. There was a P.O.B. number for a while, and I got some standard Hallmark greetings from my girls. Nothing personal, hardly a snapshot. Then, silence. I couldn't find out where my wife had gone. I heard she moved in with an old school friend from Alexandria—a woman, actually—and those two hard females shut me completely out of their lives. Shameful. They knew that and they meant to put me down. All I really missed was my three whirling little girls. Sad to imagine them dancing to pop tunes from a tinny cassette. So I left the Haynes flute factory and went west on my own.

For six years, simply taking care of myself I had about enough to take care of. Maybe I was grieving, and the kind of meaningless, broken music I played on other people's flutes soothed and solaced me, no matter how much it may have annoyed the occupants of hotel and motel rooms. If I went to occasional rehearsals when a good conductor was guesting, or got comps to an interesting program, I never heard any of the stuff: I just listened to the sound of the instruments I'd worked on. A peculiar way of hearing, and it takes an odd talent, I guess. Even a sort of deafness: my line of work would probably drive a real musician mad. In the end it seems to have crazed my wife—though when she made me marry her she was already mad for me.

About as wild as I am about Lettie now. Forty-four years old, divorced, and forgetting to tie my shoes because the woman doesn't pick up her phone at 7:00 in the morning. Cutting my face shaving because I know she's not even home to answer it, and I don't know where she is. I know what she's been doing, though. Spreading for someone; giving head, or tying him up and giving head; or offering no end of cold-hearted combinations of cold-hearted fucking. I know, because when I first came to Houston I saw this ad in the paper for a "dating service." I was feeling pretty lonely after living in motels and hotels for years, so I called the number and the service said they'd send a pretty lady to my room. In twenty minutes she was there, knock knock, and carrying a big leather bag out of which she pulled a machine and the blank VISA form for me to sign. For $100 an hour she'd do anything I liked. I said I believed we could start with the usual. Later I found a business card on the dresser:

"Hi! Remember Me? My Name's Lettie.
We Offer Service With a Smile.
A Tradition Ever Since 1985."

Remember her? I felt as though I was born again! I got up, showered, and ate a Western breakfast: steak, hashbrowns, and strong coffee with a great dollop of tequila in it. Went up to pack, but then stood at the sealed hotel window and played a Bach suite right through for the first time in how many years. Which surprised me: I had it right there by heart all along, and never even knew it.

I turned out of my way to stop off in Houston a few times after that, and when I wasn't lucky enough to get a slot on her schedule, she would meet me for a cocktail. Lettie's just as beautiful dressed as when not—even more so. Thirty-five, divorced, and there's a fifteen-year old boy in some military academy back east. One night I told her I loved her, told her I'd fallen in love with her the first hour I knew her. She said she'd kind of felt a certain something for me too. We tossed that around a bit, until I said I didn't know what I could do now—my little business was all I had and it keeps me moving on my circuit from Texas to Seattle. I have my customers and I know their instruments better than anyone else. But it couldn't be avoided: I was talking about marriage, it seems, and she listened. Until the beeper in her bag went off: my hour was up. I reached for my pants and got the VISA card out, and she ran off my receipt for services rendered. The phone rang and she got up and took it, brushing out her hair with one hand while getting the name, address, and room number of the next client. She was running a little late, so she had to go before I finished my proposal. I went to soak in the tub. When I came out, I saw she'd left her calling card as usual. No other trace of her, except the damp towel flung in the corner and—surprise!—the glossy pink print of her lips where she'd kissed the mirror . . . which I kissed back. That at least was free. Since then it's gone this way, off and on, for seven whole months.

Today I had a surprise for her: a ruby ring, white gold with four big diamonds. I turned her over face up and slipped it on her finger. She opened her eyes wide and smiled as if she was pleased. I think she really was pleased. I got out of bed, and, standing there naked, played Mendelssohn's Wedding March for her.

She reared up and then flopped back and her red hair spread out in waves on the pillow. She laughed so hard she cried. With those fat, tall, crimson nipples and that creamy white belly quivering like quicksand, she was a glory to me, a painting by some Old Master, perfect except for the ragged, dark, vertical line of the slash that ran from that winking navel to the shaggy mound of her auburn fleece.

"If that ain't some everlovin' sight! Whoever did see a man with two flutes!"

I took a deep breath. Lettie, suppose we just fix the day?

She opened her eyes and saw me with my flute still pressed to my chin.

I mean it, I said.

"Do you now."

That's my ring on your finger, so you must know I mean it.

"Why sure enough, honey."

I'll be back in two weeks. There's some urgent work for me up in Seattle. You'll be ready . . . two weeks Sunday?

"Could you play me some ole country music for a change? Have you heard that new track Dolly sings, 'When Last Seen She Was Gettin' on a Greyhound'?" She sat up and pulled the sheet around her. "This air-conditioning'll be the death of me some day, I swear." She wiped her teary eyes with the hem of the sheet and then blew her nose in it.

I want your answer, Lettie.

"No you don't."

I'll even give you two weeks to think about it.

"Well, I have thought."

All right, then. That wasn't so hard, was it?

"Nothing's that easy neither. Now just put that thing down and come over here and sit alongside this woman." She patted the bed.

I didn't particularly want to, because I knew that as soon as I got close, the odor that rose in waves from her would roll over me and carry me away from any notion I had that I could understand what she said. It was a greeny smell, with something mixed in it like the tang of leaf-mold oozing up from the earth in a shady wood.

"Come on, now."

I went and sat. I was thinking her damn beeper would go off before we got the thing settled and I'd be charged for two hours. She stood, tossed the sheet around her like a toga, plumped the pillows up, and sat down again with her bright head tilted back against the wall. She stuck her left foot out and put it between my legs and pressed up hard against me, so as to raise me up and hold me down at the same time. I let her—I even took hold of her leg by the calf and ground her callused heel into my crotch till it hurt so hard I thought I'd pass out. Lettie smiled at me. I was staring into those great green eyes of hers all the while, but still I couldn't read what she was thinking. Then the shiny red tip of her tongue came out and licked her lips. She sighed and said the strangest thing I ever heard.

"What kinda woman y'all reckon I am? You given that some thought?"

Yes, I have. From the minute I met you. I mean, when you knocked on my door and I saw you come into my room I knew right then I had to have you."

"So you had me. All right, what about it?"

You call that having?

"Mister, I'm not what you think."

I know that, Lettie

"You don't know nothing! I been on my own since I was just a scrawny latchkey kid in Colorado. I kept myself. Still keep myself. Started off by cleaning rooms in Aspen ski lodges. Waitressing.

Plenty of action up there. And no one never laid so much as a finger on me. Nohow. Least till I was eighteen. I was planning on going for a nurse, put in a whole winter changing bedpans and washing people up. Then there came that long December night. We had ourselves one hell of a blizzard: you could hear the wind screaming down the canyon and the wolves howling along with it. That spooked me. I was on duty alone. That was the night I looked in on that downhill racer. I don't know how it happened. I must have been hypnotized by that damn foreigner. The things he showed me—what-all to do and how-all—and all at once! Lost my cherry ten times over. Didn't seem to matter he was in a cast with a spiral fracture. Course they flew a Lear jet in for him as soon as the runway was cleared. Good thing—my brains were just about banged out too. Later on I went off to a cabin along towards the pass. No one to help me. Seems like I always had to manage for myself. Women don't like me. And men . . . well, they ain't much to write home about in the morning . . . if you had a home to write to. Towards the end I decided I could just as well walk away from that cabin and climb up the pass till I dropped. The wolves could have me *and* my big belly, for all I cared. I should have done it, too. By then it was too late—I did nine days and nine nights of hard labor all by myself, waiting, holding onto those old bedposts as hard as I could. I could scarce move to fetch a glass of water. Every time I came to, I thought for sure I was dead—until those cramps commenced again. Pain's no word for it. But someone up above must have heard me crying, because here came that little old widow from the ranch down the way, and she done it for me—fetched my baby out with a bread knife. Ye gods! When I woke up twelve days later down in the hospital and they showed me my golden-haired boy, well, I heard music in the air. It was music all around me. Least I thought I did. I couldn't tell you what that sounded like . . . maybe that's why you're the first man I can bear to look at since then—even across a table, I mean. And you ain't much, you know. Maybe that's why I'll wear your ring."

She gave me a shove with her heel then. The pain was like a sword rammed straight from my balls to my heart. I just doubled over, dropped face forward into her wide open thighs. She was wet, she was flooded, and it smelled of balsam somehow. I lay there while she stroked my head.

"Years later I heard it was twins. There was a girl too. The hospital had no record."

What do you mean? I muttered without looking up.

"Kiss me—there." She pressed my face against her mound. "No, further down. Lick it . . . harder!" She gripped my hair in both hands, and her nails raked my scalp.

I did what she said, until there was a hot flush and she went limp.

"I figured out it was that midwife. She took my girl and hid her away when they came to fetch me."

Why didn't you try and find out?

"Who says I didn't? Oh, I went back. That ranch was nothing but a scene of desolation. Fences down, stripped cars rusting in the yard. The main house with its roof burnt out and windows all smashed in, the barn and stables half-buried under an avalanche. And nobody in that whole damn valley knew nothing! What old woman? they said. They were merely these new-money folks, lawyers and such, or dope dealers, and there was a passel of dropouts, those hairy, dirty types with naked, runny-nosed brats squatting yonder off in the pasture by some big canvas teepees. But I believe what I heard: there was a twin child, I did birth it, and it was a girl. I could feel the two of them struggling in me during those days and nights of dry labor. God knows what that old witch done with my baby!"

I looked up then, over the round hill of her abdomen, the two creamy cones of her breasts laced with pale blue veins. Her green eyes were full of tears and she was looking out the tinted gray window into the steamy summer mist blanketing Houston.

Marry me.

"Oh sure."

I'll find her!

"How you reckon that?"

I promise you I'll find her.

"Sweet man. Ain't you just chock full of hopes. Give us a little kiss?"

I got on my hands and knees, crawled up to her lips and laid down flat on that whole landscape of her and kissed her. Seemed like it was close to the end of my second hour now. Well, so.

Afterward, she sighed and said, "All right, you win. Two weeks come Sunday. Mind if I wear white? Satin and silk?"

Whatever, I said.

"And a veil?"

Anything!

"But hear this, loverboy—I got debts."

How much?

"Never you mind."

We'll manage.

"Like I said, it's my business. So I aim to stay in business awhile."

Lettie!

"I figure I got maybe two-three good years in me. You don't mind me working?"

I didn't answer.

"Listen, sweetie—it's not like it will interfere with us being married and all. I'll arrange it so's I work only daytime hours."

I heaved myself off the bed and went and sat by the window. There was nothing to see but that blinding white fog. It must have been a hundred degrees out there. She went to the bathroom and showered. Then she strode out, made up fresh as peaches and cream, and dressed to kill as usual. Drenched with that lily-of-the-valley perfume she uses. I sat gazing over Houston, my chest blank and hollow, my heart sounding like a cracked cymbal hung inside it from a frayed string. I heard her run my VISA card through that damn credit machine. She came over and handed me the gold Cross pen and the voucher: $300.

"Well, sugar, I got to account for my time, and it is going on two and a half hours."

I signed. She stripped the carbons from the chit and passed them to me, not wanting to smudge her fingers. I shredded them. She stowed the embosser in that big red leather Gucci tote, took her pocketbook, and went to go. Pausing by the bed, she picked up my flute, hefted it, and laid it down again.

"Will I hear from you?"

Should I leave word with your service?

"You do that. It's best."

If that's the way to get you.

Lettie stopped and leaned back against the door as though I had hit her. She stared at me, and the look on her face was surprising, because she usually wore that stubborn, noncommittal expression a whore shows you when she first comes in and waits to hear what your game is. I thought she was trying to decide something that took a little figuring. Then she grinned, straightened up tall, and said happily, "Dear heart, how do you like this—after we're married, you won't have to pay me anymore!"

She opened the door, puckered her lips, and blew me a kiss. I couldn't help it: I blew her a kiss back.

Dafne

INDIAN SUMMER. The Mohawk Valley. The rolling countryside of Oneida County. On College Hill, actually, out back on the north side, beyond the football field, following the fairway as it slopes up and delivers you onto the mount of the 7th green, atop which, after putting, you can pause to survey three small valleys . . . and consider the conclusion to summer's works. A pattern of greens: cornfields, beanfields, fields of broccoli, Brussels sprouts, potatoes, hayfields, and stony cowpastures; clumps of maple, oak, ash, and beech copses glimmering aureate, blistering into scarlet, slowly burning and dropping their shrivelled cooling embers to reveal, from this height, their interwoven branches that will look like great gray nests for crows and winter snow. Among them the farmhouses stand out more clearly now, the roadside hamlets like Paris and Oriskany and Hinman corners down below where the creeks wind, those withering old New York wooden houses, shapeless and shambling, leaning together in peeling poverty for a hundred years now. Smokes curling in the still air of October, partly from fireplaces and leaf-piles, partly from the garbage dumps or car bodies forever smoldering in wreckers' pits that mark these nearly nameless places littered and dying around this harsh region. Here and there the new ranch home or redone Greek Revival specimens of gentlemen farmers, the squires and merchants and bank presidents who prefer the countryside, bleak as it is, to the decrepit cities and industrial suburbs of the long valley to the west towards the Great Lakes far away. A fine prospect though during Indian Summer. Best time of the year. For spring is melting snowpack and running red clay. Summer humid, oppressive, empty. Winter a silent frozen hell of ice glare or howling blizzard of sleet and unending drifting snow-squalls. But in autumn there is that distant view of gray-black foothills to the north, the Adirondacks; and over them, high up, the faint feathered clouds darting through the stratosphere, presaging those ponderous, black, bellying low clouds that sweep along the ridges and drop the damp, immolating snows of late November. Yet, these few weeks of clarity we have, and vision comes as revelation, as fulfillment before the end.

I am not, this late afternoon hour, mounting the tumulus of the 7th green, putter in hand, but helping my friend's wife up. We have strolled out here for our last portion of the still and limpid air. It's the Saturday of the annual Sigma Chi Halloween Party. The cars have all pulled away from the football field, crowds scurried off to their various celebrations and cocktail hours. After several years of this regular Halloween bash, we have grown weary of the Sigs of Sigma Chi and their sluttish Vassar dates back there before the first tee of the golf course. In the hall we have just left, the Sigs, suavely cheery in their Brooks tuxes, snotty and condescending, pouring out bourbon and champagne to the faculty by the insulting case, are introducing their dates, vivid twenty-year-old girls, healthy, fresh-skinned, tireless, stunning in their Bendel and Saks dresses, and flushed with roaring the afternoon away in the football stands, with booze, and brimming over with eager sex. The Sigs and their dates enjoy hosting their professors; they get a sardonic sort of kick from watching their intoxicated teachers weave off into the night, staggering among the fraternity's Porche, Triumph, MG, and Mercedes roadsters that lie parked carelessly outside like a few dozen hunters tethered at a country inn towards the close of the great Fall Hunt.

Margaret and I had left them while it was not yet dusk though, to watch the twilight come on, as well as to escape the swelling din of orgy. Her husband was standing with his nose in the 90-proof punch cup, paying court to Prexy, an unctuous ex-minister who'd been brought in by the Trustees to beef up the venerable institution by augmenting sociology, political science, and psychology —the wave of the future, as he calls these subjects. He may well be correct: we are working hard at transforming Sigs into lawyers and admen, into our social managers, our chiefs. Canny, these ex-Presbyterian ministers, who are caring properly for this world of ours. Margaret's husband was listening hard to the President, who had remained as usual next to the big bowl to dip his cup frequently and get the obedient attentions of his faculty as they came up and returned for more of the same. Margaret's husband was laughing at all his jokes: he hasn't finished his thesis yet, and his position is still unsure. He is only halfway through a study of voting behavior in the former colonies of Africa, a Harvard idealist who'd helped in formulating their constitutions as a prize undergraduate interning in Washington over the summers. Over the last six years, six of his seven countries have been restructured into native tyrannies, and he is persona non grata in them all; if the records he needs are not destroyed, they are in any case sealed to him. Between that and Margaret's six-years' barrenness, he has work ahead yet for his laurels. Still, his old preppy ties at Rockefeller and Ford keep him in firewood, and Margaret in gowns like this ivory, gold-embroidery-edged raw silk thing she has on tonight, her fine breasts floating free in it as she takes my hand to clamber up onto the 7th green. Her shoulders are protected by a thick ermine jacket from the cooling air. For three years now we have been friends. Margaret is happy here after nervous, smug, perverted Cambridge. Her childhood as a poor white in the tobacco-sharecropping hinterland of North Carolina haunts her, but these clothes, the great old college house, and the position comfort her. Great wide eyes and a fine head she carries erect above those sloping, firm shoulders: these ought to more than suffice for her here in this small closed community among the old Indian hills, populated by pigeontoed and gaunt professors' women or chapped-handed and haggard pregnant instructors' wives. Often she seems melancholy to me after a few bourbon-and-waters, wistful. This vestige of her miserable childhood is charming: she had grown up, not as a weed with tiny flowers in some briar patch, but into a handsome, big, velvety magnolia blossom. She walked with a long sway, but proudly tall, and in that white gown, pacing across the 7th green, her gait was a caryatid's.

"Did you know," she says, "the fruit of the magnolia flower's a spikey, hard, dry, heavy cone, about as big as your fist? We used to throw them like grenades when we were little kids. I have a scar from one too." And she lifts the mass of auburn hair that shades her cheek: on her left temple there is a faint round set of tiny stippled scars, like an old smallpox badge. I touch it gently.

Around the valleys strung out below us to the north, to the

east, and the south there are bonfires lighting: they look like torches lifted here and there on those slopes facing us. Too far off for us to make out the knots of children running or dancing about them like savages. The sun has just vanished behind our backs in the southwest, beyond the distant Alleghenies. Oriskany Valley, laid out beneath, is a clear gold, red, black picture puzzle. There are stone markers standing in the woods that show the border of the English colony a little more than two hundred years ago. Up here on the golf course, we are standing a few miles outside that pale, in Indian territory. Margaret has laughed at everything I've said during the last hour. Margaret has smiled at me with affection, tenderly, even when I've said nothing at all. Margaret tonight is gay, yet grave. A handsome woman, but in this twilight now, as I touch that scarred temple, her loveliness stuns me. I see beauty itself. And I tell her so. She smiles, and in that murmuring drawl replies, "Why how poetical the liquor's made you tonight." No, no, I say, it's something about you. "My new gown, child. Isn't it ravishing?"

Look at that! I say. It's perfect: the full moon has come floating up in the east. A primitive artist has painted it a deep red-orange pumpkin color, laid on for Halloween. The long hill over which it sails gives it rondure. What a pity it would have been to have missed this sight by standing back there in that Sig pen swilling hard punch. But, glancing at Margaret, I realize that she gazes up at it with no joy. Tears fill her wide green eyes; her hands lie crossed, palms cupping her breasts. Margaret, I say, are you grieving?

The bloody moon's light lies pooled in those eyes as she looks at it. We stand alone in the circle of close-cropped green grass at the 7th hole, its green now a black platform in the scarlet moonlight. From the gray, old stone mansion of the Sig House—a patch of lights beyond the golf course, behind the pines—comes only the syncopated thudding of the rock band's bass. Margaret tries to answer me. Her lips quiver, but she can say nothing. The tip of her tongue emerges to taste the tear that has trickled down beside her nose, and over her upper lip. I think, I should like to taste Margaret's tears myself. I say, Margaret, what's the matter? A reply, faint, "It's nothing, dear, nothing at all." At a loss, I try, It's beautiful, isn't it. "Yes. For the moment only." Is that what makes you sad? "I'm not sad, really. It's these headaches I've been having. I'm on tranquilizers, didn't you know?" I did not. "And they make me laugh, they make me weep. As if I had feelings."

Her words perturb me. "But," she adds, "I don't have them, you know. Isn't that awful?" With a catch of laughter or of tears, a sob, she tosses her head proudly. She is gorgeous. I turn and take her in my arms, consoling. It is awful.

She clings, burying her wet cheek in my throat. For a moment. I don't know what I hold in my arms: the ermine jacket has a thick animal musk, and her breasts against mine shake as her breath comes in broken gasps. A long moment it is, until I feel her calming. It must be some fine animal I have caught in my arms, and now it rests here, without terror. But it's unpredictable, I know. "Oh, look!" she cries out. I release her and turn. She points at the sky near the moon, suffused now with an expanding aura of shimmering golden light. "What's that!" Above the globe of that moon, and far beyond it in space it seems, there's a point of bright light, brilliant as the evening star. It is rising fast, towards the zenith. It is not Venus, for that one sparkles over the horizon at our backs, above the abyss into which the sun has fallen. This wanderer swims steadily, wavering slightly in the tremulous atmosphere. "What ever is that?" she cries again. "It frightens me." Ah, that must be a satellite, I say, one of our space stations. It's picking up the rays of the hidden sun. Look how fast it flies out there.

"Suppose it's one of theirs," she says. "Suppose it's coming for us. Suppose it's carrying the Doomsday Bomb." Ah no, Margaret, I say, stroking her arm, don't even think of it. "Suppose it is, and suppose the end of the world will come in twenty minutes. What would you do!" Her hair is disarrayed, drooping in an auburn-black shield over her cheeks. Her eyes are fixed on me. She has seized my hands in hers, and is pressing them convulsively, as though trying to utter a phrase in sign language. "What would you do if you'd only twenty minutes left to live?" Well, I say, I think . . . I would . . . "What!" She's smiling at me, curious. Well, I'd fuck.

Margaret flings my hands away, in disappointment or despair. She turns away sighing. "Oh, you!" Well I would, I say, coming up beside her where she stands poised at the edge of the green.

Deeply, ruefully, she sighs again. She's staring like a diver down into the wild ground below, the coarse weed stalks of summer gone, down along the disused, rutted path wandering off precipitously to the woods that border the golf course here, a path tangled with fallen branches, deep drifts of leaves clotted with mold and mud. Quite calmly she remarks, "I'm afraid it wouldn't do me much good. My legs are like logs for the first ten minutes, like dead wood. It's all I can do to hold them open, you know. And it takes me thirty minutes to come . . . if I do come. Isn't that awful? The world would be over by then. I'm sorry, darling." And she begins to laugh, too loudly now, pointing up at the satellite that has climbed into the velvety black zenith overhead. "Twenty minutes to go," she cries, "only twenty minutes!" I am looking up at that moving point, puzzled.

A violent tug at my throat snaps my neck painfully. She has ripped open the knot of my bowtie. And she's flitting down the steep slope off the green on her heeled white sandals, dashing along that dark path, running towards the wood, a white, weaving form. I hesitate up there on the high mound of the 7th green. I hear her clattering through that dangerous darkness down the hillside. I listen to her steps fading. Then her voice comes back, a poignant cry of pain. Then silence. She must have fallen down there in that obscurity. Like a wounded creature, she is lying in her fine white silk and fur, waiting for an end to it.

Pegasos

When my father died, I was out of town, travelling. They said they had been unable to reach me. And so I missed the funeral. By the time I finally got home, it was the day of the unveiling. My mother called to say she'd meet me at the monument, and gave me the address. Monument? I said.

"Well, memorial then," she replied, and hung up on me.

When the cab pulled up at the address she'd given me, I saw that it was near the corner of Fifth Avenue, facing the Metropolitan Museum. A bright, breezy June day. Small white clouds flew in flocks across the light blue sky, rattling the halyards against the hollow metal flagpoles, sounding like the cables that whip a mast on a ship at sea. I'd been let off in front of the Museum, so I stood there and looked at the great, square structure across the avenue, newly sheathed, finished in a matte ivory-yellow marble. It recalled the *fascisto-moderno architettura* of municipal buildings erected in the '20's and '30's in Brindisi, Bari, Taranto, and other ancient Greek cities on the Adriatic: spare and not cluttered with junky decorations like those near the tomb of Augustus in Rome, where Il Duce's government manifested that virulent infatuation with Imperial nostalgia. I saw my mother standing waiting for me there, her old sable coat open over her shoulders, its winter weight looking oppressive in June's warmth. I crossed to her.

Opening her arms wide and tilting up her face, which was feverish, beaded with sweat, she said, nodding at the structure, "It's called Pegasos. In his honor."

My god! You've got to be kidding! Pegasos! She seemed not to hear me, but gazed up at the blank, grandiose façade. I was astounded: the expense she had gone to! It would have taken all his life's earnings—and then, to contemplate that vainglory! I was speechless.

"But darling, just look!" she cried.

I looked up at her bidding, and saw that the loggia crowning the top storey carried a bronze steed, rearing, on its back a knight in full panoply, spear couched at the heavens. Just then, the hour started to chime noon: the lance lowered and the charger rolled from right to left across the entire length of the open balcony with a roar like a great wind, and struck its target, an enormous bronze dragon rampant—Clang! Back it swept, and rolled again, Clang! And again! The echoing clamor of it!

I wrung my hands, and laughed with despair at her folly.

"What's wrong?" she said quietly when the spectacle was over. Her face now wore that puckered, uncomprehending hurt expression she shows whenever she's criticized.

Pegasos! I said, raising my voice. Don't you even remember who that man was? He worked all his life to support a family. He was modest; he was decent. He slaved. And now, when he's dead, you build him up like this? Where's your sense of proportion!

"I thought you would be pleased to know at last who he *really* was," she answered, "and this shows it all."

Oh no! Furthermore, it's bad scholarship.

"Why?"

You've jumbled your heroes.

"Have I?"

Yes, the name goes back to long before Greece, to the East. Its origins are hidden.

"Well?"

What's more, the dying Medusa gave birth to him. He carried the thunderbolt of Zeus.

"Ah, you see!"

And he helped Bellerofon to fight the Amazons and to destroy the Chimaera.

"Good!"

But when Bellerofon tried to make him fly to heaven he bucked and threw him.

"Naturally. Oh, how wonderfully obstinate he was!"

When he stamped his hoof, he created the Fountain of Hippocrene.

"Yes, and Keats wrote his name in its water."

No, no, Pegasos never had anything to do with the poets at all—you've got it all confused, I repeated.

"Have I?"

The Romans thought he stood for immortality, I said.

"So there we are," she said, waving happily at the edifice.

Well, and then you've gone and taken the wings from the horse and put them on St. George's dragon—and all just to keep time for passersby!

She looked more than ever puzzled.

It's awful! I shouted. Mother, you've just mixed up all your heroes—from first to last!

She answered nothing in her defense but, "Have I? Aren't all heroes really the same?" And smiled up at me.

I could say nothing to that. People in front of the Metropolitan had gathered in little groups, whispering, staring at us, and pointing up at that high heroic bronze statuary. I realized it was far too late for me to do anything about it. Our macaronic memorial had been created, and there that monument would remain forever opposite the Museum of Art. It would strike at the hours with that rumble and roar as of subways below the earth, with that ear-shattering, head-breaking bronze clang! Pegasos! Father!

Zeno: A Stoic Dialogue

SZEKELI CAUGHT UP WITH ME again under the arch. But I was patient with him. This time it all came out. I didn't laugh and I didn't cry. I tried to practice restraint, to be fair, to do him no harm. Meanwhile, it grew dark and cold under that filthy Washington Square drizzle. All around us the Academy's effluent of students, disgorged by the thousands from classrooms, lecture halls, libraries, and labs, flowed in patchy, disconsolate streams towards subways and bus stops, or into fast-food shops all through the surrounding Village. Even in sunlight, their faces showed no purpose, little joy, and even less meaning. Faces that had neither youth nor age in them. Our little group of vets had observed them often as we wandered among the chess tables or sat on the rim of the fountain idly thinking out loud, that is, smoking and saying nothing.

Szekkitch, I say, holding the mirror of speculation up to him once again, hoping he'd glimpse some light in it, we're still young. What idea can we form regarding the one dimension of time that seems possible to us—I mean, the future?

"Ask Congress. Ask the President. Take it to the Supreme Court."

Szekkhov, I cry, they hate us youth! They have disgraced the past. They are defiling the present! Now we're outflanked—they're blockading the pass to the future! Maybe we have time, maybe not. Anyway, what is time? What are we doing, standing here like ignorant peasants on some burial mound?

"Science fiction tells us," he blurts, clutching his ragged sheaf of notes and manuscripts to his chest.

I refrain from telling him that I lost my interest in sci fi long ago. It's a game played with split cues in the smoky din of some godforsaken poolroom: everyone's too stoned to notice the crazy betting: they go on stroking the same old eight ball off the hard, threadbare cushions all night, hoping to sink a blind shot in tomorrow's pocket. But sweet, stubborn Szekeli brings me his yarns and waits for my reaction as though I'm the oracle. Towards Thankgiving he'd started to stammer something about his new science of the psyche; but then he'd hesitate and mutter that we're nothing but a bank of tapes. It works like this: To each is given a personal past, recorded live! From each comes a personal output, direct from the cells themselves!

"It's our ne-ne-never-us cistern," he seems to say.

As though nerve fibers infiltrate cells! If the proteins remember, they remember for themselves. They know us not. Nothing personal—we don't know them either. We're epiphenomena, buddy. Furthermore, beneath consciousness, beneath the subconscious, beneath the unconscious, the only emperor is sheer potential anarchy, known to the organism—if and when known at all—as the living death. Which is you, which is me. Our spinal cord has but two terminals: one's the bunch of nerves in our brain, the other is the little collection in our anus. The brain at least wears a skull to protect it.

I have attracted his attention for a moment. I go on.

Yes, Szekkovitch, we truly feel the world in those two places only. So are we going to live head-first, or preposterously? That is the question.

He tries to smile. "Man, you don't actually believe only *those* two pl-pl-places can feel . . . ?"

Oh, some secondary termini: the tip of your tongue, your finger tips, your glans . . . .

He looks puzzled. "I don't see . . . ."

Tip of penis, Szekkel. Only precious thing I had when I came to this school from Tarsus.

"Oh." He takes out his little reporter's spiral pad to get the spelling: G-L-A-N-S. "I heard you say 'glands.' Like thy-thy-thyroid. Hey—you were soldiering down in the Mekong! Where's this Tarsus?"

Rural childhood on the Island. Summers Momma cooked for the Gardners on the island off Montauk; winters she flipped flapjacks in Sag Harbor. He works at his writing, takes notes as if the world's all a vocabulary exercise. I try again to distract him.

Have you ever noticed how much low-grade porn there is in science fiction, Szekknik? Why do they like to dress those curvacious android ladies in saran wrap: boobs for the boobs? Is it because your average android has tits, but no cunt?

"Oh, she has one. She should have one," he blushes.

Isn't it because your futurological technist is filled with fear and loathing for the Great Mother of us all?

"That stuff's just stuck in for reader interest. Padding for the pulps—they pay only ten cents a word. But I don't do that. I mean, I don't try for that kind of . . . ."

You don't pander.

"I do not."

But, Szekeli, fiction should have a real cunt somewhere in its imaginary garden.

"Girls will be wearing transparent clothes as soon as they can produce a fabric that breathes, you'll see."

I should live so long.

"That's not what science fiction's about."

Or they feature low-grade Rosicrucianism, mixed with telepathic talent. Anything goes, as long as it's pre-scientific. Fairytales with fantastic zoology or love stories out of Gothic romances. Feudal hierarchies of ignorance and terror dressed up in platinum and floating on anti-gravity. What you write are good-humored conundrums. Nice.

"Is that what you think? Well, I'm still learning."

Do you know enough science to put it to work in a story? Do your pulp masters? Since when is science mythopoetic? Take science now—

"—What I wanted to ask: Do you think, hypothetically, say, it's possible to get yourself straight if you flush your circuits, wash out the misunderstandings? For instance, what my Momma said when she was three months pregnant. About me, I mean . . . ." He fades, as though a battery in him's fading.

Arise, ye prisoners of starvation! There's pie in the sky when you die!

"Funny, so funny!" His abstracted face mottles, pink against that whey-pale skin; it lengthens, angry, severe; the full lips bleach, colorless as his hair. That's the Fleming mother. And where's the Hungarian dada, of whom he never speaks, except to spell his name right? Seems Dada flew away on the shifty winds of ideological reversal. Momma told him about it in a moment of pique, or spite. Szekeli Senior was keeper of the Party's secret fund in Panama. Couldn't resist a typical Hungarian trick: absconding. With the Party correspondence, membership files, and all the gold—who knows which way the freighter he hopped in the Canal was heading? East or west, the KBG would long ago have found him . . . . Szekeli Momma at that time was carrying her own contraband, wanted to deliver in New Orleans. didn't make it. So that the little fellow got his papers only after a trip to Nam twenty years later, when all he'd known since he was three days old was American. Tagged cadavers in Saigon for two years. Now he uses the carpet-bombed landscape of that pocked, defoliated Plain of Jars for his openings: a ruined, charred asteroid hurtles nowhere through the astral storms among distant stars with a stranded Terra-born couple plunked down on it. She fair, he dark. They are out of molecular biosynfuels. They are out of luck, and out of love. An old story: the man is damned, the woman with him: he to scratch their living from that hard-scrabble homestead, she to bear him murderous brats in unmitigated travail on the cold meteoric land. Poor, fantastic Flemish-Magyar. But he perseveres in writing that stuff and proselytizing me, because he knows that I appreciate his metaphor: Paradise Lost—if he but knew the poem.

What is to be done? Such people loathe the past. They fear the future. They hate the present. What *do* they want? Eternity. They want it all, and they want it today!

So today he refuses to be diverted: "Be-be-because that three-month-old blind worm floating in her uterine broth is fully formed, provided with a network of growing nerves, right? Did you know that it clues in via the extended antenna array of its own placenta, which scans all the vibrations reflected from the invisible outside world? It hears. Not asleep, not awake. Just dreaming. And in that suspended animation the fetus hears her shrieking, 'Tibor! It's your filthy political brat—I don't want it. You hear me, Tibor! I'm getting rid of it.' Now, of course, that quivering fistful of jelly doesn't understand those words. It's all Flem-Hunky to him. But he does listen to that stabbing, squeaking, squawking voice—it's so menacing. And then it feels, oh how it feels! fists pounding on the taut drum of her abdomen. Fearsome concussions. And that whoop-whoop-whooping, as she wails like an air-raid siren, 'No no no no! I won't have him, I won't! He's not going to be yours, Tibor, you dog!' And he hears a male voice growling like thunder, 'Go ahead, you slut, you! with your fishy Flemish cunt that you never wash out. Here's another kick right in your stinking Hollander herring-tub!' But no use—pounding, jumping, poking, kicking—no use at all: the little pig's knuckle hangs to its rattling, webby net for dear life. That Dutch blood of hers is th-th-thick! That peasant womb is strong. It won't break and spill out his young life. And the crazy woman has more tortures up her skirt for it, too, all crude. Mind you, that crucial tête-a-tête is recorded in the ne-ne-nervous system, buried at the lowest level of wiring . . . ."

As he talks, he punches himself in the belly, gazing blankly over my left shoulder, his bitter Gauloise butt drooping from lips flecked with chalky dry-mouthed spittle, shreds of flaring specks settling on his jacket, flaming out on the cloth or burning black-edged holes into the stained khaki fabric. I break into his reverie. Listen, Szekkit, be serious. You're not telling me you are that scrunched-up, black-and-blue little fellow in there?

"Just su-su-supposing? How would I get *that* cleared? Is there a psychiatrist who can handle *that* case? Damn right, there isn't! It's an embryonic catastrophe. How would your card-carrying VA shrink get at the traces laid down on those autonomic tapes? It takes complete identification with the primordial trauma of this ninety-day-old creature curled in that chamber at the end of that vaginal corridor, a sort of hairless rat in an oxygen flask . . . ."

More like a chrysalid in a cocoon.

"O yah, that's good."

Waiting for wings.

"You get the idea. A worm, but alive. So, the way to wipe out that misinformation is to flush the tank and realign circuits. Otherwise, it's hopeless—humanity's finished!

Purge all personnel files, we're heading for Sector Apocalypse! Bling-bling! Blang-blang! Double red alert! (Miss Roberts, leggo! There's no time for that now—see me when we've passed over!)

"What?"

It's not exactly misinformation you're describing. More like terror in the Szekkor Sector.

"Szekeli, please. My name. But I give you only the hypothetical situation. A rat's in a trap—how should that little beast comprehend?"

A question.

"*The* question."

Chicken does not remember egg.

"Well?"

Anamnesis. Everyone seems to agree. The only cure.

"Right, sure. Whatever. Well? For *that* you need *scientific* psychology. Since all data is automatically stored, you can return to it, recall it, relive it. That corrects it."

Tampering with evidence, it's called. Get you one to ten years on the couch. Lucky to have your sentence suspended, Szekk.

"Please."

I think it's risky business.

"Try and follow me, my friend."

It's an old minefield. You can be blown away like that.

"Maps all forgotten. That's why you need a logical system. You don't understand.

Oh but I do. Socrates says you must do this self-examination in order to reincarnate better. Dante says there's no chance of getting back again anyway, so you better think about it now. Your momma's and your dada's own preacher, Calvin, says you may correct all you like, but the odds are against you: you're destined for doom and gloom eternal. While you make it sound as simple as opening a package of Jello—hot water, just stir and pour. Any flavor you like.

"Yah, foolproof is what it is. After millions of years of evolution, the human nervous system cannot fail."

So why are you sick?

"Me? Sick? Because it misinterprets. Somebody else makes a mi-mi-mistake. I'm not sick—but the system's full of crossed wires, filthy programming."

How can you know that? Szekkmann, you are off the wall.

"May seem like theory to you. But believe me, it happens to be the case. You don't get it because you're just an aberree."

I'm what?

"Hey, we're all aberrees! Since the hour of our conception we have been given nothing but misinformation. I know. I have studied the book on this technique. Just the name tells you how perfectly simple it is: Scientology. Science and Logic."

So I hear. A system you can read right off the back of the Cheerios carton. Well, what do you want from me?

"There is one problem. I need a helper to guide me along my tapes as I replay them down to the Alpha Tape. That's my first, actually. It seems to come last only because the first one is the last you reach. See? And the last will thus come first. Get it?"

You may have something.

"Then you'll kindly lead me up to the light again."

Well, I don't know if I can do that.

"Come to the Institute tonight and meet a real scientologist. I'll take you to my group leader. You'll be instructed. I can't go it alone. I need a guide."

Just a moment, Szekkio. That must be thought on.

"You clear me, then I clear you. Szekeli, if you please. It's not hypnotism, if that's what scares you. You're fully conscious. You merely learn how to scan your tapes. Then you'll be getting full recalls in real time. Visio, sonic, tactilic, and olfactoric. Kinesthetic—which is weight and motion. Somatic—that's pain. Thermic and organic—your insides. In Scientology, organic is also emotive. The fact is, you don't cry because you're sad. You're sad because you're crying. Emotion is physical, not mental like that spooky Freudian stuff."

How would I qualify for training?

"That's the beauty of it. No prerequisites. Anyone from age thirteen qualifies. The short course is enough. Absolutely. Because the method is the message: it's automatic analysis because it's geared to your nervous system. Easier than setting up a movie projector. And what a movie! Visio, sonic, tactilic, olfactoric, kinesthetic, somatic, thermic: none of that psychiatric mumbo-jumbo. The VA handed me enough crap on that Kingsbridge ward, I'm telling you. But I got out before they could torch me."

Sounds foolproof. For crying out loud!

"You'll never solve the problems of the world any other way."

Not even if we're creative?

"Creative? Yah sure, creativity—a 19th-century luxury, like driving a horse and buggy today. Man, to take power we have got to have power! Scientology is spreading. It's logical. You'll see. Ron knew what's what. The man had vision!"

I didn't know that El Ron is also to be numbered amongst the prophets.

"His teachings are sweeping the globe!"

Listen, Szekku—

"—No. *You* li-li-listen! I'm not through with you! Be honest with yourself for once, and let me finish, will you! Uh, please, it's Szekeli."

I heard him out. He grew inspired as he spoke, gazing past me through the arch, up Fifth Avenue.

"Now, what we want to do is get at the basic human powers, see? Just imagine what they will be when the billions of circuits in our brain are cleared, and juice runs full voltage! Without wasting ninety-five percent of our energy on multiplying alternate transmission lines wherever there's damage caused by fouled wires from experiential traumas. Just think if Con Ed could wire New York like our brain! Okay, can you just *imagine* the mindpower? There's no computer in the world to match it in sheer infinitude of cross-referenced hookups! Hey, when you get yourself cleared, man, your IQ will go up on an infinity curve. Like this—" and he takes out his felt pen and draws a diagram in the palm of my left hand . . .

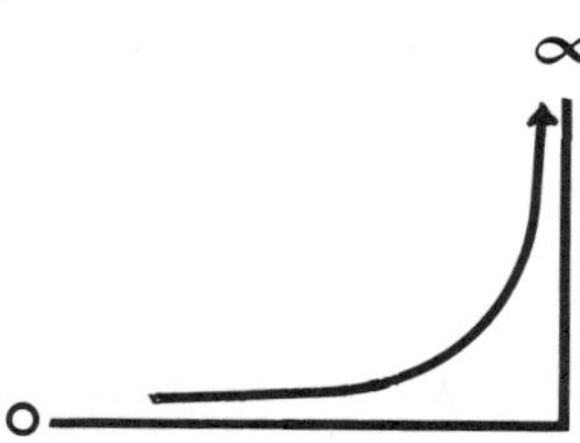

"—No telling where you'll go, because there'll be no stopping you!"

Szikki, the only thing standing between you, me, and happiness is my IQ.

"Oh yah, an IQ like everyone else has IQ! Stuffed with the random, unsystematic information they've dumped on you for thirty years, feeding you irrational garbage that sits there garbled on your tapes, as if a bunch of chimps stuck those million books on the shelves in the library there. How can you be expected to locate what you're looking for, when it could be something you overheard when you were six months old, maybe sleeping? It's all trapped down under that static of radio jokesters playing next door thirty years ago—Ben Bernie and Bob Hope and Jello Jack and Fred Allen and Fibber McGee . . . . How can you know what's shorting you out every time you think back over the million hours you've already logged in your brief life?"

It was but a little nap, an after-dinner dream.

"But you will! When you're cl-cl-cleared."

I'll sleep on it.

"How long must we wait for you to see the light?"

Till after the new year.

It wouldn't do for him. That dry spittle had collected in the chapped corners of his mouth. He squeezed my left elbow convulsively, begging me to sign up for a crash course in clearing technique over Christmas at the Dianetics Institute. In Maryland! Otherwise, he'd go forward by himself.

Into the abysmal past. Call that forward?

"I want progress! Before it's too late. But we can only go forward through the past. I'll get certified, come back and clear you all."

Clear who all?

"You and your buddies here. Intellectuals! You guys will never get anywhere. With you guys it's one big sentimental snafu."

Semimental, you mean.

"Yah yah, that's good! Hey, if you were cleared, you would take the logical next step."

What's that?

"Switch. Write prose."

Ah, what do I know—besides old communiqués from the foxhole and tax returns? Well, some other records too: birth, and copulation, and death. Should I write history?

"History?"

Everything else is mythology and opinion.

"History!" He glares at me with those weak, Flemish eyes looking the size of Dali's oyster-limp watches through those gray-tinted thick lenses. The silver frames of his Ben Franklin specs are wrapped with friction tape over the earpieces. "Nah, not history. What can history mean to the future? Zilch. Re-re-redeem yourself. Write what I write: the one possible literature: SF."

Someone's betrayed us! The First Galactic Fleet of the League of Spartacists is bearing down on our top-secret timewarp! Set battle cruiser Mars for intercept with barbarian flagship Vlad on emergence from black hole in Leda at Tau Upsilon Mu in Cygnus. Entering space tunnel. Subspace insterstitial magnadrive now going hyperspace! Secure all hatches—I said, Cut that out, Miss Roberts!—Three . . . Two . . . One . . . ZZZZZZZZZOOOOOM! Like that, you mean?

"Yah, well. Say what you like. SF's the only literature that can be written in our time. The rest is pretentious, navel-picking, deep-fried Freudian bullshit, and faggot fantasies for cornering the middlebrow book clubs or giving college professors something to write about. There's no Shakespeare around. No Melville."

Not even a Masefield, Szikker.

"Who?" Szekeli knows almost nothing beyond Hubbard, Heinlein, Anderson, Asimov, Van Vogt, and Bradbury. But he declaims the Word according to Hefaistos: "This is the age of technology. Now and to come. More so every year. New heaven, new earth coming."

God forbid!

"If you write for your own times, the only thing you *can* write is SF. SF's for the good of society as a whole. We'll teach them how to imagine the future of man!"

Szekka, are you serious? With SF? Cybering ciphers with punk operas?

"What I tell you. Listen, if you're only half as good as Bradbury, you can make a fortune. I intend to. Read him—you'll see how it's done. It's elementary. Incidentally, the name is Szekeli."

Just follow the yellow brick road. Will I win fame too?

"And find truth. But, if you live without being cleared, you'll only do more of what we've had—Hemingway, Faulkner. Passé. Heroes of Life and Time."

Once in Vogue and now they're out. Too bad.

"Across the river and over the hill. Fact is, only SF can be written honestly."

On what basis?

"The source of all true knowledge: science."

And knowledge will make us wise? When we know what we know for sure, then we'll be really good? Right?

"Right."

Because then we know what's true?

"Yah!"

So knowledge means that what I have in my mind agrees with reality?

"Oh, yah!"

And my mental conceptions give me images that correspond exactly with the world?

"Good, good."

And such images in my mind will not be illusions, or hallucinations, or delusions originating from mysterious causes?

"Right on!"

And so, I shall definitely live in harmony with nature, because nature is logical cause and effect, and I'll find out all about it through scientific reasoning, with my experiments and applications?

"That's what I mean: materialism plus the dianetics dialectic."

And the same fire that burns up the universe burns in my brain?

"I always thought you should write down what you say."

And because everything I do is logical and reasonable, it's right, not wrong. So I must not fear anything out there, or anything inside?

"That is Scientology yah! But goddammit, be logical. Get yourself cleared first! Then we can talk your kind of talk."

He was mottling with rage again. I tried to mollify him.

Szekkixx, you're probably right. *If* science is philosophy. *If* philosophy is literature. *If* literature equals scientology . . . .

"So—you'll try? Come in with me. Please!" He flips another crumpled Gauloise out of the pack, lights it and drips more smoldering ash down his chin. "We can start a dianetics cell here. I mean, a nucleus of clears. Me first, say, then you and these guys you kick back with. I'd be proud to be responsible for such a concentration of mental-verbal clears in one place. Think of it, it would be like a super-computer array flickering in front of us, with sheer power to the *n*th degree . . . power for good, power for . . . . Je-je-jesus, when I think of it, our cell could be hidden right here in Washington Square, in broad daylight! A force for spreading logic outward over the globe. Organizing and directing the renewal of mankind! Hubbard knows!" He rubs his hands together, producing shreds of skin between his pale palms, white skin that rolls out in little blackened pills.

Were it that simple, we'd have a real revolution on our hands.

"It is! Go-go-goddammit, that's the point!" His eyes actually seem to rattle behind those lenses. "The key we've waited for all these millenia since the lost world of Mu! How stupid I am, coming back and going round, in and out, all these millenia, just like the rest of you aberrees, and never grasping the key that was shining all the time right before my eyes! The very key—in the light, in the window! The fundamental technique at last! Listen to me now: clear out your circuits, you clear out your organs. Gone forever your miseries, your ulcers, your tics and myopia, your constipation and your colitis, your hayfever, diarrhea, eczema, your shooting headaches. No more pain. Because the dianetic reviews the basic sensory input-output data imprinted along the nerves. You like hearing about people getting electroshock right in their brains, being injected with insulin convulsions? Believe me, I know! Just because your memory tapes are messed up you see, well, visions. At the wrong time. Or your body acts manic when some ordinary stimulus makes you remember your own fetus thrashing about during the abortion attempt with a knitting needle and a tablespoon. Can't you see how rational a procedure it will be to unravel your circuits? You want that, don't you? Here's this ultra-fine portable mini-calculator in us being burned out by barbarous medics who know nothing about systemic nerve-engineering. Witch doctors with pseudo-medical degrees and lots of Frankenstein paraphernalia. Like when you tried to wire up the fucking field radio, and the NVA was all over you with AK-47s, and there wasn't even a manual! Firefight you have fight with fire! How I hate them!"

Now, Szekku, hatred is not good for you.

"But—"and it's running away with him—"dianetics is engineering psychology for this age of engineering. Get that straight, once and for all! Furthermore, if you want the real truth, we don't need you obsolete, old-fashioned-thinker types to confuse us anymore today. What we need now is the basic text on human engineering. Apply the three R's: Return! Recall! Relive! And we're going to apply it, whether you like it or not!"

But Szakkery, I believe, I believe you because—it's absurd.

"Furthermore, it's Sz-sz-szekeli! can't you ever get it right?"

Let us wait for a new year, Szekkums.

"You could be saved right now!"

Sufficient unto the day the salvation thereof, I said.

It had begun to sleet, a melting, icy rain driven slantwise against us from the northeast. The Express bus arrived. I stood at the head of the line, waiting for the door to open. Szekeli had dropped his bundle of manuscript on the sidewalk and was slapping his pockets for matches, another Gauloise pressed between his split, trembling Flemish pink lips. I mounted the step, waved farewell, and went back to sit over the engine for warmth. He looked down at himself and saw the holes burnt in his old Saigon-stained field jacket. Then he stared up at the low gray clouds as though he could see them—even see through them to the infinitely far black space that drew him into its pulsating, fire-filled voids. He seemed to me to stand alone in Washington Square, accusing the sky of dropping those sparks on him, as though incited by some indifferent god. And while outraged Szekeli cursed, it was Szekeli himself burning Szekeli bit by bit with his own fever.

He knows nothing of tragedy; and he is ignorant of comic relief with its cathartic laughter. He wants only one thing: to recreate himself. To realize that wish, he must return to the instant before his mother's fat Flamande ovum was kissed by his father's wriggling Magyar spermatozoan. A likely candidate for self-knowledge? I think not. I stuck his dianetics brochure into my coat pocket along with a Watch Tower pamphlet about the Second Coming that two solemn Witnesses had thrust at me just before he'd come along.

Yet Szekeli will be successful. One of science fiction's very own.

Telemachos

JANUARY, AND United Sporting Goods advertises its annual inventory clearance sale. Items from last fall's hunting season too. I am not a hunter, but it might be fun to practice archery in my own back yard.

I found a heavy double-reflex Bear bow marked down 60%. Its original list price was far too high for me, unless it were taken and used seriously. I could afford it now, though. When I asked what the double XX branded into the grip meant, the salesman replied that it was a Second. Why? "Must be some slight defect in the finish somewhere, something you wouldn't notice anyway. It's guaranteed, otherwise." We turned it about, looking for the flaw that had not passed inspection. Finally, we decided that it must be that discoloration in the varnish just beneath the grip, and wouldn't be distracting. "You could scratch it like that yourself the very first day in the woods," he said. Yes, I could, but it would be my scratch and not someone else's wouldn't it? "Take it or leave it. But if you want it, it's yours for good. As is." He walked off, impatient, and began hanging ladies' tennis dresses on a rack. I took it, as is, at 60% off list. I had to. I could also pick up arrows, targets, a straw butt, forearm and finger guards and a couple of first-quality bowstrings, and still come out cheap, and be ready for practice as soon as I got home.

It was late afternoon when I had set everything up, exhilarated and eager to begin shooting. The shadows were thickening everywhere; the sun was low in the southwest over the purpled Pacific and the sailboats were clustering at the breakwater down at the marina, heading back to their berths as fast as they could before the early January nightfall. It was very quiet, no wind at all, and only the screech of a bluejay on the naked branch of the fig tree in the middle of the garden broke the calmness of the dusk.

I strapped the guard to my left forearm, slipped the finger

gloves on my right hand, placed the heavy, longish bow behind my left calf and bent it with all my might, which was barely enough, I found, to slip the loop of the bowstring over the top catch. It took me three tries, at that, and I was panting and beginning to sweat and tremble in my knees. This might prove embarrassing, I felt. I twanged the taut bowstring at my ear a few times while I rested and calmed my breathing. The tone was low and strong, and the bow now looked very handsome. Perhaps a 56-pound pull was a bit much for home purposes? Were I out for bear or elk, it might be right, but in my own back yard? Though if I didn't work at that heavy pull now, how could I draw the bow later in the woods?

I set one of the fine, long aluminum arrows into the handgrip, and, after touching the rough plastic feathers, notched it. I placed my feet, took a deep breath, and swung the bow up to the correct position as I drew the string hard, all the way back to my right ear, and then—the bow broke in half in my hands! Was I then that strong? Or did that imperfection in the finish conceal a deep, fundamental flaw in the heartwood itself? Had I been cheated? It was branded a Second, yes. But it should have given me the same service as a new and perfect bow! I was angry. How could I prove the defect to have been in the bow, and not my powerful drawing of it? Perhaps I could glue it together again at the clean break, with one of the new epoxy resins, say? If that new superglue held, would the bow be elastic? I doubted very much.

I stood there as the moon came out, full and silver, over my shoulder, in the east. The arrows lay in their quiver on my back; my hands, laced with leather for shooting, held the two useless halves out before me; the now slack bowstring hung to my toes. I found myself fuming as I looked at the empty target leaning against the garage door. Never, never would I take a Second again! Not from anyone! Tears of frustrated fury scalded my cheeks. There were no guarantees to be had in this world anymore! To hell with United Sporting Goods! And to hell with them all!

Abraham

TOWARDS DUSK ON A CHILLY, damp January day. Everywhere, the old crusted December snows have melted off, leaving behind great smudged drifts and patches on the bare, brown-black pastures and fields and in the ditches alongside the road's shoulders. The thaw had come with the new year; but it could blizzard at any hour, even tonight, though the skies had been clear and sharp with frost.

I was tired. We'd been travelling for some days now, cooped up in the old estate wagon that was loaded down, inside and overhead, with our worldly goods. I had not wanted to drive more than two days; but somehow it had turned out a much slower and more distant journey than I could have dreamt. The roads were no longer straight, or the highways had been closed, and we bumped along detours on lumpy and broken macadamed byways or rough, potholed gravel tracks for miles and miles around mountains and through vacant valleys where only the occasional gas pump in front of a country garage that leaned away into its decrepitude showed any sign of human inhabitation. The pump outside, and the thin stream of black vapor rising from the kerosene stove that warmed it. You'd walk into what seemed a locked-up little store, you'd go on back to find some old mechanic under a tractor in the overheated shop, where the calendars featuring perky nudes had faded into the woodwork years ago, leaving only the tips of their rosy breasts, their grimacing lips and painted fingernails and bright teeth and vapid eyes still aglow with provocation. The grizzled fellow would slide himself out with a grunt, haul himself to his feet and shuffle out to gas the tank and check under the hood: how slow he could be, and taciturn, befuddled by the keen air blowing down all the long way from the Canadian tundra.

We were headed for a town near where I recalled having spent the summers of childhood, up north in the mountains. To settle there, I thought, if we could only find it again. Now, as the last of the light of day drained into that blackish-purple sump of shadowed ridge over the low bare western sky, we drove into some small town I'd never even heard of. The sign said: EUREKA Pop. 111 Elev. 999.

You know those upstate villages that have been dying for a hundred years. Giant naked elms and maples lining the narrow streets. Frame houses with bare porches and plastic sheets nailed over the windows for insulation. Paint peeling off and cheap asphalt tiles shingling the roofs. Scraggly forsythia bushes on the snow-covered front lawns all raddled with yellow stains of dogpiss. Silence.

We pulled up to a dark, shabby tourist home, a Bide-A-Wile place, its signboard out on the street illegible, though a weak bulb was burning over the porch steps. There was a wet chill now in the air, and low clouds rushing overhead in the night. My wife asked me if I knew where we were at all, and anyway, how could we go on like this without a map! I remembered then that we did have maps in our trunk, which hadn't been opened for years and years. Meanwhile, we ought to settle ourselves for the night because the boy was dropping off, asleep in his snowsuit.

Behind a countertop in her front hall stood the dim, dour landlady of this place: the usual kind of landlady. Her coarse steel-gray hair was rolled up in a bun, her squat and shapeless body cloaked in a full, chintzy dress patterned with dingy roses. Of course if we wanted to stay the night she had a fine big room for us—though there was no hot water.

We'll stay, I said.

"Where'd yehs be heading to?" she said.

Liberty. Aren't we near it yet?

"Ah, t'aint fuh," she declared. "In fact."

Where are we? I said. I haven't seen a sign all day.

"Right now yehs'd be on Route Number One. Yehs'll take Route One due north to the mawnin', and yehs'll reach Liberty all right. Yeh come up to a tee-junction with Route Number Ninety-nine."

I come to a tee-junction? I said. Where One meets Ninety-nine?

"That's right, son. Yehs'll hev to."

But what happens to Route One then?

"Oh, it joins Ninety-nine. Then yehs'll look out for One Hundred, and there yehs'll be, like as not. In fact."

I could see it in my mind's eye: a white house in the old Greek Revival style: a warm house, grand and dry and sunlit by midwinter's brilliant noon glare. There it waited, high on the hill. The sun would be dazzling, reflected from the clean new snow that was coming tonight to cover the world. The sky would be an icy blue, a blue so pale it would seem to have been blanched by frost. A fat plume of white smoke would purl up from the fireplace chimneys, and four ancient rugged oaks would stand guard like seraphs at the corners of our hilltop acre. It would not be gloomy; we would never shiver with the damp as we were shivering here tonight in this godforsaken hamlet in a dying valley.

We lugged the old steamer trunk upstairs to open it in our room and look at the old maps we'd put away before setting forth on the journey. It had split at the joints and when we opened it, it reeked—that sour smell of dead moths, and powdery mold. Nothing but mildewed odds and ends of ancient worn rugs and blankets. The clothes, our sweaters and shoes, skirts and trousers and coats were all eaten away or decayed into shreds who knows how long ago. Some broken trinkets remained at the bottom. On top of it all lay a speckled black-and-white child's lesson book. There was a faded list of items in pencil: the inventory of the trunk's contents! My wife had written it out for the insurance company once upon a time. I thought it odd to have put that list in the same trunk you wanted to know something about were it lost or stolen. But who can remember things done so long ago, or why they were done at all?

It doesn't matter now, I said. We have the trunk anyway, for what it's worth. What I want to see is that old map showing the way to Liberty. Though actually, we don't truly need it: I know the road. I know it by heart. As if it's written in the palm of my hand. I'll let you know when we're on it. I thought we'd get out the map for the hell of it, so you could follow me. Never mind now, the map's faded to nothing like all the rest.

I glanced through the copybook and saw that the handwriting

wasn't hers; nor mine for that matter. It was a child's scrawl; most of it illegible now too. On the last page I could make out these hopeful words, *Once upon a time in the beginning* . . . .

I said as we climbed into that sway-bottomed, musty bed: After all our wanderings, isn't it strange to end up in a village like Eureka?

My wife shivered and said, "Nothing surprises me anymore. Here and there, without a map, on the damned roads, all because you wanted to find some place you thought you remembered. I just wonder, where is there an end, where is there an end to it all . . . ."

She was tired. She had never wanted to start out, and she never expected to have had to come this far. Wherever we were, I knew it was much farther than anyone could have guessed. As I fell asleep, I still held in my mind's eye the house in Liberty we were headed for, that high home on the hill looking down over snow fields reaching in every direction as far as the horizon. It was there, I knew it must be there, waiting for us in the morning. Up north, beyond Liberty.

She was asleep. The boy gasped in the other bed, and then whimpered, "No! No!" Not a sound outside. The big snow had begun to fall, and immense drifts were already covering Eureka.

Sybil

STOPPED FOR A PACKAGE of L'Oréal on my way home from the doctor's. This hair can use some color. When I was twenty, it was straight, long, thick, and that hefty! A glossy, ebony lacquer. Like the Dragon Lady's. If only it would come out royale, just a shade real—it won't, of course. It will dry a dull, rusty black. Anyway.

I'm still gazing at myself through the fog that woke me with a headache like a cold round stone in my forehead this morning before the street lights went out. My heart's rattling and skipping just the way the damn clutch in the pickup does between second and third. I'm sweaty. I'm giggling and crying at the same time. And I'm staring into the black glass of an oval mirror. Its gilded frame is carved with a laurel wreath. A thick, amber, gold-flecked cloud swirls up from of its bottomless center—who *is* that in the smoky glass? I can't make her out. Closer, closer, smiling—my darling, is it you? I know it must be you . . . it *is* you—fairest in the land. Fairest of them all! My god! just to glimpse that narrow waist and flat belly, those thighs firm again, long and limber as a dancing girl's. You're dressed in a trailing black gown of some gossamer voile, black-sequinned, cut right down to there; it's got a white ruff of antique lace that stands up high behind your ivory swan's neck, and your blue-black tresses cascade over it shimmering with little silvery lightning bolts on those rich shoulders. Ah, that dazzling, satiny skin, those full, blue-veined ruby-nippled breasts! My hands slither down my slinky hips: I lift a slow, snaky leg, right foot first, left foot then, once around, and back again . . . and I am chortling like a hag, because I suddenly know that I am not only me, lovely and loving me once more, but also—Snow White's stepmother? At night into her palace bedchamber I've somehow crept. And here I am, mumbling and muttering crazy, mean words, singing and dancing into and out of that deep mirror,

Oh mirror, mirror! on the wall. . . . Who the hell cast me in this awful cartoon?

Anyway, it might help my spirits to give what's left of vanished glory a going-over with Préference #1. Then to the frozen burritos and refried beans and piccalilly with diet Coke, alone as usual with my Arthur over the yellow-stained, cracking formica counter, as if that's any kind of din-din. . . . He's plugged into his Walkman earphones turned up so high I can hear the *chiss-chinkachink chiss-chinkachink* of those tinny backups on his punk tapes all the way from his room! till now I can't squeeze out of my head that number he repeats and repeats—Dominator Soul . . . *All the time you see us, we'll be on our way, tata! Taking what is mine, cuz now I'll have my day, tata-ta! Dom-in-a-tor So-o-ul, he take what's in his way! Ta! MOVE IN ON THEM! All the time you see us, ta! we'll be on our way! tata!-ta Passive ways to pull you down, tear them up and smash them in, tata! we'll have our day, tata-ta tata-ta! Dom-in-a-tor So-o-ul!* Haven't the stomach for that tonight. Hadn't yesterday, won't tomorrow. How much longer can this go on? Still, coloring the hair takes a whole hour—which means sixty minutes I won't have to sit in that crushed Morris chair waiting for my barbarous boy to meander in from whichever shopping mall his punk friends have picked to vandalize this summer, don't have to stare at that giant Map of the World on the wall, with its corners curling under the scotch tape, and the pins stuck into it over every continent. I actually put two whole years in, meditating every night on that flat world, with its cut-up, stretched-out, pear-shaped continents, till I gave up trying to imagine I could read constellations of the Zodiac in the crawling patterns hinted at by a thousand red pins. It's a chicken-pox rash on the wall; it signifies just nothing.

Mervyn's been sticking those pins in over the last eight years. He talks to those pins—his Call Numbers. He doesn't need this map—he taped it to the wall for me, the last time he remembered he had a wife—he's got them listed in his black book upstairs in the attic. The whole roof of the house is his: it's heated and air-conditioned, it's padded with cork acoustic tiles and wired from floor to ceiling. Walk in any hour, and what do you see: tapes running, dials blinking, needles waving. He squats there in front of the mikes all day like a pale, grizzle-faced toad, his shaggy white hair sticking out from the headphones everywhichaway; he flicks switches and he twiddles knobs: 95,000 bucks worth of equipment patched into a net of cables to a rack of antennas on hundred-foot-high masts. He gets thinner, pastier, listening to that chitter-chatter, and those mysterious signals coming through—all of them out there everywhere—talking, swapping codes, playing chess, laughing through the static at something, arranging funny deals or whatever, right through the twenty-four hours and all around the Date Line. When he got the Word and turned into P535BCES, he simply stopped being husband or father. Whatever life we had in this shambles of a house since the kids started junior high, he's killed it. Him and his locos out there in the ether.

Up he goes at seven in the morning, and there he stays till midnight. Eats in there too. Never with us. The kids are grown, except for Arthur, and Mervyn never talks to him, except to curse. Mervyn kicked Madelyn out when she turned sixteen. His hope and joy. I couldn't stop him. "You walk streets? Now go sleep in them!" My beauteous Madelyn. That's when the hypertension started my pressure going up and up, till this morning it hit 240 over 175. And I had to quit the job at the Seven Eleven checkout because I couldn't stand on my feet more than fifteen minutes. And my hair went bleah and began coming away in bunches, woof, weft, warp, and all: just like I was carding a sheep. I was eighteen before it ever was cut—you could have stuffed a pillow with it, it was that thick! Menopause is no word for this. I can't find patience now to read even *USA*—barely make it from paragraph to paragraph. Their whole world looks like a ball of tangled yarn to me. As if there's sense in what they choose to print. Or as if I needed words from them! Words are for Mervyn: he's installed his ham radio in the pickup too; whenever we go somewhere for a change of scenery, all we hear's more of the same old static and screech, and all I get out of him is the same old, "Shut your face!" Getting and sending all day, he lays waste his hours. Mervyn claims he has friends all over the world. Fine for him—so far as I can tell, not a one of them has a wife. Just voices without bodies, howling.

Social life? The hibachi's rusted, greasy with crud from years ago. The wild grape's sneaking up from the creek, and I can almost feel it wriggle its way over that browned, raggedy, tattered lawn. The feeling of itch and scratch summer out here in Alexandria brings is horrible: poison ivy's creeping in along with those vines, and I've given up on our vegetable patch—let Br'er Possum finish it off, who cares! Nobody ever drops in on us. We never go visiting. As far as he's concerned, it's "Who needs them assholes!" Our kids won't come home for Thanksgiving or whatever. And Mervyn even yelled at his own grandchildren when they knocked on his door, so now they don't come to me neither. If I want to see them, I've got to haul myself into the truck and make it there on my own.

So here we are, stuck at the dead center of our fifties. What have we done with our god-given freedom? Whatever am I waiting for? And what could be worth his kind of listening—what in the world is so fascinating that anyone'll give 19 hours a day to it? What the hell does he hear in it? Shortwave's no hobby with Mervyn—it's a full-time obsession. How does he think we can go on with just a government pension and his odd-jobs—even if now and then these funny checks with pretty foreign stamps on the envelopes do come in? Self-employed expert, is he? On what? They pay him for what, advice? He couldn't look me in the eye and dare speak the tripe he tells them out there! The more he makes a philosophy out of that gossip he calls in, and tapes, and beams out again, the worse it sounds to me. His international family? His far-flung community? His new kind of world culture? Garbage! Alpha to Omega, over, in and out again—rogering, and rogered. He'll never even get to Beta listening to them hamateurs out there. First couple years after his 20-year hitch at McLean was over, okay, I carry his tray up the stairs to "the studio." Stand and listen to that jibber-jabber. Half code, half insider-jargon, half trivia, half crap: and a thousand invisible, identical Mervyns across 24 time zones sending that stuff every day and all night! Not a word of it worth preserving, if you ask me. Just doodoo, the kind of silliness we used to scream at one another over a waxed string stretched between two tin cans running from attic to attic out back when we were kids . . . Calling Buck Rogers! Come in, Buck! I read you, Wilma. I'm a prisoner of the . . . . Wilma! Come in, Wilma! Over! Buck, where are you! Sheer poetry, he calls it—the first true universal symposium, he calls it, if you please! More like a folly of fools! Check this out: he says, Together they're building the City of Man. Boys Town is what it is!

Every evening I sit in this broken-backed Morris chair, I stare at those red zits on his global-network map, and before you know it I've put away a six-pack. Then I heave myself up and shuffle these sizzling varicoses off to bed. I wish he'd just once come down and ask me to say what *I* think—as if he could ever begin to understand what I could tell him! If it was worth my trouble, I'd stick a thousand black, poison pins into them Call Numbers on his world map—let 'em bleed to death!

I was just setting the color when I thought I heard the door bang downstairs. My lathered head was wrapped up in the cellophane bag, and I'd opened the bathroom window to let out those choking ammonia fumes. Arthur? I called, Put the stuff in the microwave, I'll be down in fifteen minutes, okay? No answer. But I can hear the ball game on the TV, so I know Arthur is there. Probably busy rubbing fresh henna powder and vaseline into his Mohawk. Seven silver rings in his left earlobe.

Toes too much trouble, the bending over them till I can hardly straighten up again; so I settle for filing my fingernails and plucking out witch-hairs on my chin. Touch up the eyebrows. Might as well creme the moustache too. I'm going to slather myself with lanolin oil, neck to ankles, and paint on a blood-purple nail polish. Nothing will stop the march of time though. Still, go on and dream, darling. . . . Otherwise, all the mirrors in this house would have to be smashed. If I went to Arden, it would all be done for me: packed in mud and wrapped like a mummy for a hundred-fifty bucks. Then I could stand to look at me for a minute.

I finish, give myself a fast blow-dry, put up my hair. Hear Arthur yell, "I'm gone! Don't wait up, Lady!" Slam! I go down in my new, sheer white nightie—it must be 95° at least in this house—to clear away the mess he's left—a dabbled-at plate of congealed beans, bits and shreds of burrito all over the countertop. All the signs of a real banquet. Fine, fine. doesn't trouble with a glass, takes his Coke straight from the bottle; and there it is, knocked over on the floor, still dripping. You'd think Arthur was brought up in a pigsty, not this regular, ho-ho! home. The TV's roaring: somebody's running bases, and the crowd's going wild for a change. He'd be better off sleeping under a culvert somewhere. Might teach him to appreciate this roof over his head. Except, Mervyn's under the same roof. So am I—with nothing and no one to talk to, though I've a thing or two I might could say to them. As take, for instance, Love. And, take Beauty. . . . But first, it's time for *Dynasty* and that old six-pack. Who's hungry anyway?

The second can of brew's barely into my parched gullet when there's the phone ringing.

"Mervyn Ussery?"

Who's this?

"Miami calling for a Mr. Mervyn Ussery?"

I am Mrs. Ussery—I'll take it.

"This is Tony Alexander."

Never heard of you.

"You have now, Ma'am—I'm a Dade County public defender. I'd like a word with Mervyn Ussery."

I just told you, This is Mrs. Ussery. What do you want with him?

"Does Mervyn Ussery have a daughter named Madelyn?"

He does not.

"Pardon?"

Not anymore. But I'm Madelyn's mother.

"Oh, I see. Well, then."

Speak up, fellow, I'm waiting on you.

"Mrs. Ussery, they're asking you to post five thousand dollars bail."

For what?

"Prostitution."

Why so much? Sounds to me like prostitution plus.

"Plus possession: three kilos."

Three keys of what?

"Ma'am, let's us just call it an uncontrollable substance. Whatever, okay? It's not worth her life. The sheriff's holding Madelyn, and she's also charged with two counts of aggravated assault: he's got a couple of battered peace officers. Seems she offered a little resistance when they picked her up. That bail's not unreasonable in those circumstances. Your daughter is in serious trouble, even for Miami. I advise you to make every effort to send that money . . . fast."

Where in hell would I find five thousand dollars?

"Mrs. Ussery, if I were you, I'd get Madelyn out of that place . . . quick."

She's off the street. So what's your damn hurry?

"Listen to me, Ma'am: they're also holding a girlfriend of hers downstairs. Only it's just the body—no head. There's a tee shirt on the torso, and it says, 'Beat Me, Rape Me, Kill Me—I Love It!' All right?"

What about the head? Where'd it get to?

"It came in just now. Couple of troopers stopped a man running the dogtrack. He was naked. And he was carrying Lola's head by the hair. Tossed it into the police car and screamed, 'Arrest her—she done it!' From the look of it, he's been toting that head around by its braids for a good while now. All right, Ma'am?"

All right, already! All right!

"I'll wait here another hour, Mrs. Ussery."

I scribble Mr. Alexander's phone number down there in Miami and head for the fridge. I surely do need that third beer before I lug myself up those stairs for a little dialogue with Mervyn, one-on-one. This time he's going to hear it from me—for a change.

Iocasta

LONG DAY. Dossiers requiring my approval before going out over the Telex to managers of district stations around the country for last-minute action during the weekend. By Monday morning our campaign would be rolling, or we were lost. Market closed uncertainly, confused: bearish so far as I could tell, key indicators wobbling and menacing the week's gains. Where would the next rally develop, if at all? The spirit of contradiction rules us all now. Experts sitting on their hands while speculators slip in like sharks scattering the schools of little people. As well as scaring the great institutions who in the absence of reliable pointers are drawing in their ranks, conserving effort and resources as best they can. All day long I sensed weakening, a general loss of nerve originating not in the echelon of the leaders, as has occurred too often in the last hundred years, but lower down, at the base of the structure in fact. Plenty of prognosticators raising their voices now in a clamor of doom and destruction, just like licensed prophets. True, conditions are precipitating in which, given the presence onstage of certain characters at a certain hour, the result must be a panic. Not yet; but soon enough. In my own area, for instance, things suddenly started moving yesterday. Justice Department puts us on notice: subpoenas are flying our way: everyone in the organization who is anyone will be called in for questioning. Dismaying; sickening; saddening too: years and years of effort threatened by one man's astonishing suit! He'd spotted the very place in our entire elaboration where we could be attacked. He had bided his time; he had prepared his case with infinite detail, and was challenging us at the moment when our attention is devoted to international complexities and the domestic economy, which is now revealing signs of strain unfortunately so severe it can no longer be patched with temporary expedients. Were I writing the text, I think I should choose this very situation as the example of a classical case of catastrophe, for no virtuoso display of managerial expertise will carry us through the oncoming crisis unharmed. How much time is there? Anyone's merest guess. And now, now this one man's claim could bring heaven crashing on our heads. As though an old crippled fellow with a knobbly blackthorn stick wrenching at a crack in the wall were to cause the World Trade Center's 110 storeys to split, shatter, totter slowly, and collapse in a mountain of rubble, of marble and glass and steel flooding over Wall Street, spilling into the Hudson around the Battery, causing an eddying riptide and whirlpool to form and suck barges and tugs and ferries from their courses, pulling them down to disaster. Yet I know the World Trade Center cannot fall. I know we'll get beyond this situation too, because reality is not a dramatic episode in some chapter of the text, after all. Reality floats into the future on the imponderable. The Market will bottom out eventually, no matter how low its values have sunk: somewhere there's bedrock. Furthermore, I'll put our corps of lawyers to chorusing appeals on our case for years and years to come.

She called me away at midnight from the high windows that look out over the terrace, where a dozen potted trees stand shrouded in canvas: so many shapeless, featureless, dormant sentries. How long had I been standing there in my blue paisley silk robe, savoring my cigar and sipping the glass of whiskey as the warmth drained from the apartment . . . an hour? The great orb of the bone-white wintry moon had already shrunk to a frozen glaring disk as it flew up out of sight and hung somewhere before starting its decline in the west. But now from the zenith its harsh blued brilliance fell in a wide swath rippling over the black-running tidal current of the East River. From up here that stream swirled past, impressing me as always with its living oily violence. Again she was calling to me from upstairs, and I turned, reluctant, suddenly tired, my mind turbid, humming with the cross-talk of my nerves. After the frenzy of this week past, even the orders I'd left at the close of day hadn't provided me with repose. It seemed to me in the stillness of this penthouse, sealed from the gusts of frigid wind scouring the walls and terraces up here like slashes of invisible blades, that my ears rang. The kind of tintinnabulation one cannot avoid hearing deep in the skull, as though a brace of shotguns at a trapshooting meet had been firing beside my ears for hours.

She sat erect in bed, drinking from her red hand-blown glass tumbler: hot milk and honey laced with Spanish brandy. *Von Clausewitz on War.* A new edition, with commentary by some of our more intelligent political savants, to place the issue into our present perspective, wherever that is. At bedtime she likes history, and practical theory. I must settle for the dossiers: those raw numbers and the field reports I need to resolve before the next day's struggle. Even at bedtime I haven't leisure to reflect, although I am well aware that time is running out—one must begin by amassing wisdom grain by grain, and early on, as she had done. She's at it still. And how gracefully she shares it with me, like her life. Without her, I know, and well I know it, I should have come to nothing, nothing at all.

"You look worn out, my darling," she says, lifting her wide slanted blue-green eyes above the rims of her tiny tortoise-shell reading specs. I drop my robe and stretch out, striking in slow motion at floor and ceiling to unknot my shoulders. I am, I laughed, utterly exhausted. "Then I'll let you sleep for now. It will wait until morning, won't it." She pats my pillow, swings the reading spotlight above over to her side, and returns to *Clausewitz.* She would wake me as the gray light edges the draperies with a ghostly, trembling frame towards dawn: she would be pressed up against my back, her long arms twined about me, her smooth, fine fingers tracing invisible circles on my belly, the sharp nails catching in my hair delicately, her firm, cool thigh thrown lightly over my hip and sliding up and down, so that as I rise heavily up from the deeps of slumber I'd sense pulsing against my flank the hot breath of that secret creature between her legs. For now I'd let go of the world, that faint ringing persistent inside my head. I'd lapsed out as though I had launched myself from a height and would drop, floating and languourously flailing, and never to hit bottom. The abyss, I remember thinking, cannot be fathomed. Is it because our time in the world is a stony narrow ledge winding about a vast mountain? The base is obscured by perpetual, shifting mists below. The summit lost in light somewhere beyond our vision. The slope nearly vertical, a sheer, gray, icy, and sweating wall. We plod ahead, upward, slowly and suffering, in single file on this path for as long as we can, conversing brokenly, if we have the fortitude, with the backs of those just before us, and with the unseen faces of those just behind. Shouts, cries, snatches of echoing laughter come like greetings occasionally from somewhere above, where the track must go round again ascending, or from below, where the others are making their own way climbing after us. How bleak, to think of it like this. It's enough to make one wish to revolt, to leap away in despair . . . but then I recall those words—had I heard them spoken to me? *The abyss cannot be fathomed.*

Or was it the phone ringing that I'd thought I heard? Perhaps it had only begun to ring and she'd reached quickly out, as she always does, and lifted the receiver. I turned over and returned to sleep. Or I tried to. The room was darkened now: only the nightlamp glowing dim on her side of the big bed. "Yes," she whispers into the mouthpiece gently and without alarm, as if she'd expected this caller in the middle of the night. A deep voice answers: it is an old man's slow, deep voice. Friend of hers. I know about him. She is close to him, and has been for very many years. He seems to be saying, low yet distinct, "I couldn't sleep tonight. Will you talk to me awhile. It's so painful."

And propping her pillow behind her, she replies, sliding up to a sitting position and lighting a cigarette—I could hear the click of the lighter's cover, the pop of the flame as the quartz flint ticked,I could smell the acrid butane fluid, and feel her ribcase expand as she drew the first puff deep into her lungs—and settling herself for a long talk through the darkest hour of this long winter's night. "It's all right," she croons in her throaty voice, "he's asleep, poor thing. The trouble out there's terrible. A week of siege. The fighting's tired him so. This is the first setback he's had. Maybe he'll make it. Maybe he won't. He needs rest now."

I pretend to be sleeping as she goes on. "No, he doesn't know yet." I can hear his voice rumbling in the earpiece she must have propped on her shoulder in the way she has, so that she can hold the ashtray on her lap and smoke with the other hand. "Don't talk like that. It's not your fault, my darling. I've done what I can. You know that. But of course you are loved." I can't make out what he's saying as he goes on and on, like a man lost in drink or sorrow.

I try hard to listen. My own heavy breathing, the deep respiration of the unconsciousness I am feigning, obscures his words to me. The tones come through, though: hoarse, growling, a distant desperation. As their conversation rambles on and they exchange sentences, then phrases, then intimate keywords, it is as if he were yet her lover from long, long ago. As if they'd remained friends all this time during our marriage, meeting for luncheon dates, calling one another for news, counsel, consolation, attending afternoon concerts and strolling through exhibits, sharing a profound and vivid relationship that is as important to her as . . . anything else. But it's her affair, not mine. It doesn't offend me, or annoy me. Nevertheless, the secret endearments she whispers to him as she hears his story, cajoling his awful misery, promising him more and better days, reviewing the past, marking out the future . . . this side of the hushed, half-hidden talk makes me a little jealous. On principle. Simply, impersonally, so to speak. But not jealous of him. I know her. And I believe I know myself. Trust is all. And I trust. I try to keep awake, wondering what they are really talking of, as her voice sinks away, as she goes on listening to his ruminations, broken by endless pauses, it seems to me, in which she lights cigarette after cigarette, responding with sibilant ejaculations, "No, I can't . . . Saturday . . . Tuesday's better . . . I'll try to come . . . well yes, two, the opening . . . but of course, my darling one . . . I do . . . you know I've always . . . dearest, you mustn't go on so . . . you must believe what I tell you . . . always there . . . no, you're not alone in this . . . please, you're making me so unhappy, my precious one . . . truly, truly . . . you're hurting yourself . . . it's always been true, and . . . we know it . . . dear, dearest heart . . . . And still that voice continuing, distant, patient, droning and winding incomprehensibly this way and that, and deeper, yet farther off—she must have changed the earpiece to the other side. I wish she would speak in fuller sentences, so that I might follow their consultation. Yet even though she believes I am sleeping, she goes on answering with the guarded snatches one uses in the presence of the third person. It is something terribly important, I have realized. But what, and to whom?

I wanted to turn over, to seem to come surfacing for a moment from the depth, as if I'd been disturbed by them. Yet I found I couldn't move; I couldn't keep awake; I couldn't concentrate on her soft voice or on that man's indistinct words. Was it a dream, or did I imagine I finally heard, with the remnant of my futile effort to cling to a crumbling handhold of consciousness, the quiet clap of the receiver being cradled, the scribbling of the last cigarette stub in the ashtray, her long shivering sigh as she turned her pillow down again and slid beneath the comforter, the chilled soles of her feet pressing against my calves as she prepared to plunge into her own sleep? Perhaps I recall thinking at last, She's still here. But where am I?

Xanthippe

A RIPE OLD AGE. Overripe, actually. Then rotting at the end. Which takes him three years, dimming with the glaucoma, one dismal feature of the syndrome of diabetic degeneration. The final year was an introductory tour of purgatory: first, a cluster of light strokes that set him down in his recliner more or less for good, the right side of his body numbed, speech slurred—and as he was accustomed to scolding and instructing his patient wife by the hour, it made his sarcasms pathetically funny, because even then he never let up, not seeming to hear the vile nonsense he uttered—and, second, the capillary breakdown and resultant loss of circulation in his legs (he was a tall man, even taller than I), until there was a gangrenous left foot, so that we had to have the thing amputated above the knee he liked to pound on for emphasis. Not that he regarded it as a punishment, not that tough, selfish old cock—not for him. But if his suffering was meant to be an installment on the big and everlasting debt he'd accumulated, he could charge a lot of it off to his wife and daughter before it came through for collection. They could stand it better after all, was the way he calculated. I suppose he would have liked having a grandchild, if not necessarily by me. My children were already grown and gone by the time I married his daughter. Which wasn't that awkward: I was fifty, yet young enough to have been his son. What he wouldn't recognize was his hold on his child: she was already forty-two, and still his baby girl. In her own mind too.

Ah, what a sexy, feverish, hard-working, and learned broad. A worshipper of bookish systems: philology, lost medieval Latin poets, iconography (frames and flowers, the headgear of various kinds of guild members in woodcuts or illuminated manuscripts and miniatures or incunabula, carvings on capitals in Romanesque basilicas or English pews, women's footgear, ditto, and Mongolian and Siberian folklore with a concentration on fertility magic and motifs).

Every year she changed the color of her hair, though her eyebrows and sporran stayed black and thick. Adorably nearsighted, she's always dropping one or the other contact lens. Nothing slows her down.

He did, though, at the end. I forbore pointing out that she was possessed, and obsessed by him. That he was her mother's responsibility surely. "My mother is incompetent. She always has been." Don't you want a child? I'd inquired on each birthday. "It's unnecessary—I still have him." What an admirable sense of reality she had, I thought.

He came through the amputation, reduced but much the same anyway. It ought to have made an impression on her. But she wore only that absorbed and anxiously vexed expression—a kind of reaction to time's passage, and mortality too—and I saw she'd failed to take the hint. What with tending him and her mother, her studies, her writing . . . she had found those means to stave off time for another year. Like father, like daughter: both refused to practice death. "Do you love me?" she would whisper hoarsely, sliding her chilled legs under the comforter past midnight, stretching her long cold form against my back after coming in late from their frantic evening with him, cheering him up, sustaining him by tremendous efforts of placation of every cranky whim, and rapt attention to his speeches against the clerisy, realtors, politicians, and brokers. Especially the commodities men, because his chief means of making money was hampered now by increasing blindness: the room kept darkened from six a.m. on, as the lists of prices rolled up over the TV screen hour after hour and he studied his fluctuant fortune, hammering out numbers on his legal pad and pushing away at the buttons on the telephones beside him. While her mother changed the dressing on his missing limb, massaged his thighs, prepared his injections, washed his heavy torso, and ministered to his flaring rages between calculations, bids, and conferences with the lawyer, the banker, and brokers in Chicago and New York. He might have done all that down in Palm Springs, which I suggested—but then his daughter wouldn't have been with him each evening till eleven, listening and regurgitating her day's findings in the libraries, Yes, I would say, I love you, thrilled awake by her marmoreal legs twining about me. And I'd have to show her then how very much I loved her, or she'd never get to sleep at all. Faithfully, I replenished what he'd drained away from her.

Something to consider philosophically, marriage. Unthinkable under any other kind of perspective. Worse, absurd. Marriage of course is fundamentally absurd. It is the beginning, not an end. A start, but no true goal. Yet—the start must be made. Something she could not even bring herself to imagine, let alone contemplate. When she was not working at her manuscripts, she went shopping with her girlfriends, as she termed them. I thought their taste flashy, and in Los Angeles that's saying something, since the good designers' clothes here are rather noisy even when in the best taste. You'd never take her for a scholar if you saw her slipping into her Corvette in Beverly Hills: you'd imagine her as the rather expensive property of someone dangerous in Las Vegas.

Three weeks ago, pressure from the world of the real began mounting. I sighed to see the harried look in her eyes become fixed in wan dismay. I said nothing. One can't, one must not argue with a wife. To have lifted that mask would have revealed another beneath it. One more heartrending: the face of fear. Under it would be the blankness of impending terror, terror mingled with remorse, a visage no artist has drawn—intellectual terror. And beneath that one would be yet another mask, the rigid one of sorrow, downcast and frozen. No need to be curious about these skin-deep masks. Time would peel away each one, and in a very few days. I should see them all, one by one. And I was prepared, if she wasn't. Nevertheless, I was not ready for the last one, this face of unforgiving sullen fury she wears against me now every day. Not that, on reflection, I mind. It's better having her vivid, hating me, than drifting off lost on the burning marl of despairing grief.

His end arrived as feared, though it had not been imagined. Reality seldom is. The toes on his other foot blackened. Back into the hospital. It was possibly either/or. It was probably both/and. All discussion was finally stopped: everything is subject to the dialectic but death. Signs of heart failure. On the machine. Gangrene is slow, and could wait. He had some affairs to finish, so the broker came to visit as regularly as his household of wife, daughter, and Vye, their maid. I was present too; but he never saw me again. If ever he had. For a week everyone knew it was going to be over, though he didn't. He would not know. Be kind to him, I said. "I have been," she snapped back, "for forty-two years, and my back hurts." She'd been snapping and rolling her head around on her shoulders for months now, refusing to see a doctor, a masseur, or do anything for herself. "It's nerves, tension," she'd say, rolling her head about with pain, dementedly rolling it at meals, while driving, or reading.

Final day. Intensive care ward. Everything's hooked up, lights and oscilloscopes and graphs ticking and registering away. Nurse at the console monitoring the dozen souls at her fingertips, flickering, hovering, hesitating on the thinnest margin between this place and the nowhere that is elsewhere. The broker has taken his last orders: porkbellies, soybeans, eggs, silver and gold, and coffee—options held back and exercised, but ten new options on coffee, at $7600 each . . . they will surely come in for a half-million in six months or so, and may even cover the rest of his losses. He looks up at his daughter blindly, his hand groping in the air for hers—and missing, because she is trying just then to replace the contact lens her tears have washed out of place on her swollen black pupils. His empty palm falls on his groin with a spasmed jerk, and he's gone. Cardiac arrest at seventy-seven. Reasonably long career, after all. Enough's enough.

The rains have come, as they should in February. Inches sheeting down all day for days now, waves of rain dashing over the coast all night, sometimes pattering and sometimes bucketing and smashing over the roofs. For six years we have had very dry weather, a drought, fires and duststorms and dreary bright blazing months of bitter and polluted oily-brown smog-filled skies. Now the rains are washing the cities and deserts of Southern California clean, sweeping down the suburban hillsides in torrents of mud, flashfloods filled with cars and furniture and debris. The streets glisten black, the air is cool and sweet once more. The trees are shining with all their varied greens and greenblues, the rich foliage that had lain buried under the dust of seasons of parching winds. Our cortege departs after the viewing and service. The cars pick their way ten miles through the steady downpour, arriving at last at Forest Lawn. The efficiency of the California funeral is expected; but on this day it is not to be had. And so the last mask of my wife, hidden till now under her raw face of heavy sorrow, comes to be exposed by what happens, a scene devised by some ruthless comedian.

I am the lead pallbearer, on the right. To my left, his broker. Behind me, his lawyer; to his left the CPA. Last, the manager of his bank, a nervous fellow whose working week had long been knotted up in his affairs more than was good for his career, or the branch of the bank; and to his left, the maid's husband, a tall, scar-faced man, with new, lavender bruises and cuts on his misshapen cheeks. His eyes are swollen and bloodshot: he's still shaking with the massive hangover he's had since the police picked him up yesterday. In fact, there is a steel chain around Sam's waist, and it's connected to the handcuff on the wrist of a sheriff's deputy who's trailing along behind him, blocking the way of the women, my wife and her mother, who should properly follow the casket but are forced to stumble after the officer. And behind them, hiding her puffy face, with its newly broken-off front teeth and swollen, broken nose and half-shut eyes, is their maid of twenty-five years' loyal service, Vye. His former cronies, speculators and gamblers, are all either dead, or in the VA Hospital, or at home, safe from this blinding rainstorm.

Out of respect for her employer, who was always good to her—until this past week—Vye has come. Otherwise, the hour he died she quit. The old man was also an inveterate handicapper, and Vye had placed his bets for him, avoiding wife and daughter by some system of signals they used between them. In the morning before he suddenly worsened and had to be shunted off into intensive care, he'd sent her out of the hospital room to lay a G-note on the nose of some mare running at Santa Anita with odds of 126-to-1 against her. She'd slipped him the message herself, a tip about that mudder from a Mr. Zenophanes. "'Put suthin on that nag youselfs,' thass what he tol me, sho he did. But I dint. Cos why? Cos marol man slaps my haid upside off for bettin you fatha's damn haystoves, stead of bringin home mah wages! If ah'd stop bettin, he'd cut drinkin. Po, yass, but quiet . . . till thother evenin!" She'd been too scared to put her hundred dollars on that horse—the old man's last words to her they'd been too, and good advice from the very porch of Hades. When that lady, Pythoness, sloshed in and paid off at 126-to-1, and she went on home in tears and told Sam, you can imagine how he took the news: the beating he'd given her before going out and blinding himself on gin was all too evident. Vye quit, and she was filing for divorce, too: she'd had Sam arrested, and then fetched him out of the tank to be an honorary pallbearer. Bail was $1000 and Vye had the money in one banknote out of my wife's purse: the book's runner delivered it at the door before we got in the car this morning, and she was toting that hundred grand or so right now, rolled up and wrapped in a fat rubberband. The lawyer'd someway gotten the Court to move fast, as a charity, and here was Sam and his guard. Poor man was sick and sore and angry all at once. And Vye meant what she said: my wife knew that her mother would be without her lifelong maid when she got home this afternoon. It would be a taste of hell.

The casket was slid out of the hearse, and we heaved it aloft. The gravel road was washed out, and they'd stopped the train of cars somewhere far enough from the gravesite to give us a good walk through this drumming downpour. After five paces we were ankle-deep in mud. But still we came up to the hole in about ten minutes' trudging. Lightning and monstrous thunders bashed about the San Gabriels across the Valley, though we couldn't see them, obscured as they were by the low-hanging, billowing grayblack clouds that rushed by from the Pacific twenty miles to the west of us here on this slope. The priest had read through more than half the burial service when a messenger came splashing along from the front office: we were gathered about the wrong hole in the ground. No wonder there'd been none of the wreaths I'd expected to be cluttering up the site. I had been thinking the florist's truck had lost itself in some freeway tieup.

We got the coffin raised up again, after the grave-diggers had jumped down into the soup to get their tapes hooked under it once more. The machine they use these days runs one way: it will winch a box down, but isn't ratcheted or strong enough to haul one up again. Getting hold on it now wasn't easy. The priest tried lending a hand, and slipped face down into the side of the pit. We tugged him up covered with red mud. All of us pallbearers slid and struggled about trying to get it out and aloft. We were running liquid mud from our armpits down. No one spoke a word during this time: we grunted, fell, heaved, and stumbled about: our curses and choked-off exclamations drowned in thunder and rain. Sam didn't move a finger, the sheriff's deputy holding him on a short leash off to the side, just to keep himself from being dragged down into the crumbling hole with him.

In about three-quarters of an hour, we were finally at the right excavation for my father-in-law, who seemed to have grown heavier and heavier as we paced, falling off, now one, now another, on the detour the messenger took us on to find it in the rain. A miserable knot of people we were by then, coated with adobe-red mud, and soaked through, coats, hats, shoes: you would have imagined we'd emerged from a mining disaster. Heaps of flowers lay about our feet, ruined by the pelting rain, and the sky was quite black, even though it was just after noon. My wife held her mother up forcibly, her arms about her waist. "Get on with it, fool!" she hissed between her locked jaws. The priest was fumbling his breviary out of his pocket again, and I held a torn umbrella over his head as he thumbed for the service once again. Father, I whispered, forgive her, she doesn't know what she's doing. The old priest poked me sympathetically with his elbow as he began the prayers all over from the beginning. Listen, Padre, I muttered, let's have the shorter version this time, or we'll be drowned where we stand. I think we've had enough for one funeral already. He poked me again. I never looked up from beneath the rim of the umbrella at her on the other side of her father's grave as the priest ripped through the obsequies, skipping a half-dozen formulas and closing the affair with three breathless long sentences and amens. We scooped a few palmfuls of running mud down at the coffin, and I turned away at last to try to find our way out of this field through the raging storm.

I tried taking her arm to keep her from slipping herself on the running, rutted gravel walks, but she shook me off fiercely. "You bastard," she said, "I'll never forgive you for this!" What had I done to her, I said, what was it now? Her mother said nothing, clinging to my left arm, staggering along, poor thing, panting and sobbing. "Don't worry, darling," she coughed at me, "the child is just upset."

"Upset? Shouldn't I be upset? He was disrespectful to my father. He told the Father to skip almost the whole of the burial service and run us out of there. The whole thing's ruined. Is that a funeral? Let him go straight to hell!"

I tried taking her arm again, to keep her from stalking into a flowing puddle of water. No use. She stepped into it, heedless of the cold fouled water that came halfway up her calves. She stood there, with her makeup streaked over her face, her copper hair straggling in glistening hanks over her cheeks, and she pointed her trembling, raging arm at me, weeping and growling at once: "You botched my father's funeral. I will never talk to you again!" I said nothing.

And she has not spoken to me since, though a year has passed. She may wish to; but she is proud. I hear her voice only in the darkness now, at midnight, when she grunts, face down, sometimes tearing at her pillow with her teeth as she lifts herself to take my thrusts, crying out, in vain, "Ah, ah—my god!"

One Fine Morning in Eden

WE HAD NEEDED A CHANGE for some time now, we agreed; but couldn't decide what was to be done. I was tired of speaking. Well, not that I minded the sound of my own voice—it hadn't reached that stage—but that whatever I knew after all this time made little sense to me, and even less to the hundreds of patient kids, majors and minors in the various senses of those terms, who sat in the lecture hall, thoughts elsewhere.

Then an assignment overseas came up unexpectedly. Over there, I could administer our program of enrichment studies, whatever that means. All it amounted to was shepherding: shipping pregnant girls home and keeping tabs on dissolute boys. Meanwhile I could study language; that is, acquire some rudimentary syntax and a little vocabulary by reading the newspaper.

Yet now I couldn't make up my mind to leave. Whatever we have here, at least we think we know what it is. A month went by while I delayed my reply. Now the deadline was here. A decision would have to be made by tomorrow. My wife said she would leave it to me: Anywhere, she said, was the same to her as nowhere. And nowhere was where we were.

I slept on it. Poorly. I still didn't know what to tell them in the morning; indeed, I was not really awake. We still sat in the garden long after breakfast, going over our situation for the last time, when we heard a car pull up outside with a screech of brakes. Its door slammed. Brisk footsteps up the front walk; then a rap on the gate. We heard its latch lifted and that quick, assured tread again. A bearded man about my age stuck his head around the rose bush and looked about before he stepped forward, as if briefly wondering where he'd landed. When he saw us waiting expectantly, he ducked between the pair of orange trees and approached with those quick steps. He wore a pale gray silk suit and carried an expensive attaché case of calfskin dyed oxblood. He came right to the picnic bench and stood over us, gazing thoughtfully down. "I'm going too, you know. So much remains to be done. You understand the method and reasoning, I think?"

I could only reply, I do, and I don't.

"Not to worry. It's all taken care of."

You seem quite sure of yourself. You tell me.

"It's simple." He spraddled the bench and sat down with us, opened the briefcase and pulled out a sheaf of papers It looked as if that thick dossier was a legal document. He took out a Mont Blanc fountain pen and busied himself filling in empty lines, just as though he knew everything about us without needing to ask. I waited him out.

Finally he laid his trim hands flat on the pile of documents, and with a shy smile said, "Well, it's like this. God teaches choice—with hope."

Something about that isn't clear, I responded.

He smiled. "Listen to me! To learn a new language, you choose hope."

If one but knew the way.

"Learning a new language means—you hope to choose! No other way."

I don't understand you.

He sighed. "Hear me! God gives you hope to choose. Or else you choose to hope. Either way, it's the same."

Help me to understand, I said.

He shrugged. Turning to the last sheet and pointing to the bottom line, he passed the file over, offering me his fine pen, which I declined to use.

You came all this way to tell me that? I said.

"You know best."

He stuffed the papers back in his briefcase, got up, and walked out as suddenly as he'd come. The gate rattled shut behind him. We heard the car door slam, the motor being gunned, and the squeal of rubber as he tore off down our quiet street.

A Theban Ostrakon

LATE THIS AFTERNOON I was dressing up to go round the corner to a cocktail party. It was a fundraiser for the maverick who's jumped two parties and is running as an Independent for senator. I don't care for his politics or rhetoric: he'd inflamed masses of educated young people during the long war just discontinued, and now claims the credit for having saved thousands of lives by visiting the enemy and encouraging our college boys to emigrate instead of serving the bad war. His wife's a movie star, married often enough before. I would prefer to vote for her brand of radical whoredom and anti-sexist sexism than his kind of Children's Crusading intellectualized breast-beating guilt and pan-middlebrow antipolitics that reeks of media bad faith. In your mind's eye she's always present, naked and seductive. You know it's an unreachable imago; but it's her exploitation of her lithe body in the moving picture memory that makes her vociferous moral protestation against our military machine fascinating: she appears so vulnerable, so desirable, though she's not. She belongs to the same Establishment we all belong to. Free, rich, almost inspiring. But she wasn't going to show up at the cocktail party, so I'm attending out of obligation to my neighbors, who are colleagues of mine.

My wife was not in the mood, however. She was watching television instead. As I passed from our bedroom through the livingroom and diningroom to the kitchen, tying my tie, buttoning my jacket, and stanching a bad razor cut on my lip, the racket of the six o'clock news was deafening. A vast defeat in the Middle East is in progress: cities are being ripped apart by a dozen small armies of ideological bandits, and tanks and armored cars are machine-gunning the populace in the streets, cannonading hospitals and hotels, schools and office buildings and apartment houses, all in full color. There are earthquakes in the Alps, assassinations in four capitals; tens of thousands of men and women are parading with banners against three governments. In the Far East, the jungles are being put to the torch, and somewhere a million peasants and urban families are being marched into the swamps by teenaged troops to perish. She sits there at the kitchen table watching intently, as though it concerns us. She says out loud, "In the Southern Hemisphere, on two continents, there have been thirteen coups d'etats this past week alone. Guerrillas are proclaiming victory in twenty-one different countries." The kitchen is quiet, the canary is singing in concert with the explosions emanating from the television set.

On the table, beside her elbow, is our little son, naked, propped up in the plastic seat, his six-month-old head waggling like a rubber doll's, chubby arms flapping spastically and his legs kicking, their tender toes spread wide. Can he see what's occurring on the television screen? He seems excited by it, his eyes and mouth are working silently, his tongue pushing out ribbons of liquid and lumpy cheese in little dribbles as the explosions of rockets flare out before him. She seems bemused by the vistas of terror through the billowing smoke and flame. I think myself that the infant is too near the edge of the table; but I stand there in the door behind her, tying my tie again and watching the screen. She puts her cigarette in the saucer of her coffee cup, sets it down and reaches over to switch channels. I want to warn her not to let the infant sit there unguarded, when she hesitates, glances at him, puts her left hand out as if to touch his chest, and leans far over in her chair to reach for the knob. At that instant, the baby lurches up and tips forward, and falls—plop! like an inanimate doll, like a heavy and water-filled rubber doll—face forward, between her outspread legs, to the floor. The thud is awful. Silence. It doesn't move. She sits up, a soundless cry issuing from her opening mouth, her eyes dilated with horror, as though she is a peasant woman in a rice paddy seeing her child murdered before her face.

I stand frozen, my hands at my throat holding the ends of my tie. I feel her anger at the TV, and at herself: it is flaring out from behind the mask of her face. Then I step forward swiftly, stoop for the little creature, thinking that if it were only stunned I could give it mouth-to-mouth resuscitation. Perhaps its own softness meant it wouldn't be damaged despite the dead fall from the table top. It's all sheer carelessness, I think, and neglect of the simple rules of conduct. This infant boy, if it lives, will grow up damaged and return to haunt us, a threat somehow. I hope it won't but I know it will somehow.

As I cradle him in my arms, my wife wakes from her vision of frozen horror, her rage bursts from her, and she kicks the television set over on its face. A flash of fire comes from it as it short-circuits, and acrid smoke bursts up at us. Glass from the exploding vacuum tube and the screen flies everywhere in fine needles. She utters a scream that rises piercing and becomes a long wailing that is choked off by a breathless sob.

Berenice

AT DUSK, WE'D WATCH from the terrazzo as the ruby-red sun flattened and then slipped beyond that black desert horizon, its rays still fanning up from Arizona, refracted in tender hues of yellow, orange, rose, turquoise, purple. Sipping daiquiris to keep out the always sudden chill in the high altitude air, we would lie quietly on our chaises: she, swaddled from toe to throat in a light Mexican rug; I, draped in an old serape. A sparkling film of icy dew would materialize, imperceptibly glazing us and the flowers on the old, cracked tiling. We'd rest there as the sapphire shades of the vacant sky grew denser, deepening into a tide that swept overhead from the east. Then the big lamps of Venus and Mars, Jupiter and Saturn would be lit beneath the velvet vault of heaven and the stars finally appear, their shifting, shimmering sands filling the blueblack universe with their endless diamond-bright dunes.

Showers of Perseids flew all night long during that one August we had together in this world. Their faint, trailing afterglow reminded me of Berenice's hair. She said she had always worn it long as a horse's tail, and even when I met her it was still a silky fall of palest gold that she braided and coiled into a thick chignon. At midnight I would sit beside her bed as she wished me to and watch her at her dusky mirror as she brushed it out. Then she'd rise and stalk back and forth, talking, talking, talking as I listened, mute. That was part of the bargain; stipulated in fact, together with other particulars, in a long document I had had to sign before I could put my name to our marriage certificate. A contract for a year of service. No sacrifice, I thought then. I could spare a year of my life—what was that to me? It was just killing time, and I had little use for a property she craved more than almost anything in the world. Besides, the odds looked good—nothing to lose, and a whole new world to gain. Meanwhile, it was fair exchange: despair for despair. Or so I'd thought at the time.

She always wore a gauzy, unbleached cotton peignoir, and even sheerer beneath it a many-pleated nightgown of the same stuff. She wanted me to contemplate her through that veil, though at fifty-seven her statuesque form scarcely resembled the ancient, sacral elegance of the virgin vestal. And well she knew it. Her feet were callused, gnarled, their talons enameled a fluorescent mauve. She paced over those splendid antique Navajo rugs with the once-powerful legs of a horsewoman, knotted now over the calves and up the insides of her thighs with purplish ropes of varicose. Her fine breasts, still high and firm, were black-nippled as a nursing mother's, her belly round and heavy—she always looked six months gone to me—and it swagged as she turned. She limped slightly from the right hip: a tricky palomino stallion she'd been crazy about back in her 20's had crushed her pelvis. No children.

"—Jake had a way of lulling you with his loyalty. Then he'd suddenly slither sideways against a tree when he thought I wasn't paying attention. Perfect menace on mountain trails: I got to feeling he'd gladly go over the edge himself, if that's what it took to launch me into the Valley. The Indians said that was no horse at all—it was Santiago Cortez, a notorious brujo they'd outlawed from the pueblo long, long ago. They still defend themselves against him at their secret ceremonies in June on top of Taos Mountain: they believe he haunts Blue Lake. My foreman finally told me about Cortez the time I was laid up in hospital after Jake rolled over me twice . . . probably because that four-legged sonofabitch didn't hear enough bones cracking the first time. Gorgeous brute. My fault, people said. Why didn't I call the vet for once and all and have him fixed? My god, what good would that do! Geld a brujo? What I did, was call in Cecilia Montalban, my maid's grandmother, a tiny, toothless woman shrivelled to the size of a walnut. She must have been more than a hundred years old even then. She remembered Santiago from her childhood. That would have been, what, ten years? before the Civil War. He was handsome as the Sun God, she said. But, 'Ai, malo!' Cecilia came hopping like a sparrow out of her little thatched summer house in the pueblo cornfields. She sat by herself in a dark corner of the stable and waited till after sunset. Then she got a pitcher of salt water and paced slowly and carefully all around this house three times from west to east. She muttered incantations to the four winds, to the sky, and to the earth, and she sprinkled the water and spit as she went. I would have told Father Feuermann to cast some of his aspersions too, come Easter. But Cecilia just laughed at the idea—what did that priest know?"

I rather liked the hitch in Berenice's stride. Though that's where the cancer started too. I liked that hitch because it gave a swinging half-turn to her breasts and a lift to her belly, so that she half-stupified me with the thrust of her undulating stride. It made tolerable those late hours sitting listening to her. She seemed to be trying to salvage remnants of her life before they sank from memory forever—even though something would be left with me, I said. My mind, she said, was like sand in an hourglass: always pouring out yet always the same, nothing added, nothing lost—absolutely incomprehensible to her. She seemed to think about me in the way she thought of time.

"Anyway, why do you bother listening?"

I married you.

"Out of pity," she snorts.

Love.

"Pity, I say. And I say you don't know the difference. You won't have to pity or love me for an hour longer than the time I have left, or a year and day —whichever comes first."

I'd give you even that extra hour, Berenice.

"Why should you? What's in it for you?"

That damn contract was your idea.

"Because I know men."

You knew a horse like Jake.

"And I know my man."

You make it hard, Berenice.

"Tell me about it!"

Berenice conceded nothing. She was still warring with the absolute and kept me at arm's length, when I was merely asking to be her husband, not the hired man. That was the little extra note of surrender in my voice that she waited for. She would douse the lamp silhouetting her. I'd hear the rustle of her robe and then the gown as they were slipped off. Then she would pad towards me over the chill, sweating tiles. An old, sick tigress. As she bore me down, the smoke of her rank, brackish must filled my head: it was tinged with an iron, medicinal tang from the powerful nostrums saturating her blood. Sometimes, as she struggled hard astride me, she panted the name of Santiago Cortez into the thick silence until she came in a dry, searing flood, and subsided with a whimpered "Ai, malo!" Mornings I would wake in my room, always astonished by the brilliant, turquoise sky, the fragrant desert peace of the Valley.

Nine, ten months passed dreamlike—though they were filled with constant, secret torment too. How could such pristine spaciousness of light and such sweet air be haunted by a Santiago Cortez? Yet from our first night and through the weeks, then months, that followed, I felt moments of uneasiness: a shiver in the limpid autumn sunlight, a wash of fever in the crisp shadows of January's dazzling fields of snow. Sometimes it seemed as though she wished to draw me into herself, drink me to the dregs, sucking out whatever small, conscious will remained in my marrow, as if she fed on me, nourishing herself, so avid for mere life she was. What had I undertaken? Of course I knew why—that contract in the bank down in Santa Fe spelled it out—so I hardly needed the nightly reminder that I had made myself over to her. Of course I'd promised to help her, to see her through, which was why she had mated me to her. For at least a year and a day I would have to serve her in everything, utterly—everything! But if she outlasted the doom predicted by her doctors, if she lived for an hour past midnight, I was to have nothing to show for it. I'd be as naked as the purpled, twilit hour she had plucked me from the hot pool. That damned notarized document. Nevertheless I meant to see this through, if only because I never forgot the wealth under her control, more than anyone could imagine what to do with. To think about it was no better than trying to plan today what to do with all the time that is coming to us in heaven or, for that matter, hell.

Sometimes she reminisced about how lovely the Valley of Taos had been when she first arrived. "BB," she called those years—Before the Bomb. There was really only the pueblo, which still doesn't look much different from what it must have been six hundred years ago: that monumental adobe beehive of dark little Indian apartments (before the stucco condominiums and motels all around it sprang up in the '70s like toadstools), with its packed-down red mud square (before the asphalted parking lots for the tour buses); the clear, cold brook from Taos Mountain that traversed its heart, purling through the Indians' cornfields, branching out in a capillary network of sluices and gutters along the streets of the town to flow on alternate days now this way, now that, feeding little gardens and kitchen vegetable patches.

The congestion and racket of cars and people had exploded like a stampede, overnight it seemed to her—why, in the one summer of '61 four gasoline stations were built on four facing corners in the heart of Taos, right next to the Plaza itself! That was the beginning of the end. A little Tijuana began to materialize around them. If she and her friends could have stopped it by any means, even if it took most of the money in the Morgan vaults, they would have. The highway ran through Taos as it had since 1600, and who knows how long before that it had been the Indian trail up from Acoma, before there ever was Coronado and his soldiers or a Santa Fe. They would have had to pay off a hell of a lot of judges to prevent just those filling stations from happening. Basically the Spaniards, not the Anglos, controlled the roads, and still ran most of what ran the state. Talk about your Chicago graft! And then go on and fight Big Oil? Funny to recall how the English bohemians and the tiny arts-colony residents since D.H. Lawrence's days in the '20s had resented the arrival of her friends in Taos in 1942. Huh! as if her mother, who was after all one of the Lords of Maryland, or any of her friends, had trudged up from Santa Fe with cardboard suitcases like a miserable troop of refugees! No, they had come with agents and lawyers, uncoupling whole boxcars of heirloom furniture, precious paintings, objects, and antique oriental carpets from the train at Lamy, complete with Packards and Lincolns and Negro chauffeurs. Why, if not for them nothing would have got done around here at all, which, looking back, might have been best for everyone concerned, including the Indians . . . though nothing was ever good for the Indians, even their own vanished past. And if Santa Fe was then still a Spanish town, with its archbishop and its State Pen, just imagine this place—one hotel! Such was Taos Pueblo, surrounded by a few sleepy ranches and empty thousands of acres. Clay dust, sagebrush, and the tan-gray peaks of the Sangre de Cristo mountains looming over it just those few miles to the east.

And how transparent the glassy air at 7000 feet, how vividly green the tall, shivering aspens in May, how golden in October; and the great old cottonwoods and willows shading those long, low adobe ranch houses. For Berenice and her sister Celeste, Taos was paradise. They were lanky tomboys at thirteen and fifteen, and took right to horseback, riding the mesquite range here around Arroyo Hondo, or heading west till they came to the abrupt, abyssal trench of the Rio Grande. Their mother and aunts meanwhile visited around, getting acquainted with local aristocracy, Dodges and Wurlitzers, Howells, Phelpses, Saunderses, and such, making contingency plans to organize a last stand here when the Germans reached the Mississippi and the Japs took California. Sometimes they let their horses pick their jolting way down along a narrow, winding track cut out of the nearly vertical side of the canyon wall. It was a thousand feet to the river at the bottom; but worth it, because they'd found a little lava basin just at the edge of the stream. It was fed from below by a steady, quiet surge of steamy mineral water. There they would put off their dusty riding clothes and loll naked for an hour, soaking away the soreness of the morning's ride while their horses browsed along the sandy bank of the smooth-flowing lime-green Rio Grande.

That tub could hold more than two naked girls; there was room in it for a couple of house guests as well, and even lucky town boys now and then. Lovely in those years—not the sty it was these days. Now the gorge was more like some public nudist camp, a free-for-all, what with crazy bikers roaring along the twisty riding trail, or hippie drifters from as far as Maine or San Francisco inching their battered vans and pickups down over the rocks and potholes of the new dirt road. Nowadays you could smell the dope wafting up a thousand feet from that little beach! Candy wrappers, coke bottles, and beer cans everywhere; tattered clothes and rags fluttering from the manzanita for miles downstream. True enough. Everything was soiled, blear, and spoiled: she hadn't cared to visit the place for twenty years—except that one time, giving in to an idle curiosity, or call it nostalgia, when she returned from the oncologist at the Johns Hopkins with little but her foregone conclusion to think about.

That hot pool was where I happened to be lying, strung out, one early September afternoon. I had come walking my way, fly-casting down the river a good five miles from where the hatchery upstream lets its trout go. My creel was empty. I'd heard about the hot spring, and was glad to find it deserted. I stripped and sank gratefully back until the water came just over my chin. For an hour or so I lay there watching a pair of hawks climb in widening gyres on the thermal above the gorge. When they were almost out of sight, they would hover in one place fluttering their wings like dragonflies, then plummet down at me, to pull up with a swoop, the clap of their opened, braking wings echoing from the narrow canyon walls like shots, and start their lazy, drifting climb into the light once more. The heavy water welling from the black sand on the bottom of the little basin was nearly body temperature. Sleep came over me irresistibly.

I don't know how long I dozed. But I never heard her approach. She must have been sitting gazing down at me for a good while until the horse snorted, jangling its bridle. Belly up, all a naked man can do is smile. But she did not smile back. Berenice never smiles. Her eyes danced though—perhaps it was the flowing river glinting in them. When she nodded, I knew it was time to get out. She gazed calmly at me as I dressed, leaning forward with her arms crossed on the silver pommel of her ornately carved Spanish saddle. I broke and cased the rod, rolled up my waders and crammed them with the tackle into my creel. She stared at the stone face of the canyon wall, seeing nothing while I strapped my gear to the tall black mare's rump. Then she clucked once and turned her about for the long climb up. I followed on foot.

It was a hard three miles to the top of that steep trail. I had plenty of time to study her back: a stained straw Stetson, a white satin Western shirt, tight faded levis, and well-worn lizard boots. She sat tall and easy, never turning back to glance at my stumbling, weary progress, confident that my eyes held onto the long, dusty gold braid of her hair as though it were a rope tugging me along after her—as though everything about this had been arranged long ago and it only remained for me to come to terms.

The next morning a truck jounced up the ranch road from the highway: it was towing my stripped wagon. Vandals roamed out there along that vacant rim of the Rio Grande Canyon. I unscrewed my plates and handed the hulk over as payment to the garage. Except for the boots I stood in, they were all I owned. Berenice watched from the patio. Where was I headed—anywhere at all? I shrugged. She said, What was my hurry, wouldn't I take something for the road? I followed her back into the cool adobe darkness of that big house, intending to say goodbye. But Berenice had something more in mind.

That evening I walked round to the barn to nail my battered license plates to the door. I thought it would be well to have some small reminder of the final days of my past life. A stable wall inside was covered with rusty, fading plates. They ran year by year back to 1942. I hammered mine up in the one slot left. I would be the last man she was to know. The next morning we drove down to Santa Fe. Papers were drawn up. I signed. On the way back to Taos she pulled us off the road at a dusty, junk-cluttered Stop 'N Curio Shop just past the pueblo of San Ildefonso where there was an easy old JP snoring out back in a broken-down wicker chair. Berenice held out a crisp C-note: he shuffled on his reading specs, held the bill up the sky, sighed, shut his book, and said, "I declare you. . . ." And that was that. As we turned to leave, Berenice pointed to the dingy Indian rug he'd been sitting on and stuck another fresh banknote under his nose. That paunchy, mottled tortoise of a JP hesitated over the offer only as long as it took him to run a wet forefinger across her money to see if it really was legal tender. I tossed the rug, cruddy with years of dust, into the jeep, and we got out of there.

What kind of trash is worth a hundred bucks? I asked her.

"I know rugs. That rag back there is an old Two Gray Hills. After you hose it down good, you'll see something," Berenice said.

So you got yourself a bargain, lady, I said.

"I got me two of them today," she muttered, and put the gas pedal to the floor, her eyes on that narrow, curving two-lane road up through the pass.

That was three hundred sixty-five days ago. During these last two August weeks, although Berenice shrank in my arms to skin, muscle, and bone, she remained insatiable and conscious to the end. Only her long mare's tail of hair, by then bleached white, gloriously held its glossy weight. When I put her off me past midnight of our last night, she dropped on her back, her eyes wide open and fixed on me, a grin like death's head itself on her lips for the first time.

"Not a bad ride, for a hundred bucks."

Berenice, I said.

"You're a loser, you know."

I didn't lose this time round.

"Another hundred says you did."

She was staring through me. Then she clutched my wrists as if tugging at her horse's reins, so that my hands were pressed hard to her wasted breasts. Her heart galloped. She held me like that for an endless minute.

Berenice!

She hissed something into the darkness beyond me. Then she was gone.

About a week later there was a Certified Mail packet from her lawyers. I liked neither its tenor nor their tone. What it came to was: I was accountable and liable for anything that might turn up missing from the inventory enclosed, and that injunction included the vehicles on the ranch. Furthermore, I had twenty-four hours to vacate the premises. They had it wrong, I thought. When Berenice died, my contract with her had one more day to run. I got in the jeep and tooled down to Santa Fe to find out what the hell was going on.

I went to the bank first, and called for the safety-deposit box. There were two manila envelopes inside, one large, one small. The larger contained another envelope in it that felt strange: I slit it open and a damp, black heap of acrid paper ash spilled out. I knew what that was: Berenice had burned our agreement. The little envelope held another key, and it appeared the bank had a card with my "signature" on it. The clerk brought me a bigger strongbox. It was heavy. Inside lay a thick brown box with an envelope taped to it. Berenice's card in the envelope read: "Is not the laborer worthy of his hire?" I lifted the heavy little box out and broke it open: it contained 12 rolls of coins, and each roll held 30 Krugerrands—my wages. Six pieces short, I heard myself say. So she never really expected to last out the year. And she'd known it from the start.

Still, wasn't I her legal heir? Her pair of lawyers shook their heads. I exhibited our marriage certificate. They laughed at the funny little New Mexico document and pointed to its so-called seal. They advised me plainly and forcefully that my name was excluded from any provisions having to do with her estate: all its vast, ramified holdings were absolutely closed off. They showed me the date she signed that codicil—just two weeks ago in fact. The bulk of the fortune in any case had always been entailed to her sister Celeste and her heirs. The small income from a certain fund was provided for the church in Taos to offer a perpetual Mass to be said for one Santiago Cortez . . . did I know who that might be? I heard one sharp bark of laughter ring out in the office—that cry had apparently come from my throat, because they looked up curiously from the papers they were handing about. So, there was nothing for me. And nothing even for the Taos Indians she said she loved. Berenice betrayed them too.

Finally, they demanded the keys to the bank's vault. They reminded me that I was regarded as an undesirable, and had better immediately remove myself from the ranch as per their previous directions. The sheriff was already notified: he had been given full discretion to do whatever was necessary to secure my compliance. Did I understand what that meant?

There were twenty-four hours I still owed her, I said.

I drove her jeep back to Taos, but turned west at Arroyo Hondo, and barrelled in over that dirt road to the lip of the canyon and down that rocky, potholed track to the Rio Grande. There was no one at the hot pool—no stoned hikers, no runaway girls. I peeled off my three-piece courtroom suit, my shirt, tie, and boots, and got in. The river swam past, bright green with its lacey scum of yellow froth. Two hawks circled and circled high overhead until they were lost in the light of a sinking sun I could merely imagine from down here in the blue shadows of the darkening abyss. Nothing had changed from that afternoon my belle dame sans merci had found me loitering here. And it was already a year. I let myself drift off. I knew better than to think there had ever been anything like hope for me.

Esau

I'D BEEN TOLD to keep out of Nazareth. Or if I visited, not to stay the night. Nothing good ever comes out of Nazareth, runs the saying in Israel. Or if I stayed the night, not to set foot in Shechem: there would only be trouble. Well, I stayed in Nazareth. In the last decade it's been built over in Wonderland style, with special viewing spots in the religious compounds, great openings in the floors so that you can stare down into the underground warrens, the cave doors and foundations of the ancient little stone houses. All above ground is new stone, Italian-designed, slick and solid kitsch. Arranged to facilitate people-moving, as the saying runs among the aerospace architects who construct our Disneylands. I stayed in Nazareth, ate lamb kebab, drank the raw 777 brandy, and slept poorly. The next morning, right in that vast and vacuous cathedral built over Mary's Well, I ran into my own brother, whom I hadn't seen in twenty years, and his sister.

It was a surprise. Slight shock too. He didn't look well. His great bony frame wasn't clothed in fine muscle as once it had been, in the days of our youth. He'd shaved that woolly russet beard, and lost most of his thatch of dark red hair: liverish tufts stuck out over his ears and hung down in hanks over the soiled color of his checked shirt. And he obviously hadn't shaved for a week: the scraggly stubble was a patchwork of white and tobacco-yellow, red-black and gray. He was nervous-looking, his hands trembled, those formerly rocklike hands. And the way she behaved with him, she might have been his wife. I had never met her before. She'd been born to some father or other after he'd been carried off to Israel by our mother, when the marriage broke apart. He'd visited us a few times, finished work on his degree, and dropped from sight. I'd been busy with my own life, which was unstable as it was, moving here and there every year or so, getting settled only to have to uproot us all and move on again as opportunities called.

"Come stay with us," she said, resting her hand on my arm.

Hot little fingers, and moist. She was tanned, or very dark; her hair thick, black and worn long like a girl's; her breasts high and hard. She wore her jeans tight; her lavender chiffon blouse was rolled and tied in a knot over her midriff. Full of silver jewelry she was: bracelets, anklets, rings; necklaces of old ivory, amber, and topaz on gold chains draped her neck and swung heavily on those fine breasts. She was a woman with whom you were promptly a friend, and soon a lover . . . if she wished to take you. Her voice was hoarse, low, guttural. Well . . . I said.

"Don't be foolish. You're coming to us, and that's that!" my brother growled. "We have no time for manners."

They lived near Shechem, a field away from the hilltop, the ancient place up there. It was quite illegal, he said, and he didn't give a damn. Let them come and try to evict them. His writing was more important—he had to be at the source. So far, there had been letters, warnings, and threats. But this morning the notice had come from Jerusalem, Registered and Special Delivery, handed through the door by a smirking Nazarene lad on a donkey, who'd had the impudence to tweak her nipple as he passed her at the gate. "Things are coming to a pass," he said. How much longer he could hold out against the local population of Druses and Muslims, and the Jewish State as well, he didn't know. But I could help. How could I? I said. "You'll see when you're home with us," he said mysteriously. She laughed.

As we drove over goat tracks in the jeep, the air grew very still. The morning sun was blazing near the zenith; the sky had retreated to infinity, and the earth seemed to heave up solid tides of heat. The *chamsin* wind that had blown in from the high desert to the east for two days now had suddenly stopped, and the land sizzled in blinding silence beneath the heavy pressure of that mass of unmoving air.

The path wreathed about the base of the high hill of Shechem. We turned off due east of it, about 7 km. from the highway running north-south on the west and bisecting the Galilee. On a low mound his house squatted, a shack of white stucco, three boxes around an ancient olive. Down the slopes to the east were groves of olive trees. Out front there was a rickety bench, some geraniums in pots of hard clay, some cactus along the walls, and a swinging wooden gate tacked together from old shipping crate planks. A miserable pair of date palms shaded the front door.

We skidded up, his sister and I hopped out, and he parked the jeep round the back. We went inside and sat under the olive tree with beers. It might have been Arizona or New Mexico, a shack like that, the kind you see on the back roads in the desert, abandoned years ago.

He was very nervous. Three long-handled spades leaned against the wall. He pointed at them. "We're going to work now. They're coming at sundown to get us out, if I know those *chaverim*!" What kind of work? I wondered. "You'll see, my fine smoothie brother." He spat into his palms and rubbed them. His sister came and sat next to me on the old collapsed divan, put her arm round my neck and squeezed me, laughing, "We are all together in this now." In what? I wondered. "Just wait," he gloated, "there's only one way to win, and it's starting now. Listen!"

I listened. In the silence out there I could hear the change in things. I could feel it in my prickling skin. My hair seemed to erect itself, each strand separating, rising, and tingling. The atmosphere seemed to grow denser, darker and hotter, if that was possible. What's happening? I asked. "The sandstorm's coming." What? I didn't believe him. They took me by my arms and led me outside. They pointed to the east. Sure enough, the horizon had changed: a great yellow-gray cloud loomed from the very earth, from the hills beyond the Jordan; it billowed into the sky.

"It's coming!" they both shouted at once in my ears. And she bit my ear, rubbing her breast against my right arm. He stood pointing at that cloud. She put her hot little hand under my belt as I stared at that incredible horizon, that smokey cloud that was all whirling sand, not vapor. Her hand thrust down behind me, wriggled down to my buttocks: her finger pressed into the cleft and scratched. She was playing. "Now, now," she muttered in that low vibrating voice, and patted me in front. "Let's not get excited—there's work to be done." My knees were watery as I followed them into the house, where we locked the windows and sat for a supper of olives, bread, and cheese.

Then, as we crouched at the low wooden table, finishing our sweet mint tea, the storm struck the house and went over with a terrific roar, the sand drumming on the tin roof, the sound of pouring rain. For an hour we didn't move, but sat on that sunken old divan, smoking and waiting in the dimness of the early dusk inside that dark storm of sand, waiting for the night to come.

When it faded out, my brother jumped up and handed us the spades. "Let's work before they come for us!" We stepped out the front door, rather climbed up into it, for the sand was heaped about the house clear to the tops of the windows, and we had to scrabble up and pull our bodies through. I thought we were going to try to clear it away from the windows, but I was wrong. "There's only one way to keep the house from filling up with sand," he said, "and that's to close it up ourselves." It puzzled me, but I accepted his logic: after all, it's his country; he should know what he's doing.

For an hour we worked madly, shoveling sand from the heaps that lay everywhere outside now: fine golden desert sand scintillant with sharp white crystals. We covered over the windows completely, up to the roof. "Now, when the storm returns in an hour, nothing will get into the house. We're safe: it's sand against sand!" He laughed.

Then we could hear motors gunning up from down below, sirens crying, and we saw the lights flashing red from all sides. "The soldiers have us surrounded," he yelled, but they'll never get in, and they'll never get us out of here now!" At that moment, the storm swept back over us from the other side of the house with a tremendous, biting blast. We slid back in through the top of the door, and set to shoveling and shoring the sand up from inside. We could hear the furious shouts of the officers and the troopers calling outside in that howling, burning, dry hurricane of sand. We almost pitied them out there, standing up under it and trying to scrape the sand away from the windows and doors, if they could find them. It was blowing back and covering us over as fast as they could shovel it away.

"You see?" she said, "he's right. It's sand against sand." Now it was still inside, the air soft and quiet as a tomb. We sat down, all three together, on that broken old divan to wait for the morning. I put my arms about them both. Their heads lay on my shoulders, and they slept like children on a long journey. I remember the candle on the table guttering out.

Medea

IT SEEMED A GOOD IDEA for her to travel this summer and for me to stay at home for once. To my surprise I felt lazy, I'd had enough. Sleep, eat, play with the boys on the beach, catch up with my reading. Wednesdays we'd rent a boat and go fishing out in the Bay. Long summer evenings, cigars, playing through the record collection undisturbed. Restaurants; movies; in a word, relaxing. I've seen enough forts, enough statues, enough pictures and tombs; I'm tired of excavations and cenotaphs and the gabble of foreigners, always about money if you listen to what they say. You can never bring anything back but yourself, and you're lucky not to get fleeced. In the end, it's all just menus and dysentery.

But she was happy to be launching off on her own. She's been angry, restless; the boys wore her down. Her girlfriends had set her up with this all-expenses-paid junket by recruiting her for a conference of psychoarchaeologists. Two weeks of papers and discussions by researchers from all over the globe: THE THRESHOLD—MAN, WOMAN & PRIMAL PERCEPTION. She would pretend to collect their words and make them over into some kind of book. The money came from a Swede munitions tycoon who'd made his fortune selling armor-plate steel and guns to the Nazi Teutons, and was atoning by throwing exclusive seminars in his rebuilt tenth-century Alpine schloss. I kissed her goodbye, wished her luck, and put her on Transworld's Flight #1 at noon. Already she looked gamesome, dressed for adventure: handsome, clear-eyed, fluttering free in her bright blue travelling suit.

After three weeks had passed without a card from her, I began to wonder if she were all right. The boys never thought about it; they were swimming, playing along the beach, reading comic books all day, and addling themselves with extra TV, staying up as long as they liked.

The fourth, then the fifth week passed. I had written to the schloss three times. No word came back. She must have been too busy. The conference was closing; she was due home after a week's sightseeing around Istanbul. This wasn't like her: she wrote messages of love loyally. Had something happened to her in Paris, at the schloss, or, more likely, in Istanbul? I kept calm with the boys, who were asking when she was coming. They'd remembered they'd had a mother, I suppose. They were fed up with hamburgers and pizza and chop suey and sundaes, I suppose.

Seven weeks to the day, Transworld's Flight #3 landed on time at 11:11 pm. The boys were asleep, I hoped, after the potion of warm cocoa I'd fed them. I stood at the arrival gate with a bunch of white carnations in my fist. And, yes, there she was, filing out with the three hundred dishevelled, worn tourists after a seventeen-hour hop from Turkey.

But how good she looked, fresher than the day she'd left me: tanned, thinner yet without seeming worn—except about the eyes, which were, I noted, ringed, hollow . . . but glowing with excitement, or passion. She wore a dress I'd never seen before: crimson, a silk brocade with green shadows of spirals visible in its luster.

I thrust my bunch of flowers out. She took them, reluctantly, her lips smiling, but only as with a faint memory of what her smile was. My stomach turned. She was here, safe; but something had changed. As we waited downstairs for her case to tumble from the chute, she took my shoulder and gripped me hard with her left hand, half-turning away. "I have something to tell you," she said in a low voice, "so listen to me well." Did you have a good time? I asked. "Wonderful, but hectic." You're looking great, I said. "Thank you. And I feel great too."

The luggage came. I picked it up and started for the exit. You must be tired out; you must feel like sleeping a week. "I do . . . but I won't." Well, till noon then. "I'm leaving at noon," she said.

I set the case down. My legs wouldn't move. "Flight #1 leaves at noon." May I ask where to? "I'm booked. I'm packing tonight." May I ask where to? She takes a deep breath; her face appears suddenly pitiless. The vacant terminal lobby, the late late hour, the long trip, the cruel fluorescent illumination? No, it's something in her.

"I met a man," she said. "I'm leaving. Everything's yours. The children too." I see, I said. I suppose I sounded utterly resigned. She expects resistance; she is prepared for bitterness, violence. Yet I know the inevitable, even before it comes. I always have. It's my gift. That's why I chose her. May I ask who he is? "Yes, of course. A wonderful man. About your age. I'm terribly in love with him. I don't know how it happened. I hardly recall how it happened. But it has been like being carried off by a tornado, for a month now. I can't live two days without him." Oh, I said. May I ask who he is?

She sighs, forlorn, as though reluctant to share even that with me, so fully has she departed from our life into this new one of her own. "He's the Director of West German Television. A producer. A genius. Busy everywhere in the world. Rich. Handsome. Clever. Strong. He's taking me with him this week on his own yacht to film a terrific archaeological find. It's called the *Argo*." Ah, I said. "And we'll start our settlement: I don't need anything from you anymore. You'll keep the boys." Ah, I said. "And don't worry, you'll be taken care of too." How? I said. "I told him everything about you. He's very generous. He'll throw you a couple of scripts a year to write. You'll make out." Thanks, I said.

We got home at two a.m. She never woke the boys. She was in a quiet fury. She went right to the bedroom, opened all her drawers, and began laying out what she wanted, which was little enough—some fresh lingerie, a pair of shoes, a white suit. "He's waiting for me in Istanbul. You'll see to the paperwork here. No, no, don't touch me!"

Her mouth was set. There were tears in her eyes. But her mind was made up. She strode like a panther around our bedroom. And what is his name? I said.

"He's called Herr . . ." For the first time, she laughed, her skin flushed with warmth, her hands raised, opened with pleasure. And, as though daring me to smile, she cried out, "Herr Blumenpflanz!"

Saul of Tarsus

We are a smart bunch of moneymakers out here. Rolling country, small hills, lakey dales, winding pikes, and historical roadhouses that saw Revolutionary battalions tramping and camping. Somewhat more than ninety minutes from the Street, it's a commute; but worth it to have golf and tennis for the wife, a barn and horses, some sheep and goats for the kids, a thirteen-room ranch house with remote control stereo laid on in each one, including the laundry. As for donations, per capita we give equal to Beverly Hills, and they are showoffs. Among our notables we've got some smart ex-Yeshiva *chaverim* who can read your Torah forth and back again while figuring fortunes in silver, corn, soybeans, eggs, and pork bellies. Don't ask what we need. Here we do all the asking. And answering.

But it was the Ladies' Auxiliary that heard about this *wunderrebbe* and made the offer to get him out for the high holidays. Could he sing, they said. Not even a Jan Peerce could sing like he could sing, they said. In three days they pooled ten thou. A trifle. Sent off a cashier's check months in advance, on Passover, in fact, as demanded by his agency, and talked of nothing else for six months. When he came, we would all hear something. As though a Messiah was going to stop by.

They picked him up early Friday morning at the station near the Pennsylvania border, outside New Hope. Showed him off at their annual Founders and Donors Luncheon. A plump and glowing son of a bitch, was what I thought: not a shiny patch on his fine serge of midnight blue—banker's stripes; silk vest, oyster-toned; textured silk shirt; a ruby cabuchon stickpin popping out of his gray tie, also of a silk woven heavy enough to be tapestry; a fawn-gray homburg; and Bally boots of satiny calfskin as fine as his silk socks. Pinky rings: one diamond set in white gold, surrounded by rubies, the other a star sapphire the size of a robin's egg. A golden goatee, and thick golden eyebrows over black and Byzantine eyes. If he weren't a cantor, well then he'd have to be the bagman out of Vegas. There goes that ten thou—with Rosh Hashonah and Yom Kippur into the bargain. Go trust our Sisterhood, women who live on rep and rumor. Yet, I must admit, so do we in the Market.

Friday evening. Town empty and Temple packed. The hard core is our Seventy Families. Such great expectations for this New Year. Sitting among these folk, well fed, handsomely groomed, and dressed with overflowing stylishness, was in itself exciting. But the richness of their mingled scents was intoxication. The throaty, spicy odor welled up radiating from the women in the warming air of the Temple: its dark muskiness palpitated from them until your head floated from your shoulders, adrift on waves of fat, animal incense. Their vitality heated us all, and their glowing moist skin swelled, supporting their heavy necklaces and bracelets, which made a faint tinkling sound as they swayed in their seats. These splendid women of the Seventy: these wives and daughters with fine torsos like ripe fruit in the finest of cashmere and sheer camel wool: their glistening coiffures, from black to flossy platinum: they were an autumn garden among us, and all our wealth seemed to emanate from the darkness between their full and weighty thighs.

Their marvelous Reb Saul has mounted the stage. Behind him, the satin-gowned singers are choiring. He has a fine voice. But compared to Peerce or Tucker, this is no cantor at all. Why should anyone notice, though? Their money is singing in their skulls.

For our sermon his text is, "Hear, O Israel." In a bright-edged, *heldentenor* pealing, he calls "Hear, O Israel!" And stops. The quiet grows until the indrawn breath of our thrilled matrons can be heard sighing out once more. At the rostrum, before the altar, standing in the purple-shadowed vibrant spotlight, he shimmers in his midnight-blue robe. The white shawl over his shoulders plays cold blue flame as his stocky chest rises and falls. Diamond and sapphire sparks flash at us from his pudgy fingers. Everyone waits for him to speak. At last he does. "Do you know what I shall now say?" And the women and the men of the Seventy Families, ranked in the costliest pews before him, cry out involuntarily, "Yes, yes." "Good! Then I don't have to speak any further!"

Briskly, he turns and strides from the dais, and vanishes in the wings.

A long silence in the Temple. The entire congregation is dumb. Our rabbi scurries forward to close the service, his hands fluttering as he intones, "And thou shalt love the Lord thy God with all thy heart, and with all thy soul, and with all thy might." We all know that line. "Omayn," the crowd responds in mutters as it rises, disappointed, and starts filing out as to a funeral. No one says anything. Outside, there is the sound of the doors of Cadillacs, Mercedes, and Lincolns slamming, of motors firing up and the swishing of heavy white-walled tires as they pull away.

What transpired that night at our rabbi's, I don't know. But the service on the next evening begins again in the same manner, as though nothing unusual had occurred. The Sabbath is being closed, the first Sabbath of our New Year. Everything is as it was the preceding day. Once again, the choir choiring, and our guest, the *wunderrebbe* Saul, letting loose that tenor in a rather impressive *cantilena*, something it seems to me this time that sounds like another ten thou. His round face glistens with the effort, his throat swells mightily, yet his eyes, seen from the last row where I sit, are not caught in that passionate ululation—they are fixed on me, on my forehead, or fixed through me. Frankly, I have not shut mine in prayer nor cast them on the book in prayer: hence I can observe him, even though he never sees me: his focal point is deep inside the back of my head. Which is nowhere, really, neither here nor there.

Tonight his text is "The Horn." Once more he cries out, "Our God, and God of our Fathers!" And stops. And waits, just as he waited yesterday. Everyone waits with him. I notice that our rabbi, and the seven who advise him, the Rolls Royce gang we call them, are glancing at one another, faint smiles struggling free at the corners of their mouths. They are going to put him in his place. There must have been telephone conferences this morning, Sabbath or no Sabbath. Our glittering guest smiles too, and then coos to us all, "Does everybody know what I shall say now?" The seven head men, these chiefs among our Seventy Families, rumble challengingly, "No, no!" Looking as though he's hanging onto his own prayer shawl for support, his polished toes an inch or so above the floor of the stage, Reb Saul clasps his *tallith,* lifts his eyes to the candelabrum over our heads, whirls about once to survey the Ark behind the altar, and shrugs, speaking not to us but to the emptiness of the Temple ceiling. Simply, truthfully, he says, "If you don't know, then how can I ever explain it to you?" Then, as briskly as the evening before, he skips into the wings.

The departure of the congregation takes place anew. Only this time it's faster: there is frustration and rage indoors, and a loud unholy buzzing outside. Limousine doors are wrenched open and violently shut all over the parking lot, and cars tear away with tires squealing. It is miraculous that no one's knocked down and killed within the Temple grounds.

To my surprise, however, we are not done with the fellow. Had I been consulted by our wisemen, I should have counselled them to swallow it and forget the whole affair. This trickster may be a holy guy of some kind, but he is more than a match for our brokers of pelf and power. I was not consulted. In our community, wisdom is measured, as elsewhere, by those who own most of everything. The rest take our tips from them. There are few enough crumbs strewn about the high seats, though: they lick their plates clean.

So that here we are at last a week later at the Day of Atonement. All our beauties have fasted: yet they glow more than ever like the sleek and full-bodied kine they are. Hunger has flushed their cheeks and touched up their eyes with light. Many have come and gone out of the Temple all day for Kaddish services: we all have our dead, even the rich. And we have our *wunderrebbe* back again, lo! for the closing service on this Sabbath afternoon. Judging by the serious mien on the faces of our leaders and rabbi, real business is in order. We gather that there is actually a double-or-nothing bet laid down—the service and sermon will go through as it should, or he shall refund everything, tonight's fee and the first twenty thousand bucks. We are at the bottom line. It is his single wit against the collective smarts of the seven of the Seventy.

The day is our most solemn. The autumn weather has been filled with glory: dry, bright, colorful: Indian summer commencing here in Indian Hills.

And his voice is glorious too. The famished choir chants from the pit of their empty bellies. A Kol Nidre to end all Kol Nidres. Truly, Reb Saul has a rare voice! In it we hear not merely the chant of ages, but the chanting of Israel's sorrows, twenty-five hundred years of sorrow. Such a song must make good all the vows made to Him, vows unfulfilled and unfulfillable. It will make good, moreover, the ghosts of promises made but not kept since Moses smashed the Tablets against the Golden Calf at Sinai. When the *wunderrebbe* finishes singing, everyone in the Temple weeps, even our tough leaders whose eyes had not moistened even at the funerals of their fathers and mothers. Oh, he is a pro!

And the text? Surely, a thirty-thousand-dollar text: "The Lord our God, The Lord is One." For the third and last time he intones, half-crooning, half-pleading, "On this day of fasting, I beg Him to pardon my sins. May he answer me! May He say, I have forgiven!" And he stops. The bosoms of the wives and daughters rise and fall, making the light itself tremble. Down in their front rows sit our leaders, waiting him out, confident they have won. He is confident too. His hands lift, palms up. He gazes down at them. Finally he says, "Do you know what I am going to say to you this evening?" Half our congregation, by prearrangement, nod, "Yes, yes!" and the other half shake their heads firmly, "No, no!" Reb Saul beams at all of us. His bejeweled fingers grip his silk shawl, flaring white, pink, blue darts of flame into our eyes.

"Excellent!" he says in that clarion voice. "Your troubles are over. Those who know will now explain it to those who don't!" Before anyone can react, he skips back, reaches up and closes the Ark, spins around thrice on tiptoe, puts the *shofar* to his lips, and blows a mighty blast that pins everyone into their seats.

The High Holidays are ended. The New Year has begun. No one's moved. A silence devastating. Then, an inarticulate murmuring, the susurration that comes from inside a nest of hornets, hums through the Temple. But louder than that, from outside, sounds the brilliant burr and gargling roar of the exhaust pipes of his Ferrari as it ignites, shifts swiftly through the first and second gears and into third, accelerating now into the dusk, heading towards New Hope and the setting sun.

Jacob

ON THE MORNING of my fortieth birthday, we woke in London. Back home it was Thanksgiving Day, just as on the day I was born. It's no holiday in England, though. Sitting over strong tea and damp toast in Durrant's Hotel in Mayfair, my wife said that she would buy me a present—I had only to name something I'd always wanted. A houndstooth sportcoat, I said. That was what occurred to me as she spoke. She smiled. "Then a houndstooth jacket it will be!"

Off to Regent Street. Cold, raining, a dreary day, just as it usually is on my birthday. Into Austin Leeds, Ltd. Up, up to the third floor. The salesman is tall and elegant in his proper pin-stripe suit of black. Long ash-blond hair, ruddy cheeks with a network of fine crimson whiskey tracings on his nose. He knows just what I need, and leads us to a quiet corner. My wife seats herself on a comfortable leather pouf, crosses her legs splotched with oily spots from the messy weather, and lights one of her oval Turkish cigarettes. I stand waiting before the triptych mirror. He brings out a beautiful jacket, trim in its detailing and cut perfectly. It is a subtle green, like young grass, hatched with silver houndstooth checks. It is a fine cashmere tweed, light, shapely, lined with red and gold silk paisley. It fits me as perfectly as if it had been bespoke.

And yet, it feels not right somehow. She sits smoking, patiently observing me as I turn about in the mirrors, and she smiles with pleasure. But I find I am growing angry. "What's wrong?" she asks sympathetically, kindly, concerned. Perhaps she's thinking I am not going to accept this gift from her after all. At last I realize what troubles me. I had been feeling the heavy weight of the shoulders: it is padded. I mention this to the salesman. I ask if the tailors will remove these lumps. I can sense that if I cannot carry them now in the fitting, I certainly shall not bear them when I return home.

"But, my dear fellow, this is the way it's styled, you see?" he says with what seems to me a mellow condescension. Take them out, I say. "We call them angel's wings," he adds, "and we cannot remove them from your garment." Well, you must. Do it for me, I plead with him: they won't do in America. "Quite out of the question," says he, sneering at me now. "I can't change the correct style only to suit you, and I won't have that splendid coat altered to suit you either. It's one of a kind, so far as I am concerned."

But the weight of these wings will oppress me at home, I say. I find that I am also somewhat worried about the extravagant price of this jacket, but I say nothing to her about it. Instead, I say, I am buying it, and I'll have to wear it, so it ought to be done as I wish it.

The man is silent. "It's you must choose," he says finally. "Well?" my wife chimes in. "Take it or leave it," he announces, his teeth showing in a harsh grin, not at me, but to my form in the mirror. My wife sighs deeply.

It is already darkening outside, and the evening rush hour has started on Regent Street. It is very chilly and wet: weather that cuts like an ax into the bone.

Corinth

AFTER A TIME ON THE WAGON things got better, despite the drought. The first months seemed even good, I thought. Or good enough. I'd returned to my old friend for some repair work on the analysis, and after nine months I saw that there was no table I couldn't drink myself under. Now I knew that even the one single martini before dinner heralded brandies till midnight, sleeplessness, and empty dreams. For the past seven years things had gone very well with me, I thought. Or well enough. So when like most good things it ended abruptly, I was rather startled. It had all been delusion. Yet receptions, parties, dinners, business conferences and luncheons, and just plain friendly occasions for boozing still come remorselessly along in the ritual round of the calendar. I take sodawater now: I ride on the wagon up high. It is, after all, a desert that stretches only as far as the horizon, though that's as far as one can see each morning. What lies beyond, we don't know until we get there.

Christmas week: surprise party for the twenty-fifth anniversary of our nuptials. The door's opened wide to us by her parents, smiling, beyond their golden celebration: patient, quiet, all quarrels done with. The parcels, holding silver things for us, are hidden behind the Chinese screen, with its phoenix and dragon flitting forever through a mountain mist somewhere: a tea service, a carving set, salt & pepper made of antique heavy Russian silver, cruets, wine goblets, an old heavy tray of high relief showing in the playful manner of Fragonard a pair of mature, naked lovers coming together beneath an oak tree; a coffee urn, a pair of richly carved seven-branched candelabra, an ornate empty picture frame. And finally a silver nymph, her arms held out before her, offering a laurel wreath. She stands on tiptoe upon a radiator cap, and will replace the chromed steel three-armed star on the hood of her Mercedes. I sit with my iced sodawater at one end of the long dinner table; at the other end, she grows gay with the heavy, sharp Burgundy, boisterous, rather giddy.

On her right hand she's placed José, our fosterling. José Mendez is a handsome boy of nineteen from New York, a Costa Rican kid who's been shipped west on our recognizance. Oldest of thirteen, father locked up for life in Attica on a junk-pushing conviction, mother struggling vainly to keep the two next ones, girls, off the street and slaving honestly behind sewing machines in the garment district to support her and the rest of her tribe. José had been slipping into trouble, despite his clubbed foot. War Minister though he was for the Delphians, he didn't want any part of that short, desperate life of the gangs up there in East Harlem. He'd already shown prowess with the machete against some hapless Thebans; so said the white-bearded social worker who'd shepherded him our way. Now he was gainfully employed in San Marino here, a bagboy at the Alpha Beta Market. Nights he worked at his remaining highschool courses, doing other chores for us around the place at odd hours as well. A clever boy, José, quickly fitting with no difficulty into our big empty house, which must feel like a palace to him. Three swift months pass, and she was doting on him. José this, José that; in every sentence, José. Her new son.

Perhaps he is part of the reason I'd finally quit. Perhaps not. There were those ten years when we'd been busy establishing ourselves; seven when I'd refused; seven she, afraid of her age. Yet here we are with a grown son. And there she sits at the other end of the sumptuous board, with its thick padded linen, stiff napkins, sparkling crystal, good vintages, and a succession of festive dishes four of our oldest friends carry in triumphantly. Laughter, gay talk. No one hears much amidst the chatter and music. But I can hear everything she says down at her end, as though we were alone. Next year José is to have her Mercedes, with its new silver radiator cap. When he marries, José shall have our silver. José is going to go to a college nearby, so she will have her eye on him. José's a golfer. José sits his horse like a hidalgo. Girlish giggles, her hand reaching out quite unconsciously to squeeze the boy's or to stroke and pat his shoulder. Exhilarant with wine, her eyes filling with fond tears, affection rampant in them; her rounded dove's breasts puffing up in that lowcut white gown; the emeralds in her small earshells setting off her wide green eyes wonderfully, eyes that appear blind to me, unseeing, as twenty-five childless years brim over with tenderness. José is abashed by this demonstration: the handsome, reticent fellow turns to glance at me, he smiles shyly as if to beg my pardon for her extravagance. Where he got such good manners from, I don't know. Not up in East Harlem among the warring gangs. Even TV could never have revealed to him how we really live here in San Marino, this paradise of stockbrokers, executives, lawyers, and doctors below the San Gabriel Mountains, just east of Los Angeles beside the Santa Anita track. He's adapted very well, I think. Or well enough. How many years has it been since I sensed that moist heat fulminant between her thighs, making her restless in her seat: from my end of the long table she seems a bird bobbing on its perch. Well, well. But our old friends, and her own parents, show me visibly that they notice nothing, nothing at all as she exhibits her foster son and herself to them like this, even though no papers of domiciliation have been signed as yet during this trial period.

Next, New Year. She is Chairlady of the San Marino Rose Bowl Parade Float Committee, working till dawn the last three nights, supervising the team of twelve women decorating our entry with 500,000 chrysanthemum blossoms. This year the theme is World of Mystery, and she's designed our sixty-foot float: GOLD COAST. The long platform has a sort of magic isle, with a bower, surrounded by flowing waters. Miss San Marino's a nymph nearly naked in the chill of New Year's morning. Servant boys in flower-printed loincloths bring her tribute, among whom is José looking like Ariel, only lacking the butterfly wings: a gilt tiara glints with rhinestones on his curly head, gold dust flows from his body. San Marino wins Honorary Mention for Original Concept. The blue ribbon is laid away that evening in the desk drawer somewhere.

Thus in brilliant fancy we enter our twenty-sixth year. Others will come, although I cannot see them now. This week has been enough. It seems there are other ways to make a lot of money easily besides expanding real estate holdings. The lengthy board meeting this afternoon proves that, if I need proof. I had opposed the Corporation's use of venture capital, no matter how high the interest and fast the turnover, for the support of certain kinds of publishing: namely the glossy magazines for men and women spreading everywhere these days, those featuring ten to twenty-five pages of photographic collections in full color. Picture stories of naked young people in various postures of genital display, pantomiming the erotic. Mostly girls, however, viewed close up through soft fuzzed light, pudenda opened, engorged and glistening, or stroked by their own amorous fingers, the nails long and painted, the limbs and torso propped at angles impossible to sustain steadily or long in our gravity, except for such still-life portraiture. Twenty pages of Letters to the Editor, all written in the one style of schoolyard porn, summarizing incredible escapades in that monotonous prose, and offering imaginary climaxes in which the one thing inaccessible to language is declared: the sense of the act of union. With another person or thing. Or perhaps even with oneself. But the board graphed our activity, and the bottom line is clear: we'd loaned out $10 million last year to three different magazines with a gross, combined circulation of twelve million copies, meaning up to forty million readers—and we had recouped nearly half of our principal in interest charges alone! Nice work if you can get it. I am surprised a staid bank like ours derives such pleasure from loansharking. Of course, we'd borrowed most of this capital from a friend of the Chairman of the Board. It should be as obvious to the examiners as it is to me that we're being used as the conduit for money with a higher than normal temperature, neutral green to the touch though it seems. Examiners are not concerned with the pathology of our money yet: the ethical thermometer has not been patented that might reveal a problem here. I had thought I was the manager in charge of the Loan Division. During all these years I'd believed I had independent powers of decision, and could run things as I liked. As with so many other matters,it turns out I have no such powers. Exasperated at my helplessness in the face of that bottom line—the chart's carried round the table, and whoever saw a profits graph pointing up at 45 degrees—what I finally remarked at the board meeting, about cabbage and cunt, though meant to be comical, seemed to me tragic. Money is the only oracle. When it begins to talk, the best, the proper thing is silence.

That board meeting over sooner than usual, I make for home early. The printouts will be stacked neatly folded on my desk

Monday morning, and I shall initial them: OK OK OK. . . . I leave my chariot for servicing at our garage six blocks down from Alma Real. And home I stroll, thoughtful. Below me to the west, vaguely visible in the depths of a heavy sulfur-brown lake of smog lies Los Angeles. That slowly undulant swamp of polluted air is drifting by just below San Marino towards the east, to slosh through the pass and spread out over the hundreds of square miles of citrus and avocado groves of Riverside County too, its fringes lapping now at Palm Springs far out in the desert, and its topmost froth withering the tall pines atop the peaks of Big Bear Mountain, Mount Baldy, and Arrowhead. If this inversion persists another day, it will accumulate and pour up over us here in San Marino. The sun of late afternoon is already coppery, it will glow scarlet and burn invisibly away as it descends through the smog into the ocean beyond. Only a few months during the winter weeks do we see it set in the Pacific from here, if we're lucky. Yet our lawns and gardens sparkle freshly, and all kinds of exotic trees, flowers, and plants flourish around these houses. It seems pleasant to walk home, even if it's uphill all the way on Alma Real. I carry my coat, my sleeves are rolled, my tie loosened.

I am not thinking of money. Nor am I thinking about the three dozen-odd numbers of the magazines strewn over the conference table for our considered inspection, not merely to lie there exposed but also to remind the Board that important novelists, significant social philosophers, even scientists and high-ranking national politicians supply the texts for much of the printed matter distributed in columns between the ads for clothing, cars, deluxe furnishings, high fidelity components, and other esoteric gadgetry. The Board can see, and know, if it wishes, how the emergent American mind is serviced by these slick organs: everything from yoga and Benin bronzes to Linear B and Sanskrit epics goes to support the Consumer Index through the medium of sensuality. I am thinking instead about comedy and tragedy, trying to remember what distinguished them from each other. Something about fate and failure, I think. And something about escaping fate after all. Could it be simply the difference between failure and success? Which was more interesting? Or, more true? I recall objecting once, It's hard to know, if you are in the drama, which kind of drama it is. They laughed at me because the prof said cuttingly, "You are not in the play, Mr. King, not ever. The play is played for you—so that you will see, and in the end know." It's the same thing in the end, it seems to me, I replied. "So it may seem to you, Mr. King. But things are seldom what they seem. Class?" And the class chorused, laughing at me, "Things are seldom what they seem!" So much for literature. Yet here am I, half my lifetime later, murmuring to myself that I should like to review the matter, just one more time.

José and Miss San Marino have been dating steadily since they rode the float up Orange Avenue to the Rose Bowl on New Year's Day. She's a bright-eyed girl, tall, with heavy, silky black tresses flowing to her hips. Yolanda Graves. Father's a plumber just down the slope of the mountain, in South Pasadena. Oval black eyes, wide and liquid; long, fine nose; full, plumdark lips; willowy, with narrow and long breasts turning up like twin cones. Taller than any of us, and clever too, for a girl in the Rose Bowl category. Admitted to Stanford last year, and claims she's studying Astronautics. I see her straightening up alongside her ivory convertible XJ V-12 Jaguar across the road. Crossing to our home, she smiles down at me, radiant-toothed: the polished slanting cheekbones seem to glint in the afternoon light like scars: she walks with dignity, a mahogany idol. We meet at the front walk. A surprise visit: she wants to take José out tonight. Before we go in, I ask Yolanda what she thinks is the difference between tragedy and comedy. Or don't such questions come up for a person majoring in Astronautics? "Oh, Mr. King, naturally," she says in that whispering contralto voice that holds reserve powers beneath the curving clavicles that dress her wide shoulders. "Only, we don't use those terms anymore today." Oh? I say, opening the door quietly to let her in.

The house is cool, still. The finches flick about and chirp in their wicker cage; the parrots chat burbling to one another in their brass cage. The air-conditioning is the endless sighing, barely audible, of a sleeping giant, and through it comes the burr of the pumps for the big salt-water aquarium embedded in the wall separating us from the livingroom area and the other wings of the house. I like my collection of salt-water creatures—fish, molluscs, arthropods, anemones, sea horses. They stay put; they drift with grace through this imagined habitat; they demand no loving care, and acknowledge none that they are given, neither seeing nor knowing the terms of their existence here. And if they did, they could not understand.

"Those are really outdated ways of looking at drama," Yolanda continues as we go to the bar and pour ourselves long glasses of quinine soda with slices of lime. Really? "You see, Mr. King, that whole complicated business of dancing around in horned masks and goatskins and all, and sacrificing someone, with everyone laughing and weeping and singing—that's all too primitive. We call drama today by different names. We call it irony, and resistance."

Irony, and resistance? Interesting. But don't you think, I say to this heifer-eyed, subtly made-up young woman, who is puckering her caterpillar-smooth eyebrows and pursing her full purplish lips with abstract concentration as we sip our drinks and pace about the thick, peach Chinese rug covering the shining black slate floor, she in her silver sandals and shimmering in that slippery red synthetic sheath, her wide bronzebrown shoulders cut by the thinnest of strings —I can see she wears nothing beneath that dress—don't you think, Yolanda, that those terms are too restrictive? Human affairs aren't that limited. Surely, irony, and resistance do not suffice to describe the great plays in our repertoire? "That's all right, sir," she responds kindly, taking my arm unselfconsciously, as though I escorted her, and repeating, "Irony, and resistance. They are what we'll have to use from now on."

Well, it makes some sense, I admit. Given the way things are for us. But suppose—"You just think about it some more, Mr. King." She presses my arm, her hard young breast laid against it, quite unconsciously. Such as this are the girls in the glossies: chemists, computer technicians, psychologists, majors in Astronautics. The categories have changed, I suppose.

Conversing amiably, we have arrived at the wide threshold of our bedroom. Where we halt, side by side, rigid, and silenced.

On our bed there are two figures. José, dark as teak, fine-boned and with supple muscle articulation over limbs and trunk, lies on his back, supine. The soles of his feet are dark brown, the left one twisted, knotted. His penis is erect; it is thick and long. His balls are tight, furred with hair as wiry as his own head of black curls. His penis pulses slowly, his left hand at its base gently holding it to point up at 45 degrees.

Beside him on all fours, my wife. Her blonde hair down and dishevelled, damply matted, her smooth pale skin contrasting with José's flat brown. The dark blue veins of her thighs are traced miraculously as in marble columns. Her nails are polished vermilion, glowing with a wet fluorescence. On her fourth finger, the big diamond glittering even in the dimness of this room. She has lifted her leg in the air. She is about to cross it over his thighs to mount him. Her dense breasts swag from her round chest. Her butt waggles teasingly up and away from him. A pink, soft, and pearly O, her anus. From this angle, she seems twenty years younger. Her woolly, dark blonde shag is visible in her crotch, a tuft of it thrusts out behind, almost a little tail.

José looks away from her towards us standing in the doorway. Surprised by his glance, frozen as she kneels above him, my wife looks back over her left shoulder. José does not move. His face is calm.

I'm sorry, I say. I don't mean to spoil your pleasure. No, no, please. Do go on.

Still, they do not move. They seem to hesitate, embarrassed. I step back, gripping Yolanda by her right elbow.

I lead Yolanda away. She is pensive, her eyes shaded. She's breathing short and hard. I take the glass of quinine soda and lime from her hand. I open the front door and she walks out to the street, her sandals slapping on the brick path. Then I shut the door carefully again.

Isaac

GRAY, COLD SKIES. Old streets. Vacant lots and swamp smell. Brooklyn. A visit. Immigrants, relatives on my father's side. An old linoleum on the splintery floor, roach-brown gashes where it has been scuffed away. Oilcloth on the kitchen table, and flies on the oilcloth. The feeling of dirt. Not poverty, but dirt. A smell of unwashed bodies, or clothes, or feet. Another kind of smell, bitter and sour. An old man sitting by himself at the window of an empty room. The window gazes onto an alley of broken bottles and rusted cans, a stained mattress, its clumps of stuffing dribbling out. A scabby mutt pokes its muzzle through clotted, gelatinous newspapers and a rancid compost of cabbage stalks, pigeon feathers, blackened, shrivelling orange rinds.

The room holds only a sagging iron cot, bowlegged and rusty, unmade sheets, rough blanket, dingy pillow. The old man, wearing a black coat down to his ankles on this damp rheumy day and a heavy black homburg tipped back on his spotted bald head, the old man beckons me into that room with a lifted hand, crooked fingers urging me towards him. He seems huge. He seems a massive shadow hulking over the plain wooden chair in which he sits, unmoving but for the fingers waggling at me. I stand with locked knees, holding back, stubborn. My father shoves me forward, his knuckles harsh between my shoulder blades, and shuts the door behind me.

It is only today that I realize the family was in the other rooms. I could hear them laughing, talking loudly: dinner was about to be served. But then, there seemed to be no sound at all. Still hesitating, I lean stiffened against the door that my father has closed firmly behind me. I am betrayed. The silence thickens about me. And the old man, without moving or even half-turning round, beckons me. He seems to stare at the windowsill. I hold my breath. Is he blind?

His long white beard is stained and blotchy gray around the mouth, streaked tobacco-yellow down the chin. His thick lower lip hangs pendulous. The mouth is open; but he is not breathing; or he's breathing so slowly it's terrible to listen for the sound of his breath. White *payis* join the beard from a fringe of shaggy hair ringing his skull, hair white though singed yellow and gray, those sidelocks dangling from beneath the scurfy brim of his hat. His coat has a collar of dull black lamb's wool, patchy and faded by age. His high black shoes are cracked, worn paper-thin, tied with extra string around the ankles. I can see his long underwear splaying over the tops of his shoes, gray and dirty cuffs of frayed cotton. Still he beckons me. I can scarcely move. Because I am aware that I had already seen something even while I was led to that door, and it had frightened me. I force myself to inch down the small room that seems to loom like a high-ceilinged, endless corridor leading towards . . . what? I cannot imagine what, although I know somehow. And as I inch ahead I seem to hear a small, still voice, a muffled buzzing somewhere in the silence. Then I see.

He is watching flies on the windowsill. And I realize that in his other hand he holds upright a long narrow shining knife. His left beckons to me; his right holds that blade. I see how the light glitters on its edge. How keen it is. My heart is swollen; it pants in my chest. My heart hurts. But I go to him, scared, driven by a will not mine, to face what I must face, an urge stronger than fear. And at last I stand beside him. His hands seem a giant's. Huge-knuckled hands with folds of fine skin over the lumpy black ropes of veins. Those hands cannot possibly belong to this old crippled man sitting hunched in hoary age: those hands are not stiff: those hands are alive and unafraid. I realize then that although he's aware of me next to him, he is not thinking about me, and certainly not thinking I could be nauseated by his unwashed age, his garlic and nicotine, his musty clothes—the sour felt, and damp, greasy, furry stink.

His lap is strewn with shreds of tobacco and ashes of burnt paper. On the floor lies a bag of Bull Durham with its blue draw-string and yellow tag, and a packet of ZigZag cigarette papers. Dozens of bent stubs are littered on the floor about his chair, one acridly smoking by his heel. And still he shows no sign of recognizing me; although that left arm is held up, its fingers moving ever so slightly, moving me closer. His hand now settles on my shoulder, a dead weight, and grips me hard. I freeze.

It is flies—he contemplates flies. One crawls along the sill, pausing yet continuing as though impelled towards him: cautious, fearful, alert, hesitating, hopping back and starting again. I see what the old man is doing. Before him lies a lump of sugar surrounded by more of them. Dead, though not crushed, flies. Fragments, rather; bits and pieces: heads, wings, legs lie splattered everywhere, some still twitching, curling and snapping as if in agony. As this latest victim, hungering, anxious, timid, nears the sugar, something seems to trouble it. It should flit off; yet it cannot. It is fixed on that sugar. It smells the sweetness. Desire holds it there. It stops and strokes its face. Preens its wings. That pause proves fatal. The knife hovering in the air somewhere far beyond its ken slashes invisibly down, so swift and subtle that no sound, no tremor warns of its coming, and its edge, honed to razor thinness, slices the fly neatly in half. No mess of squashed thorax or mush of fly guts. How does he do it? What knife is that, and what hand?

The old man half-turns his face to me, and smiles. A sweet, kindly smile. A smile that was there already, had I been able to glimpse it. His contemplation had always been a smiling one. His hand had not lost, his right hand had not lost its cunning; nor yet his bleared eyes their sharpness. And now the left hand with which he had drawn me to him is lifted and laid upon my head, which it covers with his warm, dry, and heavy palm. It is a kind hand, soft and knowing. It strokes my hair lightly, gentle despite its size and weight. Pleased, he smiles a little wider from the corners of his tobacco-fouled lips, and says, "Tzott!" And his eyes beneath those shaggy yellowed brows open wide with a quiet hilarity.

Later I learned he was my father's great-uncle, and had been a famous schochet. The throats of innumerable lambs, bulls, heifers and calves, rams and ewes, chickens, geese, and turkeys had been honored by him swiftly, painlessly—slit by that same airy knife whose work is ritually done before it is ever seen to lift and flash, the hand descending before the heart has beaten even once. He was retired, a refugee, an old man, an old, old man squatting by the windowsill, waiting out his last days in that decayed rented house next to a dank and foggy Brooklyn canal.

"Tzott!"

Asklapios

IF AT THIRTY your eyes are closed, and if by forty you still haven't opened them, tomorrow you'll find yourself fifty, and it's become uncomfortable, this being sealed. You toss about, bruising yourself in the dark. Time for a cure.

Hegel says somewhere, *Denn warum sollte er (das heisst Gott) uns nicht offenbaren, wenn wir einegen Ernst mit ihm machen wollen?* At thirty I regarded his question as naive. I decided by forty that he had lost his nerve and fled cowering to shelter in the arms of the Fathers. But tomorrow came, and I heard the ironic challenge in Hegel's question: *After all, why shouldn't he (God, that is) come through for us, if only we'd try leveling with him?*

I stopped right where I stood: I had been marching in place, turning right, turning left, blocked by an unseen barrier, erected, perhaps, by some immemorial, innate despotism. Merely midlife blahs? Time for a cure?

Mathematics and History suggested themselves as a likely Rx. I enrolled myself in those two disciplines. However, after the first weeks I ceased attending. Where time went, I cannot say. Before I knew it, the examination period was here. Gathering up my texts, I went to the Holiday Inn and crammed. My meals were sent up, and I ate them sitting at the window, looking down at ten lanes of traffic streaming north and south, east and west, along the intersecting interstates below me. Day and night, cars, trucks, vans, pickups, motorcycles, campers, and long-range semis—unceasing. It seemed as if the whole vast production of East Asia was pouring through this emporium. Never mind: it will never fill the deserts of our Southwest.

But when Monday morning came, I was no wiser. I packed up and went to petition the Advisor to let me drop everything. Too late, I was told. The system requires complete records, success and failure alike. The finals must be faced. Outside the office a long line was waiting: red-rimmed eyes in wan faces. They leaned against the wall or sat slumped on the floor, outstretched legs making a gantlet of the corridor. They were staring into their scribbled notebooks or skimming marked-up texts with their fingers: they were smoking, eating sandwiches and fruit, and spooning yogurt; they were sucking straws stuck into cans of soft drink or sipping coffee or cocoa from styrofoam cups. All waiting to see the Advisor.

Once home, I sat heavily, suffused by a lassitude, a fatigue never before experienced. I laid two fingers across my left wrist: the pulse staggered, now trotting, now stumbling, now fading away altogether. I breathed deeply: no pain. Yet half my heartbeat was missing, or rattling at a syncopated wallop. I stood up, but wasn't dizzied. Nevertheless, telephoned for an ambulance and ordered a bed at the Cedars. Intensive Care was ordered for me.

I took six days of deep rest. Nurse brought me a letter on the morning of the seventh day. My transcript. It read: MATHEMATICS = 0. HISTORY = 0. For an hour I added them up. This way and that way. No matter which way. . . . When the Resident paused on his rounds to ask me how I felt, I told him I still felt like myself. "I'll do you a favor," he smiled. He rotated the console that sat on the little wheeled cart at my bedside and revealed its face to me. The wires that were attached to my temples, my chest, my wrists, and my ankles all fed information into its minibrain: the result was displayed on the oscilloscope. I was looking at a glowing grid. A green wave moved over it: my life-functions. Passing by on that wave was my heart: a dot of green light. Wave and dot entered at the left and flowed evenly across in leisurely fashion, up and down: my life was a six-inch strip, a mere segment of an endless, invisible, undulating serpent manifested here, in the present, marked by that beating blip winking along its crests and troughs, measured minutely by the grid. A digital clock read out the rate at which I rested. A fine instrument. I thought I could hear a faint high musical chime as the dot came in at the left from nowhere and vanished at the right into nowhere once again. "This will amuse you for a little while," he said. "Maybe you'll learn something from it too." He patted my shoulder benevolently and turned away to resume his tour of the ward.

Fascinated, I watched the oscilloscope. I tried various breathing rhythms, offered isometric clenching and release in an attempt to change the impulses my body sent through these wires into the machine. It took far too much effort to make any impression on its display. Finally, soaked with perspiration and trembling, I gave up and lay there watching my life-wave go by, counted by the green dot that was my heart. I slept.

When I woke up, I found that I was lying in a comfortable and warm bed that yielded everywhere, yet supported me in a weightless suspension. I was no longer alone. There were many others breathing in that silence. I listened: it was a silence filled with silences. I opened my eyes then. It was very late. Above me was a sky glutted with stars. I lifted my heavy head and peered about me. Stretching into the distance were tiers of beds, all white, with white bedding. In them were the sleepers, and they were all swaddled in white too. At the horizon, in a vast circle, stood the silhouettes of tall buildings, some faintly sparkling with lights here and there. The air circulating through this place was pleasant, cool and moist, scented with roses. The sound of our low, even breathing filled this incubation chamber with a nearly inaudible hum. But for its music, it might have seemed that space and time had been annulled in that deep slumber. I thought, I must leave here, no matter what the cost. But I found as I struggled to lift myself that I grew only heavier. The harder my effort, the greater the weight pulling me down. Sweat trickled from my scalp; it stung my eyes. I ground my jaws as I thrust against the tender grip of my bed. And then at last, with a great wrench, I fell over, staggering on my legs—but freed. The lofty dome above had paled. Where the east must be, a band of pink, the false dawn of this false universe.

I walked barefoot on icy tiles in that direction down the dim aisle of sleepers sighing in those tiered beds. Suddenly I saw someone approaching out of the depths of the shadowy wall before me. I never hesitated, but went on until we were face to face. It was a tall figure in a white robe. He was masked by a thick, curly black and silver beard that covered even his high cheekbones. As the light of the rim of an imitation sun rose over that black city skyline, and he held his hands out to greet me, nodding gravely and smiling at our reunion, I saw that this stranger was myself.

I woke in the obscurity of the Intensive Care Ward. The only illumination shone from the low-lit dials of the grand console monitoring all the sedated persons in here. The plump ebony nurse who sat behind it, illuminated by the greenish light of its dials, was fast asleep in her chair, her jaw slack as she snored gently. Her ivory shirtwaist dress was half-unbuttoned and twisted awry, her pendulous left breast blooming—she must have unhooked her bra for comfort. Her hands lay open in her lap. Her white-stockinged legs were spread wide, her feet in her white shoes bent crookedly as though she were a big rag doll. The face of my oscilloscope was blank, its light extinguished. One by one, I stripped away the electrodes taped to my body. My cheeks were stubbled, my mouth parched. On the night table there was carafe of water, and I drank some. There was also a basket of fruit and thick honeycake made with walnuts that my parents had had sent as a gift—they were far away, retired to some tropical isle. I broke the cake and nibbled at it. I bit into a glossy red apple. Delicious. Nurse slept on. I quietly dressed myself and tiptoed out.

It was bitterly cold on the street and very clear. The late hour was deserted except for an occasional taxi jouncing through the night along the boulevard in the distance. I walked away, towards home.

Kassandra

IN TEN YEARS, you'll forgive this night."

Never.

"Another ten, and you'll forget it."

Never.

"Ten more, and you'll wonder what the fuss was about."

Never, I said, finally.

Cocksure. But it went beyond that with him. Decathlon Silver Medallist. I'd watched him scoring all those years at school. He knew it, too. And after a triumphal return from the Games, he came to me at Thanksgiving. I was alone in our Newport place, Mother and Father away at St. Moritz, my future husband grounded in San Francisco. Years of adoration—now there he stood at the door, the very form my eyes had admired in action on the fields. My knees quailed. Who wouldn't have let him in, and be glad to. We made drinks and talked, gazing out into the gray, deserted lagoon, where hundreds of shrouded boats rocked their masts in unison, swayed by the pelting of the season's first storm.

Though fame had just come to him, his reputation was really long-established with me: my Sisters had each taken him on, and boasted of it. Charming, all muscle and rare skill—who wouldn't have. Yet I'd held out. Still here he was, as if he were keeping a card on our class in my sorority, all of us scattered around the world now a year after graduation. For five years I'd eluded him. It was the only promise my mother ever exacted from me: not him. Not that I possessed the strength to keep that vow. Twice luck was with me because of the ways things fell out. The first time, Dad's plane to Los Angeles was scratched, and he stayed on in Palo Alto to take me to dinner. The next time my turn came round to be initiated into the mysteries, Mom's mother died in her sleep, and I took flight for Syracuse. Close calls.

Two martinis towards the evening, another front of the storm pouring black, heavy clouds in low from the wild Pacific everywhere to the west, the fireplace burning mossy oak logs. The Silver Medallist lies glowing at ease on our thick buffalo robe, the orange light glancing warmly over the harsh facets of his unmarked face. No escape this time. My belly seems as hot as the flames pouring up into the chimney. Between my legs a giant rose opens slowly, its petals twisting, rustling almost audibly. An hour and more I hold out, until the docks and the boats vanish, drowned in the dark and pounding rain. I don't want him, though that rose sighs. I keep him off, making him tell me about the Games. No use. He simply stands and removes his clothes. After which it is nothing for him to strip me naked. Yet, in some infinitely small place somewhere behind my forehead my whole, true self is compressed, concealed from him. Before I slip, frenzied, into the net of his arms and am grasped by his wall-hard thighs, I am capable of one thing: I take my grandmother's diamond from my throat. I can recall that I managed to unfasten that tight antique catch on the fine platinum chain, despite my trembling fingers. And that I placed it on the night table beside my parents' bed.

Nevertheless, I fought him all night. What it was really like, I cannot say. Not since then, certainly not before then, have I experienced such a long, dark night. Rape, we call it nowadays. Perhaps it has always been rape. Yet to be truthful, I wasn't violated. Passion, and possession too. Not union. We entered it consciously and, after a short sleep as profound as coma, emerged at dawn fully conscious again. Knowing him, rather knowing his track record, how could I have been surprised. Or blamed myself. We become utterly our bodies in such hours. All right. But it may also happen that we are outside them at the same time, watching. You read of people who die, and say they have looked down at themselves and said farewell—only to return, to be called back or forced once more into the partnership through the intervention of a doctor or some passerby that found them just in time. So with me that night. Not right away. After our first bout, before the ecstasies that were to come.

Where was he? I heard my hidden self ask. He'd come for me; he was taking me; I'd taken him to me—yet I sensed that he was not there at all. Though not a machine, the self-loving stud you meet and even take on sometimes for the hell of it. Something else. I was afraid, not of his absence from me, but from himself. I could endure the not having him—almost all of us have known that agony. But not the horror of the latter. For one night, I'd thought, I would have that beauty I'd missed for five years, just as my sisters had had. This was unimaginable. Towards morning, hatred—its metallic taste filled my throat—turned what the sweet, rich flesh gave to sudden harshness. And even then, not to the lips and tongue: but towards the one who woke and watched us; my self in me. All through the dawn, through the hour of dropping silence between two waves of the vast storm that kept on coming in wet masses from the tumbling skies, lit at last by a cold light in the gray east from a sun that would not be seen for three more days.

What was it? I wondered. What was so terribly wrong? I was too young then to know. And he was aware of it; he knew. It made him cruel. I had come to, raw, weeping. I didn't know that it was despair, that I had been destroyed somehow forever. After twenty years, I know what a night like that should end like—not with uncontrollable weeping and a body that is one great torn wound. Quite the opposite, in fact: a body that may seem to be crushed, powerless to move, but nonetheless a body that smiles, humming with quiet praise as it knits itself miraculously again and rises as though just created like beauty itself from the spume of the black waves rolling against the shore. No, it was not like that. And he knew it. He was cruel, never drying my tears, never consoling me for what he'd done to me. Unlike the others, I'd guessed his secret: all the gifts were his but one. He had no . . . what? No soul. His prowess, his fine form, his irresistible charm—it was monstrous. He knew I'd glimpsed that emptiness even before we sank through midnight. Yet I'd gone on with him, knowing what I did, until morning. Out of what necessity, because I was too young to know better? Perhaps. Now I guess that it was compassion. That, or perhaps unable to believe that such a thing can be, needing to hope that it might not be. Or, miserable that I could have been so deluded, mistaken in my longing, in my body's response to him.

He was cruel because he could be nothing else. Perhaps he wanted to disclose that secret to me, as if my sharing it could lessen the burden of nullity. Had he soothed me in his arms, had he pretended that all was well with us, that our night of hard loving was something to be remembered as one of the possible fulfillments of life, the sort of thing that comes into existence and remains, he'd have been kinder than most men. Though I should have hated myself for letting him pretend. Instead, he showed me truth—and it was too cruel to be borne. Adding those hateful words, "You'll forgive," and, "You'll forget . . . ."

And as I swore, I've never forgiven, nor forgotten what I suffered that night. Rape's such a weak word for it. A thing without a soul in my arms. A thing like that in me.

When he left, he took something from me. Not what he'd come for—although there have been moments when I was nearly ready to give it to a lover. He took my grandmother's diamond pendant. He didn't think I'd seen him pocket it while he dressed, as I lay on my parents' bed, tear-blinded, my legs and arms strengthless. As he went out, he said, "At least you'll never have to see me again, if that's how you feel."

I'll see you dead first! I choked out.

Down the hall, laughter. Laughter as the door blew in under a gust and was yanked shut once more. Outside, laughter through the cold sheets of rain,the sloshing of his deck shoes on the wooden planks as he trotted away.

I couldn't know how much I'd meant what I'd said in my rage that morning. After twenty years I realize it, neither having forgiven, nor hardly forgotten that night. Now he lies here before me in the Hyacinth Viewing Room. He did well in life for twenty years. He made a fortune in yacht brokerage right here in Newport, more than ten million a year in sales. He couldn't have missed. Today there's not a foot of dockage to be had for money or love. And I am down here by mischance, clearing up the estate after the fire, only to see the obituary. He died by water. Aboard some plutocrat's 220-foot cruiser, the *Palace*, that runs aground in a fog off Anacapa and breaks up in the darkness. He was found drifting in his lifejacket two days later, miles and miles away. And he looks marvelous: the soft blond hair silvery after twenty years, the squares of the bronzed face hardly needing the cosmetician's brush. Dressed appropriately: the sportsman's blue blazer, the white flannels, the graceful black patent leather slip-ons. Calmly sleeping at ten in the morning. Viewing's set for eleven. I'm quite alone with him in this air-conditioned chamber heaped with floral arrangements: anchors, cruisers, sailboats. The ventilators purr; the lights are very low; the electric candles flicker beside the bier.

When the sad Muzak comes on, I realize it's late, almost time for the obsequies. Nothing is changed; nothing is solved; nothing more is to be known. It comes to me then, like an inspiration: my jewel's with him still! I want it back. Against the force of my loathing, I reach over into his coffin—oh, it's fine polished rosewood, with heavy antique bronze moldings for handles—and put my hands to his neck. Yes, beneath the knot of the crimson and white silk rep, there's a lump. My fingers thrust through the shirt—my eyes, I realize, are shut tight against the vision of that immobile carcass full of cold blue chemical fluids—and they yank. The big oval gem, with its large old-fashioned facets, comes away in them with a bit of chain, not the fine platinum of my grandmother's legacy but some contemporary 18-karat goldwork in flat S-shaped links. The Muzak turns up: his family and friends will be filing in any minute now.

I have to get away. Through the exit on the other side of that coffin. The door's flush in the wall, without a knob. How does it work? Behind the recessed panels around the ceiling, the lights are brightening. A plate beside the door has two switches in it—which one's for what? I flick one. The door doesn't budge. But there's the sound of machinery somewhere near me. Turning, I see a panel in the far wall slide away, and then, the whoompf! of a gas furnace igniting beyond it. A sudden whoosh, with a flare of intense fires. Whirring of belts. The far end of the coffin drops away, and his body begins sliding out, as though on some plank, head-first through that opening in the wall. The feet tilt up in their shiny black shoes, and he slides helplessly, steadily down towards the flames. As the feet disappear, another panel with a thick quartz glass window comes down, sealing the chute. The whole room flickers as the body seethes in the blast of that incinerator. Now the top panel of the coffin is swung up again, and the empty box remains here with me, its satiny white padding molded in the shape of his missing form. I don't know whether I'm laughing or crying; but I fumble at the other switch. The door slides away noiselessly before me, and I step through and down the narrow corridor as fast as I can, my heels turning in the thick brown carpeting.

At the other end, the heavy door yields easily, and I find myself out on the black asphalt of the parking lot, dazzled by the August sun overhead. Lincolns, Cadillacs, Mercedes, and a notable number of Rolls Royces are moving sedately in line towards the entrance of the mortuary and chapel: many are coming to pay their respects. Getting into my car, I drop my grandmother's diamond into my change-purse. My hands are shaking, and it takes a little time for me to get my key into the ignition. I can hardly see through my sunglasses. But I drive out as fast as I dare, trying not to think of the fuss that is being made back there behind me now.

Perceval

SO FAR, SO GOOD. The dossier shows progress from kindergarten on, all my doings sans hitch or blemish. But how's the selection made? A competition free to all comers, yet who are they? Your life an open book; theirs a mystery, sealed and silent. Until the story's finished, when what was hidden is revealed: their works and days: error and wastage disguised as life. Meanwhile, you apply, and apply. You wait for the interview, which is the first real step, or perhaps the last. You must be ready, though there's no particular way to prepare.

When the letter came by Special Delivery early this morning, my eyes began to be opened, I thought. I was requested to show up at Seneca. So, that was the fortune behind the Fellowship! Gilded Age, Robber Baron money: railroads, shipping, coal and iron, and the banking that absorbed it all in our century. A massive segment of it now philanthropic, living its own life. For each lucky Fellow it offers freedom from care. Riches given to all through that singular award of freedom to an individual. Not quite first prize in the lottery, but it should suffice. A gift's a gift. Take it. Use it. Even if it's tainted by irregularity.

The small irregularity is, I suppose, this invitation to Seneca. Unless I'm too careful. Perhaps my journey there, which has taken five long years from my life, will lead to the interview? At the tiny dilapidated station an hour up the Hudson, I hire a taxi. After a mile of driveway winding out beyond the high stone wall's automatic iron gates that opened and closed again with a quiet, well-oiled rumbling, there's the place. A low fieldstone carriage house below had been shut up long ago: the lock on the door was rusted through and the windows dusty and darkened. There were fine views along this gravel road: copses of ancient oaks, tall stands of firs, plantations of grand sugar maples; a few deer browsing at the dark fringes of the woods in the distance, does and fawns; rabbits hopping over the green meadows that opened among the trees; and, on the thick lawn sloping up to surround the great granite sculpture—a Beaux Arts castle for a magnate—a scattering of peahens with their cock in full display strutting before them, uttering harsh shrieks. As the cab pulls up, two black and white Great Danes bound alongside bellowing at us. They're friendly fellows, and I climb out unharmed—except that one of them rears to lick my face, leaving muddy pawprints the size of a child's hand on both shoulders of my jacket. A man steps forth and pulls him off, pummelling him and smiling, and directs me under the postern at the end of the open drawbridge that spans a dry moat full of blossoming purple and white lilacs.

We have all seen a place like Seneca, in old movies or dreams, or read of it in childhood: the plutocrat's demesne: its empty suits of polished armor flanking the foyer, pikes, halberds, and crossbows on the black oak-panelled walls, the massive antique English and Spanish furniture, the sumptuous Persian carpetings on the slate flagstone floor. Vast rooms to right and left. Cool on this June day: a hush that is palpable. It's still early afternoon, yet it's dark in here. In the sitting room on my right, sunlight plays through the leaded glass of the French windows, some of them opened to the rose garden flashing its blobs of crimson and white, and beyond them the red clay of the tennis courts, and then the shimmering light green of the swimming pool, from which a groundsman is sweeping leaves and insects with a net on a long pole: the light sparkles in the water dripping from it. In the sky swallows swooping, twittering as they hunt.

I'm about to follow this footman—is that what he's called? he wears a blue linen dustcoat—upstairs, when the master of Seneca himself steps out of a door that should be the library there, off that sitting room—I glimpse books going up out of sight, a moveable oak ladder, a red leather Morris chair. . . . He's slipping tortoise-shell reading glasses off with his right hand, fumbling them at the pocket of his blazer, a blue-green tartan with embossed golden buttons. He carries a thick sheaf of papers in a brown manila folder beneath his left arm. Baggy white flannel trousers; bare varicosed feet in denim espadrilles. I hadn't imagined him bearded: scraggly white fleece, his white hair shaggily cropped, a wen the size of a pearl onion above his left eyebrow. Rather scholarly looking, in fact. Why should I be surprised? What do I know? I am ignorant. He also seems surprised to see me, as though I am not only a stranger but unexpected too: he throws his head back to look up at me, squinting, and makes me feel loutish, towering over him here like this. His head waggles with the tremor of Parkinson's disease, yet he bears it with the authority of one who not only proposes but disposes as well. Have I come at the wrong time? Surely there must be a regular traipse of guests over this wide threshold, what with the complexes of interlocking duties and business affairs to be managed, including the media conglomerate that is in effect his voice, worldwide.

As he approaches, hesitant, taking scuffling steps, as if he'd prefer to slip past me, I hold my hand out and announce my name. His eyebrows arch, vaguely quizzical. At his throat a blue polka-dotted silk ascot is held in place by a cabuchon ruby, seventy-five bloody, coruscating karats at least. My name seems not to have enlightened him. Nonetheless, he welcomes me instantly with his clasp: a broad palm, warm, dry, gentle. Though his fleshy pressure seems somehow impersonal too. In a low apologetic voice, he says, "I'm sorry. Wasn't expecting you. Perhaps my secretary's made a mistake." I feel myself flushing: I have made the mistake, and not my first. I, who've never arrived at the right moment. Taking the letter from my breast pocket, I unfold it. No, this is the appointed day. "Well," he sighs, "it's all right then. You'll excuse me: I keep only a skeleton staff here now. And things are a bit rushed. It's one crisis or another. You won't mind being left on your own?" Well, sir, I begin, I'm sorry I'm a burden to you. "Not at all," he protests, kind yet absent too, holding onto my hand, "no one's a burden to me, my dear fellow, no one and nothing." He casts his eyes around this entrance hall, suggesting that there is room in this mansion for us all. "But I am in fact somewhat distracted these days. Too many plans. Never time to see them through." He has not let go my hand. He bites his upper lip: he's trying to think of something. "Tell me," he blurts, as if eagerly seeking my judgment, "while I have you here, what would you say to the establishment of this place as a reserve for a select group, so to speak . . . thinkers, and such? Is that idea obsolete?" Well, sir, I've just walked in here, and— "Ah, it's a waste, you mean. Much too late to devote ourselves to that quest. I thought so." I venture to contradict him: Isn't that why I was asked here? "Oh, you do thinking then? Really?" Again, I feel my face flame with the fire of embarrassment—do I? "Never mind, we'll come to it later. Just now there's no time, is there. You'll think I'm indifferent to your fate. I am not. Believe me."

To this politeness, I nod gratefully. He releases my hand at last and turns aside, saying we're to meet at supper, I must make myself at home here if I can, and disappears through another heavy oak door on the left. The footman escorts me to my suite upstairs, tosses the overnight case on a stand, throws the narrow casements wide, and leaves. The scene offers a wonderful sweep of lawns, woods, and land rolling up to a ridge on which a hill bursts steeply out of the treetops, bare, glowing umber in the afternoon light, a crenelated tower on its crown, its windows flaring. That is the only structure visible, about five miles off: everything out there is Seneca, stretching to the high horizon.

By the window, there's an elegant kneehole desk of inlaid wood and mother-of-pearl: the top shows a stag at bay, one hound tearing at his throat, others fastening fangs into his flank. A Waterford carafe and tumblers stand on it. I pour one full of whiskey and wash three aspirin down. The profound quiet here, after the clattering, filthy commuter cars, empty on the midday run up the shore of the Hudson, has unmasked a throbbing headache I was not aware of till now. It will take a while getting used to the spaciousness here, the atmosphere drenched with moist light that fills up this basin among the old hills . . . after ten years' confinement in the roach-raddled rooms I call my home on Avenue A at 13th Street, just off St. Mark's Place. While I wait for the aching band to dematerialize in my head, I dab a soapy towel at the black pawprints the beast left on my jacket. Unsuccessfully. I give it up—no point in wetting it through and having to wear it damp all evening. I have nothing else with me but a pair of shorts, a new polo shirt, sneakers, and swimtrunks. I own nothing but this old seersucker suit, the worn white suede bucks and the frayed tie. A wanderer hardly needs that much, in fact.

I could read. Or write: a quire of handmade paper and a good pen are laid out on the desk, on which there's also a silver bud vase with a perfect red-yellow rose, freshly cut: a dewdrop sparkles in its heart. Was I expected after all? I can't focus my eyes for reading, and I have nothing to write. After ten minutes, I've finished the rich malt scotch, and the utter tranquility of the room, the slow drift of small white cumulus clouds past the tower out there, begin to be oppressive: the jangle of my nerves, my own pulse in my head, and my breathing are too audible in this peace. I must move about.

The hallway's empty. My wing of this castle seems devoid of life: the other eleven bedroom suites are vacant, as I find on opening the doors on rooms like mine, each with its lovely rose in its slender vase. No luggage anywhere. I am the only guest then, truly unexpected though my invitation was correctly written? I'll have to accept it, since I am here.

Over the lobby, a wide, curved balcony. Paintings adorn it, some good, some great, in fact, the sort you might see in books, not in the museum. I pace down the grand stairs, following the pictures hung along it. At the turning, there's a Renoir nude that must be seen to be believed, so full of light is it, brilliance that even in this darkening afternoon seems to well up from the depths of its surface. She, rather it, is incredibly effulgent, the smile she wears . . . my coming here's already amply rewarded by this sight of her, even if it's error in the end, pointless waste. I can go back where I came from, sustained: this vision is enough.

Once down, I continue pursuing the wall of art back along the hall beneath the staircase. And then I hear remote voices, from somewhere below. A door's ajar, hidden in the gloom under the balcony. A stairway, narrow, steep. The voices are hollow, not in conversation: remarks, or commands, punctuated by feet dragging and stopping. Thuds, clinking. I decide to sneak down and see.

The stone steps stop in a large pantry, cool and filled with the purring of a bank of freezers and refrigerators. This pantry gives onto a great, low, vaulted kitchen furnished with hanging racks of pots and pans, and long-handled culinary tools, tables, benches, ovens, and paired heavy-duty ranges and stainless steel sinks. It's not a basement, however. The land must drop away on this side of the building, because the honeyed late afternoon light pours through its glass wall, filling the whole place with cheery radiance. A chef with his tall white hat, his cheeks glistening pink above a pouting mouth, his apron tight over a nice round belly, is trussing a goose. Beside him on his maple worktable lies a shiny pink haunch of veal, a fifty-pound loin at least. Beside it, three blue-white capons, necks and heads still feathered and dangling, bleeding on the immaculate black and white tessellations of the tiled floor, waiting their turn to be dressed. The chef's assistant—a lanky and sallow fellow with long thin moustaches, apron hitched round just under his armpits, white tee shirt torn at the neck, his long sinewy arms tattooed with flowers, anchors, hearts and bannered mottoes, and, yes, a fat Cupid with drawn bow over the right triceps—notices me standing in the door. A cigarette droops from one side of his mouth: his eye winks against its purling smoke. He faces the chef at an adjacent worktable, and goes on swiftly chopping big red onions. Near them is a wire basket of peeled potatoes, bunches of thick carrots, a colander of sweetpeas, bowls of wax beans, and heaps of tomatoes, cucumbers, celery and lettuces and red radishes. The man who'd carried my bag sits at a low table, polishing flatware: a coffee service waits to be rubbed bright too. At one of the sinks, there's a chubby blond potboy, violently pimpled and crewcut, swabbing out a copper cauldron, sweating and grumbling to himself. These were the voices I had heard as they hummed, joked, responded to the chef's curt demands. This, the skeleton staff? Serving an empty house? For whom is this feast being prepared? Who will break the sweet loaves yeasting on the range? taste the cherry tarts glowing in those little aluminum pans? Who will drink these three jeroboams of Chateau Petrus '59 standing uncorked to breathe out of the way here in the pantry?

I have been enjoying their orderly activity and am about to cross the kitchen to look into the huge stockpot steaming on the other range—its sharp scent of herbs and fatty marrow wafts across this breezy chamber—when I notice a long table next to the wall just to my left, and remain fixed where I am. On this marble slab, half-covered by a rag of stained sheeting, a body, the nude body of a young woman. The sheet's carelessly, even hastily, draped over her. She lies crumpled there on her right side, arms and legs askew, bent brokenly at elbows and knees, as though she's fallen from a great height. Her flesh is pale cream, bruised with splotches large as my hands. Her head's tilted up at a cruel angle. I drift sideways towards her, tempted to lift the sheet from the face it masks. I'm afraid to. Yet I cannot prevent myself from touching the part of her upper arm showing from beneath the cover, or pressing that portion of her thigh protruding over the edge of the slab. Her naked flesh is firm, not yet cold.

Inside my skull I hear my own voice whisper—she's been killed. But in fact my lips are sealed. I'm here in their midst, after all. And they know she is here too. They know where I stand, what I've seen. One of them must have tossed this poor covering over the beautiful cadaver, the bit of drapery a Bathing Artemis clutches to her in one dimpled hand as she steps unprotected and shy from the secret pool . . . to conceal her modesty from me, the unexpected guest. The chef's carving away at the haunch of veal. The chef's helper chops loudly at carrots with his great blade. They all go right on with their tasks. These people make their own rules, I murmur soundlessly.

My fingers tingle with the sensation of her flesh; my ears are flooded with the silence of her smashed form. Taking a deep breath, I go on ahead into the kitchen to inspect the makings of the banquet. They can appreciate my *sangfroid.* I have seen what I should not: I know what I must not know. A missing girl. I, who was not seeking her, have found her. The damage is done. I must not betray myself. Still, silence is testimony too.

I walk confidently through them to gaze down into the swirling broth of the stockpot, to sniff up its fragrant vapor—pepper and salt, parsley, marjoram, cumin, and thyme—and to contemplate the big bones knocking and bumping at its bottom. I shall dine well here.

Salome

SIX MONTHS IN Los Angeles, and I'm still alone in my place. But not too depressed. No longer mourning the loss. Ready for the present, perhaps, if not my future. Let well enough alone. If it's well. If it's enough. I sit at a good though monotonous job at Technetronics, Inc., assembling microcomponents for the guidance system of what must be the latest model of cruise missile.

We have all been cleared to work here, some forty men and women on this line. At 08:00, we file from the locker room into our places, wearing gauze surgical masks and caps, covered up by sterile white jumpsuits, our feet shod in canvas booties. The badges over our hearts show our names and our polaroid portraits, both profile and full mug. This room in the plant is sterile: sealed, air-conditioned, bathed in soft, graywhite fluorescence, and permeated by Muzak: cocktail-hour dance tunes, slowed-down old jazz standards—a flattened-out, tinkly noise played at the one low volume that wears away the day and fills the night and sleep with its tinny, discreet jangle. Nauseating. We sit at the long bench, working with tiny bits of gold wire and hundreds of minuscule chips under stereo-microscopes. This little brain we're assembling will guide a stubby-winged missile a thousand miles—skimming over hill and dale, streaking along just above the surface of the earth, darting through valleys and touching treetops, up, down, up, winding in and out at a tall man's eyelevel—until it sees its target, plunges abruptly down to detonate a small, strategic mini-holocaust, and obliterates a city somewhere.

During lunchtime we get to chatting, more or less. My co-workers are like me, more or less, young to middle-aged, all from somewhere else, too. We talk movies, TV, the sports page: sex, religion, politics are no-no's. At 17:30 there is the slamming of car doors, the roaring of exhausts as we file out and head for the freeway. And then the long evening: each locked in his or her own unit, alone for all you know. Turning the key confirms a solitude. But the pay's very good, the job more or less assured. It's a fresh subcontract: Technetronics, Inc., is in on the ground floor of this latest development in weaponry. So not to complain, I adjure myself. Maybe someday soon I'll return to the studies abandoned in despair after the breakdown. I know that this time I have got a hold on things. Damned if I ever let go again.

About 16:00 this afternoon the fellow to my left, Peter Fuerst, says to me, "Kingsley, how about coming to our party tonight. Most of our bench will be there."

Well, I say.

And Sally Johns, the girl to my right, a girl with a pair of hips if ever I saw hips, even in her full, loose white jumpsuit, says, "Come on, Kingsley, give it a try. You bring your wine, and I'll bring mine." Her luminous blue eye winks at me above her white mask. I'm persuaded.

It's Friday. April again. It's even rained this week: Los Angeles is clear, washed, glistening: there's snow on the peaks of the San Gabriels to the east, and the many different kinds of green foliage everywhere that fills this city are fresh and tender. Life may be possible, who knows. I need something more for myself.

A shabby stucco cottage in Venice, gabled and low, with a Midwest sort of front porch and some splintery rattan furniture on it. A half-dozen cats prowl about or sprawl lazily, cleaning themselves. It's on Rose Avenue, a few doors from the Pioneer Bakery. The street's lined with decrepit houses just like it, all with fenced, hopeful patches of front lawn. Bougainvillea vines, rose and hibiscus bushes mask their peeling age, and the cool evening air is tainted with the nightblooming jasmine, a sharp scent that mixes pleasantly with the delicate yeasty odors of bread baking in the nearby plant. A few blocks to the west, beyond the flat, broad beach, the Pacific lies calm and gray, not a boat or ship anywhere in sight. It's nearly 22:00 when I open the front door, and the party's underway. I straighten my tie and step in. The usual scene. Outside, the quiet of late evening; inside, hi-fi cramming the small rooms with thunder and screeching. I set my jug of mountain red on a sidetable with the rest of the booze offerings. People are dancing, or talking mouth to ear. I have the feeling I have come to the wrong party: not a soul in the place do I recognize.

Or else I'm not as well as I have believed myself to be. By 23:00 I'm slouched on a bean bag in a corner, an observer, sipping at my seventh glass of wine. Plenty of action, yes; but it baffles me. I'm sure I must know these folks from Technetronics, Inc., by name or face or form. Yet somehow they are now all strangers. One tells me he's a movie director, up for an Oscar. Another is a state senator down for the tax hearings next week. Another's on the Governor's Special Commission for Environmental Protection: Toxic Wastes Committee. That gal's a well-known sculptor in epoxy resins, getting into advanced laser holography. Another, a little Chinese, is a minimal conceptualist: she shows me the razor marks on her wrists: a famous art work she created the other year in the elevator of the County Museum. The tall black girl is a ceramist: lingams and yonis and omphaloids three meters high. I have spoken to a familiar-looking man from my own bench who tells me he's a psychotherapist specializing in addicted call girls. There is a pair of Sufi dancers in orange pantaloons and gauze blouses, their heads in blue turbans, and a pale, married couple of Sikhs in white, wearing tall white headdresses and drinking only Perrier. I have poured my wine out to a woman who's the best-selling author of Gothic bodice-rippers in paperback: she's just passed the ten-millionth mark. Peter Fuerst himself has red hair now, not mousy brown. Sally's cropped black head is hidden in a long, silky, synthetic blonde mane, its tresses compressed by a band of sparkling rhinestones, hanging below her backside—I know those hips—and the rest of her full body hardly covered: shiny platinum patches on the large nipples of her heavy and free-swinging breasts . . . and she's not Sally now either . . . she's Salome Head, Coptic belly-dancer from Alexandria, Egypt. Mark, who assembles to the left of Peter Fuerst all day long, is introduced to me as a stockbroker: he's offering me a new issue of preferred stock in a valve factory: a steal now at seven dollars, shares bound to triple and split within the year . . . it's new pipeline-building for Baghdad, he says. And it *is* Mark, I guess, behind the curly chestnut G.B.S. beard. Though it's not Mark's nose propping the heavy frames of his thick, clear glasses.

I have tried talking to these people over the buffet, in the kitchen, even while faking a hootch with Sally, who has pressed her quivering, naked abdomen and buttocks up against me more than once. Yet none of them seems to know me, and we have to get acquainted all over again. Hi there, it's Kingsley, I've said, only to be met with blank looks: "Kingsley who?" It's finally too much for me, and I have to go squat in my corner to nibble at hardtack and drink my wine in peace.

Towards 24:00, things start to get wild. Not rough, just a little wild. I can guess what is going down soon. Arabic slam-dancing. Group swinging. Whatever. Sally—Salome Head—crouches in the center of the room, gyrating to the sounds of Ali Baba and his Middle East Assassins: a long album with six endless, authentic ethnic tracks. The place has been darkened, the lighting undulating blue and purple around the walls and ceiling.

And I don't feel at all well. I am holding a brimming glass of wine, staring at it as it runs over my cupped hands. I look up, and Sally's standing over me, her long, thick blonde hair brushing the top of my head. Her forehead's sweat-beaded, the mascara's sliding down her heavy cheeks, the lids of her big black eyes painted a cobalt blue and powdered with flecks of gold dust. I realize that she must be wearing black contacts. And when she unpins her muslin veil all embroidered with hearts and roses and smiles at me, a gold tooth glints in the front of her mouth. Maybe it's not even Sally. No one here tonight has the same name, or same anything I remember from Technetronics, Inc.

"Come on now, John," she whispers throatily, "Dance with me, okay, man?

John? Kingsley here, I say.

She stares at me and replies brusquely, "Kingsley? Never heard of him." And then she bends above me, her pendulous breasts powdered white, sweat-streaked, rank musk reeking from her deep armpits, her heavy gold-glittered thighs trembling from her exertions on the dance floor. She thrusts her hands under my arms as though to lift me from my collapsed, bean bag seat. But I am too heavy, too firmly planted. The heat radiating from her hits me in the face, dizzying me. She grins, full of zany lust. There is a bright zircon-crusted star winking from her belly-button. "Come on now, John, won't you join me in the dance?"

Tell me one thing, I say.

"And what should that be, my darling lover?" she croons, panting.

Just tell me—what gives? That's Peter over there, isn't it; and that's Mark; and this is our bunch from Technetronics, Inc., isn't it?

Silence.

Well, isn't it? I insist.

She lets go of me. Stands back erect, her plump belly, its hollow, starry gash of navel thrust at me, her bangled wrists planted firmly on those hips, their painted talons gripping her thighs in anger. She gazes down at my forehead, not at me. And she speaks in a new, acid voice, mocking. "Look, Kingsley, you better leave L.A."

But why? I ask surprised, suddenly anxious despite myself.

"Because you just ain't gonna make it here, man."

Oh?

"No, man, you ain't. For why? Because you lack a persona, see?"

But Sally . . . ?

My protest is cut short. She digs a sharp nail into my heart, saying, "Man, you got nothing but your own self!"

That's all I want! I hear myself shouting back at her.

Her other hand slices across my Adam's apple, and she snorts, "That just ain't enough, man. Never was. Never will be."

There's a sudden silence in the room. They haven't changed the cassette. I can hear the loud, low hum of the amplifier putting out its silent, roaring sound, like the white noise of nothingness. Salome hooks both hands into my belt and heaves me from my seat; she leads me through this congeries of pure strangers, not one of them resembling the disciplined, skilled workers I know during the week at Technetronics, Inc. They watch me being yanked along. They stare at me with pity, and with contempt. As she thrusts me backward out the front door into midnight on Rose Avenue, I see their turned heads. They have watched my expulsion, but said nothing. As she closes the door, slowly hooking up her yashmak again with one hand, leaving visible now only those black-stencilled brows arched over those great black blank eyes, the Sufi has already flipped the Assassins, dropped them into the machine, and turned them loose. Their drums erupt with a wallop, and the door is shut in my face. The Princes of the Earth will go on partying without me.

I walk to the car. There's a damp breeze flowing in from the Pacific a few blocks off. It's salty and it's sour. I am chilled in my light suit. I have nothing but myself now. And I am wondering what there is to do with it.

Gnosis

I WAS DRIVING THROUGH the midnight in my little white Fiat convertible. Thirsty, deathly tired, I'd pulled over and parked on the crumbling shoulder of the road, climbed out with some difficulty, and walked here up a steep hill through a ruined, black park. Now I stood looking back to get my bearings, and saw dimly that I'd stopped on a kind of causeway running across a vast swampland whose watery tracts glistened beneath a night sky full of low turbulent clouds lit up and glowing fitfully, blood-red, as though illumined not by sheet lightning but by silent, distant explosions, great fires burning in towns behind the hills around this valley. On the dismal plain through which this causeway ran there were scattered leafless trees, gnarled, twisted, dead and broken stumps, and fallen, rotting forest giants. I stood in the middle of a wooden bridge over what seemed a deep moat far below. I turned about again and looked at the high wall and the gate on this place: an age-slimed, rough-hewn stronghold. A fetid wind blew around it, breathing in damp gusts now hot, now cold. I realized I was not alone, that men and women were walking past me silently, going in and under the rusting portcullis, each one alone. They wore formal attire, dark coats, gray trousers, patent boots, and long dresses, velvet and satin jackets, jewels, and silk shawls. While I am buttoned in my white belted raincoat and wear twill trousers and a cashmere turtleneck sweater, suede boots—driving clothes. Obviously I am only passing through, not dressed for the occasion.

In heavy silence they come up the hill on paths leading from the dark swampy plain. They file by on both sides, as though heading to a state wedding or state funeral, or a congress of nations. I am tired, in need of some refreshment—it seems as though I have been driving forever. I shrug. I am here. I go on in too.

Having passed beneath the hanging portcullis, I find I am in the Great Court. And yes, someone is in charge here. A giant of a man, taller, bulkier, more powerful than I have ever seen—a Goliath. Bearded, wide-mouthed, square-toothed, someone out of the lost, epic days. As the men and women in their fancy dress file towards him, he receives each in turn, grasping hand and arm, embracing each one, his deep voice giving them low and hoarse directions, it seems, for each one enters the castle by a low small door, each alone, and through many doors, like rat holes. I come to him and look up into his glaring deep-set red eyes, round as saucers, as the Grimms would say. He waits for me to speak. His thick tongue lolls over his fat lips with amusement. I insist, I'm just passing through, you know. I don't belong here. I've got a very long way to go yet. Then he replies in a rumbling basso voice, "Welcome, my friend! My name is Cacooethes!" Graciously, he smiles in his stubbly beard, inviting me to join his organization. "Come in, my friend, this is my headquarters. My group is now in session. I would be pleased to have you become a member. You've arrived just in time."

Flattered by his deep, good-humored, and reassuring words, I am about to say yes. I hesitate, and, as I pause, thinking about my choice, I seem to see him without his black jumpsuit. His body is hirsute, bear's tufts of thick, curly, black-brown hair sprout from his shoulders, his chest is a morass of rusty boar bristles. Something about this makes me suspicious, perhaps the way people vanish through those little low doors. His name puzzles me too. Perhaps I should turn and leave right away. Then it comes to me: this fellow is Satan's chief devil. Or, his name is a name for the Adversary himself! He seems to guess my apprehension. He smiles at me ingratiatingly, as if to excuse himself for not having shown himself directly to me—as if he could never be so rude. Soothingly, he says, "Don't worry, my friend, it's all right here." Opens his arms to embrace me. As our chests meet, I feel that I can discern his true form: he is not a flesh-and-blood giant. I see him as though suddenly gifted with vision: this doorkeeper is a boiler, an iron-plated mechanical monster with eight arms, long steel rods with powerful steel grappling hooks for fingers! Inside this boiler is a sea of orange-white flame. I hear his whispered roaring in my ears, "Caca, they call me." Oh yes, I say aloud, I know who you are!

It's too late! What is that roaring about my head, in my ears? A furnace. I am melting into him. He is absorbing me in the red-white flames leaping inside that boiler of a body. And I too will become a devourer of souls. But this is an accident, I think, a misunderstanding! Because I was thirsty I left my car in the middle of my journey. Because I needed to relax, to stretch out a bit and rest. I had been driving alone so hard and so long. I only happened to stumble onto his operation—I hadn't come directly to his castle in this desolated district. I don't have to join his organization. I don't have to stay here. And I think, he's only just who he is. He just does what he does. And I can walk away before I'm utterly possessed by his flame . . . through which I am now able to see all those who had entered before me. They are no longer clothed in their formal attire, but naked now and joyous, cavorting about with limber glee, carrying on wildly, dancing and leaping in the fires like children in a swimming pool. Out there on the drawbridge, they passed me in silence, filing solemn from all directions of that cold, scorched moorland, while now here they are radiant with passion, with demonic intensity, released and transformed into souls shouting, singing amidst the flames.

Oh no, I think, I have to get back to the car before that gate crashes down! I break away from the clasp of that cast-iron boiler-body and dash for the drawbridge and the outer darkness of the world—and my freedom there in the empty night.

Moses

FROM THANKSGIVING ON, another winter of ice-age snows. With the solstice a cold wave moves in over the entire region: by day the skies are white and void. The bleached sun rolling low in the south and glancing off the endless billowing drifts never lifts the temperature above zero: the thinned air hisses and shimmers all night with the utter transparency of 20 below. The constellations are packed with so many more stars that had never been guessed at before: they are sharp as needles, and their faint blue radiance floats back from the vast, endless mantled earth. Then, for a week in January, the auroras spread their filmy veils flowing between us and the heavens, pulsing with cold and brilliant ineffable hues. At midnight the stillness is broken by the ripping groans of trees splitting here and there through the woods and orchards. Nightlong the owls hoot, mating calls floating now near, now echoing far off invisibly. The crust of ice forming roughly on the snow is covered every day or so by a new powdery fall of crystals materializing out of the empty air and whirling off in dazzling coruscations all afternoon, keeping the paralyzed world freshly swept with whiteness, layer laid upon layer again. The fences have sunk from sight, and all the fields and pastures merge into one expanse. A few cardinals light our feeding tray with bursts of crimson; the bluejays crash savagely down, scattering poor and ragged sparrows; the waxwings pluck vainly at ice-glazed berries.

Two hundred years ago there had been longhouses in our orchard. All winter long Senecas or Oneidas lay wrapped in pelts, pots of squirrel or dogmeat stew simmering on the embers of hearths down the length of their one great room where two dozen or more families endured such freezes. It is so cold now there are not even rabbit tracks to be seen. Too cold to ski, too biting to snowshoe or toboggan. We pass in muffled silence along these walled paths plowed for us between the buildings. We drink far too much on the weekends. Heavy icicles fringe the eves, some a yard long. And the frost persists, week after week. In February, a week's moist and warm air flows in from the sea two hundred miles to the southeast, bringing a sickening slump with it. Midwinter thaw. Underneath the white world things seem to shift about as though the frozen ground heaved, turning and slowly swelling and reshaping itself before our eyes. Then other waves of storms come in, blizzards from the Lakes to the northwest burying us again in drifts six to twenty feet high. In late March, finally, when everyone is down, bitter and miserable with cabin-fever—and even old, true friendships taste the dregs at the bottom of our exhausted being—there are moist breezes from the south and southwest, with sleeting rains slushing the bottomless snowpack. For days, icicles drip and run like faucets, then crash down dangerously. Crows sit ranting from the empty tops of the oaks. The sun vanishes altogether, hidden behind low, tumbling black clouds that roll endlessly over, pouring sheets of cold water down, torrents running over the rotting fields and broken roads until the clay shows through at last, red mud sliding from the banks, leaving slashes everywhere.

It is over. People are coughing, their shadow-rimmed eyes watery with fever and bronchitis. The old among us stand up better—after seventy-five years in this hard country, they are immune to all but time. Their minds hold out too; only their brains seem to decay, to rot out like the trunks fallen in our woods. Yet even this hateful sort of spring is precious to them. To them only, perhaps. We wait, saying nothing. What good after all can come of this cycle of death and rebirth each year. The soul is not nourished by seasons.

We had heard nothing from Liz and Leo since last summer. There was a card with a Mexican stamp on it. It had taken months to wander up to us here in Arcady, just below the foothills of the Adirondack Mountains. A garishly inked blur of the usual empty beach fringed by swaying fan palms, a striped umbrella in the background, and a coffee-tanned Azteca in a string bikini who stood grinning ferociously at the edge of the strand, her arms held out with longing to the flat, copper-green lagoon. Such winters separate old friends like fossil strata in which a couple of centimeters of sandstone suggest the passage of a million years and more. Yet the past is always present, locked up in the dead record below us. And even to the living, what is time? Another thin deposit between us now, like this fading winter. Liz and Leo—what were they doing so far away there on that blank western coast of Mexico? Hadn't they been journeying to Seattle for the summer? Had the rain been too much for them? And were they still there, slung in hempen hammocks under a thatched roof, sipping margaritas while the tepid tropical rain fell all the afternoon, or watching the kids ransack the tide's edge for crabclaws and cockles or run screaming like macaws into the small surf?

Just at the end of April, though, the crocuses up and blooming below our windows, there comes a battered yellow Buick wagon jouncing along our rutted driveway. The maples are sprouting small green leaves, all alight, a milky furze that dresses their mossy gray limbs. The willow on the lawn is newly dressed, a dryad in a shining, transparent, pale green shift. The oaks are budding too. The last patches of snow are shrivelling, running over the lawn in clear trickles on the downslopes, surrounded by dingy, matted grass that shows signs of life once more. And we too are here still, blinking at the creamy sun that rides every day a shade higher, gradually filling out. We're ready for them, not because they bring us any news of the great world, but because a letter arrived the other day, declaring an outing for us all. Liz wrote it in her detached manner. It told us, that having at last reached Seattle, Leo seemed tired, complaining that he hadn't recovered from that Victoria virus. That hour after hour he'd gripped the wheel of their new International Harvester wagon, white-knuckled, chewing on the inside flap of a cheek, no longer talking to them. That he'd grown changeable, preoccupied. Then irritable and absent-minded. Finally, withdrawn. No sooner lodged on the small rented islet miles out in Puget Sound, their larder stocked, the salmon rigs readied, than he'd insisted on packing, ferrying back, and turning south, south, and south again, driving over three thousand miles as though pursuing a rainbow whose foot was planted somewhere thataways. As though a pot of gold waited in Mazatlan, that billboard paradise. The only gold was dysentery, paid out by herself and the children. Leo suffered not at all in his gut. When they were taken to the hospital for two days, Leo was lost . . . it must have been a suicide. What else is 57 Quaaludes? But in the end he refused to lie down at all after having paced the beach fourteen hours, dazed, tranquilized, and also horny as hell. He came in himself for the stomach pumping—she'd found him at the other wing when she was discharged. Meanwhile, their Harvester wagon was dismantled right beside their cabana. Nothing left but the logo, which Leo skimmed off into the sea. They were permitted to fly out only after the doctor had written a very expensive report certifying to the authorities that it had been merely food poisoning. Not to worry: all was well—after a round of twelve electroshocks and eight months of intensive therapy with a hardheaded psychiatrist. And Liz meant hardheaded—the guy had read nothing but textbooks all his life—he thought everything Leo had ever thought he'd thought was a myth. And he has a point there at that, Leo agrees. Not that he remembers much if anything of the whole year. Otherwise his head, ha ha, is clear. So they were driving up for an outing, she wrote. And here indeed they are, pulling up to the house.

"Let's see if Leo's still cracking his knuckles," my wife remarks aside, as the door swings open and Liz heaves her thick thighs sideways to get out. Poor man, it occurs to me: drove all the way down to that hot sea, where Charon's barge lay hove-to outside Mazatlan waiting, and it's passed him by. All he will have had forever now was the midlife crisis, that dreadful pilgrimage expunged from recollection. Liz, however, chain-smoking and hacking, will remember it to us in every detail. Yet the story will lack the one detail one cares to hear: what it felt like to stumble, to go over the edge: that prolonged moment's months of dying as things silently lifted themselves from their places and drifted outward, removing themselves from him in all directions. That agony unknown, one lives in the poverty of mere ignorance. Yet one lives. There is that. They have given him life. Life in ignorance, in exchange for the knowledge of death. His year they can never return to him. Her letter had closed by saying that Leo was even taking an interest in things again. And here he is, extricating himself from behind the wheel as their boy and girl clomp up the porch steps to where ours are waiting for them. Leo still looks like Leo. Well, we are all changed, yet no one knows.

I know. He is a frightened man. That much I discern from our conversation late that night in front of the fireplace after the rest have gone to bed. Doc Hardhead has cured him of the illusion that whole being is possible, let alone desirable. A naïve wish merely. Everything is only things. Their presences have been removed. They never were. To will is false, dreaming. Willing, we add increment to increment as day is added unto day. And we? At best, a sum to be totalled never. That is how things seem to him now. Not too bad at that, either. And grace? I say. Leo is stocky; his hair has gone white suddenly, a thick, short-cropped thatch. The ancient acne scars are deep pocks now. He doesn't even smile at this. "What is grace?" he returns. "You surprise me. Really." Sometimes I surprise myself, I say. And go on: It's the one thing the world cannot supply. "You surprise me," he says again. But we ourselves can supply all the rest: realism, *le tacte des choses,* even, at the end, clarity, acceptance, resignation. "Enough for me," Leo murmurs, finishing his bourbon, "no more, please. There is no other world now." But I pour myself another measure of Wild Turkey and, laughing, tell him: The path to the possible lies right here at one's feet. We are always and right now too on that unmarked path. And surrounded by the presences of every thing unrevealed, luminous as these glowing coals. Grace may descend and open our eyes. Or grace may erupt from within. "Thanks, but no thanks," Leo says, holding his empty glass upside down. "I'm going to sleep. You've had enough too, brother." Just trying it on for size, I say. No harm done? "Enough is enough. What more could you need?" Myself, Leo. "Wish I could help you," is all he says.

The next morning's clear. You never can be sure around Arcady though. We'd travelled fifty miles north by noon, climbing up into the mountains. There's a place in the National Forest I know, a campground that would be empty this time of year. I am driving; Liz is beside me; Harriet's behind me and Leo next to her; the four kids are playing poker in the back, the dog between their legs serving as the support for their board. The trip's pleasant, traffic light. I am glad to find the narrow access road into the upper valleys open. The water from the snowpack above is trickling out under the snow banked on both sides of the road, and steams up on the midday warmth. Twenty miles away from the main road, the mountains are altogether deserted. We are winding along, a little too fast for comfort as Harriet keeps reminding me by taps on my shoulder, when there is an angry beeping from behind. Liz has been rattling away with her stories about their junket across America last June, and I'd not paid attention to the rear. There'd been a glint of sun off a windshield earlier; but I had not been aware that now there was a muddy jeep tailgating us, weaving from side to side. Now its horn is beeping at us. From the look of it, they were two fishermen in green and brown camouflage jumpsuits—their assembled rods are clipped to the roof. They are too late to do any fishing today, I remark; and besides, most of the fish are gone up here—the rain and snow is polluted by sulfuric acid from the Midwest and the streams are dead. "Let them pass," my wife urges me. I can't, the road's too narrow and the shoulders are oozing mud: they'll have to wait. They keep on pushing me, though it should be plain this big Chrysler wagon fills the road. They'd have to wait for a turnout. And five winding miles go by, up and down, the wide places blocked by mounds of melting snow, and they pressing just behind, not letting up with that beep-beeping. I hold steady and hog the crown in the center of this road. Too damn slow for them: I can see them in my rearview mirror mouthing obscenities.

Then it happens. There is a hairpin on a downslope, and I enter it staying close on the left, even though anyone coming down from the mountains must be invisible to me if he's going to come around that bend just now. Right there that jeep makes its move, comes roaring along passing on the right. Are they crazy? I yell. As they draw alongside, the driver's shouting and thumping his horn. These upcountry Kallikaks! I laugh. But just ahead, we suddenly notice the road's broken right off the side of the mountain. And these two red-faced and squinty-eyed characters, half-turned round at us and shaking their beer cans threateningly, never even see the jagged edge of the crevasse yawning there. The jeep just hurtles out, turning end over end, and vanishes. The women gasp, but I keep on, hugging the half of the road that remains on the left, not even tapping my brakes.

"Goodbye, you guys," our boy calls, and the other three kids laugh, as though it's the climax of some TV chase. The curve goes sloping wickedly down into a half-mile of straightaway, where I can see a shiny slick ahead: a ripple of ice where water freezes on the asphalt in the shadow of the mountain. No choice. We hit it coasting. "My god!" my wife wails from behind me. The snow tires whir as the heavy Chrysler slides out, and to our silent horror we also find ourselves flying in slow motion off the road.

Somehow, nothing more terrible happens. The car simply tilts, nosing forward, and slithers grumping down the long wet scree of slate and granite shale blasted from the flank of the mountain when the road was cut through up there. Down, down, down. We come to rest a thousand feet below on a soft, wide spill of gravel where a stream runs clear beside a naked stand of second-growth birch and alder. A calm glade, the young spring sun slanting into it from the south through the vee between two snow-covered peaks. Just right for our picnic! I hear myself announce.

For some minutes we sit there, stunned. Then Leo opens his door and gets out. Liz lets hers swing wide, but doesn't move, half-consciously flipping a cigarette up from the ever-present pack in her fist, bringing it to her mouth and stroking her lighter across it. My wife pushes her door open wide, lets her long legs hang out, reaching to touch the solid ground. I turn and see that she has her right arm on the shoulder of our girl behind her; but she is staring at the toe of her boot, which makes a slow and thoughtful circle over a layer of rotting brown birch leaves that covers the wet pebbles. I stay in my seat, holding the wheel hard after having cut the ignition. Leo walks around the car, kicking the tires. Three times he circles the car, inspecting the damage. His hands are on his hips. He stops finally, looking up at the mountain vaguely. He sighs deeply and says to no one in particular, "Now whose fault was that?" Liz must recognize some oddness in his tone, for she lays a restraining hand on my arm, leans across me heavily to look up at him, and says sharply, "You know better than to blame anyone, Leo!" Leo turns his unfocussed eyes down and says sweetly, to me, I think, and not to his wife, whose tousled head lies on my chest, "What do you think of your god now?" I respond, startling him, But I have no god. "Then where in hell are we!" Somewhere, Leo. "Not good enough!" We're two hours north of

Arcady, I continue, and still alive. “Not good enough!” he shouts. “Leo darling—” Liz cries.

He turns, striding away to the southwest, where the weakening sun is drifting towards the shoulders of the mountains we entered an hour or so ago. The shade that lengthens over this gorge into which we have fallen seems to drop the temperature ten degrees: a sudden chill without a breeze. The sweat springing from my body runs down icy inside my clothes. “Where are you headed?” Liz calls out plaintively. He halts, half-turned towards us in farewell, to observe, “We'll never get out alive.” None of that! I hiss after him. I'm thinking of the children, who are just clambering out the back of the wagon after the dog, who sneezes violently and strolls over to the stream to lap at it. “Someone's got to pay for the accident, or we're done for. We need a scapegoat. And I'm it. So long.” A wave of the hand, and he heads off.

Leo! I'm angry with him, seething with indignation. Liz shoves me violently out of my seat, and I am up and trotting after him. He turns slowly, smiling blissfully. I never do see his balled fist coming up, in fact: he has not swung, but only lifted it, locking his shoulder as his heels plant themselves to meet my headlong rush. I am knocked sprawling, the wind out of my lungs, by the blow to my heart. And he resumes his deliberate stroll away into the wilderness. “Stop him!” Liz croaks. “Oh my god,” my wife moans again. But the children are laughing at the tableau: this isn't serious. Yes it is. I get to my feet. A smooth stone, the size and shape of a goose egg, in my hand. Without consideration, I hurl it after Leo. It flies true; it catches him behind his right ear. He drops face down on the edge of the cold purling brook. Harriet's voice from the car, bitter, “That's stopping him.”

Leo's face is drained white; against the dingy basaltic sand where he lies, it's like the upturned belly of a dead fish. But a line of blood oozes from the corner of his mouth, congealing purplish on his chin. There is a tear welling in the corner of his eye, and its lid trembles faintly. A slow pulse in his throat beating stubbornly tells me he is coming to. He's alive, I call over my shoulder to the women.

Leaving Leo to them, I set out in the other direction, following the water. The four children trail after me; they insist on helping me search for the way out. The last thing I see, as we turn the bend, heading upstream into the woods, is Liz kneeling, cradling Leo's head upon her lap, and my wife dipping her blue bandana in the clear water. Our black mastiff's glad to be out of the car and running ahead, quartering the rudimentary track as though he were out for bear. Silently, the children file behind me. Save your strength! I have admonished them. "Why?" my son said, sceptical as always. For the way back. "Ah," he replied, as though he knew what he was saying, "I forgot about that." How could you? "Because you're always saying there's only one way to go—forward."

If that's what he's learned from me, I muse during the next hour's trek over broken ground where the winter's debris has blocked the way along the noisy stream—timber, boulders, slides and snow-filled gullies, mushy soft ground covering the wide places around the little tributary freshets from above, full of melting ice and brush—if that is so, then I've taught a hard truth to these children. Will they remember it, or even understand it later?

Then we stand, surprisingly, on a road that comes out of this wood, fording the brook at a natural dam made of gravel and flat stones, a rapid on our side, a pool below a fall on the other, and it leads away, still following the water, but on higher ground. On our left, the mountain slopes vertically up to where the paved road rides its shoulder a thousand and more feet above, and fades away into a cold white mist that is already descending from the peak. This track's perhaps an ancient logging way. The going's easy now, and we gladly march along. Up ahead, a bend; when we approach it, the dog's on the other side, planted squarely in the middle, his hackles bristling with alarm. He sniffs the air, his great fierce head turning this way and that; his hind legs quiver visibly. That's not like this brute.

And there's a light ahead. We keep on, the dog bringing up our rear now, reluctant. The children haven't remarked his odd behavior, but follow me humming a tuneless anthem together. The light appears to come from inside a house now visible through the trees. A dark, dank place it seems as we come up to it, though rather large for these parts. Gabled with Victorian scrollwork everywhere; a lofty porch, built up twelve feet with fieldstone, mossy black with age. The wood once painted red and white has long since faded to a blackish carmine, wide swaths of mildew everywhere, and wet rot. At the roadside a mailbox on a crumbling cedar post; gothic script: Peavy. A signboard propped against the trunk of a great hemlock that stands beside the sinking, overgrown flagstone walk: Peonies—Honey—Flowering Judas—For Sale. Off to one side there are indeed old hives scattered among the unkempt growth of what must have been an orchard once upon a time: the hives are tumbled about, broken, buried in leaves and trash and rotten snow.

"What a witchy place!" croons Leo's girl, and they all giggle with her. On the sagging moldy post at the top of the twelve broken steps to the high porch there's another sign, scrawled with a brush dipped in tar: Do Not Disturb. Yet another board tacked beside the screen door: No Trespassers. The hell with that! I grumble, and rap firmly at the lintel.

No answer. Knock again. The dog, who has kept back and waits below on the muddy walk, growls low and warningly. Sounds from inside. A light now edging the door on the inside, a heavily scarred oak door, its once white-painted surface all peeling, the gray grain's whorls and waves napped, roughened by long exposure. It opens slowly, scraping along the splintery threshold. An old woman stands there, shawled with an afghan, a sagging gray cardigan buttoned over a gray flannel shirt. A black and stained serge skirt hangs to her ankles, which sink into loose, unlaced workshoes. She holds a kerosene lamp up towards us.

Have you got a telephone? I ask her. She seems not to understand me. I say that we have been in an accident, that our car has come down the mountain, from up there. She looks at me with anger. Doesn't she believe me? Nobody's hurt, I add—but we have got to find a way up again. Can she tell me where to go for help? Behind us, the dog's barking now, barking and whining at once. "Yeh'd be Jews," she mutters then, and spits with contempt. She makes to swing the door shut. But my boot's planted there. She looks down, baffled. Then she raises her lamp to peer at us again, lifting her wrinkled brown face to study us from under the ravelled rim of a black straw bonnet she wears perched incongruously atop her head; its fusty old satin ribbons are tied beneath her chin as if they held her loose jaw and clacking dentures in place. She is angry. Her head shakes with rage. But my boot stays, holding open the door she's pressing at. Her voice grates, "That's the way for yeh now." I turn in the direction she has pointed, and the door is slammed shut.

We march down from that rickety porch. The dog's happy to be running again, away from that place. On the road once more, and pursuing it to the right, we see through the thinning trees what look like distant lights. They flicker from what seems a low valley.

Setting out briskly, we emerge after a few hundred yards to find ourselves on sloping ground. It's darkening, and a chilling wind sweeps at us as we move quickly down. Is it a sunken meadowland, a floodplain ahead, or deep water? The children are flagging, so I slow our pace. We can only go where this track leads us anyway. And in an hour we discover what was barely glimpsed from the high ground we'd left behind: our way ends, abruptly, at a black lake. In fact, the road runs right into the lake, into ice-strewn waters that splash against the short, driven by the wind. The shore is littered with water-logged old trees, half-floating, half-snarled in great heaps and tangles to right and left. Impassable: swamp: mud, dried calamus and sumac brittle in the cold wind; withered; dead.

No lights anywhere. Wherever that village was, it's utterly hidden from sight now. The dog stands silent, his tail tucked between his legs, head down. The children cluster against me. Beside the road, there is a stack of old railroad ties. I am thinking that I had been hoping for salvage like that, railroad ties to shore up the borders of a rock garden I had planned once. Here they are, free for the taking. What a fortunate fall! I say, smiling. The children look up at me, puzzled. The littlest one whimpers, trying not to cry. I stoop, and take her in my arms.

Valley

It is axiomatic, my old teacher maintained, that to do good work demands submersion in, and identification with, your subject. My silence in his seminars signified resistance to his lesson. He warned me, that although I might go on to make a name for myself, sometime, somewhere, I must find myself faced with the choice: either accept the human condition, or abandon all hope of understanding.

What if I refuse? In that case I should be finished, he said, and my life would have been wasted. I raised my eyebrows. "You think me a coward for not refusing." I sighed and said nothing. He tilted back in the old oak chair behind the heavy-grained, dark, scarred oak desk he'd brought to his new office. These relics of the last century, the legacy of his teacher, didn't go at all with the new bronze, anodized aluminum bookcases and functional office furniture the University had installed in this air-conditioned, glass and stainless-steel showcase for social science, flush with grants of millions from the Institutes of Mental Health and the National Science Foundation. "And you even think I'm a fool. Why? Because I've accepted the human lot? Let me tell you this: it's the only way to learn anything worth knowing." He stuffs that rough shag into his sour, burned-out briar, and lights it with blackened, horny fingers, their long nails yellowed and caked with filthy dottle. Still I say nothing. Which upsets him. Which seems a continued denial. He adds, absolutely, puffing away, "And the only way to live. You'll find out. Whether you like it or not."

And it is twenty years later that I have recalled that late spring day in his office just before noon. I can see, as if I were still sitting facing him, the sweet fresh green leaves of the ancient elm trees on the wide lawn surrounding that building. New leaves of milky light green that made the great canopies glow with the dewy and moving light that poured into them from the Midwestern June sky. Tall elms with thick yet graceful, finely ridged, gray-black trunks that soared up and outward like the slender forms of caryatids, like silent women with arms that extended in long, drooping branches, immense women. I'd forgotten that hour for twenty years. It comes to me now in this darkness, in this waiting solitude in which I sit, seventy feet below the surface of the earth, at the bottom of a smooth round shaft in the Valley of Sacrificing.

He'd taught us well, actually. Our group, his choice students, coming to him at the end of the epoch of discoveries, had succeeded everywhere. Meticulous observers, prodigious collectors, respected recorders and analysts of the peoples with whom we had sojourned. Our books were many, immediate classics. We'd done splendidly for science and humanity. What it cost us, even we did not know. How could we? What is there but success?

And yet all along, in many difficult situations, I knew that the choice he'd said awaited me somewhere, sometime, had not presented itself. Where was it then? And when it would appear, blocking my way, must I believe that I should have to give up human understanding? Was there truly no other way to live?

My stool is a rough block of granite. The vertical shaft above me is about six feet in diameter: there is no means by which one could hope to ascend it. The daylight up there, visible as a pale shimmering blue-white disk no larger than a silver dollar, is brightening. Soon the sun will pass over and send a dazzling beam straight down to illuminate my spherical chamber.

I know quite well, after years of visiting these people, what this situation is. And I know as well as they do what it means. Once a year, for the wellbeing of the nation, when the sun shall come to pass directly over the mouth of a shaft sunken into the earth, there will be a sacrifice. This nation is not cruel or wanton. Neither is it stupid, insensitive, or savage. The people will soon enough be indistinguishable from the rest of humanity, getting, spending, producing and consuming more or less efficiently. In such a matter as this, however, some things remain the same, and time has no significance. The Valley of Sacrificing is a wide plain beside a round, shallow lake. It is surrounded by the high walls of a long extinct volcanic crater, mile-high walls terraced by concentric rings that run right to the top; fertile, planted with orchards and gardens. Thirteen villages lie in this basin, linked in a circle of twenty-eight miles. At the center is the lake, surrounded by this plain, dotted with many thousands of these shafts, each covered with a carved stone like a manhole cover, or sun disk. The whole mosaic constitutes a useful calendar of great antiquity and unperturbed accuracy, although there may be shafts that have been used more than once in the long millenia. The people, however, insist not. They assert this calendar of yearly shafts the one constant, the only truth in the world they know. Great skeptics, my people. But I am a greater skeptic yet. Perhaps my eyebrows lifted and revealed my thought. Perhaps that is why I woke to find myself here at the bottom of this shaft.

I never suspected they would punish me in this manner. I am not suitable either, I had thought, as victim or hero. Or hero-victim. In their own way they are gentle, even civilized. If fixed in this ritual. They must have set me down here as I slept; for that, they must have put me into a deep, long slumber.

I have climbed down a dozen of these shafts. At the bottom of each there lies a skeleton. There are the usual utensils for sustaining life, or comforting it afterwards: a dish, a flask, a cup. Nothing more: no jewelry, no tools, no weapons. Except for a well-made knife of flint, or a sharp obsidian blade or horned antler. The meaning of that instrument is obvious: the victim had been given food, but he was also expected to become a hero—to offer himself to the sun at the hour in which its blinding glare stands overhead filling the hole on the one day of the year. How many of these bones, though, had been heroic?

For some years I'd wondered what the sacrificed underwent, what it meant for him? One knows what it is worth to the nation, to the way people are situated in the world, to the structure of organized social life: by this one constant they have persisted from the beginning. Yet who has discovered what it is for the victim? Without that knowledge, what is all the rest worth? You have been sent out, offered up to the goal of our human existence—and what you achieve remains absolutely unknown to those for whom you had gone ahead. So here now is my opportunity to learn what we should know. It is in fact a gift, a great gift. I am not surprised to receive it, after all.

But where is my dish, my flask, my cup? Where the knife for my food or my self-immolation? I am naked and cold and hungry instead. But, knowing my people, I am patient too. They will do this right, as in everything else, or so it has seemed to me over the years of my study.

And it is good to think that while I am given my chance to know what I have always wished and thought essential, I shall also be conferring the usual expected benefits upon the people. Nothing better can be imagined.

At last, sounds from above. I look up. The round opening is darkened: something blocks the light. It moves. I watch, trying to grasp what I see. Finally, as the occluding form seems to be turning and dwindling, I realize that someone is being lowered down the shaft. As he descends, he seems to dwindle, because his approaching body doesn't fill the cylinder. A trick of perspective? But also apprehended truly, for finally, seated in a loop of thick rope, there is a boy of no more than twelve. Naked, beardless, beautiful; innocent of understanding. He has been washed, polished with oil. On his lap, the dish, a loaf of bread, the flask, containing whatever fermented drink is thought suitable—I can scent its vinous fumes already—and the cup, all of rough, undecorated, unglazed clay. Also a fine, long blade of steel. My own knife, in fact. They have displayed their subtle thought and gentle courtesy. They have honored me.

Seated, dandled in the swaying rope, the boy recites a formula, singsong as children do with words they have memorized. These are secret words. Ancient words. They can have no meaning for the child, of course. To the one who hears, they are everything. And I listen carefully. I must not forget them. I must remember them. I must take them with me.

He finishes. He hands me the dish, the flask, the cup. As for the knife, he hesitates. It lies across his smooth thighs as he swings in the loop, turning easily, swaying like a pendulum.

Tell me again, I say. He smiles and repeats his strange recitation. I have it now. I do not know what the words signify, but I have them by heart now. What more is needed?

I take the knife. The child smiles. I have never seen this lad in my village. He must be a changeling. Human sacrifice has been outlawed for many years by the great world, but some remote nations still practice it in this way: they exchange children between villages. It is not proven; but one intuitively knows it.

With one swift thrust, I have severed his neck from ear to ear. The sun at that moment stands overhead; it fills the shaft with light. I am so dazed that I am spared the terrible sight of the child's ruined body, which with one swift motion I have thrown from the cable's loop and replaced with myself.

I am winched up, slowly, slowly, to the surface of the world again. When I step forth among my people, my hand and arm crusted with blood like my knife, they step back, withdrawing from me in a widening ring, appalled at what I've done. In silence, they turn away. I know that I shall never be able to speak with them again. I have made the great refusal. I have left all community behind me for good, forever. I do have the old words, words that came from the remote past, words that lead to a future unimaginable. But nothing else. And to whom should I ever utter them? Yet what was most important to know, the knowledge that could be gained only by the having remained below to die, I shall never have the chance to earn again.

Siren Song

IN VENICE for a couple of days, lecturing for the Department of State on American Civilization. I've come up from Rome, given one talk this morning at Cà Foscari, the University of Venice, and am leaving for Trieste tomorrow. Approaching the Ponte Accademia from the Rialto, I notice a familiar name on a kiosk: Lenore Heller. The placard's current: the concert is tonight at La Fenice. Well, she's made it this far. Heller has certainly done well.

Lenore is the girl downstairs in the building I'd lived in as a child. We'd walked to gradeschool together from the time we were six years old. Junior and senior high too. I had gone off to college in the Midwest, she to some conservatory, Oberlin, I suppose. She had a voice. We'd dated occasionally: movies, dances in Poe Park, walks by the Hudson. Heavy petting in the waiting room—her father was a doctor, and his office was next to their apartment on the ground floor. Now to my surprise I recall—how old had we been, eight? nine?—I recall Lenore lying supine. I see myself dropping to my knees there in the basement coal room, a vast chamber that was filled to its lofty, arched ceiling beneath the marble checkerboard-square lobby each September with tons and tons of anthracite, an Olympus of small, damp, hard black stones. The trucks would back up on Mace Avenue, and for a day or so the coals would be sent pouring down a chute through a little window grate that opened on the front garden. At one end of the coal room the great roaring furnace stood in a wall of firebrick, its iron doors hooked open with a long rod every few hours by Jimmy or Frank, the elevator men who stoked them.

And there we are one sleeting afternoon in late November, an hour or two before my birthday party. I'd broken open a carton, laid it out on the slope of coal; and Lenore lay back on it. How we got there, or why she had led me there, a light in her eyes, I do not know. Nevertheless, here is the sight of her, an oozing scab on one of her pudgy knees. She lies still, her head at rest on her left hand, gazing at me, her wavy light brown hair spread out over the black pebbles. She draws her red tartan kiltie up with her right hand until it lies rucked on her white crepe blouse. Her naked, creamy, round little belly swells and sinks as she breathes evenly and deeply. Her legs are sprawled. Her feet are held down by her saddle shoes, her thick white socks coated with coal dust. I kneel and lean towards her to press my cheek against the bare skin of her virgin lips, which grow hot and moist, opening to me. As the roaring crackle of the furnace fills the place, her voice, melodious even then, seems to be singing my name from far above me somewhere; and now her drumming heels send coals rattling down the slope.

I walk heavily over the boards of the Ponte Accademia, concentrating on that vision. Yet hard as I press my thought, my memory remains dark as that coal room: there is nothing more it can yield me. I pass a few nasty alleys and stand at the box office: SOLD OUT. I leave a note with a clerk in the manager's office and board the *vaporetto* for the island of Murano, where I eat a leisurely dinner. Venice is not that filled in early May, so there is no line at the Campanile when I return by late afternoon. Up there, I walk the parapet, enjoying the sight of the Queen of the Adriatic spread out below me.

In the evening, an envelope awaits me at the *pensione;* a heavy card inside it, its border embossed with a wreath of bay leaves. "What do you take me for?" it reads. "Of course I remember! My dressing room: 11:00. Lenore." More than half a lifetime ago. Yet she's no stranger to me.

Supper I take alone, meditating on nothing in the nearly empty diningroom of the Accademia, walking out afterward to the Piazza San Marco for a liqueur and a cigar at Florian's. The sun's already gone, leaving a mauve band over the west, fading into the black pall over Mestre. An ivory moon, full and benign, hovers just over the Palladian façade of San Giorgio, lighting the long line of the Lido strand with a ribbon of silvery blue. Gondolas are cruising out on the Lagoon, their lights bobbing in the wakes of the vaporetti and taxis. The air is crisp yet mild, the vast Piazza strung with strollers, tourists uttering their low and pleasant cacophony of tongues, the laughter of many languages rising through the flutter and whirr of pigeons flocking and wheeling overhead. I head across the piazza about 10:45, enter a narrow vicolo leading from the cathedral, and thread my way to La Fenice.

The doors to the opera house are closed; but the lights tell me that the program is still playing. I show the usherette my card from the great diva, and ask my way to her dressing room. I'll have to go out and around to the rear of the theater, where there's another entrance for Staff. I do that. The rear of La Fenice lies on a narrow *canaletto* bordered by a pavement wide enough only for two; there is hardly any flow, and the viscous surface of the black water is oil-daubed, flashing velvety rainbow colors where the lamplights strike it. Trash wallows on it, rotting vegetables, pulped oranges and banana peels, parts of crates bumping against bottles, rocked by the wavelets made by cargo barges passing in the adjoining alleys. A fat rat scuttles past my shoes and plops from the edge into the reeking dark. The walk is protected by a thin, rusting iron railing. A dim lantern illuminates the stage door.

I open it to find myself in gloom. There are worn stone steps leading up on my left, a stairway winding along the outer wall of the building. I ascend, heading up into darkness. One flight, and music is audible, filtered through the wall on my right, and through barred windows and closed little doors at each landing. I can't quite make it out. At first, only the grand thumping tympani, blaring brass, muffled, distorted strings. Otherwise it's quiet as I climb these walled-in steps.

At the third turning of the second stair, there are voices singing, and a chorus discernible too. And then, coming to the landing where I stop to breathe, the music flows through from the hall inside: the last part of the Ninth Symphony: the Ode to Joy! I had arrived just as it commenced. Eleven o'clock, the climax still to come. I halt in my tracks, entranced by the music's growing glory, fitful though it is from backstage, and garbled by the intervening baffles of old stage sets between the orchestra and myself. And, wasn't that Heller's voice, rising, sinking, swelling and swooping exultantly above all the others? So that's what's become of her—my Lenore!

I am not, however, to hear the last, triumphant measures.

There's a tumult rising from below: the confused thunder of many feet. I turn and see a mob of fans pouring up the dark narrow stairs, all laughter and chattering. They too could have heard the finale of the Ode to Joy, with her voice like a phoenix flying above that prayer of hymning celebrants. Yet to them it seems unimportant. They gabble, they squeal, and it's all lost as they flow around me, blocking my way, filling the vacant corridor ahead in their excitement. They wave papers, photographs, album covers over their heads. I can scarcely make out the clamorous applause coming from inside the house, so noisy is this claque of heedless youngsters.

Still, I try to elbow my way through. A girl turns furiously on me. I must get through, I say. Let me pass, I say, I have an appointment with La Heller. I knew her once in person, I say.

"Up yours!" she snorts, and the two boys with her lock their arms against me. The packed crowd of two or three dozen Italians will never let me pass, that's clear. No reaching her now. I can wait, but how long? Who knows if she'll be even there when I finally attain the door to her dressing room? And why should she wait for me? And won't we both be gone tomorrow?

Down the strait winding stairway once more. The way darkens, the lights are dimmed. I place my feet cautiously before me, testing the dangerous steps with care, hoping to make my way down unhurt out of La Fenice.

Courtly Love

AND SHE WROTE ME a letter after she'd run away from him. To say she wanted me but couldn't have me. To say she was unlisted. To say, if you please, she needed to be by herself. Not that she desires being alone. No, she aches for me from head to toe. As an ontological proposal she puts it. To be by myself. *By* meaning "beside." *By* signifying, too, the cause of which she might come to seem the effect. "A white phantom is what I am now," it reads, "though between us, true-tempered as ever, the sword of passion lies. My darling, you must abandon the quest, abandon all questing if you wish to find me again. You will need to hunt for me no longer then. There's nothing to be found; there is no one to seek. Then I shall be for you." Nice letter for your mistress to write. The woman thinks to liberate herself by hiding. So she had left him for good—and me too, imperfect as I am. How could anything be good this way?

And it was not good. Summer had passed. Autumn brought little change. New York never cooled: the days shrank drearily in dust and gritty touches of feebly circulating air. No rain or frost, no currents of piney wind from the Adirondacks or Catskills, already frozen and gray, no sleet or hint of storm from the North Atlantic. Only a stationary mass of high-pressure hot air blanketing the entire zone until it seemed as if we were to have to live floundering at the bottom of a pool of acid industrial waste and the exhaust pollutants produced by all the machines that kept us going. An emergency that had not yet been conceived and grasped as the onset of a state of disaster. Rich and poor, we were all in this together. Yet everything proceeded as usual in our mighty metropolis. How could it not?

And I too went on as usual. Each morning I rose and went off to work with all the others under that sere yellow-brown pall enveloping us. Struggle never ceases. The quality of life had altered, not its style, since we can know no other here, where the poor believe themselves richer in fact than they would be elsewhere. I did not know how I missed her. We were through with one another, but not finished. There seems to be a difference. When this occurred to me, I understood that what grew in me day by day was wrath, a charge accumulating until it filled me. Where was there place in me for my bones, my organs, my muscles and flesh? Yet in the mirror this scarred body seemed whole, its clothes fitting as well as ever. Was this dense wrath unreal? I knew better. One night in late November I read her letter again. There should be a clue.

And suddenly there it was: the zip code stamped on the envelope! Flushing Meadows, in Queens. I'd never replied to that horrible farewell statement of hers; nevertheless, I thought she would use a post office box for protection, that it would be in the station near the park that had been the site of the great New York World's Fair of my childhood, erected on top of the garbage dumps that had filled the swamps of old, making marvelous futuramas out of the midden of the present. If *I* could, anyone would find her, even he, the husband that sent her an allowance. No matter what it cost him, he was satisfied to support her; he's that way; he loves her; it's all he knows. By keeping her, he kept me too; and by keeping me, he kept her. That is what she believed.

And thought would last forever. However, we changed, if she did not. Whereupon she had disappeared, upsetting the whole world. To find her again now is not so easy. I could try. If it weren't too late. Although it was past midnight, I'd never get to sleep: that numeral would dance in the darkness before me. I dressed and went out.

And it was 1:00 when I reached Flushing Meadows, in Queens. The nighttime was less suffocating than our days: the inversion had lifted and let some of the ruined atmosphere drain away. Overhead hung the rancid half of the old moon, sagging, jaundiced. The borough was quiet: Sunday night, and people getting whatever rest there might be for the week to come. I found the post office: its empty flagstaff stuck out over the sidewalk. She should be holed up somewhere within walking distance, and not in an apartment: she needs space to dance in. It would be some loft. Alongside the

El tracks were old factory buildings, garages, warehouses. In five minutes' cruising I spotted the only light left in this sleeping world. She never sleeps. There she'd be.

And was. I ascended to the seventh floor in a freight elevator large enough to carry my car, too, and knocked on the iron-sheeted factory firedoor. Music inside somewhere, muffled by thick walls: her radio playing as always. No answer. I kicked at it three times. She knows my kind of banging. No answer. I am turning away for good when there is the scuffling of slippered feet. Five complex seals are unbolted, the door lever is wrenched from my hand and the heavy door heaved at me. I am stunned by the blow to my nose and forehead, blinded by the bank of glaring spotlights. Confused, rocking on my heels, I hear her singing out, "Darling, is it you?" As though she had never changed utterly, had never broken it off, never fled and left me. Which she had.

And leading me by the hand, stroking my forehead, kissing my nose and eyes tenderly, she reproached me for my silence. "I knew you'd find me—if only you looked. But you didn't." As though I'd given up, refused, rejected, betrayed her. Which I hadn't. I'd accepted her loss and gone on alone with nothing, certainly not myself. She was my being, wherever that is. This occurred to me as I brimmed with that fossilizing wrath that filled my soft inner parts, which were life. Love's anguish. The cloying incense of chrysanthemum and cedar purling up from a little bronze frog on the floor near her bed reminded me of it all again. I stood gazing at the wide, quivering waterbed from which she'd been aroused. It was covered with a shroud of cloth-of-gold: millefleurs decorated its ground, ruby- and sapphire-petalled, and the center was emblazoned with a great red stag that held suspended between its nine-point rack a blazing emerald the size and shape of the heart. The rest of the studio was drab, the ancient factory walls painted the gray of cinderblock. The floor was all new hardwood, bleached and finished for dancing. And she in a gauze saffron robe with winged sleeves, its hem falling to her thick-sinewed dancer's ankles, revealing the knobs and calluses of her dancer's feet. Patting, pinching me, she circled round, laughing and restless, removing my clothing.

And her voice, hoarse yet musical as always, though I never

could hear its melody: she pitched her words strangely, so that the clear words she spoke were a language that said something else again. What, exactly, it was hard to know. Was that her powerful attraction? Perhaps. The face, with its heavy bones and wide green eyes, the heavy lips and large square teeth, was not beautiful, nor even handsome; the body was dense, strong, still carrying its weight easily at forty. Not a comfortable body, and never graceful on the stage. She had failed at dancing, though it was her life. Dignity was all she owned. What is that today? A thing unknown. Yet I'd missed her truly when she was gone. Was it that barren pathos that attracted me? Perhaps. She was out of style, even her obsessive lust an anachronism in this world of frenzied, shallow greediness. Pointless, really. Too late: I was naked now.

And standing gazing at her bed. She dropped her robe. As she bent to strip that cover from the bed, I saw that her hips were blemished with yellow-green bruises the size of fists, the flesh of her inner thighs traced over by a network of fine purple varicose, the ochre hair in her crotch a long coarse shag tufting back between her buttocks. Even though the incense was drifting about her, the rank odor of her spread, dominating this space: slime-sour, salt. With a moan deep in her chest, she threw herself down on the low bed, rolled over on her back, and stared up at me from her great green sunken eyes as she opened herself wide—mouth, arms, legs. I fell upon her like an oak tree.

And we never slept. Later, I rose to void behind the partition at the other end of the loft. My watch read 6:00. Outside, the streetlights burned in the hazy air before dawn; the trains were starting their morning run, clanking past hollowly below. The sweat of our struggle was crusting on my body in the stifling wintry morning. I was tired, but not eased in body or spirit. Something was terribly wrong. What had I found here?

And returning slowly from behind the partition, I see something that stops me dead. She kneels in the middle of that wide, trembling bed, her arms crossed over her breasts, her head lolling, her deep-set eyes half-closed as if tranced. Two men squat on either side of her. I know them. One is her husband, that stolid broker of office buildings in midtown, a gray man with rough gray skin. The other, his nephew, a lawyer and Mafia bagman, wiry, short, hook-nosed and beetle-browed. They lean against her. The older one presses close to her right side, his chin resting on her shoulder. The younger one presses one hand on her smooth knees, the other cupping his mouth as he whispers in her left ear in a low droning rapid mutter that sounds as though he is instructing her by means of a formula repeated over and over urgently. She sways forward and back, responding to the incantation with her entire being. They are taking possession of her, body and spirit. The words are indistinct: Nebrekkakka Membrekkakka, Membrekkakka Nebrekkakka. Seductive syllables.

And despite everything, despite my indifference, my freedom, my loathing of this whole evil time, I must save her. So intent are they on their filth, they never hear me as I sweep on them, naked as I am. Him I take by the throat in one surge, crushing the life's breath in him, lifting and flinging him aside like a wax figure. On the swing back, my joined fists catch that ferret between the eyes, knocking him cold. As his body tumbles to the floor, it seems to shrivel into a twitching ball of empty clothes.

And she remains kneeling, unmoved, unwakened, unknowing. Sunken into their power, sunken deep, deep. I slap her twice, hard: a right, a left. Her head rolls on her shoulders, her body stays poised, upright, firmly balanced, the arms still crossed over her breasts. I am too late. She is lost to herself. The glassy eyes see nothing, the cheeks are inflamed, swelling, marked by my fingers, and blood trickles from her cut lip. The wreckage is appalling. Nothing is left in this place for me. The old man is as good as dead. His nephew will come to sooner or later, and put a contract out on my life. The year is ending purposelessly. I dress myself.

And as I left, I looked back once: in the weak light of the morning filtering through those dusty frosted panes I saw her kneeling still, as though at prayer. Naked, her dulled yellow hair strewn about her head in tangles like briars, the eyes closed now, her body swaying forward and back on that fluid bed. She seems made of some clayey rock. What kind of being is that?

And at last it is raining. The winter drought has ended, thank god. Sheets of grimy water run over the pavements, black currents coursing along the curbs, dragging paper and rags and bits of wood, the oily sludge flashing rainbows everywhere as the puddles back up from the clogged sewers. Things have not been thrown right. Things have fallen out this way instead.

Prometheus

I WAS SORTING THROUGH the safety-deposit box. I seemed to recollect an old bond that should have been due. I was surprised not to find it. Perhaps it had been redeemed already, the money long spent—yet I had no recollection of it. So our past vanishes utterly and in vain. Something I did find amongst the deeds and certificates and wills, something I'd forgotten was there: a sheet of paper I had brought from an old house in Princeton, taken as a memento.

Each year I used to go East for a week to slog at reading through thousands of wretched college entrance essays for the Educational Testing Service. One afternoon, taking a break from that smoke-filled room we all worked in to enjoy the crisp late September breeze outside, I'd met Mr. Einstein strolling along and accompanied him home to that large, old, dark-panelled house hidden behind the trees near the Institute. He invited me in for a cup of tea. It was pleasant to sit there on the brown plush sofa as the afternoon faded into a weak gold light that burnished the oak walls, glowed on the old furniture and lit the keyboard of the Bechstein with its fringed silk shawl embroidered with flaring poppies, leaving shadowed a sidetable in the alcove that was heaped high with journals and treatises, all cobwebbed, dusty, and apparently untouched for a long while.

Mr. Einstein spoke about his despondency. About the slow, increasingly painful thought of his last years, the incompletion of his general Field Theory, and the difficulty of dealing with metaphor, which lives, he said, a life of its own with no regard for Space and Time. There was something about metaphor, he said. He told me how he had studied English upon his arrival in the United States, taking grammar texts to bed and memorizing the dictionary column by column into the early hours of the morning. For three years he had done that.

So that was how he had got such a command of English, I thought, and so swiftly: that fine restless brain at work day and night. I began to say, Professor, with your mind . . . .

"Nah—ja, ja," he said, puffing away at his acrid pipe, "It's impossible to say anything after all, my son."

But, Mr. Einstein, surely you don't . . . .

"Ja—nah, nah," he said, and smiled kindly at me.

And then, when I dropped by on my own the next afternoon, he was gone. The door stood open; the day was ending in autumn gold again; the garden beyond the French windows was silent, dry, desolate. I roamed about that dim livingroom, touched the piano, the middle *C* I twice sounded rang out blindingly bright in the echoing void. I glanced into his study. A sheet of white paper called out from the typewriter, a letter he'd begun the previous evening. Just a few lines were written there: "My dear children—Although I profoundly regret my role in the invention of the terrible, ultimate machine, I am confident that in the end it may turn out not to be the means of your extinction but that you can find a way to control the powers I have given you and contain them in that infernal box . . . ."

I slipped that letter to us from the platen and walked out the front door again, leaving it ajar. He had never finished it, never signed it. His sorrow and his benediction will go unknown, I suppose, to everyone but myself.

Elijah

I AM STROLLING BY NIGHT like Elijah through one of those narrow passages in Old Jerusalem. A moonless darkness: the shops are shuttered. A curfew stillness: shabby cats sidle along the walls, melt like shadows into cellars. Around a corner a strange light suddenly glares: a harsh propane lantern set on the ground. I can see dark figures by it; they seem to be squatting at an intersection of two of those strait lanes called streets in the Old City's Arab Quarter.

Approaching, I see it is an excavation: three men are not squatting but standing in the pit as in a shallow grave. Hasidim. I stop to watch what they are doing. They have been scrabbling at the earth with their bare hands and have dug up basalt tablets, black stones the size of folios. They seem to be puzzling together over the inscriptions on those stones. Their expressions are a comic mixture of doubt, worry, and bafflement.

I stand there looking down at them, a stranger passing in the dark night. Their black caftans are stained by the dung-colored clay, their high black shoes clotted with lumps of red mud. I am dressed in my casual California clothes: blue espadrilles, orange golf slacks, a white polo shirt worn outside. They look up surprised, when they hear me chuckle.

The first Hasid says in a hoarse, guttural voice, *Why does he laugh? What does he know about these things?*

I reply that there is nothing very important in such writings. And anyway, I know it all by heart. *Nu, so how does he know?* the second Hasid grumbles, annoyed.

Laughter wells up deep inside me, and I hear myself saying, How do I know? I know, I know! I know . . . because . . . I am . . . who I am!

I'm startled to hear these words come from me, actually uttered by my own voice. But they are appalled. Jerking his arms up, cruddy palms outward as though to ward me off, the third Hasid groans a hoarse Yiddish groan, *Vos zogt er?* He lifts his face towards the old smoke-fouled ceiling of the souk, the whites of his eyes turned up in desperate prayer, *Gor meshuggeh iz er! You didn't hear him, Lord! But if you heard him, Lord, don't listen! Oy, oy! Vay iz mir!*

Mystified, frightened, all three shrink against the dank muddy wall of the pit they have dug for themselves in the night, averting their faces, seizing the broad, mink-banded rims of their black hats to shield their eyes from the sight of me standing over them in the white glare of their lantern.

Now that I've said it, now that the secret is out, my laughter brims over, huge laughter echoing out along the dark stony walls of this sour passage. Everybody will hear it, everybody will know. Nothing can be done about it. I had not intended to say anything to anyone ever again, yet the voice spoke of itself. I am laughing fit to be tied. Things are simpler than anyone could have guessed.

The Bird Cage

THE STORM MUST HAVE SWEPT IN some time before dawn. When I woke, I lay listening in the darkness to that metallic December rain lowering over the city, pouring in cold gusts of shrapnel against the windows. The morning turned gray, but never much less than gray; the rain fell full of razors against the walls, as if it meant to scour this century's bitter grime from brick and stone, and wash away the sludge coating the town like an impenetrable callus of lacquer laid on year by year and fixing everything we are in a sterile waste.

I didn't go to work. Towards noon I put on my rubbers, wrapped myself in my fleece-lined raincoat, unfurled my umbrella, and went to keep a lunch appointment at the Four Seasons with an old friend who is a professor of political science. Alex is an urbane, skeptical fellow, and his third book on naval warfare has just been named a Pulitzer Prize volume. It is also a Book-of-the-Month Club selection, and already a Bancroft History Award-winner, which has helped it sell over a half-million copies. Alex is suddenly rich. Today is his sixty-fifth birthday, and he is celebrating alone with me, in honor, he remarks, of my silence.

I toast his inevitable, if late success. We order oysters, a brace of squabs stuffed with wild rice and accompanied by braised morels with a '61 Margaux, baked pears for dessert, espresso. He tells me now that he has never been to sea, and the only battleship he's ever seen was parked at the Brooklyn Naval Yard. His career began with a dissertation in Classics, an analysis of the confusion at the Battle of Actium. His mother had read *Antony and Cleopatra* to him when he was nine years old and semi-delirious with rheumatic fever. His damaged heart put him at a desk in naval intelligence during the war, where he fiddled with battle reports far from any action, and wrote up commendations for commanders. His colleagues have always resented his top clearance; the reviewers call him a crypto-militarist. His work, he avers, is simply dispassionate analysis of webs of lies woven about the accidental maneuvers of masses of men at the mercy of wind and wave: neither art nor science nor tradition rules the warring fleets, though he has never said so before. His laurels surprise him. It means that no one knows anything about anything. "What can we extrapolate from ignorance? Now, Caesar understood the language of the birds, and he taught it to Mark Antony. But Antony was rash: he insulted the Pythia at Delphi. The hag silenced the birds from that time on. Not even sparrows would chatter in his presence afterwards. He was doomed."

Alex took a cab over to the Century Club: he wanted to smoke his cigar and browse through the Audubon quietly until cocktails, when he will be honored by a reception and banquet laid on by his publisher. I went out and walked up to the park through that freezing rain. Outside the Plaza, one old closed hansom stood forlorn, its lantern glowing weakly, the nag covered with a poncho, his head drooping to his knees. A half-dozen ragged sparrows cowered in the poor shelter of his belly, waiting for some grain to spill when he tossed his muzzle to get at the mash sogging in the bottom of the nose bag.

There was no one but the animals at the zoo. Under that pelting black sky towards four p.m., the gray light was fading into an evening that would never come. The air wallowed with blasts of icy wind circling from the east and hurling the rain in drowning sheets. I turned into a doorway and waited. The downpour grew heavier. I went inside. It was the aviary, warm and steamy. The place had been changed since I'd last been there. Now it was all one great cage with narrow winding paths among tiny pools and artificial rivulets under a thin forest of bare trunks and low palm trees and bushes. The collection seemed to be general, composed of waders, raptors, mountain and forest birds, tropical and temperate alike: parrots, macaws, toucans, small ducks, curlews, cranes, herons, flamingoes, doves and ducks, guinea fowl, hawks, ravens, crows, vultures, and eagles. The small birds paddled about and splashed, the waders stalked sleepily, and the greater birds of prey skulked on their naked branches. One great horned owl hooted now and then, frightening none of the others: food was abundant here, and the birds paid no regard to the people who walked about among them with cameras on bright days. I was alone here, though. I sat on a little cast-concrete bench beside a six-inch waterfall, and watched the peacock preen himself, his tail spread out over a patch of dull brown sand. The rain poured steadily on the glass panes of the roof. I looked at the bank of thermostats and hygrometers attached to the trunk of a palm tree and thought, I have not thought a thought in years.

Footsteps on the gravel. A tall woman approaching. She paces very slowly, and stops every other step to gaze down at the waterfowl standing on one locked long leg, heads tucked beneath a wing or beady eyes fixed on nothing. A long gray leather coat wraps her; it is buttoned and belted, despite the lush warmth in the bird cage. Her hair is thick, white, brushed back from her high forehead; it is that stained white of women whose hair was flaxen in youth. Her face is masked to the cheeks by the fur collar of her coat, a yellowish muff now, soiled by the filthy rain of this city, and tatty with age. She does not go by, but rather stops to stand facing me at arms' length. She is very tall: my head, as I sit, comes only to her thighs. Looking at her uptilted face, I see only the large nostrils of a fine aquiline nose: she is staring at the great owl high above me. I turn to see what he's doing. Nothing: he perches on that bare, polished limb of the dead tree, a big motheaten clump, his enormous yellow eyes full of shattered crystal, hexagonal unblinking orbs steady under her gaze.

I break my silence. I come here to look at the birds. I come to hear them. "I know you do," she says. "But I come to see the birds. I come to listen to them." I've come ever since childhood, I add. The place has changed, hasn't it. "I've always come. But it's the same." No, we can be close to the birds now. "Close, but not any nearer." Oh? I say.

She looks down at me, smiling to herself, as if amused by our words. Her face is round and full, with high, slanted cheekbones. I stand up, and find she is a head taller than I. She wears no makeup: her yellowish complexion shows a velvety skin, covered with a network of furred, fine lines. She was, once upon a time, not unhandsome. Wide gray eyes, flecked with faint ochre. As she stands there she seems to sway from the waist, the way a tall pine sways in the breeze on a mountain-side. The scent that comes from her is resinous too, heavier and softer than the turpentine essence some soaps exhale.

How did you know I come here? I ask. “I am a poet,” she replies, still gazing at the owl over my shoulder, “and I know things like that. I’ve come here since the beginnings. I saw the first and I saw the second levels of these walls built on.” She describes the hidden foundations here, as though this dingy granite-bricked building in Central Park were erected upon the lower courses of hand-fitted cyclopean blocks, and those blocks themselves hewn from the knees of Mount Parnassus and laid down like the floor of the temple sanctuary. Kidding her along, I ask, So, you can remember what’s buried beneath our feet? “If poetry must be made, it can be made from stones,” she answers simply, “even out of stones, since bare stones are all we have.” I wouldn’t know, I say. “We veil ourselves in our own darkness,” she adds, speaking to the owl with that low, oracular, yet indifferent voice. I wouldn’t know, I say again, stubbornly.

The peacock screams twice and, folding his great fan of purple eyes into a long train, paces carefully away from us. For the first time, she looks at me, her eyes filming. Her lips curl with mere contempt. They are full lips, dark red lips. She turns from me, whispering, “No, you wouldn’t know, would you.”

I watch her move slowly away. She is really an old woman: her torso is propped upon legs swollen from ankle to hip, as thick and as shapeless as columns of stone. She swings one forward heavily, then the other, her long body rocking from side to side as she progresses, scouring the gravel. Her hair flows down her back like a bleached, coarse mane.

Suddenly the alarm bell sounds, warning everyone it’s closing time. The prolonged clanging disturbs the mixed population of birds; they leap fluttering from the ground, splash up distracted from the shallow wading pools. The smaller birds swirl around the great cage with a flittering of wings; the larger ones flap and float about in random circles and criss-crossings, cawing, crying, clattering their beaks in a terrible discordance. The owl lifts his wings and beats them emptily, shifting the grip on his perch from foot to foot.

I button up and step outside into the dark December downpour. There is no one and nothing in sight.

An Evening in Babylon

THE AD IN THE *Times* announcing the preview of my play perturbed me. The show isn't ready to open. In my opinion, it's nowhere near dress rehearsal. The producer, however, will not listen to me: he dimples with frothy cheer. A born optimist, this Cy Richter is a curly-headed fellow I'd known back in high school. After flunking out of Columbia's College of Physicians & Surgeons, he'd gone and taken a dual degree in Jewish Studies & Sociology, a popular combination nowadays. The director Cy picked for my work is none other than Ezra Pound. Ancient, wrinkled, preoccupied, Pound never speaks. One afternoon, after a garbled reading of my climax, he took me by the elbow and led me aside, only to mumble, "I have talked too much in my life. After all, silence is best."

The theater's located in an old Moorish-style building, once a deconsecrated temple that later belonged to some now-extinct lodge. I catch a cab and head downtown. By the time I get there, an expectant audience fills the hall; many others are scattered through the loges and even up in the two balconies, where I can see their distant, dim faces. Cy stands in front of the lowered golden curtain. I stay at the rear of the theater to watch the proceedings. The house lights are up and Cy is catechizing the audience: he asks it to come forward with ideas for the title, the theme, the plot, the climax, the catastrophe, the resolution, and whatnot else. A mimeographed questionnaire has been handed out at the door, its broad questions marked with multiple choice boxes: POOR, AVERAGE, ABOVE AVERAGE, EXCELLENT, NO BASIS FOR JUDGMENT. People think it's part of the show—everything is entertainment today—and they actually, seriously join in: professional- and academic-looking folks, artist-types, students, the middle-class political characters who attend presidential conventions—just the sort to be excited by a power play like this. And they all have opinions, too! Whenever someone wants to speak, he or she gets up to struggle through the thicket of knees, brushing coats askew on laps, knocking hats off, and striding self-importantly down the aisle to the empty pit where the mikes stand. Hands eagerly wave papers, people volunteer questions, suggest amendments, offer hints to the actors, advice for the director, and even bits of dialogue for the author, whoever he may be.

An hour passes while I listen, pacing back and forth at the rear. At this rate, my drama will never begin. I'm getting annoyed. I fret, anxious to see how the play will go, ready or not. Still the curtain remains down, the house lights bright. I feel as if I were not at a play, but attending one of those tumultuous sessions during the French Revolution. I am beginning to regret the day I committed myself to paper.

Finally Cy Richter gavels. The audience hushes. He leans forward to announce that because of the many thoughtful propositions put forward, he is forced to suspend this great, this masterful, work. He will write out checks to all those who purchased their tickets by mail; for those who bought them at the box office, he pulls a fat wad of bills out of his hip pocket and lays them under the hammer on his little lectern. With a banging of seats the audience begins to rise and file forward to the stage, queuing for refunds.

At my observation post in the rear I am fuming. Why, even at his last gasp, Antonin Artaud would have better managed this absurd theater of cruelty! As the audience passes me on its way out, people remark to one another how it's been such an interesting preview—they might even return for the play—whenever and if it opens—oh, absolutely!

When the house is empty, I go down and sit near Cy in the first row, expecting to see the play rehearsed. I am hoping the evening will not have been an utter waste.

The theater darkens; the curtain slowly goes up on bare boards, a cinderblock firewall upstage rear. Downstage center, a rickety ladder, an empty packing crate. Where is everything? Richter pats my hand as if to say, "Patience." Now Pound shuffles in from the right. Beneath his elbow he clutches a sheaf of scribbled-over manuscript, meaninglessly marked with arrows, crosses, circles. He never glances at us, but shambles downstage left and descends the stairs muttering and groaning into his goatish beard, *Pull down thy vanity/thy vanity pull down* . . . .

That's all? I say.

Pound stares vacantly about; then as if recognizing me at last, he smiles sweetly, the senile remnant of his once-sonorous voice reedy: *If the hoarfrost grip thy tent/thou wilt give thanks/when the night is spent.*

Look, Cy, I expostulate, when you offered to produce my *Mosaics* I was grateful to you. But none of this business is in the contract. You have not kept faith with me.

Cy dismisses me with a cluck of his tongue. "Oh, faith. Leave it to me and Ezra. We'll make it new. From the ground up. Everything's for your own good, you know."

A fine pair: the silly rabbi and the anti-Semitic master poet! They will do what they will do. My works and days mean nothing to them. Strive as I may, in the end I have no choice but to give up the ghost.

Grace

WHEN I SHOWED HER THE BOTTLE, my wife raised her eyebrows but said nothing. It was a Premier Grand Cru, 1929. I'd picked it up in some cellar up a cul de sac near Mont Parnasse. Paid less than 12 francs for a wine that should have cost around 600 francs, if you could find that vintage. A vineyard right between Chateau Gloria and Chateau de la Tour Blanche. A treasure—when carefully drawn, decanted, allowed to breathe for an hour, the bottle proved to be everything it should. So the label was genuine. Now do you believe me? I said. She only looked at me with sceptical eyes and pursed lips.

We were living in Paris. Our cash had run out. But things changed when I found that little cut-rate shop. A check arrived every second week, and it was good, more than enough for us to get by on. She asked me if I knew where it came from. That was a question I couldn't answer, except to say that without it we'd have had to go home again, and we couldn't do that, could we. I must have been recognized. Perhaps it was some grant, I said, something I'd forgotten I'd ever applied for? Perhaps I had been on the waiting list? Perhaps my turn had come? After all, why not? Manna falls from the skies She seemed to doubt that, just as she had doubted the truth in the wine. Anyway, what difference does it make? I said. She folded her arms and turned away from me.

And then, there was the wine, too: that dark little man in his basement caveau saturated with the musty sweet smell of spilled liquors supplied us with a bottle a day. Fabulous. I merely took my afternoon stroll a bit wider through Mont Parnasse so as to pass that hole-in-the-wall. And she shared its greatness with me each evening. We'd never had it so good. Not a care in the world, I said. We were free. Only, when I went round to rue Scribe twice each month and the check would appear in the mail I picked up at the American Express, she would raise her eyebrows and nod pensively, murmuring that I was living in bad faith. For the time being, I'd reply. Besides, what choice did we have? She'd shrug, a glint of contempt in her eyes. I reminded myself how easy it was for women to judge, one of the more delectable, unearned luxuries they enjoyed. For some reason—no, it was pure contingency, it was gratuitous, an accident; it was existential, absurd; there really was no reason; given the nature of things how could there be any reason?—I had walked out of my way one afternoon on my usual meander and stopped to look down into that cellar at the end of a cul de sac. I had asked if by any chance there was to be had a good cheap ordinary to go with my daily bread. And was handed, not some metallic *picquette*, your common bulk *vinasse*, but that great vintage, one of the greatest in history. The grapes had been crushed and were fermenting the very month I was born. And now, some foundation or some anonymous benefactor was coincidentally contributing to our well-being. Only a woman would suspect the source. Clearly there was no way to know. The only source was the facts themselves. Wasn't that good enough? Facts? she laughed, the facts alone will kill you! Now that was nonsense, I thought, because in the last analysis we were just living for the day.

A good and happy year passes in an hour. This sunny morning, as I step out onto the plane-tree-shaded sidewalk of the Boulevard St. Germain, I am seized and pinioned. A low voice snarls in my left ear, "Sureté Nationale!" It's so fortuitous that I don't even flinch. Planting my boots firmly right where I stand—there's a torn page of yesterday's *Le Monde* under my right toe, stained by wine or blood—I say quietly, And for what offense?

"Your crime is unspecified, Monsieur. But you know what it is." Rather nonchalant, I smile at hearing that. You cannot arrest me for an unspecified crime.

At the same time, I realize I'm caught: they have indeed arrested me. I see it instantly: it is in fact merely accidental. It is my existential way of life: altogether gratuitous. Though that wine may be true, no, the wine is a good, a great wine—how can I afford to drink this vintage? I carry it down from Mont Parnasse, yet I don't even know what it is. The bottle is therefore new—hence it must be a false bottle. We drink an old wine each evening, and throw out this new bottle with our refuse every morning. Who picks it from our refuse? Is there something more valuable than this heavenly wine in these bottles? As if it would pay for us to drink our cup to the dregs. Nevertheless, we don't know what it is that is secreted in it.

No, I am innocent! Guilty objectively, you could say; but as subject, innocent! Oh if somehow I do know; yet I could not have known . . . given the circumstances of our lives. That is my defense. I'll fight to the end to maintain it. Who can prove I was willingly engaged in crime? What crime? Surely I have been used? I am an innocent. Or the Sureté Nationale's pulling a Kafka on me. I won't stand for it. I'm not your confused K, your oh so meek and patient J.K.—just let them bring me to trial! I hold my ground, protesting, even laughing at them too; but this pair of flics refuse to say what the charge against me is. One continues to snarl quietly into my left ear that I am very well aware, and that I'll confess. I'll confess all right—after a French interrogation.

Never! I say.

"Sooner or later," he replies. "It's logical."

I think of breaking loose. I'm head and shoulders taller than these two wiry, iron-sinewed little Gauls: I weigh as much as both of them together. But as I flex my arms, looking to left and right, I see a Frankish blond giant step up behind me out of the hallway. Prepared for my move, he lifts me in the air by my elbows and shakes me, bellowing like a moronic cyclops, and bangs me down again so hard I bit off the tip of my tongue. Then, grabbing me by my scruff with one great paw, he hustles me forward to the curb and throws me head-first into the back of the black Citroaen that has just glided up to the curb.

The car dashes off through the morning streets, vibrating over the cobblestones of St. Germain. My eyes are covered en route by a black hood, and I see again only when I am stood up, my wrists manacled behind me, in the large airy kitchen of some four star restaurant as the day's work is commencing. The cooks are preparing their cauldron of stock, the assistants chopping and sorting vegetables, the butcher and his helper disjointing, slicing, and pounding meat and trussing fowl. The place is sharp with onions and garlic and parsley. The chef at the far end directs his crew in a low voice. Beside me, the two flics; behind me stands the giant.

There is a long steel-topped table against the wall, cleared of pots and pans: only an auto battery sits there, its terminals wired, the wires leading to red clips. And there's also a fat man in a blue suit, an old, crushed hat on his head: the typical detective of French movies. An acrid-burning Gauloise droops in one corner of his thick-lipped mouth, a thin gold band encircles the pudgy fourth finger of his right hand. His bulbous watery eyes glare, accusing me. Indignant, I speak out for the first time, What the hell have you against me? Give me some reason! Well?

He shrugs, the same sceptical gesture my wife has made all year long. Even his eyebrows go up like hers. Without uttering a word, he seems to suggest, "You are bluffing." Well, maybe I am living in bad faith. But, logically, how could they know? They couldn't. Therefore I can take their interrogation.

Which goes on all day. The cigarette burns on my cheeks; the 12 volts of direct current into my wired-up genitals; the iron rod against the soles of my feet. The fainting; the pitcher of ice water dashed in my face. The usual. The cooks, the kitchen help, the waiters and busboys go about their business through the whole afternoon, paying no attention to my gagged moans and silent writhing on that table. But I am innocent. Bad faith or no. I hold out.

They quit by late afternoon. To the two flics who've worked me over, Monsieur L'Inspecteur remarks, "This unfortunate has been syndicated and doesn't even seem to know it. In this day and age, too. I wonder what the true story is . . . ." Well, I think, they may as well take me away, since he can tell I won't crack.

This time, they half-carry, half-shove me into the back of an open car and drive it slowly through the warm, bright July dusk. We are going along the rue St. Honoré towards the Place de la Concorde. There are police barricades set up along the sidewalks, and no traffic: the street is as empty as though it were expecting a parade. The populace is gathering as we cruise along in second gear. They crowd the route, waving their little tricolor flags and streamers. Am I then that important a subject? Through my torn lips and shattered teeth, I say to Monsieur L'Inspecteur, Am I the key to your operation? Is this why you have taken me prisoner, tortured me? What in heaven's name do you want me to confess?

Monsieur L'Inspecteur smiles faintly as he gazes out at the crowds now standing ten deep. He does not answer my question. Is he ashamed?

The car slows, shifting down to a crawl in first gear as it approaches the Place de la Concorde. Only now do I realize that all the way, despite the waving flags of the mob pressing against the barricades and the police linking their white batons to restrain them, there have been no smiles, no cheers, no shouts of *Vive la Liberté!* The children held up to look over people's heads have been silent too, wide-eyed and solemn. In fact, the throngs are grave, their faces melancholy. It means that I am not being transferred to prison, not going to be tried. I am instead being conducted to the guillotine.

As the car turns left down the rue Royale, it creeps. At the Place de la Concorde, it halts, blocked by the masses that have filled the square. I stand then, and shout, But, I am an innocent! What is the charge against me? You cannot, you must not permit them to commit injustice! It will be the ruin of your society and the end of your civilization! I am in fine voice now. It is noble speechifying. Hear me! This is a crime against the individual by a state! Therefore, a crime against your children! And thus, a crime against the future! Against humanity itself! You must stop them, before it's too late! *Aux armes, Citoyens!*

Silence. No one moves. Have they heard me at all? Monsieur L'Inspecteur rolls his eyes at the purple sky above. His lips purse, whispering his opinion to an empty heaven: "*Oh là là!*"

The Old Muse

MIDNIGHT. I have returned to the Bronx. Allerton Avenue as it was nearly forty years ago. And I am forty years older, standing waiting outside that mausoleum, the Manufacturers Trust Company. No one is about under the yellowed street light. Overhead, the empty El station. Across the avenue, a lone Checker cab parked at the taxi stand. An old woman comes out of the darkness towards me. She is gaunt. She wears a loose cotton gown, a muumuu printed with large dark flowers, blurred purple bruises. Her gray hair is wild, splaying over her shoulders in greasy hanks. Her eyes are hollowed with grief, her face creased with sleeplessness. She raises both skinny arms like an ancient votary approaching an altar and comes directly to me, her eyes fixed upon my breast as though she looked through me, as though I were not there at all, and she drops those stiff hands on my shoulders, dead weights with clamping fingers. Her right arm slips downward slowly, tracing its clawfingers on my skin, over my heart. Yet I am not frightened: I stand still, frozen, patient. The magnetic force of her gesture is a silent thought, a command: *I must speak the truth. I must speak it out.* I am startled, but resigned to it too. I think, Why me? And I also think, So be it.

ATTRIBUTIONS

ORFEOS: There came that moment when his wife, dying yet again, speaks for the first time—and the last.

A PROPHECY: Despite our paleolithic nostalgias, we can never return home.

AFRODITE: For the Greeks, the realm of Love and Beauty was ruled by this goddess. Fertility too. She had come originally from the East, and what her name really means remains guesswork.

RHADAMANTHYS: In Greek mythology, Judge of the Underworld.

IKAROS: Another famous Greek legend. Ikaros is the name of the young man who did not take the advice of his ingenious father, the engineer Dædolos. Escaping with his father from their island prison on wings made by Dædolos, Ikaros was seized by a rapture of the heights: he flew higher and higher towards the sun, and found death—the beeswax that held the feathers together melted, and he tumbled to his death in the sea below.

PROTEUS: Originally a minor sea-god. Homer considered him an Egyptian spirit who served the ruler of the sea, Poseidon. Proteus is a shape-shifter: if you could just hang onto him, you would see him as he truly is. And then, oh then he will answer your questions! As it is said, you should only be so lucky!

PSYCHE: The Greeks aptly named the little princess of the fairytale Psyche. Eros himself was her secret lover. In the Greek romance about Psyche, we learn that to look upon Eros is to lose him, and Psyche did. Her punishment was extreme: but she willingly endured severe trials in expiation—the woman's version of the Labors of Herakles.

CHEIRON: Half-man, half-horse, the Centaurs lived in the woods and mountains of northern Greece. Some are famous, and Cheiron is the wise and kind old medicine man among them. They were attracted by the fumes of wine, a drink of which they were indeed over-fond. Cheiron taught medicine and various arts to divine children and to heroes.

TO KOLONOS: Just where *is* our hero, poor blind Oedipus, when we glimpse him wandering between sin and expiation? Where most of us sometime may find ourselves, condensed into a word within all our words, swaddled in silence, unable—and unwilling—to speak a word. As for that woman, she's long dead.

AEAEA: The island where Circe entertained visiting wanderers but then also detained them as her swine. Odysseus and his crew were her guests for a while.

CALLIOPE: Muse of the heroic epic. There she stands. Will she, won't she, can't she sing?

HERMES: Once, procreation and fertility were aided by him, and he could be seen along the roads in the form of a priapic milestone. He was invoked by travellers for protection; commerce was supervised by his eyes; he went before souls into the regions hereafter. Hermes was a civilizer, and he also ruled dreamland. His is the name given to the god of transitions: of translation, so to speak, from one condition to another, from one form of being into another, from one place to another. Rogues and thieves were also his devotees, for they followed merchants and goods along the way.

KRONOS: An Asiatic mythologem surely. After all, fathers don't try to devour their sons. Or if one did, it was that defeated giant who was the youngest child of Heaven and Earth, that youthful warrior who castrated his father so as to make room in the world for his great brothers. And here we are today, so reduced that Freud thought every son must fear his father's sickle in the night—when in truth we seem to try our hardest to maim, kill, and bury them *and* their achievements. Or else was it that Kronos is imagined as having ruled somewhere far off in a wonderland, King of the Age of Gold? Where on earth might that have been, and when? The dust of time has blinded us. And yet here we are, almost at the end of time, wearing expensive chronographs, if we can afford them, still reviewing old histories from God to Man, from father to son, mostly tales of mortal struggle. Some sons, and many daughters today, seem to think we are still threatened by our poor fathers, those almost forgotten patriarchs. Perhaps, as the poet said, the Child is Father to the Man, and it is such as these, our strange children who will kill the poor, rickety, ancient king.

TEIRESIAS: An ancient man who was a blind seer. Having lived as both a man and a woman in his time, he understood something about men and women. It was he who finally answered Oedipus's questions concerning the root and cause of the malaise in Thebes.

BACCHAE: One day things shall have come to such a pass that men can no longer distinguish between the warning of an ambulance, the wail of a fire truck, the yowl of police in hot pursuit of crime, or wailing women.

PAN: A vague creature from Arcadia; of little account in his own time, and rather a failure in his notorious pursuit of two girls. Even those tales were late inventions. He was essentially a small-time loner who had few relations to the Higher Ones. He is known as a player on a reed flute, which he probably tootled to while away time and let his flock know he was around. We see him depicted with a man's body and arms and goatish head, legs, and tail, almost cousin to the creatures he herded. One thinks of him as amorous, which is to be expected of a fellow whose main business was to inspire fertility in flocks. People used to beat him when he failed at that. Poor Pan.

DAFNE: A nymph Apollo desired and pursued. But in his arms she turned into the laurel tree. Its leaves are a bitter and aromatic herb used in stews and soups, known to the cook as bay leaf. Heroes, warriors, and athletes wore a wreath of laurel.

PEGASOS: Legendary flying horse. Alexander had a famous steed, too; together they covered a lot of ground, sans wings.

ZENO: There were a few notable philosophers so named. I was thinking of that Semitic Zeno who lectured in the Stoa of Athens and founded the Stoic school. Principally, he claimed that the only real evil was moral weakness, the only true good being virtue. How to find that good and avoid that evil remains the challenge. Holding to them both is helpful in a world of logical manias.

TELEMACHOS: Odysseus's son. He is a man by the time his father returns to Ithaka, and helps him clear the palace of its unwanted guests. A great bow was drawn there.

ABRAHAM: The man packed up his worldly goods and took his wife on a long trek west, forsaking big-time Ur's noisy chivaree. And for what? The better to hear the voice of his god. The rest is history.

SYBIL: A long time ago there were prophetic women uttering oracles. As many as ten famous sibyls were recognized all the way from Italy to Persia. Their ecstasy was systematized and written down in Greek hexameter verses, which lent a certain glamor (and formal veracity) to their words. While a raging man often looks foolish or mad, an angry woman is terrible to behold, since it usually takes much provocation to put a grown woman out of patience. True sibyls never lost patience, I believe, only their consciousness.

IOCASTA: Queen of Thebes. She had a son called Oedipus. What happened to them is known to all.

XANTHIPPE: Socrates' wife. Legend has it that she was something of a scold.

ONE fINE MORNING IN EDEN: Everyone has imagined such a place. What was it like? and why did it fail us? Surely something was lacking there—or in us.

A THEBAN OSTRAKON: A potsherd. In Athens, *ostraka* were used as voting tablets. After Alexander conquered Egypt, they were used for tax receipts; later, we find them with all sorts of scribbling on them: orders, lists, letters, school exercises, magical spells, and bits of Pagan and Christian religious texts. They are most common in old garbage dumps and the ruins of homes.

BERENICE: There were several formidable women named Berenice in Classical times, among them some tigerish queens. One even had a supernova named for her hair by her husband, Ptolemy III, only to be murdered by her son (and spouse). Edgar Poe wrote a frightful story about a woman named Berenice. I have redeemed that hapless bride in this tale.

ESAU: Twin brother to Jacob the Patriarch. Born first, as it happens. We are told that they began their quarrel even in the womb. In Hebrew his name signified *the hairy one.* Esau sold to Jacob his rights as first-born for a pot of boiled lentils. Otherwise he would have perished of hunger where he stood.

MEDEA: A Greek adventurer named Jason went to Colchis in the East, on the shore of the Black Sea, in search of a trophy called the Golden Fleece. This princess and sorceress helped him get it from her father, it was said. Euripides wrote a tragedy by that name.

SAUL OF TARSUS: Known in later life as the Apostle Paul.

JACOB: Son to Isaac the Patriarch. Once, while on a trek, he slept at an altar he'd put up for the night. There he dreamt that he saw a kind of ladder by which angels came down to earth and went up into the sky. Later, he had many sons, and those sons fathered the tribes of the Hebrews.

CORINTH: An ancient Greek city. Oedipus, rescued by a shepherd, was a foundling who had been left to die of exposure, his ankle pierced by a stake. His name is a sobriquet for his crippled foot. He was brought up as the son of the King and Queen of Corinth. A dutiful son, he left home rather than risk harming his (supposed) parents and taking their throne.

ISAAC: Son of the first Patriarch. While still a lad, he had a bad scare.

ASKLAPIOS: For difficult decisions, one is advised to "sleep on it." For matters of life and death, Greeks and others used to go to a hospital/hotel/spa like Epidaurus, say. After suitable preparation such as diet, exercise, bathing, counseling, prayer, and the rest, one was ready to bed down in the healer's temple and sleep on it. That was called incubation. It entailed dream analysis, too, if one were fortunate enough to be visited by the hoped-for, god-sent dream. Over the millenia, faith and tough moralizing have been substituted for the Classical moderation that treated the whole person. Then psychotheraphy came along. And now—the aerobical workout. My story is titled after the God of Medicine. It speaks of integration, that consummation so devoutly wished for.

KASSANDRA: Priam's daughter in Troy. Homer never said she had any gift for clairvoyance, although he did single her out as the most beautiful of the royal princesses. She is said to have been mishandled by one Aias the Locrian. It was not until the time of the tragic poet Æschylus that she was given some foresight by Apollo, who hoped for a bit of loving in return. She cheated him of that desire, with the result that the god caused her words to be met with incredulity and downright disbelief. A hard fate, to be able to tell the truth of things to come, and be ignored by everyone—perhaps even worse than violation.

PERCEVAL: A hero of old Romances. A simple lad, raised by his mother in the woods. Serving King Arthur on the Quest for the Holy Grail, he is unbeatable; and, being an innocent, he manages to make his way into the mysterious castle where it is hidden and to ask the right questions. Some, however, say he *failed* to ask the right questions.

SALOME: Southern California has daunted newcomers for decades. It may not seem so to some anxious skeptics; but even here your Genius Loci manifests itself in memorable forms.

GNOSIS: Greek for *knowledge*. Those who were called Gnostics seemed to believe that there is a secret kind of knowledge, access to which was hidden from all but themselves. It may be true for all we know.

MOSES: Said to have been a Hebrew brought up in the Egyptian royal court. He led the Children of Israel in the Exodus out of Egypt and into the desert wastes of the Sinai. Also known as The Lawgiver.

SIREN SONG: Said to be irresistible, the song of the Sirens lured wanderers to their death. We are told that one who sealed his ears and kept going saw the shore of their isle glittering with the bleached bones of those who had been fatally drawn too close by the music of their singing. Edgar Poe speaks of a lost Lenore. Eliot's Prufrock thought of them as mermaids who wouldn't deign to sing to him! I sometimes think that the price would be worth paying, could that song be heard today, and assuming our currency is acceptable to Fate.

COURTLY LOVE: A Medieval pastime. Said to have been encouraged and developed by Eleanor of Aquitaine into elaborate codes governing the proper behavior between ladies and gentlemen.

PROMETHEUS: An early patron of mankind. Without his help we still would remain cold, wet, and naked, for he thought ahead. With his help, humanity got fire, and so we're no longer necessarily cold, wet, and shivering naked. But we may yet explode this world with our fire. It's a problem.

ELIJAH: A figure of Jewish folklore since post-Biblical times. A full-to-brimming glass of wine awaits him at each Passover table, and the door is left ajar to welcome him, who epitomizes the wandering angel that is everyone's benefactor. He has a way of revealing himself in mortal form, the unprepossessing, modest stranger who can perform the miracle all of us need at one time or another—and seldom receive.

AN EVENING IN BABYLON: One can only sit by the waters and weep, it would seem.

BACCHUS: One of the sacrificial and annually sacrificed gods of antiquity, Attis, Dionysus, et cetera. His blood was the wine of pure and innocent pleasure-giving. But of course we are all innocents, aren't we?

GRACE: According to some 20th century thinkers, you are what you do. That is the problem in a nutshell.

THE OLD MUSE: The Greeks distinguished *nine* daughters of Mnemosyne (goddess of memory) and Zeus, the All-Father. Nowadays, *the* Muse is merely a cant term suggesting the source of "creativity" in the writing of poems, while her "absence" is an explanation for writer's block.